BURN IT DOWN

AMERICAN MAYHEM, VOL. 1

GUERNICA WORLD EDITIONS 72

BURN IT DOWN

AMERICAN MAYHEM, VOL. 1

PERRY GLASSER

GUERNICA
World
EDITIONS

TORONTO—CHICAGO—BUFFALO—LANCASTER (U.K.)
2023

Guernica Editions Founder: Antonio D'Alfonso

Michael Mirolla, general editor
Scott Walker, editor
Cover design: Allen Jomoc, Jr.
Interior design: Jill Ronsley, suneditwrite.com

Guernica Editions Inc.
287 Templemead Drive, Hamilton (ON), Canada L8W 2W4
2250 Military Road, Tonawanda, N.Y. 14150-6000 U.S.A.
www.guernicaeditions.com

Distributors:
Independent Publishers Group (IPG)
600 North Pulaski Road, Chicago IL 60624
University of Toronto Press Distribution (UTP)
5201 Dufferin Street, Toronto (ON), Canada M3H 5T8

First edition.
Printed in Canada.

Legal Deposit—Third Quarter
Library of Congress Catalog Card Number: 2023936021
Library and Archives Canada Cataloguing in Publication
Title: Burn it down : American mayhem. Vol. 1 / Perry Glasser.
Names: Glasser, Perry, author.
Series: Guernica world editions (Series) ; 72.
Description: First edition. | Series statement: Guernica world editions ; 72
Identifiers: Canadiana (print) 20230220428 | Canadiana (ebook)
20230220436 | ISBN 9781771838566 (softcover) | ISBN 9781771838573 (EPUB)
Classification: LCC PS3557.L335 B87 2023 | DDC 813/.54—dc23

for
the Moofky–Boofky Mob
with gratitude to Sam, Crowbah, Ketch, Bro, and Kels

Plants that cannot bloom by day
Must flower in the night
—Jack Traylor w/The Jefferson Airplane

The Summer of Love

SEVERAL CARS PASSED THEM WITH horns blaring, most with
drivers vigorously pumping a middle finger salute. The speed
limit was 50; but James did 35 on the straightaways, less on
any turn. Buckles wondered if being chickenshit caused acne or if
acne turned a boy to chickenshit. Whichever, in the dictionary next
to chickenshit was a photo of unsmiling James with his slit-grim
green eyes, his ginger-hair crewcut, his invisible eyebrows, and his
pimply neck.

The Bear Mountain Bridge became only one lane wide in each
direction. Once the Volvo was on the bridge, there could be no turning back. The car behind came right up close to flash its lights again
and again. They were going too slow. James' grip on the wheel went
defiantly white-knuckled. He drove no faster, but whined about the
trip already being more than he'd bargained for. Now that he unex-
pectedly had to cross the Hudson at lunatic speed, if they did not
get killed the odometer would surely give him away and he would
be grounded until he was thirty. He hoped Buckles understood all
he risked for her, by which he meant she would feel she had to act
on her gratitude. For her part, Buckles considered braining James
and liberating the Volvo for a few hundred more miles even though
she had no experience driving. There could not be all that much to
it if James, the Master of Chickenshit, could manage it. But instead
of committing several felonies, Buckles sweetly smiled and asked if
they could go a teensy-weensy bit faster.

James very gradually accelerated to 45. Horns behind them blared.

On the western side of the bridge, the Volvo rolled to rest on the shoulder of a long crescent of road, a spot that kept the car hidden from view from ahead and behind. A close wall of pine trees on their right cast sweet-smelling shadows over them. Buckles was sure she would soon learn all she needed about hitchhiking, but she supposed James had chosen a terrible spot for her to start her San Francisco journey. She'd want drivers able to see her from a long way off with time to slow, not come tearing around a bend and have to jam their brakes when they first caught sight of her.

They sat in the idling Volvo. No words came.

Buckles still hoped James might change his mind and, if not go with her, at least take her 50 miles, but her heart knew James did not have it in him. He had less balls than Ira, his pet gerbil that, when it ran itself to death, James had lifted by its skinny tail to drop it into the toilet. Back when James and Buckles had been classmates in junior high, they would suck on a Pepsi can bong and exhale weed onto Ira, then giggle while The Amazing Stoner Rat ran crazy on his wheel. It probably killed him. Now in a Volvo at the side of Route 6 she missed the stoner gerbil more than she could ever miss James, and she wondered: *Who in fuck names a gerbil Ira?*

Buckles and James saw each other only rarely after her troubled ninth grade, and even then only in summers. Buckles had been plucked from Scarsdale's public schools and packed off to Dobbs Academy, the posh boarding school in Dobbs Ferry that was supposed to rectify her chronic underachievement. Her parents had opted for the school's hybrid residential plan. She spent four nights each week at Dobbs and weekends at home, leaving her a transient no matter where she was. Worse, by late June every year, boarding school kids scattered all over the world. When Buckles returned to her parents' home, what few Scarsdale friends Buckles had now thought her a prep school snob. They were right, but knowing they were right did not keep her loneliness from becoming a crush.

In early August, Buckles decided she needed to make the break. She'd hitchhike to San Francisco where she could listen to some music, smoke a lot of dope, and with luck get laid by mature boys with longer hair and better arms than the fish-belly white preppies of Dobbs or the knuckle-dragging losers of Scarsdale High.

The last time James and Buckles had seen each other had been a joyless reunion the previous June. He was celebrating his new driver's license. They talked a little about the old days, but all James really wanted to do was smoke grass and get his hand in her pants. They'd parked his mother's car on a cliff in a park overlooking the Hudson where James tried to persuade her to climb with him into the Volvo's backseat, an idea so absurd she'd laughed out loud. Was there a chapter in the *Boy Scouts Manual* about how to get a girl to make out? Had James studied it? Did the chapter recommend preliminary nostalgia about dead rodents? At least his weed had been fairly good.

Exposed to conversational skills the equivalent of Novocain, Buckles surrendered to the moment by allowing James to pop the cap from a bottle of root beer for her, but she did no more than touch her lips to it or, Godforbid, him. All manner of legends in the Hudson Valley had given place-names to a point where some Indian maiden had thrown herself onto rocks for the sake of honor rather than spreading her legs, so the weed had Buckles wondering if she hurled herself into the river to be free of James, might they re-name the parking lot? *Buckles Landing. Buckles Point.* Or maybe for her real name: *Abby's Leap.* When his hands reached for her thigh and then her chest, she slapped them away, in the end avoiding a front seat wrestling match by pointing out he would not want to be driving around in his mother's car after dark, something strictly forbidden and fully possible if they got too stoned and went too far.

The sad fact was that they had grown older and no longer had anything in common except memories of a dead gerbil. Though James was a half year older, Buckles had matured sooner. It was time for her to move on. James was destined to die a virgin dweeb, succumbing to terminal virgin dweebitude. If he did not have the keys to his mother's car, she'd have never seen him again, but he'd volunteered to be the first step of her long journey.

In the Volvo at the west side of the Bear Mountain Bridge, the dweeb's eyes locked for the last time on her chest. He'd known her in the summer days when she ran shrieking around her patio pool in boy's undershirts. Buckles was certain that he'd agreed to drive her north of Westchester to have his hands take a last chance at fondling her breasts, and he was annoying enough to believe that in some way the drive indebted her to him. Admittedly, James had put on a little more muscle since ninth grade, but his only real physical change seemed to be the angry razor burn festering on his pronounced Adam's apple. If the dweeb had guessed her sexual status had changed last year at Dobbs, he'd have believed her debt to him was an absolute entitlement.

The directional clicked. James needed to bang a U-turn to head back to Scarsdale. Buckles wondered if he might bounce the car across the grass divider rather than go forward to the next exit to turn around. When they kissed goodbye his tongue tried to pry open her teeth, but her jaw locked. Before she could crack open the car door, he gifted her with the last of his stash, a going away present he'd dumped into a Baggie. "It's mostly stems and seeds," he said. She grabbed her gear, stepped from air conditioning into soupy air, heard James say that he hoped she'd remember him, and slammed the creaky Volvo door, though her plan was to forget the little chickenshit as soon as she was on a commune.

To be fair to James, they both knew his life was now worth less than fly shit. His parents were sending him to a military academy to make a man out of him, meaning he would be trained to kill without remorse. Pity had stopped Buckles from breaking his wrist when his hand tried to travel between two nickel-plated buttons of her denim vest. Sooner or later, he'd be fertilizer in a rice paddy, but only after he spent a few years in a gray flannel uniform with shiny brass buttons, shiny brass epaulets, and sharply creased scarlet-striped-pants, toting a wooden rifle in circles on a snow-covered parade ground with a bunch of other acne-plagued boys whose parents were willing to condemn their own sons to becoming stone-cold killer porker-fascist baby-burners. James had tried and failed at copping a quick feel. What of it? Maybe his last dying thought when he stepped on a landmine would be of her never-touched boob.

Buckles walked backwards on the side of Route 6, thumb out, her rope macramé rainbow tote bag colliding with the back of her knee with every step, the plastic handle of her phonograph in her other hand slick with perspiration, her red backpack crammed with 45s heavy on one shoulder. The backpack was decorated with an American flag, but with a peace symbol instead of stars. The peace flag matched the bandana she'd knotted over her hair.

She had to leave. Never mind that everything that was happening was happening in far off San Francisco, Buckles required distance from Dobbs, a place where a girl organized a suicide pact for girls whose thighs touched. No one had gone through with the idea, but when Buckles told them they were idiots, she'd been ostracized for being sensible. Girls at Dobbs had all the independence of a school of tropical fish darting through underwater weeds.

Had she been right to offer her mother the details of her route? She did not have the heart to simply vanish. Mom needed to believe her daughter had a plan. That's what the Sinclair women did: they planned. They did not actually do much, but they sure did plan.

As for Daddy, well, good luck to him and his slut. Dropping April's name and a lie about Daddy bragging about his open marriage into her goodbye note was a parting gumdrop of bitchiness sure to keep her parents busy with each other while Buckles conquered America. Let's see how Daddy the Lawyer talked his way out of that one.

The awful reality was that Buckles had not thought to plan beyond where she now stood in the late-August morning, her thumb out, perspiring, walking backwards, burdened by a tote bag, a record player, and her backpack of 45s. She swatted at her neck. Shouldn't mosquitoes be asleep waiting for dusk?

She squelched her excitement when what could be her first ride slowed and then stopped. Maybe her plan was not all that bad. The big lady swung open the squealing rusty gray pickup passenger door. She wore a red and black plaid flannel shirt stained with soil. In the pickup's bay was a one-eyed dog that was some Irish Setter but much more mutt. "Call me Beth," the big woman said. Her truck smelled of dirt and cigarette smoke. Her loose breasts swayed under her shirt. "That's Sandy," Beth said, "the same as Little Orphan Annie's dog." Buckles nodded and wondered who Little Orphan Annie could be, never mind her dog, but she kept in mind her Dad's advice: "When you have nothing good to say, say nothing." Daddy-the-lawyer was a mouthpiece-for-hire, probably a good one. People paid him a lot to lie for them, so his general counsel might not be all bad even though he was a total scumbag.

The American countryside slid by on her right, growing less green and more clay-brown as the truck climbed foothills. Buckles had never been in any kind of truck and should have realized it elevated its passengers. She was able to see farther and down into passenger cars. From that height, Buckles imagined she was a queen destined to rule all she saw. A little more than two hours after chickenshit James picked her up at home, Beth, Sandy, and Buckles crossed into Pennsylvania to begin their slow climb over the Appalachians.

"Coal country," Beth said, lighted another Marlboro, and offered one to Buckles, popping it from a soft pack by a tricky flip of her wrist. Buckles turned it down. She'd develop a tobacco habit some other day. She wondered if Beth would mind if she rolled a joint, but then decided not to ask.

Beth rambled on and on and on about how the roads these days were lined by nothing but naïve hippie girls who thought the world was safe as a cradle when the world in fact overflowed with danger. Buckles tried to seem interested. Beth had nothing against hippies, had no problems picking up a hippie-chick like Buckles, but woman-to-woman felt it was her moral obligation to caution her. "Don't you never get into no car with a man alone, and if there are two men, drop your bags and run, just run," she said. She crushed her fifth Marlboro since Buckles climbed aboard into the overflowing dashboard ashtray.

Buckles liked being taken for a hippie. Now that she was traveling, really traveling, it felt accurate. She would never again be a playacting suburban weekend day-tripper hanging out in Washington Square Park.

"Don't even think about riding boxcars unless you want your ass raped by faggot hobos or railroad bulls. So get a knife. You need a knife. Every woman on the road needs a knife. If you can't get a knife, you can use a Bic lighter to soften the plastic handle of a toothbrush enough to hold a razorblade, then wrap the toothbrush in adhesive tape, as a grip." She took her hands from the wheel long enough to pantomime the action. "That's free jailhouse knowledge," Beth said.

In the pickup truck's bay where Sandy rode with her shaggy face into the wind were a rusty shovel, a pickaxe, and a hoe. Whenever they hit a bump, Beth's tools rattled and crashed. Beth was either a gardener or grave-robber. Buckles smiled at her silent joke, but what if Beth was a real grave-robber?

"Most people pay dear for jailhouse knowledge, so you'd best be thankful you are getting it for free. You need jailhouse smarts to survive, and not just in jail." She leaned across Buckles to pop open the glove box. "But I would not recommend a toothbrush and razor if you can do any better. See that there? That's a switchblade." The handle was pink mother-of-pearl. "You press that silver button and the blade pops open. Five inches of tempered steel is sharp enough to slice some asshole's nuts off before he knows you have his business in your hand. Just remember, a man who does not do you dirt is thinking about how to do you dirt."

She smacked the glove compartment closed before Buckles could touch the knife.

Beth was good enough to drive half around Scranton to a highway truck-stop where she fueled up and dropped Buckles. It was out of her way, but not all that much. She was headed for Syracuse. Beth refused money for gas, but was generous with her tedious advice. "You don't want to look like some kid on her way home from a day in the sun by the lake. You need long haul rides if you are headed for California. Long haul. Don't be shy. You ask where a driver is bound. You want plenty of people around when you ask, too, 'cause if the son-of-a-bitch gets vague about where he is going it's 'cause he don't want no one to overhear. That's why you want a crowd nearby." She screwed the pickup's fuel cap tight. "Look deep into a man's eyes," she said. "Eyes never lie." Then Beth pursed her lips like she was blowing a kiss, slammed her pickup into gear; her tires raised a plume of dirty white smoke as they found traction, and Beth and Sandy headed north.

The buzzkill that came off Beth and people like her was the negativity that caused the war in Vietnam. Expect the worst, and that's what you'll get. The Beatles were becoming old-fashioned, but *All You Need Is Love* said it all. If John and Paul ever hung out with her, they'd get high and rap about this and that as if they always got together to shoot the shit over weed. Buckles had things to share with John he needed to know. Paul and Buckles might write a song. George was good for rapping about philosophy, and Ringo, well, Ringo was a goof, but a loveable goof. She wished she could plug in her phonograph, lie down, smoke a bowl, and play records. Life was simple if you allowed it to be.

Surrounded by her stuff, Buckles sat a long while on the granite curbstone on the shady side of the truck stop convenience store. Her knees rose higher than her head when she crouched like a peasant. She'd made it west of Scranton on her first ride from Beth the Grave Robber. It would be hours before the summer sun set. The map of America was vague in her mind, but at this rate she believed she'd be skinny-dipping in the Pacific in a matter of days. Beth might have been a buzzkill, but she was right about long haul rides being the ticket.

Buckles made an early dinner of a pint of very cold milk and a small cellophane package of chocolate-chip cookies. She chose to pay for the cookies rather than risk being caught shoplifting and so being sent home. Food should be free like water and air. The last of the soft cookies crumbled to dissolve over her tongue. *The Village Voice* said that the Diggers served nourishing meals in Golden Gate Park. Free food was just another reason to be in San Francisco. If she were there now, her belly would have been swollen full by brown rice and healthy vegetables.

She untied her red, white, and blue headband with the peace symbol on it, shook her hair free to allow her scalp to breathe, and then reknotted it. She took the rainbow tote but left the rest of her stuff on the slender cement walkway when she went inside again to pee. She changed from her Wranglers to the shorts she'd cut with pinking shears from an older pair of full-length jeans, then took a moment in a lavatory stall to roll a joint from James' stash. James had also given her some Zig-Zag rolling paper. Smoking from her dope pipe outside would be too obvious. *The Village Voice* cautioned that there were places like Arkansas and Louisiana and Texas where an ounce could get a person locked up for years, so you could not be too careful. The privacy of the lavatory was important.

Her stuff on the walkway remained undisturbed, proof that Beth needed to trust people more. The frayed threads of her shorts floated wavy shadow patterns on her tanned thighs. Even if it had too many seeds and stems, Chickenshit James had given her some most excellent shit. When she ran her tongue under her upper lip, she could hardly feel anything. She pinched her nose; it was numb. Buckles extinguished the last of her joint with a pinch of spit before she ate the roach, eliminating all evidence in case there were cops eyeballing the hippie kid sitting on the walkway concrete. That was her, now. The hippie kid in an American peace flag doo-rag. A psychedelic Volkswagen bus would carry her off on a moonbeam. Once she found a commune, she'd change her name to Storm or Chrysalis or Starlight.

She watched trucks from the highway shiver to a stop like giant dogs escaping rain. Buckles near wet herself laughing when a cement-mixer roaring back to life sounded like a farting elephant, the funny part being that she had no idea what a farting elephant might sound like.

A huge rig squealed to a stop on the concrete apron directly before her. A puff of black smoke escaped from a rear wheel well where something burned. The truck's friendly name, *Donna May,* was painted in a fiery orange script on the engine's white hood. The driver peered into the wheel well, spat disgustedly, and went inside. Twenty minutes later, after what had to have been a hurried meal, the driver adjusted something at the smoking wheel and waved for her to join him as he pulled himself into *Donna May*'s cab.

Buckles wondered if what she had seen was real.

But when the driver leaned out the passenger door to wave to her a second time, she hoisted her backpack to her shoulder, grabbed her tote bag, and gripped her phonograph's plastic handle to run to catch her first ride in a real truck. Running in sandals cut from truck tires was not easy. She prayed the driver would not become impatient and pull away before she crossed the distance, but he waved again for her to hurry, leaning to hold open his passenger door, grinning down at her through his black beard like some crazy lumberjack. She tossed her phonograph up to him, pitched her backpack up after the phonograph, and swung her tote onto the red leather passenger seat before she grabbed a chrome bar to haul herself over the one big step to the cab from the running board. The driver's belly laugh convinced her she'd made a right choice.

"I'm Big Bill," the driver announced, his rough hand encircling her wrist to haul her up the final foot. She weighed nothing. His black leather gloves had no fingers. They were already rolling when he patted the wheel. "This here is *Donna May.*" Then he smiled wickedly and said: "Then again, *Donna May* not, if you get my meaning. She is a gal with her own mind. Just like me. I'm an owner-driver, by God, free as the wind, and sweet *Donna May* here is the love of my life!"

His horn blasted twice.

Donna May's cab smelled of diesel and sweat and onions, but not so bad it made Buckles sick. She unknotted her headband again, this time using her knobby hair brush to massage her scalp and untangle her hair. Like liquid gold, strands of her hair cascaded around her shoulders. She felt Big Bill's eyes on her, but that was all right, he seemed nice, waiting for her and all, practically lifting her aboard. *Donna May*'s air conditioning was a relief after the gritty August air, though the cold of the cab was so strong and so sudden that her nipples stiffened. She was glad for her jeans jacket and wished it had sleeves or that she had not changed into shorts or had at least taken the time to push her head into one of her black T-shirts, but she could not worry about every little thing if she and Big Bill were going to get to know each other for a long time in his truck. She wondered where he was from, where he was going, if he had a family, if *Donna May* was named for someone he loved.

Big Bill checked mirrors on both sides as *Donna May* gathered irresistible speed on the broad acceleration lane ramping onto the highway. They were off, and the next chapter of her adventure began.

Big Bill tucked a pinch of tobacco into his cheek, offered her some of his Longhorn Straight Cut, then told her everything about his Peterbilt, the lights, switches and dials, the tiny sleeping alcove behind their seats, and how he being an independent he could pick up passengers if he had a mind to. "My truck, my time, my rules. *Donna May* and I have been some places and done some things, haven't we, girl?" Big Bill sounded the horn again for the sheer joy of the noise as the sun before them drew them off the Pennsylvania hills and into the flatlands of Ohio, pursuing a horizon so distant Buckles was sure the world's edge lay under the haze. Maybe she was still a little stoned, so it was all she could do not to become giddy at her luck and the promise of it all.

"I run the scales, darlin'. The only way a working man can make a living is to be an outlaw," he said, spit out his window, and whooped. He explained that meant he had no choice but to dance around rules. "Me and Jesse James are brothers under the skin." What with the payments on the truck and the payments on his house, he had one hell of a nut. His payments on the truck were more than the payments on his house, if she could believe that shit. He owned his private piece of Creation in the foothills west of Albuquerque.

Bill's life was living proof that America was going to shit. "Never mind no Vietnam. I'm fighting my own war just to keep my head above water, and I am here to tell you an honest man will drown. No rest for the wicked. No rest. But it makes me no never-mind. I'll just redo my log. With spit on an eraser and balls, a man can accomplish most anything." He glanced at the dashboard clock. "We are running way behind, so best be ready for me to keep the hammer down all night. *Donna May* will see us through, won't you, girl?"

An all-night ride was more than Buckles had hoped for. She might be in Haight-Ashbury in a few quick days depending on how far she rode with Big Bill and how far San Francisco really was.

"That sounds great," she said. Maybe he was headed home to Albuquerque where Buckles might meet his wife and children before pushing on to the coast.

Big Bill was making up lost time because his schedule had gone to shit days before coming east. Some broker sumbitch shaved a few dollars for himself by leaving Big Bill short-handed at a dock in Wichita where three men loaded sealed crates marked *Lockheed*, though they were nowheres near any Lockheed building Big Bill could see. "There should have been five hands, and the three that showed up weren't hardly no Cracker Jack, neither. That sumbitch pocketed two men's pay and left poor old Big Bill sucking wind."

Later that same day, Bill had idled two solid hours in some godforsaken rest area outside of Emporia. "Emporia might not be the end of the earth, but you can spit over the side." He was waiting on Ezra and Ezra's product bound for Buffalo, New York, product that could not appear on no manifest, if she knew what he meant, same as the phony Lockheed crates. If they stopped for any kind of inspection, his damn papers indicated *Donna May* by rights should have been mostly empty and he'd be royally fucked. "Poor old Big Bill ain't nothing but a mule in a world of quarter horses." Then circling Bright Lights, he'd lost two more hours. Genuinely curious, Buckles asked, and she learned that pretty much every city had a trucker's nickname. "There was road repair around Bright Lights. That's Kansas City," he explained. "And there weren't even time for no steak or ribs at some choke-and-puke." He laughed. Before she could ask, he said: "That's a restaurant, sweet darlin'.".

So he was most of a day behind hauling nothing but contraband, and Ezra, not a patient man, waited for him on the flipside. Ezra would not care a rat's ass about Big Bill's troubles, so now that he was headed back to that sumbitch, he had to keep the hammer down. The only good thing to happen to him in two days was running into his Little Cherry Lollipop outside Steam Town.

"Little Cherry Lollipop?"

"That's you, darlin'. That's you."

She was unsure if she liked her nickname, but it seemed sure that truckers called everything by a name that only they knew. To keep Big Bill's respect, Buckles said, "Going far and fast suits me."

Big Bill whooped and slapped his own thigh. "I knowed you was the right girl. I just knowed it." Miles of Ohio reeled by as Big Bill explained his problem was how he was too good. "When you start bending over to hold your ankles for friends and friends of friends, you get jammed up." His eyes strayed from the road only long enough to drink in one more time those bare honey thighs he'd spied in Scranton, flesh so smooth and tight it hardly jiggled as *Donna May* roared flat out.

"Now tell me true, Little Cherry Lollipop," Big Bill said. "You ain't no narc, are you? What would you say to a few whites? Just for some inspiration, is all I am sayin'. I got a few racks real cheap in that bag. Help yourself. I don't see no rubies in the rearview and ain't no bear report coming to us, so while *Donna May* blows the doors off every vehicle in Ohio, Indiana, Illinois, you and me can party and cross the goddam Mississippi without stopping for a breath. Ezra is a mean motherfucker who don't need no excuse to kick serious ass, so I'd hate to disappoint the sumbitch. Like the Good Book says, there's a time to love and time to boogie, but in *Donna May* we can make up a half day and do both at the same time. We never need to stop. What do you think? Can we try it? Are you ready to party on the move all night? Will you be my Little Cherry Lollipop 'till the sun comes up?"

Buckles understood no more than half of whatever Big Bill said, but she understood enough that the last of her marijuana high seeped away like rainwater into dry sand.

Through his curly black beard, Big Bill scratched his chin with five fingers. He swore his rack of whites were pharmacy grade. "This ain't No-Doz and it ain't none of that home-cooked shit, neither. My Little Cherry Lollipop and me are going to have us a time!" His big hands slapped the wheel. "No reason to stop. All night. Whites ain't no worse than strong coffee, maybe five cups a pop is all. A touch of crank never hurt no one. Am I right or am I right? Take a few, sweetmeat. Don't be shy."

Buckles was growing uneasy, so she risked turning him down. "Not yet," she said politely. She might not have been the smartest girl in Westchester County, but she was smart enough to be wary pills and needles. Pharmacy grade or not, whatever whites were, she wanted no part of them.

Big Bill scowled, but then smiled, still expecting to hear her say *Yes* eventually. A little teasing was just fine with him, just fine. But the longer they drove, the darker the encroaching night became, and the more Big Bill scowled. The fiery orange, red, blue, and green colors glowing from *Donna May*'s dashboard flickered determination in his beard and black eyes. Each new shadow that passed over his face blackened his mood.

He seemed a little better when he bragged at how much strength a man needed to turn *Donna May* and work the old girl's two gear shifts. Big Bill assured Buckles he would never float shift. "If *Donna May* and my ass did not belong to the bank, I might. I just might. But only a fool would risk burning out his own clutch." To see how strong he was, he asked Buckles to squeeze his bicep with her two hands.

Buckles had squeezed a boy's bicep plenty of times. It was not a big deal. Boys seemed to like it, and truth be told Buckles liked the feel of the muscles in a boy's arm. It was like giving a backrub, a kind of body exploration that did not have to mean anything or go any further than what it was. A boy might offer his arm to display how he was hardening into a man.

But Big Bill was no boy; Big Bill offered his arm to display his irresistible strength, strength enough to control *Donna May*, Buckles, or anything else. That bicep was thick as her waist, a steel-hard bulge swelling from the short sleeve of his black T-shirt. It was tattooed with a naked lady looking out at the world from under her bangs while she rode a coiled red snake. Big Bill's black eyes had shrunk to dark pins. It was an August night outside, but it was freezing in the cab. Despite the cold, a sheen of perspiration glistened on his forehead. Big Bill could bend her easy as a bobby pin.

It was too late for Beth's advice. Buckles felt stupid. Why hadn't she looked closer at his eyes before she hauled herself aboard? She touched his bicep hoping that would be enough to satisfy him. His arm and all the rest of him was iron. There was no fat on the man. Big Bill's narrow waist funneled into his grease-streaked jeans behind a tightly cinched black leather garrison belt. She scooted over as far from him as she could without throwing herself out the door of the speeding truck.

Donna May's twin cones of blue-white light reached through the darkness, light filled by clouds of bugs that rose from the endless cornfields on either side. Bugs pattered the windshield like hail made from jelly. Big Bill's open denim vest was identical to the one Buckles wore, except Big Bill's was lined with plaid red flannel where she had Sherpa wool. On the shelf between their bucket seats lay an open railroad watch that held down his crumpled brown bag of whites. Suspended under the dashboard was a two-way radio that squawked a language she could not completely follow. Big Bill called it the See-Bee. Whenever he picked up the mic he'd said: "This here is Big Bill and *Donna May* westbound, hammer down, with the one and only Little Cherry Lollipop, the lot lizard who stole my worthless Tennessee heart. Come on back."

Where Daddy always counseled silence, Mom counseled to keep smiling. Buckles' smile wobbled with uncertainty. This was no time for her to lose control of herself. If people truly loved each other, no matter how crazy they were, what could go wrong?

Someone on the See-Bee mentioned a bear taking pictures. *Donna May* slowed from 90 to 70. "Now you watch," Big Bill said.

Five miles later they passed a state trooper on the grass divider leaning from his car window with a radar gun. As soon as the radio crackled a report that the road was now clean and green, *Donna May* surged back to 90. Someone named The Oklahoma Heathen asked if that Cherry Lollipop would need a ride on the flip-flop. Big Bill laughed.

"Don't you wish, good buddy!" And switched the radio off.

Summer lightning flickered before them, far off silent flashes crackling out of a cloud-free heaven that illuminated nothing but for moments extinguished the stars. *Donna May* careened through inky darkness beneath the dome of a cloud-free heaven. Big Bill said the soft glow off to their right might be Cleveland, the dirty little city perched on the edge of the greater darkness that was Lake Erie. Way to their south lay Akron, the shithole Big Bill prayed never again to see because it had been the start of his bad luck, though he would say no more about that. "You look out for shooting stars, though. You'll see plenty. It happens every August for a few days." Buckles thought he was fooling with her until she saw her first meteor, and quickly after that a second streak of silent light scraped a short-lived white line across the sky.

Meteors, lightning, a cloudless night, bugs the size of birds, Buckles wondered if she were tripping. She might be just fine. One second she was fearful, but the next, everything must surely be in her head. Big Bill could be nice enough that she wondered if he'd mind if she napped.

She had no time to ask because Big Bill lunged toward her. She jumped, startled, but he was not reaching for her, but for a shallow brown cardboard box of 8-track tapes behind her seat. "Pick one," he said, shouting over *Donna May*'s engine. He aimed to be hospitable, and every party needed music. All he wanted from her was some good company. A man had his needs and a two-person party would be perfect. "Music will get you in the mood, am I right?"

Among the tapes, Buckles recognized Linda Ronstadt, but Big Bill said he could not abide any more of that hippie Mexican bitch, so he instructed Buckles to find a solid American. Without his narrow eyes leaving the road, his big hand fumbled around in the box on her lap until he found Hank Williams. All she knew of Hank Williams was that his music was jingle-jangle whiny stupid, but Buckles smiled and said he had always been her favorite, especially the part with the violin.

"That's called a fiddle, sweetmeat."

Then Big Bill smashed Linda Ronstadt against the steering wheel until the green plastic splintered. When the tape sailed out the window, it uncoiled and fluttered like a party streamer. *Donna May*'s horn bellowed. "That's how I treat a bitch I don't like."

Panic tasting of puke bubbled up her throat. Buckles could no longer kid herself. Her ribs and arms quaked with more than cold. She'd never known such a feeling. Back home, she was the Sinclair kid, the smart petulant preppie blond who read too much but everyone said should be a model. At home, any time she needed, she could retreat to her room and slam a door. At home, a list of phone numbers could be called to summon someone to her rescue. At home, trouble could only mean police, a boy, or alcohol, all easy to dispense with by a quick call to Daddy the Lawyer. His business card was her shield. Its printed front was for the cops; the fountain pen in blue ink on the back guaranteed one hundred dollars to anyone who, day or night, no questions asked, delivered his daughter to the front door of Mr. John Sinclair, Esq.

Back home there were rules, but there were no rules aboard *Donna May*.

Earlier that day, Buckles returned home from who knew where with dead weeds limp behind her ears. Her mother, Kelly Jo Sinclair, said, "You know dandelions are weeds, right? Buckles, you are wearing weeds in your hair."

KJ's daughter smiled vacantly. "Mom, they make wine from dandelions."

In little more than crotch-length denim shorts that should have been illegal, Buckles jiggled braless, her chest not-quite-adequately

covered by a huge maroon and green paisley kerchief knotted behind her neck and knotted again at the small of her back. Her
black rubber sandals were carved from truck tires. Though her hips
and legs belonged to a woman, the exposed flesh on KJ's seventeen-year-old daughter's arms and back rippled under a stubborn
layer of smooth baby fat. The kid would be eighteen in October. KJ
did not like to think about having a daughter living at home who
was eighteen. Seventeen was bad enough. College could not come
too soon.

Buckles grabbed the stair rail and stomped up to her room, every step booming like Clydesdales charging across a drum. When
her door slammed, first Mick Jagger sang how dandelions could
make you cry, and then Ringo's booming drum introduction to
Sergeant Pepper's Lonely Hearts Club Band rattled the entrance foyer's chandelier.

The kid's record player had three settings: *Off, Unbearable,* and
Attack.

KJ forked chicken salad from a plastic container onto lettuce
leaves. Before the kid had barged through the creaky iron gate and
passed the hedges, KJ had stepped down submerged stairs into
their swimming pool, cooled herself, and then gone to her kitchen.
Wet footprints marked her path across the kitchen's burnt umber
Spanish tile. They'd evaporate in minutes.

KJ set herself a simple goal. She needed to ambush Buckles
into a simple conversation about dinner plans. But because KJ had
greeted her only child with a stupid impulsive observation about
weeds, Buckles was now barricaded behind a closed door and a
wall of rock and roll noise. What had she been thinking? Two years
ago, KJ's remark would have been laughed off, but these days even
the most innocuous comment was a fingernail drawn over a chalk-
board. At least they were not screaming. Not yet, anyway.

KJ scraped her uneaten lunch into the trash, her appetite gone.
She thought to fix things. Or at least try, but KJ was intimidated by
her daughter. Worse, her daughter knew it.

Her hand clutched the pool towel tighter to her chest. She grew chilled on the staircase, knobby toes gripping the beige hallway shag. Gooseflesh puckered her shoulders and arms. Her ear against the solid wood of Buckles' door detected only that damn song about flowers, gentle people, and San Francisco. Buckles played the song constantly. Was it possible for a phonograph needle to carve through the vinyl to the other side of the record? She'd have to talk again to Jack. The kid had too much leisure and too much money, and Jack saw that only as a mark of his own success, not that it was warping Buckles into a spoiled brat.

Two years ago they'd agreed that the nearby tony private Dobb's Academy upper division would be ideal for the kid. She was gifted, and both of them saw no reason she would not attend Radcliffe or, like her mother, Wellesley, but the public high school left her bored and uninspired. They agreed to the Academy's requirement that she be set back a half year to catch up to the school's intense curriculum. "It's a money grab," Jack said, "shaking us down for a little more tuition." But they'd agreed to the condition when Buckles shrugged and said, "Whatever." They opted for Dobbs' 4-day per week residential program open only to nearby applicants, but the plan precipitated unforeseen problems.

Come summer, the international student body scattered all over the world, leaving Buckles at loose ends. She did little beyond reading *The Village Voice*, swimming dozens of laps, sunning herself more brown than any blonde white girl should be, occasionally taking the commuter train to the city, and, unknown to her father, smoking enough marijuana for a New Orleans Dixieland quintet.

At a guidance counselor session months ago, the counselor suggested that Buckles had too few friends because she was intellectually gifted as well as being effortlessly gorgeous. She'd need to overcome the curses of wealth, good looks, and brains if anyone expected her to attend the best colleges. The counselor made notations on a record sheet, beamed her smile, and pronounced Buckles an underachiever.

Back in their Mercedes, Jack said, "Underachiever? That means they have no idea of how to educate the kid. Maybe we need to scar her face to make her less pretty. Can't have any advantages, can we?"

Buckles said, "Fuck that cunt."

God's most precious angel had silken blond hair, cobalt blue eyes, and the vocabulary of a Saigon streetwalker.

Jack kept his eyes on the road, but failed to suppress his grin. KJ spun to kneel in her seat. Buckles' eyes took in the world passing by her window, her eyebrows so pale they were invisible. The kid's valentine-lips belonged on a porcelain cherub imported from Germany.

Jack said, "That's no way to talk, young lady," in a tone that meant *You tell 'em, kid.*

For KJ's husband, the matter had ended that day, but for KJ, the situation worsened as spring stretched into summer. It was time to reset some boundaries, but KJ had no idea how.

She followed Buckles up the stairs, but her fist hovered over Buckles' door, hesitating. The last time KJ had entered her daughter's room unbidden, she'd interrupted an Advanced Geometry tutoring session that somehow required a boy named Spencer to lay face down and shirtless across Buckles' bed. Jack had been off on one of his week-long trips to London. Though Buckles had to be younger than the boy, she was tutoring Spencer for an AP exam that would smooth his way into Harvard. Later, KJ learned that Spencer was the son of an American diplomat stationed in Belgium, which was why the Academy had granted Spencer permission to combine home cooking and tutoring with a Friday overnight to the Sinclair home. KJ had allegedly signed the permission form; Buckles' forgery must have been credible.

When KJ opened Buckles' door, Buckles was straddling the boy's narrow hips to work his neck and muscled shoulders with her hands. Her tennis shorts had been more or less on, though a zipper gaped open. The boy's white tennis shirt was bunched into a roll just south of the Lacoste alligator. Buckles' eyes ignited with indigo fires of furious defiance as KJ spun a retreat to the safer hallway. Either geometry had radically changed since KJ pondered triangles at her New Orleans Catholic school, or KJ's nuns had deliberately overlooked some of Euclid's more earthy theorems.

Spencer spent the night in a spare bedroom; KJ spent the night listening for footsteps. In the morning, the boy made pleasant sophisticated conversation over a breakfast of scrambled eggs, rye toast, and fresh fruit, all prepared perfectly by Buckles. Spencer adored Brussels and urged both his breakfast companions to make the journey. Then KJ with Buckles drove him back to the Academy where a lacrosse match was scheduled for late Saturday morning against Deerfield. KJ had even cheered when Spencer scored a goal.

That night, KJ had insisted that Buckles and she have The Talk.

Long before Buckles enrolled at the Dobbs Academy, the Scarsdale progressive public schools had attended to the mechanics of human parts. KJ drew a deep breath to venture beyond stamens and pistils as Buckles stirred clover honey into her ginger tea, but the kid preemptively said, "He's a dork, Mom. He gets really good chocolate, but he is nothing special. I would not let him get to second base." The patently false reassurance convinced KJ that third base must have at some time at least been visited, and Spencer almost surely had knocked one out of the park. But why catch her daughter up on it? There was nothing to be gained, and even if the lie proved true, it would not be a lie for long. What American girl in 1967 wanted or would heed a mother's advice on when and who her first lover might be?

Buckles' pink tongue licked honey from her spoon. She said, "Don't tell Dad, please."

Buckles censored herself only for her father. It went back to the day the great romance began, the day Jack came in from shoveling snow, left his boots in the mudroom, and discovered his three-year-old daughter, christened *Abigail*, had scraped that same tongue bloody by licking the salt from the metal stays of his galoshes. She'd looked up grinning for her Daddy's approval, her perfect tiny teeth stained crimson. Jack named her *Buckles* on the spot.

During The Talk, Buckles had finished so many of KJ's sentences that eventually KJ went mute. Buckles was definitely, assuredly, unequivocally not pregnant. Buckles claimed she was a "technical virgin," a term her mother hoped still conferred a Catholic girl a range of activities that left her in a state of Grace without leaving her lonesome on Saturday nights, though KJ knew a teenage girl lied to her mother with less effort than baby ducks swam. Buckles enumerated events worse than pregnancy, ticking them off one at a time on her fingers, an annotated list of the perils in the life of a Flower Child. Had the good sisters in KJ's New Orleans school known of *chlamydia* or *gonorrhea?* KJ understood little of venereal disease until she was in college when she first read the foil on a condom and had a roommate explain the packages' contents and use to her. Nevertheless, here was her clear-eyed child almost out of 11th grade displaying an encyclopedic knowledge of syphilis, which, Buckles noted, since it could be spread even to technical virgins via oral sex, required not only close visual inspection of a partner in search of dripping discharge, but the sensible precaution of an oral dam.

"And how do you know all this?" KJ asked, genuinely curious. It might be the Summer of Love, but did well-prepared teenage girls in 1967 carry their oral dams in a purse beside a supply of ribbed condoms? Did they walk into pharmacies and say, *I'm giving head tonight. What flavor oral dams do you carry?* Dear God, did oral dams come in flavors? Spearmint? Peppermint? Cinnamon? Strawberry? Or did they come from the same soulless vending machines that dispensed condoms in seedier bar lavatories?

Buckles rolled her eyes with exasperation. "Read *The Village Voice*, Mom. Like, the times they are a'changin', you know? Don't let the classifieds shock you." Her teacup and saucer rattled into the stainless steel sink.

The Talk ended with a promise that Buckles would not soon "get horizontal" with some boy whose sole claims to adulthood were pimples, hair falling over his eyes, and a lacrosse stick. In exchange, KJ agreed to accompany Buckles to a doctor to obtain a prescription for the Pill. Since the only physician Buckles had ever known was her pediatrician, and since they agreed that having the same gynecologist might be too weird, KJ promised to ask around rather than agree to Buckles' initial plan to ride a bus to the free clinic in Yonkers. Finally, KJ conceded she would never ever again enter Buckles' room without express permission. Buckles ended The Talk when she retired to her room, Janis Joplin, and a German novel KJ knew nothing about, *Siddhartha*.

With an inviolate guarantee of privacy, as long as Jack was not home, the scent of marijuana now frequently emanated from Buckles' room. KJ, for her part, trying to keep up, did locate a copy of *The Village Voice*, and yes, the classifieds, pages of ads seeking anonymous, kinky sex, shocked her.

So on the August morning KJ stood immobile outside her daughter's bedroom, the aroma of reefer seeping from underneath her door was not unusual. The door cracked open three inches. One red-rimmed eye half-covered by a glossy cascade of freshly ironed blonde hair examined KJ.

"Wha-aat?" Buckles made it two syllables.

"I'm going out. That reading club. Do you need anything?"

"No."

"How about dinner? Pizza? Chinese? I don't want to cook. It's hot as Hell and your father will not be home for days. How about a nice Waldorf salad for us girls? I'll stop at the deli."

"Who gives a fuck?"

"Watch your mouth. Please. Profanity isn't grown-up. It's coarse."

KJ casually leaned her hip into the door, but just as casually on the door's opposite side Buckles did the same. Counterpoised in perfect balance, mother and daughter stood separated by a plank of solid white oak.

"Sorry, Mom. Really." The breeze coming through Buckles' open window carried marijuana smoke further into the house. A joss stick burned beside the kid's hookah. "When will you be back?"

"No later than eight. Anything after that, I'll call."

"Groovy." The door snapped shut.

But before KJ reached her own bedroom, Buckles charged down the hall behind her mother. The kid's arms encircled her from behind. Buckles whispered, "Love you, Mom," at her ear, squeezed her tightly, and before KJ could turn to see her daughter's face the kid had vanished again behind her door, her fog of reefer, and her wall of loud, loud music.

Charlotte said, "It's summer, am I right?" Their bartender, Timmy, nodded. "Summer means white shoes and Gimlets. Gin. Go easy on the Rose's. That stuff is fattening."

"Not vodka?"

"Vodka is from Russia. Communists live in Russia. I'm a patriot, Timmy." Charlotte's long fingers scooped salted peanuts, pretzels, and Chex baked with Worcestershire from a teak salad bowl, then sucked each of her fingers clean. "It is officially cocktail hour."

KJ said, "It's two-thirty."

"I am on Paris time."

The girls of the library reading club met from eleven to noon on the second Wednesday of the month. They'd fallen into the habit of ending their monthly chats at *The Village Lantern. The Lantern* was a short walk across the library's paved parking lot and down a narrow tree-covered street. Timmy was a generous pour, easy on the eyes, and the subdued lighting flattered the aging girls into believing they were ten years younger than they were. Even in summer, the place was colder than a meat locker.

But lately only KJ and Charlotte made their way to the pub. It was a sweltering August, so most of the girls headed home to private swimming pools, tennis club pools, country club pools, or sought out some volunteer activity that allowed them to feel useful. The steamy August reminded KJ of her New Orleans childhood when on the worst days she and her mother spent afternoons and evenings in movie theaters for the only public air conditioning available. The summer of *Gone with the Wind,* they sat through three consecutive continuous showings, only leaving when Atlanta burned a fourth time.

Outside, her armpits had run soup. Immersed in the restaurant's chill she wished she'd brought the off-white sweater with pearl buttons she left balled on the rear seat of her Ford wagon. Her tennis culottes left her legs exposed; from calf to thigh she dimpled gooseflesh.

The library discussion was supposed to have been about *The Arrangement*, the bestseller by Elia Kazan. KJ had read only half. Charlotte had dog-eared the good parts, by which she meant several sex scenes. Instead of the book, they half-whispered gossip about their neighbors, all of whom Charlotte assured her were doing it with gardeners, pool boys, tennis instructors, and even grocery delivery clerks not yet out of high school. According to Charlotte, the men passing through Scarsdale ploughed the women who stayed in Scarsdale with more skill than Porfirio Rubirosa ploughed Hollywood starlets.

When no one else had anymore dirt, Charlotte clapped her hands to pronounce the meeting would continue at *The Lantern,* but only Charlotte and KJ went there. On the strength of two Manhattans, Charlotte then confessed that her husband, Howie the dentist, was drilling his office hygienist.

"How do you stand it?" KJ asked.

"The Mercedes convertible soothes most of my pain—"

"That's crazy."

"And then there's the country club and the house. After we buy the lot next door and put in our own tennis court, I may consider a divorce. But for now, I suffer." Her lipstick left a crescent on the lip of her glass. "I like my life, KJ. I even like Howie, the cheating prick. I like how my boys are turning out. Besides, what would I do? Open a flower shop? Declare I was an interior decorator? I could specialize in hand-carved wooden eagles, I suppose. They sell like hotcakes wherever there are split-level ranch houses with flagpoles on the front lawn. We are women of status and position, and why would anyone walk away from that? We don't actually have to *do* anything except be rich, and I am getting good at that. Why throw away a lifetime of faking orgasms with an impulsive flight to Reno? I mean, at least we do not live in Mamaroneck. Do you know the Mamaroneck town motto?"

"No."

"'Almost Scarsdale.'" She drank most of her gimlet.

"What about your self-respect?"

"Self-respect gets in the way." Charlotte withdrew an American Express Gold Card from her purse and snapped it to the bar. "That's my name on it. See? That's my self-respect. Do you have one?"

"I have Jack's credit cards."

Charlotte peered at her over the lip of her glass. "Oh, now that's precious. Get your own credit, Kel. Women are lousy credit risks. No jobs, no skills, and when we do work we earn *bupkis*. Jack will need to cosign, but after that you will have your own credit line. You can't rent a car or sign a lease without credit, and you can't get credit without a husband who cosigns. Suppose Jack is flattened by a bulldozer?"

The plastic in KJ's purse indeed had Jack's name on it. "I won't worry about it," she said, smiling; but, of course, she worried instantly.

Timmy replaced Charlotte's gimlet without being asked. He raised his eyebrows to ask if KJ wanted another, but she shook her head. They were regulars. Regulars did not need to speak.

Time passed. Charlotte's glass refilled and was emptied and refilled. KJ sipped half of another round. KJ did not realize how long they'd occupied bar stools until Timmy asked if they wanted him to turn up Huntley and Brinkley, the dinner hour NBC news. Charlotte said: "Leave the damn thing down. I am tired of riots."

Staring up at the silent TV and videos of Detroit in flames, or maybe it was Newark or Buffalo, KJ said, "I don't get it. What do you suppose is happening? I don't understand anything anymore." She made the mistake of telling Charlotte of her tiff with Buckles.

"Times change, dear. Drink more gin; things will make more sense."

"It's more than that. When we were kids, life ran in regular channels."

"You mean 'ruts.'"

"No, no, no. We were regular people. I was in the South, you were up North, but things were pretty much the same for us. We knew what to expect and how it would work. We married young, we had babies as soon as we could. We were educated in New England because that was where a first-class education was to be found."

"Also high-earning husbands."

"That too, but what of it? We smiled no matter how bad things were, and we worked hard to look good. Curlers, pushup bras ..."

"Herringbone stays were invented by the Marquis de Sade."

"How about that we touched each other when we danced? Being in a man's arms meant something. Have you seen how kids dance today?"

"It's St. Vitus Dance. They're stoned out of their minds, of course, but why not? We have alcohol; they have marijuana. It's all the same."

"I don't think so. My mother's people went to cocktail parties to bad-mouth Roosevelt, not to conk out on the floor. Roosevelt was supposed to be president forever. We were in a war, but there was no doubt about who were the good guys. I knit socks for servicemen. I danced at the USO. Buckles thinks if you knit socks for a soldier you are a warmonger."

Charlotte emptied the teak bowl of nuts and crackers onto the bar to extract Brazil nuts. She sighed. "Do you still own a girdle?"

"I think so. But that's not my point."

"No, that is my point. Buckles doesn't own a girdle, does she? Maybe you mouth off to her because you are jealous?"

She was a ways from drunk, but her drink made KJ fuzzy. "I am not jealous of her. That's the kind of thing she would say. It's ridiculous, Charl."

"She'll have options we never dreamed of. That's why you ask her nasty questions about weeds in her hair. Wait a second. God, I hope she's on birth control."

KJ nodded. "For months."

"Well, there it is, dear. Before she is out of college, she'll have taken more lovers than you and your mother and her mother had in all three lifetimes, and she will never have to worry about consequences. I've lost count, but how many lovers have you had? Five? Six?"

KJ did not answer her. It was two, actually, but she was not about to tell Charlotte about her anemic sex life. She'd hear no end of it. But Charlotte was making sense. Was that why KJ compulsively challenged her daughter over sexual details that transformed into blood sport? Charlotte's explanation lodged in her mind like a pebble in her shoe on a two-mile hike.

Every woman in their reading group had a theory as to why their kids were adrift and the fabric of the country was shredding. Cosmic forces were at work. They blamed the Pill, drugs, colored rock and roll singers, Martin Luther King, that horrible Harvard professor Timothy Leary, Bob Dylan—who was really a Jew, so at least that theory made sense—fluoride in the water, the Beatles, the Democratic Party, or Dr. Seuss, yet another card-carrying Communist who plotted to win the hearts and minds of American children with his clever little tales of fair play that were really socialist parables. Walter Cronkite nightly reported on the Generation Gap as if each new outrage was as common as head lice among second graders. Generation Gap? It was more like Generation Abyss. As for the fashion model, Twiggy, no one had an explanation for Twiggy. Marilyn Monroe singing *Happy Birthday Mr. President* in front of 18,000 people in Madison Square Garden was sexy and easy to understand—stick your ass out, pop your boobs, and purse your lips—but Twiggy's appeal was unfathomable. Charlotte called her *the human ironing board with a hole in it*.

Charlotte kept her eyes on the TV, glommed a handful of nuts, and asked, "Do you remember where you were when they bombed Pearl Harbor?"

"Church. With my mother. The news was on the radio by the time we came home. The president declared war the very next day."

"And exactly where were you when Vietnam started?"

"I haven't the slightest. When did it start, anyway?"

"No one knows, dearie. No one knows." Charlotte touched KJ's wrist. "I pay attention to this stuff because I have sons. Vietnam is like the clap. We caught it from the French." Charlotte consolidated her drinks, pouring the last into the new. "When we were kids, John Wayne could knock the stuffing out of anyone. But I swear to you, if Duke himself comes for my boys, after I kick him in the nuts, Howie and I are packing our bags to escort the boys across the bridge at Niagara Falls, just four happy tourists who are never coming back. Howie can bring his damned hygienist as long as we can get our boys out of the country. We hear McGill is a lovely college. We'll make a huge donation and take up cross-country skiing." Her swizzle stick traced a wet line on the bar.

"Really?"

"Really. We opened an emergency account in Montreal three months ago. All we have to do is wire ourselves more money. Do you realize, KJ, I am the only person in my family without a penis? Penises are less marvelous than men think, and they have a way of straying where they do not belong, but these penises are my penises. Today my three penises are attending a Yankee game. Isn't that swell? They invited me to go along, but I prefer getting stinko with you. I like my penises, and they like me, and I do wish the Penis-in-Chief was not humping the hygienist, but I know it can't last. Howie gets bored easily, even if the little tart sucks like a Hoover."

"Sometimes I am grateful I have only my Buckles."

"Girls are great until they are eleven; then it's PMS all day, every day for several years. Buckles must be past that. She goes to college in September, right? Things will calm down when she is out of the house. You'll see."

"Not yet. Another year. She's taking all these AP classes to get a leg up."

"At least you'll never need to worry about her coming home in a box." Charlotte sucked in a breath and leaned over the bar. "Why do you suppose Timmy isn't in the Army?"

"I think he may be a homosexual," KJ whispered.

Charlotte sighed. "With that tush, I should have guessed. Such a waste. Do you think Timmy can teach my boys to fake being queer? Basic fag lessons, enough to pass a physical. Or fail a physical. It depends on your point of view." She glommed the last pretzels and Chex. "And now I have to pee." Charlotte wore Tretorns with no socks, but when she slid off the barstool she staggered as if she were balancing on ball bearings.

KJ's swizzle stick stood at attention in the melting shaved ice of her final Gimlet, still half full. Chet Huntley stared down at her with his sunken, disapproving eyes condemning all of America on its express rail trip to Hell. People in green khakis led by a priest in vestments had broken into a Selective Service office to pour pig's blood over draftee files.

Smelling faintly of vomit and strongly of fresh perfume, Charlotte returned from the Ladies Room.

"Should Timmy call a taxi?"

"If we sit still, I'll be fine. It's the spins, is all."

Charlotte placed her folded hand on the bar and then her forehead on her hands. She soon lightly snored. Timmy pretended not to notice as he lined up Old Fashioned glasses mouth-down on a dishtowel. On the TV, a bloom of napalm and black smoke immolated a peasant village; Chet Huntley and then David Brinkley bid America a good night.

KJ dropped some crumpled bills on the bar. She could not leave Charlotte at *The Village Lantern*, but with all three of her penises attending a baseball game there was no one to retrieve her. It was not the first time that Timmy agreed with KJ that Charlotte could not be allowed to drive. After he made the phone call, while they waited for Charlotte's taxi, KJ used the bar phone to call home, but Buckles did not answer.

Buckles was either stoned in the hammock or topless hidden by hedges on a chaise and too comfortable to get up. She had to be on the pool deck. It was too steamy to be anywhere else. Then she had Information connect her to Antonio's. Once Charlotte was folded like a sack of grass seed into the taxi, KJ went to her rust red Ford station wagon and drove to Antonio's for her pizza with mushrooms, artichoke, and extra garlic, Buckles' favorite.

Home, she carried the pizza across the lawn and through the iron gate out back.

Buckles was not at the pool.

The pizza box burned her fingertips. The house's glass kitchen slider was unlocked. KJ made it into the kitchen where she dropped the pizza on the kitchen island. She blew on her fingers before she opened the box, near swooning at the aroma. She was starving. Extra garlic had been the best decision of the day, maybe of her entire week.

"Artichokes!" she shouted. "Extra cheese. Buck?"

The big house swallowed her voice. If Buckles had grown impatient and gone out with one of her few friends, she'd have pinned a note to the refrigerator's corkboard. The kid was a pain in the ass, but she was a considerate pain in the ass. It was not like her to leave no word. At heart, Buckles was a good kid with a head on her shoulders, for sure smarter than her mother. She would straighten out. They'd become great friends again. KJ was sure of it.

She shouted a second time from the base of the stairs before she returned to the kitchen to sit on a high wicker chair. She scarfed a second slice of pizza and chugged a cold can of Tab.

"I'm putting it away, now," she called.

Nothing.

KJ climbed the stairs. For the second time that day she came to Buckles' door, but this time after a single knock she did not hesitate.

The room was more impeccable than a *Good Housekeeping* cover. The last sunshine filtered through the off-white damask curtains. Gold dust motes drifted in the still air. The sateen shams were centered and puffed on the queen-size four-poster, the cream-colored coverlet smooth and tight as if it had been ironed.

A brown legal envelope was propped against the stacked cushions. The seal parted easily. KJ's hands shook.

Dear Mom:

Don't come after me. Please.

I don't want you to worry. I know what I am doing. I don't expect you to understand. I am so excited! Like Bob Dylan said, *Your sons and your daughters are beyond your command.*

I have a good plan, I promise. By the time you read this, I will be far away. My friend with a driver's license will use his mother's Volvo to get me north to the Bear Mountain Bridge. It's only about an hour straight up 9. The boy is not going with me, so don't worry about that. I am not stupid enough to get married. I'll hitch on Route 6. It's a great road, a little twisty, but it will take me west. No one hitchhikes across the George Washington Bridge or the Tappan Zee, right? They are too crowded.

See? This is a good plan.

I don't want to miss California, not this year, and I know you and Dad would not let me go. I can do it. I have some money saved up and please don't hate me but I have been taking a few dollars, just a few at a time, from your purse or Daddy's wallet for most of the summer so I should be all right. I bet you never noticed! ☺ When I get to Haight-Ashbury (that's a neighborhood in San Francisco) I will join a commune. Communes are the future. If everyone lived on a commune, no one would need money ever again. We will live off the land. If everybody loves everyone else and shares everything, we can really do it. All you need is love, right?

It's like you and Daddy and April. Daddy said you know all about her, so I guess it is all right to say that I like her. Daddy said not to mention to people that you and him have an open marriage because most people would not understand, but someday because of kids like me marriage will be over and everyone will be happier. You and Dad are the coolest parents anyone could have. April is cool, too. We had lunch that day I took the train to the city and we talked all about you while we waited for Daddy at O'Neal's. He was late, as usual. She told me that you have not yet met her, but I am sure you will like her, too. I promise I will come back to visit all three of you someday when you all live together, but not for a while.

Tell Daddy I love him, but I just I can't sit around today waiting for him to come home from wherever he is because today is the only day my friend can borrow his mother's Volvo. It's a very safe car. I need to start my real life. If I wait, I will miss everything!

I promise I will call when I get to California. I just don't know when that will be. Time is just an illusion, anyway. And nobody should come after me because I really will be OK.

> Peace out and bliss,
> Buckles

The note was in a childish scrawl, half-print, half script, written with a smudgy pencil on a sheet of lined yellow legal paper that had been unevenly folded to fit in the envelope. The smile face was drawn in India Ink by a calligraphy pen that had smeared on the fold. She had not waited for the ink to dry.

KJ's legs folded under her. She sat on the floor, faint, weeping. Her head rested against her daughter's bed, the yellow notepaper slipped from her shaking hand to the floor.

Her baby was gone.

About two hours after KJ's teeth parted a slice of pizza with artichokes and garlic, Big Bill, *Donna May*, and Buckles careened wildly across two westbound lanes and the dirt shoulders of the road into eastern Ohio. Bill's teeth ground fists of crackling whites easy as Tic-Tacs. He'd blink and blink and blink; his eyes bulged; the muscles of his neck wound tighter and tighter.

He suggested that Buckles needed to meet Little Bill, the reason

Big Bill was called Big Bill. A shooting star split into three silent fireballs in the sky to their left. Buckles tried to concentrate on the scenery, but the Ohio night revealed nothing. She could not avert her eyes. The zipper of Big Bill's pants rasped open. When he reached into his pants, *Donna May* swung violently from one side to the other and back again. Big Bill described in precise detail what Little Cherry Lollipop would first, second, then third do for Little Bill.

Buckles' eyes brimmed and her nose ran as Big Bill elaborated on how parts of him would explore parts of her, an experience that had to happen at 100 miles per hour. She could see that, couldn't she? With goddam Ezra waiting for the shipment in goddam Kansas, there was no goddam stopping. But they could do it all, anyway. They could. Buckles instinctively knew that crying would drive Big Bill even more crazy violent, so she choked back convulsive sobs and tried to think what to say. If *Donna May* were moving more slowly, she'd have jumped, but at these speeds the road would scrape her to hamburger, a point Big Bill was happy to point out at her hesitation. His plan was to cross into Indiana and run the scales by blasting by a weigh station he knew would be closed. Since his Little Cherry Lollipop was with him all the way, they could push on. "Little Bill is at his best in the morning and *Donna May* runs best at night. Everything is working for us. As long as we don't run out of magic whites and we see no bears, we don't never need to stop. We don't even need to slow down. Ain't that something? Is that a plan? I know you want a man who can last all night, am I right? Come on now, admit it. Every gal does. It's your lucky day. Look at Little Bill here. He's ready. I'm ready, and you are ready enough. Just take a look."

Big Bill sounded *Donna May*'s horn again, the blast a long lonesome moan that dopplered over endless dark fields. He suddenly pressed the accelerator so hard that Buckles fell back in her seat. *Donna May* lunged forward on the straightaway, her engine clatter deafening. The speedometer needle quivered above 110. Big Bill tucked a fresh chaw into his cheek. Came a bend in the road, the 18-wheeler scarred the earth when its wheels left the shoulder, scattering gravel and dirt until the tires found purchase and seized the rig back onto pavement.

Big Bill spit tobacco juice through his teeth out his open window. The wind roared. Buckles' throat clamped shut with a crab of panic. The globe of golden light that floated through the August night was *Donna May*'s cab. If she fought him, Big Bill would have his way no matter what she did, and when he was finished with her, he'd drop whatever was left of her, broken, out the truck cab door.

But what if he locked her in the back of the truck? What if his plan was to take her along and use her again and again as *Donna May* hauled them across all of America?

Daddy the Shitheel claimed that crying never accomplished anything and that everything was negotiable, so she inhaled past the lump in her throat to draw enough breath to speak. She marshalled every bit of strength in her five-foot-three-inches to say as plain as she was able. "Bill, that plan is not agreeable."

His hand rose to strike her, but her voice seemed to somehow calm him. Big Bill said, "I get it. I get it. I get it, sweetmeat. No need to play hard-to-get. You'll get paid, darlin'. Ask anyone. Big Bill is a fair dealer. Cross my heart and hope to die, I swear. You get your ride, you get your money, and I get what Little Bill needs. All I ask is that if Ezra wants a taste for my being late, you cooperate. Now, that's fair, ain't it? You earn, I earn, and we are all square."

His belt buckle clanked as it fell open, his zipper rasping. Trade her to Ezra? She should have seen that. For a half second, she went blind with new panic, and in that half second Big Bill locked both her wrists in his right hand. He steered with his left and his knee.

Buckles struggled free and managed to swing her big tote up between them. The tote was not much, nothing at all, to have between them, but it was better than Daddy's business card. *Donna May* blew by isolated passenger cars, threatening to blow them off the highway. Big Bill twice had to release her hands when *Donna May* began to fishtail across two lanes, the truck's rear outrunning the cab; it was all Big Bill could do to wrestle the 18-wheeler straight without blowing his tires or flipping the truck rolling into a cornfield. Orange and red sparks flew skyward from the diesel exhaust when downshifted, but as soon as the truck settled back on the road, Bill goaded their speed back up to 100 and returned to the details of how he'd use Buckles, how Buckles was going to thank him when he was done, and if she cooperated real good, why there'd be no reason at all to invite Ezra to have a taste. He'd hide his Little Cherry Lollipop somewhere a mile away from Ezra while he negotiated a fair price, and then come back for her. "Now how does that sound?"

Donna May seemed to develop a mind all her own. Buckles pulled her feet up onto the seat, coiling her knees ready to kick out at Big Bill. He whined. "You are going to get us killed if you keep this shit up. Now, it is time, darlin'. It is past time. I don't care if you suck or fuck, but it is time. Will it help if I tell you how pretty you are? Is that what you need to hear? Big Bill is agreeable. Sweet talk is never a problem. You're about the prettiest girl I ever saw, but I swear, if those lips and tongue aren't wrapped around Little Bill in another minute, that pretty face will be a memory. I hope to God you took a good look in the mirror this morning, because you ain't never going to look that good again. You understand what I am saying to you?"

Bill leaned closer for a kiss. His breath smelled of rot, tobacco, and menthol. When she did not put her lips to his cheek, his voice rose to tell her she really wasn't as pretty as she thought. Her tits and ass looked damned fine, why else did she think he'd brought her aboard *Donna May*? But his voice rose to a new higher pitch when he asked how pretty she thought she'd be if he sliced through her nose or took an ear. "I can do that!" he shouted. His eyes bulged. "Who is here to stop me?"

He emptied the paper bag's last whites into his mouth, grinding them like ice. Then his voice dropped to a whisper as he pleaded with his Cherry Lollipop. Bill was truly sorry that they disagreed, but he was not about to stop in darkness in the middle of West Bumfuck to let her out. There was a contract between them the minute that sweet ass touched *Donna May*'s red leather bucket seat.

Night time was running time, by God. He'd stop long enough to screw her blind by day once he settled with Ezra and his boys in Kansas if that was what she wanted, but he needed what a man needed and he needed it now, no mistake. He gripped her wrist, but when she kicked his thigh his hold on her went slack. He had to downshift for what should have been a gentle curve but at 100 was a tight turn. *Donna May*'s rear wheels started to slide out from under the truck. Cursing, Big Bill struggled for control. The 18-wheeler fishtailed. Buckles smelled burning rubber.

Big Bill wept and begged. Ezra and his boys could give less than a fuck about his troubles. "They want product. Late is late, and they have their way with baseball bats, blowtorches and pliers. They don't need no goddam excuse. To them, it's all sport. Don't go thinking they will keep you out of it. A pretty little girl like you can keep those boys entertained for days. And they are not near as kind as me. Not near."

Buckles grabbed the crackling walkie-talkie and thought to shout *Help!* but all that did was make Big Bill's eyes narrow to slits before his yellowed teeth bared. "You dumb cooz, you have to press the button to transmit," he said, and yanked the pig's tail connector cord out of the unit.

By the morning's small hours, Buckles was crying most all the time. Big Bill had managed to tug her shorts and underwear below her knees, but he could not get Buckles to mount him with one hand on her and the other on the wheel. Buckles was being worn down from slapping at his insistent hand reaching into her denim vest, grabbing at her thighs, and trying to jackknife her legs apart. Her left breast was spotted by a purpled bruise. Her hands had gone to Little Bill two times, but Little Bill stayed soft. Big Bill blamed her for not trying hard enough, though she was sure it was the drugs he took. She could not bring herself to do more than touch him. At home, a touch had been enough for James or Spencer, but they were boys and Big Bill was a man. If Big Bill had been sane enough to stop at the side of the road, he'd have had his way despite her terror, but crank, his fear, and his schedule had him believing he had to take her behind the wheel at 100 miles per hour, an acrobatic goal easily achieved if she'd just swing a leg over him like he was a goddam bicycle and Little Bill her goddam bicycle seat. She knew how to ride a goddam bicycle, didn't she? She could face forward or back, it made no never mind to him. Both in turn if she wanted.

Buckles could not breathe. He apologized that he did not have the time to fuck her good and proper, and he was sorry for that, but it was time to get down to business. Big Bill was, after all, a family man. All that Little Bill needed was a little fun, but she needed to keep in her mind that Ezra's idea of fun involved power tools and ropes. Was that what she wanted? Big Bill raised his clenched fist to strike her.

Buckles rose to her knees on *Donna May*'s seat. Far away heat lightning flashed. Big Bill clutched at the back of her neck and pulled her head into his lap. She breathed the sour smell of him. She was able to pull her head back long enough to shout a desperate lie, "Mister, my Daddy is a lawyer and I am *jailbait*."

Big Bill heard little more than the amphetamine powered tom-tom of his heart, but he did hear that, plain as the Final Trump and twice as ominous. Lawyers, jailbait, and Big Bill had a long and sorry-ass history in Ohio. The cooz's age, if it were true, ordinarily would do nothing but pique Big Bill's eagerness for several forms of non-consensual sodomy, but they were close to goddam Akron. From the moment she'd climbed aboard, he'd been blinded by available pussy, bare arms, and bare buttery thighs, but now he peered into an abyss of endless torment.

Sensing his momentary hesitation, Buckles lowered her eyes and whined, "I am fif-*teen*."

His pinhole eyes went from the road to steal a new glance at Buckles in the cab's dim light. Sweet Jesus, Little Cherry Lollipop *could really be* fifteen, if she was that, and here was Big Bill with a four-year-old bullshit rap in goddam Akron, the shithole where a little no-name whore with a juvie sheet longer than a right-handed gorilla's right arm near put Big Bill away by claiming rape. The amphetamine curtain over Big Bill's eyes dissolved before this new terror. The Ohio prosecutor had twisted the little tart into claiming forcible rape because statutory rape could get Bill no more than a year with her record, time he could have done standing on his head, but it never got to trial. His asshole good-for-ratshit lawyer negotiated a plea, and the prosecutor agreed once the two thousand dollars Big Bill borrowed against *Donna May* was in his brief-case. Ezra, that blood-sucking son-of-a-bitch bought the paper on *Donna May*, and the good people of Ohio had been happy to see Bill let off with time-served and parole, provided he made a weekly phone call to his Ohio parole bitch. Big Bill was free as a bird, but if he looked sideways at a Girl Scout in Ohio, the parole-bitch would have his ass in Beaumont where some weightlifting Black guy would make Big Bill his wife.

The Emporia-cooked meth wrapped in a loose canvas tarp that near caught fire from the heat of *Donna May*'s brakes was bad enough, but though young pussy was the best pussy, and young head was the best head, Little Cherry Lollipop was nothing but an open trapdoor above a world of shit he did not want nor need.

His brain broke into a cold flop sweat. What if this bit of jail-bait had been sent by the parole-bitch? Could Ohio be trolling for Big Bill? It was entrapment, for sure, but down in Beaumont no one would give a shit. The situation needed to be fully analyzed.

The crank clogging Bill's brain bled away. His first thought was to fuck the little jailbait bitch, snap her neck and throw her from *Donna May*'s cab, but nothing motivated County Mounties more than a blond, blue-eyed child's corpse at roadside. Big Bill already knew he would never see Paradise, but he feared the certainty of Hell, Hell being located inside the walls of Beaumont prison where baby-rapists were passed among inmates who had kids outside, probably too many kids, probably more kids than they knew, proba-bly kids who looted and shooted for the joy of looting and shooting, and here the state of Ohio plotted to deliver the baby-rapist Big Bill so they might settle their bad accounts with God. No, kill-ing the jailbait bitch in *Donna May* might put him behind the big walls where Big Bill would live a week before his front teeth were knocked out for the easy access, ever-ready blowjob. His ass would know the feel of being fucked by a locomotive.

But that very moment Little Bill was trying to convince Big Bill to take his chances. Just do the bitch.

That was when Sweet Jesus trailing Celestial Glory showed Big Bill His infinite mercy. The Perrysburg truck-stop rose on their right, a glowing island of Divine luminous green rising in Ohio's morning twilight. Big Bill sobbed his gratitude to the power and mercy of Heaven. Praise God, but Jesus loves the sinner! Big Bill could find another Flower Child in Indiana or Illinois. They lined the roads that summer like hitchhiking daffodils.

Whites had drained his spit, but his mouth went into an over-drive anyway. He needed to explain. He'd meant nothing by calling her Lollipop. Shit, didn't he have a girl of his own that was near her age?

"Admit it! Admit it! I can't be expected to think some hitch-hiking hippie-girl could be only fifteen. Every trooper in the state would agree with me there. Look at you! I ain't but flesh and blood. You look twenty at least. Maybe twenty-two. Fuckable, too. Suppose I'd forgotten myself and done even half of what you had in mind? Where would I be then, I ask you?"

He had only been trying to help her out. It was Big Bill being too good again. Snares and traps awaited Big Bill at every mile marker. He was too good, far too good. Once he dropped her off, best not mention Big Bill to anyone, ever. Nothing about Big Bill, nothing about any Peterbilt named *Donna May*, and for goddam sure nothing about goddam product that did not appear on no manifest. He'd been making up stories to pass the night. Did he say Ezra? There was no Ezra. Ezra who? And if there was no Ezra, he was damned sure not in Emporia. No, Ezra would be in Boise. But he weren't in no Boise, neither, because there was no Ezra, not in Boise nor Emporia. Big Bill had made him up, a story like Goldilocks or Snow White meant to pass the time and keep her amused. But now it was time for her to leave and his playacting was finished.

Rapidly downshifting, *Donna May* damn near blew her engine. Sparks flew from the diesel exhaust. The truck crept up the exit ramp and trembled to a stuttering stop. Big Bill hardly tapped the brakes. He did not want to be around long enough to have no trooper notice no bare-legged blonde child leaping to the ground, a minor child that had crossed state lines with him, after begging her way onto his truck back in Scranton offering all manner of favors just for a ride to Ohio. Did she still have her panties on? She had no bra, but bare tits was not so unusual these days.

Buckles tossed her rainbow tote to the concrete, grabbed the truck's chrome steady bar, and quick as she could leapt from the cab. As her sandals touched the tarmac, Big Bill threw crumpled money at her. Before the folding cash could be swept off by the wind, Buckles slapped her foot down on a ten.

Under a plume of white exhaust, Donna May shuddered back to life. The Peterbilt lumbered up the acceleration lane, the truck's amber running lights flickered once and then once more, and then, followed by a great rush of wind, *Donna May* and Big Bill punched a tunnel westward through air.

The sound of crickets settled on her. Buckles breathed the oily smell of fuel. Her record player, her backpack filled with her music, and most of her money were gone, vanished with the truck.

The jaundiced windows of the diner at the Perrysburg truck-stop were unseeing eyes under a Biblical plague of moths. A final shooting star scratched heaven. The rising east wind carried the smell of crumbling earth, manure, Ohio corn, diesel, and the new day forming itself under a smudge of barely visible haze at the horizon. It was 3:30 in the morning.

Buckles was beat, bruised, friendless, broke, and fourteen hours from home.

Buckles ordered her first pot of tea and went to the Ladies Room. Though she had no memory of it, she'd pissed herself fighting Big Bill's hands. She washed her crotch before she soaked her cutoffs, helicoptering them over her head to dry them before blotting her shorts with coarse brown paper towels. She stepped out of her only pair of underpants and then stepped back into her damp cutoffs. She could go commando in short cutoffs, but unless she was having a period, no one really needed underwear, right?

By 7 in the morning, Buckles had been perched on her counter seat for three hours, the cutoffs drying on her. The cold cloth reminded her of the week it took to break in her Wranglers. Twice each day, she'd worn the new jeans in a freezing bath, then kept them on until they dried completely, then wore them again in the bath until they shrank to a perfect fit. For a while, her puckered skin had stained blue. The whole process went easier if she lighted a candle in the dark bathroom before she smoked most of a bowl wondering why no one made jeans for girls. She shopped in the Boys Department where a conversion chart told her what size boys' waist fit over girls' hips. There was always too much material at the waist and never enough in the seat, but after five baths in three days the Wranglers were so perfect she could get them on by lying on the floor and pulling up the zipper with pliers.

The wrinkled teabag at the bottom of her porcelain cup looked used up near as bad as she felt. With hot water and patience she might squeeze a drop more tea from it, but truth to tell neither Buckles nor the teabag had anything left.

Every time she thought the shakes were done with her, they returned. Safety was an illusion for rich spoiled brats from the suburbs, the girl she used to be. She felt ridiculous for not having known what should have been obvious, but she resisted blaming her parents for having kept her more sheltered than a cocker spaniel. This adventure was on her. The cosmos had sent Gravedigger Beth to warn her, but she did not listen. It was only a day, but she was already no longer the stupid Flower Child who left home.

Her wallet, records, and phonograph were running west, but she was trapped in Perrysburg, Ohio, anchored by a rainbow tote bag that held the few crumpled dollars Big Bill threw at her. Two more tens were clipped together at the bag's bottom hidden beneath some T-shirts and her rolled Wranglers. The small Baggie of grass James had given her was down in there, too. That, the cutoffs she wore, and the sleeveless Sherpa-lined jeans jacket on her back were all her possessions in the world.

Articles in *The Village Voice* about how to live on the cheap had recommended Uncle Ho's Victory Sandals not only to make a statement of solidarity with the Viet Cong, but in admiration of the practical artistry required to carve a one-piece rubber sandal from a used tractor tire using no tool more complicated than a bayonet. They were durable, too. The *Voice* neglected to mention her feet would be cold, itch, and pick up crippling pebbles.

Her sandals came from a sketchy head shop near Sheridan Square, a place called *The Crystal Ship*. It throbbed with the music of The Doors, of course. The sandals cost eight dollars, a long way from free or even inexpensive. Buckles paid with money liberated from her mother's purse and pushed the penny loafers she'd worn into a sewer. The store also sold Zig-Zag rolling paper, prisms, hookahs, black light posters of Hendrix and Joplin, incense, joss sticks, dream catchers, all manner of dope pipes fitted with plumber gratings, tweezers or surgical clamps to hold the smallest roaches, but the guy at the counter with a red Jewfro who looked like one of the original Fuzzy Freak Brothers said he'd throw her ass out if she asked again about a place where she could score. The bells on the door jingled like Christmas when he opened it to look left and right. "Where are the pigs who sent you?" he'd asked, raised his middle finger to the world, and shouted, "Fuckers!"

That same day she caught a fleeting glance of Daddy and a young woman as they dodged into a Spanish restaurant on the corner of Bleecker and MacDougal. Buckles often wandered about nearby Washington Square in hopes of spying Joan Baez and Bob Dylan. They lived close, just a short walk from *Gerde's Folk City*. The one time she tried getting into *Gerde's*, the bouncer had peered at her, peered at her fake Wisconsin driver's license for which she'd paid five dollars, peered at her again, and laughed. "Nice try."

"What's wrong?" she'd asked.

"This is one of Eddie's," the bouncer said. "The guy around the corner, right? Every girl from Wisconsin can't be named 'Florence Goodbody' and every one of them have a crisp, new driver's license. Don't feel bad, kid. He rips-off a lot of weekend hippies. Did he sell you his oregano, too? Trust me. It will only give you a headache." The bouncer returned the fake ID to her, advised that she dip it in hot tea and then crumple it up a little to make the license seem older if she ever thought she might try to use it again, just not with him. "Keep it as your souvenir of Greenwich Village." She tucked the license into her wallet. As soon as she was out of the bouncer's sight, she sniffed at the baggie Eddie had sold her. It smelled like pizza.

She loitered an hour to be sure the man was truly Daddy. He was supposed to be far away in London on business, while she was supposed to be at Dobbs. Neither of them were where they were supposed to be, so she hesitated. Maybe it had not been him, but she lacked the nerve to cross the street to look into the restaurant or so much as go through the restaurant's white doors, the old-fashioned kind that swung in or out like a saloon's in a western movie.

But then Daddy boomed back onto the street. His arm encircled the young woman's narrow waist and the young woman leaned back into him. That was confusing. The slender woman had dark, short hair, wore a pale yellow miniskirt, and a wide, white patent leather belt, matching go-go boots, a lavender gaucho jacket, and a ton of eye make-up.

Daddy hailed a cab. Buckles was ready to slip away unseen when DNA closed a proximity circuit and Daddy made eye contact with his daughter across the narrow street. It was too late to pretend they did not see each other. Arm extended, palm down, like he was steadying a skittish horse, Daddy gestured that Buckles wait. He leaned into the taxi to receive a long, lingering kiss from the young woman. Like a woman drowning, her arms went up to encircle his neck. It may have been across a street and through taxi glass, but Buckles knew an open-mouthed kiss when she saw it.

Once the cab pulled away, after wiping his lips with his sleeve cuff, broadcasting his widest shit-eating lawyer smile, Daddy crossed Bleecker. Buckles readied herself for the bullshit-cascade. Daddy-the-lawyer was talented at whipping up custom-made bull-shit. People paid him money for effective lying, enough that he could maintain Buckles and her mother in a two-story Tudor house with a backyard pool in Scarsdale, with money for her to attend Dobbs. Being rich was a shame she endured.

His first words were to marvel at the incredible odds of two people bumping into each other in New York City. "Eight million to one," he'd said, chided her on playing hooky. "So now my best girl knows a secret."

He said that as if she'd discovered an unwrapped Christmas gift under a T-shirt in the back of his closet, rather than having been discovered with a young woman who'd strained upward to slip her tongue down Daddy's throat. He promised Buckles he would explain how it was that his London client had chosen at the last second to come to New York, but he had no time to talk right then. "Business," he said, a word that could cut any conversation short. He kissed his bestest girl's cheek; his breath smelled of fruity wine, his neck of expensive Bay Rum. Then, as if it were an afterthought, he asked Buckles to promise she would mention nothing to her mother. "There are factors you don't know that I have no time to explain."

"I'll try," she said, fully aware that *factors* was lawyerese for cov-ering his ass and setting Mom up to be dumped.

He pushed a ten into Buckles' hand for cab fare back to Grand Central, reassured his bestest girl a third time that the situation was not what she thought, though it unquestionably was, and then slapped the top of the taxi. Two blocks later, Buckles instructed the cab driver to stop, gave him a dollar, and walked the rest of the way to the commuter rail station to conserve the rest of Daddy's bribe while raising blisters on her feet where her sandals proved less than flexible.

Buckles wanted to believe him, but she knew that, most of the time, her father, John Sinclair, Esq. was full of shit.

The Ohio truck-stop reeked of fry oil, pepper, and onions. Buckles' seat was a mini-sea captain's armchair that swiveled on a post, though it could not spin a full circle. Her toes barely reached the floor. The breakfast crowd pushed through the revolving door and were lining up. The diner would soon want her counter seat, probably the reason the waitress crossed her arms at her chest and stared at Buckles as if Buckles were a cockroach swimming sidestroke in the mayonnaise.

Buckles tried to formulate a plan, or at least waited for one to come to her, but her mind was stuck. Big Bill popped in and out of her skull like a scary Jack-in-the-Box. She was unable to separate what was trivial from what was crucial. In her heart, she knew Big Bill was trivial, or should be, but every time she believed her ugly night aboard *Donna May* was behind her and it was time to take on whatever was next, a flash of new memory returned. Beth the Grave Robber had known what she had been talking about. Buckles promised herself to never hitchhike again, but right then getting off her seat and making it to the revolving door posed more of a challenge because she did not trust her legs to carry her. Plain and simple, she was screwed, stuck on a chair on a post in Nowhere, Ohio.

Where could she go? What might she do? Her mind blanked.

Sleep would have been good. A few hours' sleep might straighten her out and stop the shakes that came and went through her in waves. Fatigue invaded her arms and legs and neck and shoulders and back like India ink slowly soaking into a paper napkin. Buckles could not remember ever being this tired, but she could not very well put her head down on her folded arms to nod off like some junkie on a Greenwich Village bench.

At least she could observe.

Buckles sat in the crotch of a U near the neatly stenciled red sign: Professional Drivers Only. Professional drivers were mostly men who wore faded caps and talked softly into the payphones reserved for them on the wall in their special section. A few were old, a few were young, most were in the middle. A few women drivers came and went, all looking like Beth, her ghoul friend who was smart enough to carry a switchblade and had given Buckles all the right advice, never get into a truck alone, look into his eyes. All the sage advice Buckles ignored.

Women drivers were big wide girls with bulky tattooed arms and short hair that never needed to be brushed. Like Beth, they wore loose green or white Dickey T-shirts with pockets over their loose chests. It was not a fashion; a woman had to be strong to turn a big truck's steering wheel, and they carried pens and wallets in their shirt pockets. There were never enough pockets in most women's clothing. In voices as deep as the men's, they traded information with the male drivers about road conditions. They also spoke a little louder than the men, laughed a little louder, and walked with a deliberate swagger that said they would accept no nonsense from anyone just because he had a dick between his legs.

Every detail could be important; Buckles just could not yet tell which, and until she could, no plan could possibly come to her. Look how Linda the waitress arrived for her shift at 4 a.m., shortly after Buckles had shoved her bare shoulder against the cool glass of the revolving door and parked herself on the red vinyl seat at what had then been an empty breakfast counter. It had to mean something, but what? Doreen joined Linda two hours later. Their uniforms were buttercup-yellow polyester. Something in those observations had to be important, the universe exposed its secrets if only people knew what to see, but how any of that might matter to Buckles right then Buckles could not guess. All she knew for certain was that any girl who ignored Beth's advice and climbed aboard trucks without looking deep into a driver's eyes had to be a complete fool.

Now she had no money. She would not ignore the universe and its advice again. Without money, she would have to hitchhike even if she'd sworn to never try that again, but as Beth had advised, she'd need a switchblade knife. Could Beth have been sent by the Power that lay at the heart of the universe? Had the grave robber and her dog been ethereal messengers? She could not pay for a knife, so she'd need to steal one.

A knife. A knife felt like the beginning of a plan. Clean, dry underwear was good, but a knife was far more urgent.

Buckles sat on her shaking hands.

Linda hovered. "Anything more, honey?"

Buckles said, "No ma'am, but one more hot water if it's not too much trouble. Please." Linda looked at her peculiar, slipped her check-pad back into her doily apron, and went to refill the little steel pot.

Buckles calculated she had exactly $32. There was twenty-two dollars in her tote bag and Big Bill's crumpled ten in her pocket. Could $32 last to San Francisco? It probably could not, but thinking about how it might was at least some sort of planning, and that was better than remembering the hopelessness and terror that gripped her in Bill's hands. The secret compartment in her records backpack held fifty dollars more, but that was on its way to Emporia, Kansas. Big Bill had come out ahead, taking more from her than he gave.

How unfair was that? What did *fair* have to do with anything?

Whenever Daddy tried to sound with it, especially when he had an audience of the few people Daddy believed were Buckles' friends, her Dobbs swimming teammates, he'd say, "That's the way the cookie crumbles," and Buckles would cringe. They were hardly more than acquaintances, but Daddy came close to flirting with those girls. That was so creepy she did not like to think about it. Her girl friends grinned at her with amused pity. They knew from the get-go that her father, John Sinclair, was a total dipshit, living proof that no one over thirty could be trusted because anyone over thirty was either an idiot or a sleaze, and her Daddy managed to be both.

Two days after the accidental meeting near the Spanish restaurant with the old-fashioned saloon doors, at Daddy's insistence she ditched school and again rode the commuter rail from Dobbs Ferry to Grand Central. He asked that they meet for lunch at O'Neal's. He'd bring April, his friend; all his bestest girl had to do was show up.

Buckles left Dobbs three hours earlier than she needed to leave to get to O'Neal's, though. Killing time in the city, Buckles found the rainbow macramé tote bag. It hung from a metal coatrack on wheels on the sidewalk before a consignment shop in the East Village. If you did not mind the slight fraying of the handles, the bag was in perfect condition. The salesgirl claimed it was woven by peasants at a very special ashram in Madras, India, the same place where George Harrison studied transcendental meditation with Maharishi Mahesh Yogi and Ravi Shankar taught George to play sitar. Every thread and cord was enlightened, maybe even woven by George himself. As she left the shop, Buckles shoplifted the jeans jacket with the Sherpa lining from the same rack out front, stuffing the jacket into the macramé bag and casually heading away. She broke into a flat out run for two blocks before she slowed, breathless, and rested before the hike from Alphabet City up to Lincoln Center and O'Neal's.

Somewhere around 38th Street she jammed the pink angora sweater she'd worn for the luncheon into a sewer, stripping to her bra right there on the street, but moving swiftly enough that almost no one noticed the half-naked kid slipping her arms into a sleeveless denim jacket. Under the vest, she wriggled out of the bra to ditch that, too. She was left in soft faded denim from neck to toe, looking tougher than any girl in any pink angora sweater ever could possibly look. Even her sandals tough. Daddy's friend needed to see Buckles was someone to be reckoned with. Mom might be a wuss, but Buckles was not. To accessorize, she planned on shoplifting an ornate cross with a bulky chain, soon.

The stolen vest gapped a little between its nickel buttons, but was otherwise a perfect fit. It turned out later to be the best possible garment for hitchhiking, warm after sundown but cool in the day. It had a gazillion pockets. Most of the grommets stayed snapped closed no matter how she twisted or turned. Whoever had removed the long sleeves with a seam ripper might also have been the person who embroidered the back with a yellow comet and two silver stars. The macramé bag was woven from rough red, green, blue, and yellow cords, each cord run with a metallic gold thread. The red cord was faded worst, though, and the color bled onto her hand when by 53th Street it started to drizzle. The salesgirl with eyes that could not focus may have believed the bag was from an enlightened holy ashram, but later, when Buckles dumped the bag's contents, she discovered a small tag: *Made in Japan*. Since it turned out to be a pretty good bag anyway, she decided not to write a letter to George Harrison. Though Buckles and her generation stood for Truth, some lies were not as bad as other lies. Hypocrisy and lies fucked up the world, and Truth was what Buckles planned to insist on the day she met April the Bitch and Daddy the Pathological Liar at O'Neal's.

Daddy would arrive late, as usual, but Buckles expected that. Lateness was his way of making everyone else edgy. It was about his need to control everyone. Especially her. Buckles hardly noticed anymore. So she went right up to the lady in a booth at O'Neal's by the plate glass window.

Buckles recognized her, so she enjoyed a brief advantage because the woman could not know Buckles was Buckles until Buckles said, "I'm Buckles." The woman toyed with her pearl choker and drank a Whiskey Sour, a drink Buckles recognized because it was one her mother often ordered.

"I'm April," the woman said and started to extend her hand, then stopped when she saw Buckles made no move to extend hers. Shaken, April smiled stiff as the Toby jars Daddy collected or the Lladro sculptures Buckles' Mom preferred. April offered Buckles the stemmed cherry from her drink, a gesture that made Buckles despise her even more because her mother always did exactly the same thing. She and April the Bitch were forever going to be great friends. All it would take was a maraschino cherry.

Yeah. Sure. Right.

As expected, April turned out to be a type, a woman whose mouth dripped honey that was really nitric acid. She smelled like the Bloomingdale's cosmetics counter. Living in London was only temporary. She was really from Connecticut, which figured. She probably owned a thoroughbred, those stupid pants they called jodhpurs, and one of those protective black metal helmets, though it was hard to imagine there was any brain in there to protect. Her horse probably knew she was stupid, too. April explained how she had returned to the States to be with Jack because they shared some mystical overpowering connection that Buckles was too young to understand, but might, if she were lucky, understand someday. Men as good as Jack were difficult to find. He deserved the best, by which, even Buckles knew, she meant no one but herself.

Buckles strained not to puke.

Climbing into a taxi in Greenwich Village, April had looked like Goldie Hawn at a Be-In, exposing plenty of skinny bare thigh and calf white patent leather boots. But now she was uptown and wore sedate black pumps, white gloves halfway to her elbows, and a pink dress that if it had bloodstains might have been Jacqueline Kennedy's on the day her husband's head exploded. April went on and on about how lovely a girl Buckles was, how her name was so unusual, and how her Daddy bragged how pretty she was, though to be sure, now that she saw Buckles with her own eyes, she saw how Daddy's descriptions fell short of the reality.

Buckles needed to hear she was pretty like fish needed to know water was wet. Who gave a crap about pretty? The times, bitch, they are a'changin'.

Captivated by the speck of lipstick marring April's front tooth, the growing realization came to Buckles that April was sugar-sweet because April was terrified of her. Buckles and Mom looked so much alike that April must have felt as if she gazed into a magic mirror that revealed Jack's wife when she was young. All the women in Daddy's life were icy ash blondes; only April had brown roots. Mom was a pain in the ass, but she was the most beautiful woman in the world and always had been. Daddy had to be a moron who liked getting laid by morons. He probably had told this April-creature he was going to marry her, and April was shit-stupid enough to believe it, like she'd be the last woman in the world to find ash blonde by Clairol.

Poor Mom. Thirty was over the hill. Buckles loved her father, most of the time she really did, but she saw how Mom was stuck with a shitheel who was banging a phony Carnaby Street bird really from Connecticut.

Daddy showed up at O'Neal's, shook out his umbrella, and apologized for being late. Wholesale bullshit, every word. Daddy was late for his usual reason. It put him in control. Not only did other people have to wait for him, but he was maneuvering April and Buckles to get to know each other. There was no telling if April was in on it, though Buckles would bet she was.

Buckles' vague determination to escape and start her own life formed at the precise moment April wobbled away on her heels to "freshen up," by which she meant "pee." Daddy leaned over the table to whisper, "Isn't she terrific?" He filched a French fry from Buckles' plate. He expected he and April might be together for a while, so he hoped Buckles and April would get along.

Buckles wanted to believe him, she really did, but then Daddy told Buckles that he and her mother were into free love. He really said *into*. The stupid lie hit Buckles like ammonia revived a groggy boxer. Her mother was a lot of things, most good, but free love was off her map. If that was the best story Daddy the Professional Liar could concoct to smooth it over with his daughter who had seen the Connecticut tart with her tongue so down his throat she must have been tickling his tonsils, then Daddy's opinion of his seventeen-year-old was bargain-basement low. Buckles was not that gullible; Daddy was not that hip. For God's sake, Buckles would turn eighteen in October.

It was pathetic.

Honesty might have impressed Buckles. *I'm fucking the tart because it's fun.* Buckles would not have been happy to hear that, but a plain confession would have been a sign of Daddy's respect for her. She'd have considered blindness and amnesia for her mother's sake. Buckles was no virgin, but Daddy could not know that, and she was not about to tell him, so he treated Buckles as if she were forever a child. *Don't allow the house and pool in Scarsdale to fool you. Mom and Dad are hippies in an open marriage, and, oh sure, he and April, who was the right age to have been Buckles' babysitter a few years ago were* into *free love.* They'd turn the Scarsdale house into a commune, serve brown rice, pull up the hedges, and plant marijuana.

The worst part of lunch at O'Neal's was the moment Buckles looked across her burger to where Daddy held April's hand and Buckles had to acknowledge that April could be the image of her own future. Dobbs Academy had for a hundred years educated young women to be the compliant wives of important men. In the Dobbs cosmos, Dobbs girls either became compliant first wives and faded to invisibility, or Dobbs girls thrived as vipers sucking dry the souls of someone else's husband.

The only other role in the triangle was to be like Dad, a glad-handing shitheel who followed his dick. Buckles was not equipped to grow a penis, though she wondered if April could manage that trick. It was all Buckles could do not to ask April if she intended to plant Daddy's penis in a ceramic pot, like pothos, watering it regularly but not too often.

That same week Buckles began her study of road maps and discovered Route 6. She'd shared her plan with James who said, "Oh wow, that's so Zen." Buckles realized the boy whose hand was in her pants was a drooling idiot. At least she could jump start her life if he had the use of his mother's Volvo. That was Zen enough for her.

But in Perrysville, Ohio, Buckles understood there was more to planning than tracing a finger across a blue-line highway headed west.

Linda, the big-hair bleach blonde waitress in a pink polyester uniform, bent to rub the back of her calves. When Buckles needed the Ladies Room again, she asked Linda to watch her stuff until she was back. It was not much to watch, but Buckles did not want to emerge from the Ladies Room and no longer have her seat.

In the lavatory for the second time, Buckles peered beneath the stall doors, casual, until she was sure she was alone. She peed out her tea and then killed a few minutes reapplying mascara and eyeliner to make herself look older. Ripples of nervousness and fear came and went, gripping her whole body with the shakes. She squeezed her eyes shut and bunched her toes to not fall down, more from a hangover of terror than from growing hunger. She was just unready to think about her night with Big Bill. She might never be ready for that.

The last thing she did before returning to her outpost and her counter seat was to inspect the deepening purplish bruises on her breast. They were tinged green. She washed her armpits with warm water and hand soap, and blotted herself dry with coarse brown paper towels. Her parents would be looking for her, of course, and that meant that no matter how bad things got or how far she'd come, she could never give up but had to keep moving. Even if they did not give a crap about each other, they'd come together to pursue her. She hoped Mom did not hate her, but was sure Mom would, at least for a while. That little note Buckles had written was napalm on her only bridge back, but really, all Buckles had done was deliver news Mom should have already known. Someday she'd send a note or make a phone call just to let her know her little girl was not dead, but no apologies. None.

Her damp palm met the metal plate on the Ladies Room door. She wondered where she could shoplift a knife with a pushbutton blade.

August—December 1967

K J'S LEGS WERE WATER; HER head rested on the bedspread. She inhaled the last of Buckles, still lingering in the folds of white poplin.

Not trusting her legs to carry her down a flight of stairs, KJ took Buckles' Princess phone in her lap and dialed Jack's office. His receptionist deigned to answer after eight rings. A fire raged in her chest. Calling the traitorous bastard was bad enough, but the habit of years that made her depend on him in crisis was worse. Self-loathing surged in her heart.

The receptionist explained hurriedly that she'd been at the elevator waiting to leave the building, but had sprinted back through an empty office to pick up. Mrs. Sinclair was lucky to catch her.

"Just connect me to Jack."

Mr. Sinclair had departed hours ago. If he was not yet home, he might be staying somewhere in the city.

"I know your voice, Rochelle. The one so stinko at the Christmas party, everyone heard you whining about Prince Whathisname, the boyfriend who dumped you." Rochelle had pitiable stringy hair, dull brown eyes and a cluster of blackheads on her forehead beneath her greasy bangs. She'd been at the punchbowl with her ass that started in Weehawken and quit at the western wall of Central Park, spanning the Hudson and all of the West Side. "You find that son-of-a-bitch. Don't you dare tell me you can't. Tell Jack that Buckles is missing. Buckles is his daughter, if you do not know, and don't forget to tell him to call me at Buckles' phone. I don't care if you crawl through midtown on crushed glass, you find that prick this second. We both know you know how to find him. We both know he told you that if his wife called to pretend you do not know. If this phone does not ring in ten minutes, it's your job. Am I perfectly clear?"

She slammed the receiver into its cradle and stared at the yellow phone a full four minutes before it rang.

Muddled by panic and incinerating rage, KJ's mind couldn't keep it all straight. There was Buckles, there was Jack and an affair, and there was fat Rochelle from Hoboken who would never get the life she believed she deserved. Did everyone at Jack's office know that Jack stayed in the city to sleep with women not his wife? Were the elevator operator and the women who mopped the executive toilets exchanging gossip about good ol' Jack Sinclair, the cocksman *shtupping* legions of women not his wife?

"Relax. Buckles will be home before me," Jack said. He asked her to calm down. She emitted a wordless scream.

"Jack, she wrote a note. She said April is nice. How long have we been in an open marriage? I forget. There are a few gardeners I'd like to screw. I have a list." The hum on the otherwise silent line became audible. She strained to hear if there was another faint sound on the line, probably April tugging down her skirt zipper, maybe Jack's zipper.

"I can explain," he said at last. "Look, I am on my way."

KJ's whole being wanted to believe that Jack really could explain, but she was certain he'd use his time in the limo back to Scarsdale to concoct a just-believable story thin as tissue. Her whole being also wanted him to be completely right, that Buckles would be home before him. They'd laugh and go out for Chinese food. Her whole being also wished to believe that Buckles simply got it wrong, that Jack was KJ's faithful provider, her loving husband, a perfect father, and not a shiftless shitheel in expensive neckwear. Her own father, the square-jawed Yale man smelling of Bay Rum who secretly advised Limeys on how to withstand Hitler had been blown to pieces in the London blitz before America entered the war. He left a closet of white shirts, five boxes of perfectly polished black shoes, a dozen magnificent ties, and one great lesson: clinging to an imagined past never made it so.

KJ paced until she made it down stairs to wait on the sofa in their darkening living room. A Lincoln limo circled their driveway and left Jack on the portico. When he bent to kiss KJ's cheek, she drew back. "Let me see the note," he said. Despite the growing gloom, KJ saw his face was ashen.

"Did you call the police?"

Why hadn't she thought to do that? What was wrong with her? Every second could count. She was an idiot.

Jack went to his home office and his private telephone line. KJ stood uncertainly at his French doors. He gestured that she come closer, and so KJ placed her ear beside Jack's. A police dispatcher said Buckles could not be declared missing for three days.

"Don't hand me that shit," Jack said. "This kid is a minor."

Jack fumed his way to a captain who said a lot of kids were running away, all this dope and sex. Jack gave him the gist of Buckles' note, omitting any mention of her father's love affair. The captain agreed with Jack that in all likelihood Buckles would be back any minute; at worst, she'd show up in the morning. But since Mr. Sinclair was a lawyer with influential friends in county government, the captain agreed to reach out to a contact at Stoney Point up in Rockland. Little could be done in the gathering darkness. "She might be a minor, Mr. Sinclair, but she is above the age of consent."

KJ understood that fine point of law to mean that, while Buckles could not sign a contract or borrow money, she was free to get laid, a difference KJ did not find mollifying. The dispatcher would issue a back channel APB. A lucky patrol car might spot her in a convenience store or someplace like that. They'd look for her strictly as a courtesy. Did the Sinclairs have a description? What was she wearing?

KJ seized the phone from Jack. She spoke rapidly. No, she had no idea what Buckles could be wearing, but she described her:

magazine-model drop dead gorgeous, blonde, powder blue eyes, long straight hair with a center part. "What every hippie kid wants to look like if every hippie kid was a surfer." KJ did not care that she sounded like an idiot. It was all fact. She handed the phone back to Jack, but kept her ear near the speaker.

The captain thought he was reassuring them when he said, "If she does not have a lot of money, she will be back in a day or two. She is most likely with someone, and they do not want to be found." She could not be declared a missing person for at least three days. If something came across his desk about an unidentified blond girl in a hospital, he'd call the Sinclairs immediately. "Give it a few hours, Mr. Sinclair. But take my advice; if your daughter willingly ran off with someone, she is not going to thank you for pursuing her. Try to relax."

The Sinclairs sat in smoldering silence. KJ suddenly stood. Doing nothing was impossible. At the front door she glared at Jack. "Are you coming or not?"

The Mercedes broke the speed records north on the Taconic, crossing the Bear Mountain Bridge where the car slowed to a crawl. Jack twice asked her, *What did you say to her?* which overlooked the whole thing about this April-creature. That was Jack, all over.

Of course, KJ also blamed herself. She had followed the path of least resistance, backed off when she should have leaned in. The marijuana, the weekend trips alone to the city, the lavishly appointed room, the summer of leisure, a prep school and a life so distant from theirs it was no wonder the kid took off. KJ's misery was the price for being a progressive parent intimidated by her seventeen-year-old.

On the west side of the Hudson, the Mercedes pulled onto the gravel shoulder to allow cars to pass; drivers cursed at them. The roadside pines were dark, tall, and forbidding. The August night buzzed with crickets. To cover more ground more carefully, they walked in opposite directions on the shoulder. Their shouts of "Buckles!" were swallowed by deep shadows. Then they drove another quarter mile and did it again. And again. And again.

After two hours, they were exhausted, frightened, and out of ideas.

Still in their car at their front door, Jack asked, "What was the name of the kid who drove her?"

Miserably, KJ admitted she did not know. It was shameful how little she knew about her daughter. Her eyes fell closed with fatigue. Her aching forehead rested against the car's cool window glass.

"The police know what they are doing," Jack said.

KJ flung open the house's front door and shouted Buckles' name, but though they had left the lights on, the place felt empty, eerily abandoned. KJ checked the pool patio, and held her breath when she switched on the underwater electric lights, but no blonde corpse floated facedown in the pool. Upstairs, she opened and closed the door to Buckles' room, hoping to see the kid asleep. She checked the closet and under the bed to be sure the kid was not indulging in some sick joke.

It was over. Jack piled spare pillows onto a downstairs living room couch. KJ stayed in their upstairs bedroom. She lacked the strength to undress. Eyes wide, any time she began to drift off, she jerked up awake. By dawn she finally slept, but those two hours brought no rest.

Detective Masselli, the short overweight beak-nosed policeman who never knotted his woolen ties, was nominally in charge of Buckles' case. The little waddling man had wiry hair growing out of his ears and nose and a habit of clearing his throat of tobacco-congealed phlegm before he spoke. He was smug and could not bring himself to so much as fake urgency. Unless body parts started showing up at a roadside or in the Sinclair mailbox, Masselli was inclined to dispose of the jacket on Buckles by burying the file in a drawer with a hundred identical jackets. The kid was of age, she left a note, she knew just what she was doing. "It's a free country." His hands were tied. He'd do what he could, but that was very little.

The most recent picture KJ had of Buckles showed her lounging at the pool in a red bikini with her long blond hair half over her blue eyes. Her wet hair was slick, rich, and barely covered the cleavage of her breasts pressed flat beneath her on a canvas chaise lounge. She looked more like the Playmate of the Month than a runaway high school kid who might be victimized.

Masselli located the boy who drove Buckles to Bear Mountain. There were just so many Volvos in Westchester, and only a handful that belonged to people with a kid the right age.

Masselli interviewed the little puke named James twice in three days, the second time with KJ and Jack on the other side of one-way glass with James' parents on seats that flanked their boy. James was not under arrest, but cooperated. Leaving the station, James' mother came to KJ and hissed, *My boy did not rape your whore daughter* and escaped down a flight of steel stairs before KJ had a chance to scratch her eyes out. His parents at least agreed to allow the cops to take Jimmy the Puke to where he'd dropped Buckles west of the river, though Masselli later reported the little puke was not one hundred percent certain of the spot. The little puke had not waited for Buckles to get a ride. No, the little puke left her alone in the dark. For all he knew, Buckles was snatched up by a band of roving Gypsies who trafficked teenage sex slaves. Buckles had not called or written to the little pimple-faced moron puke since she vanished. Eventually, Mr. and Mrs. Puke packed Baby Puke off to military school right before Labor Day, threatening a case of harassment if the Sinclairs' troubles pursued him there. Their future brigadier general needed to be free of this complication that had him somehow implicated in the disappearance of the little slut who'd bribed their angel with drugs to take her away from the embrace of Westchester. KJ hoped the little puke psychopath would enjoy a military school culture of forced buggery. That might clear up his complexion.

KJ discovered the small blue address book in Buckles' vanity. She called every number in it, but most were kids who'd lost contact with Buckles since she enrolled at Dobbs. She seemed to do nothing but read books and swim. She was an isolated, solitary kid. KJ blamed herself for being blind. She tossed through sleepless nights reviewing all the places, real and imagined, she had gone wrong.

She'd been the dutiful wife, hosted the necessary get-togethers for the senior partners, flirted with several, a meaningless gesture understood by all to be fun and undertaken for the sake of Jack's advancement. His colleagues adored her. She'd borne his child. All right, the passion department had diminished since then, but that was normal, wasn't it? Had KJ's loss of interest in sex pushed Jack away, or had Jack lost interest in sex with her, and so he'd gone? She'd been the ornament on Jack's right arm whenever he needed her to be, she had cheered his victories and wept at his defeats, and though she was bored to stone she expected to grow old as dutiful Mrs. Jack Sinclair.

Jack was handsome, rich, vigorous, and had a profile fit for Mount Rushmore, but somewhere he had turned into a shith-eel. Jack's closet emptied of Brooks Brothers suits, tailored Italian white shirts, and black wing tips when he moved into the firm's Manhattan apartment "until all this clears up," a phrase he sincerely believed meant KJ would soon forgive his adultery, Buckles would return, and everything would revert to Jack's fantasy of normal. The Second Coming was more likely.

Soon, Jack and KJ met only in the offices of their respective lawyers. Since Buckles would turn eighteen in October, custody was not an issue. She had an irrevocable trust fund waiting for her if she ever surfaced. The only issues at disclosure were Jack's hidden assets that he denied existed, his future income from the law firm that he maintained could not be calculated, the intrinsic value of his part-nership he would not estimate, and the ultimate ownership of the Tudor, despite the fact that technically he'd abandoned it. In other words, he disputed everything.

For weeks, the farthest KJ traveled was to the end of the drive-way after the Post Office truck left. She lived on yogurt, lettuce, and cottage cheese, whatever could be delivered that was more than pizza or Chinese food. She needed to be able to sprint to a phone before the third ring. Well into September, The Dobbs Academy called to ask if they could delete Buckles from their annual roster as there was a long waiting list of applicants; they needed the bed. It was the first KJ learned that Jack had stopped the tuition checks.

Near Columbus Day, KJ hit on the idea of phoning a police station in San Francisco's Fillmore district. Not wanting to sound like some feebleminded housewife, she asked a sergeant to issue a bolo, police jargon for *be on the lookout*. She held the wire while the sergeant checked. A photo of Abigail "Buckles" Sinclair was indeed pinned to a bulletin board among hundreds of other photos. "The kid in the bathing suit? We'll do what we can," the sergeant said, and then supplied KJ with the phone numbers of local social services and some hippie priest who dedicated his life to ministering to runaways who were, no offense, whoring. "If your girl still looks like she looks in that picture, she's caught someone's attention," he said, thinking he was being reassuring. KJ wept for two days before she could bring herself to dial the number of the hippie priest. She convinced him she was a practicing Catholic and that Buckles was not the victim of family molestation or physical abuse. The priest was familiar with that damned photograph and plainly did not believe her, but he read her a list of alternate newspapers that included Cleveland, Chicago, Denver, and Omaha, as well as *The East Village Other, The Village Voice, The Berkeley Barb,* and *The Bay Guardian.* "There are no guarantees she made it here," he said when KJ asked why the newspapers were so far afield. She hung up with new determination and purpose. At least she was not sitting on her hands.

Jack wrote the checks; they blanketed the country with ads. Buckles might never read any newspaper except *The Village Voice,* but maybe someone who knew her did. Their kid's name was too distinctive for anyone to think the message was not for her.

BUCKLES. CALL HOME. WE LOVE YOU.
NO QUESTIONS ASKED.

The first day the ads ran, she drove to Yonkers and waited a full morning for the *Village Voice* to be delivered. Their notice was among two dozen similar boxed notices. Every kid on the west coast was migrating to Greenwich Village; every kid on the east coast was migrating to Haight-Ashbury. A great tide of American children sloshed to and fro across the continent because some asinine jackass told them to put flowers in their hair and that life was beautiful. An asshole professor from Harvard, of all places, was urging youth to turn on, tune in, and drop out. If she could have laid hands on Timothy Leary, she'd have diced his grinning face into small bits using nothing but her fingernails.

The private detective they hired in October proved to be a complete fiasco. Buckles' imminent birthday filled KJ with a never-ending mixture of low-grade panic and hope. Birthdays brought people together. Buckles might be homesick. She expected Humphrey Bogart, but the man from the Edelman Detective Agency looked more like an overweight balding elementary school teacher. He took the photo of Buckles in her swimsuit and five thousand dollars, flew to the west coast, spent a few days strolling through shabbier San Francisco neighborhoods to push the photograph under the noses of every kid in every pizza joint and dive bar. He searched among addicts, pimps, and whores. Then he came home to present the Sinclairs his bill for additional expenses, another fifteen hundred. "I'll take more of your money if you insist, but I won't kid you. If your girl does not want to be found, she won't be. On the good side, your girl is a real looker, so she will be hard to forget. On the bad side, those are the looks that attract the wrong kind of attention."

He kept the creased photograph.

At a particularly bleak moment amid a succession of bleak moments, KJ phoned Jack and burst into tears. "I don't know what we can do next." Jack drove up to have a face-to-face without divorce lawyers in the room. They agreed to talk strictly about finding Buckles. KJ brewed tea while Jack sat on a high stool at the kitchen island. He too was out of ideas, and he wondered if it were not time to simply accept that Buckles had made a decision they would need to accept. "I am sure she is all right," he said.

"You're sure? I am so glad you are sure!" she heard herself shrieking. "You and your damned girlfriend. What did you expect? Do you know what happens to girls alone in this country? Do you? Do you have any idea of what a girl's life is like?" Jack stonily stared at his folded hands. He covered up while she slapped at his head, arms, and shoulders. "She'll run out of money, but she won't come home. That's not Buckles. You think she is a marshmallow, but her spine is made of iron. Girls have one asset to sell any time they need to, and it brings in more than any shitty job. You think maybe she's packing groceries in Omaha? Filing books in a library in Kansas? Are you an idiot? She will need drugs to dull the world. Maybe a pimp will put them in her veins to make it simpler for him to teach her what he thinks she needs to know. Blonde, blue-eyed, and young. That ought to bring quite a price. But why worry? John Sinclair, the father of the year, believes his girl is all right! Buckles will think she's filth who can never come home. Her problem isn't herself, it's us. You fed her some crap about an open marriage. Look how well that worked. You think she is stupid? She is not coming back, Jack, and she is not all right. There's no happy ending for you because you cannot keep your mouth shut or your fly zipped. You set up your daughter to have a chat with the cunt you were banging. All those nights you never came home. How could I not know? Now my little girl is out somewhere fucking strangers for her next meal!"

Blows rained on his back until her arms were tired; then she fell against him. He turned to embrace her to comfort her, but she found a last bit of strength and jerked away. Jack fled. KJ hurled a Toby jar from a foyer knickknack shelf. It smashed to skittering ceramic shards on the driveway, spinning to a stop under his Mercedes. Though Jack drove of sight, KJ hurled two more. Then she threw his cashmere overcoat onto the gravel driveway. Her station wagon went over it every day for a week before she stuffed the coat into a trash barrel for collection.

October 19, Buckles' birthday, was the worst day she'd ever known, worse than the day Buckles disappeared. KJ had lived in a hope-filled fantasy of how Buckles would appear, there would be a tearful reunion, they'd embrace, KJ would refuse to hear anything about an apology from her child. They'd go pick apples as they had at every birthday Buckles had until she was twelve. Instead of cake, they'd bake an apple pie. KJ bought the ingredients three days in advance.

The emotional crash was near fatal. KJ sat in dim light, curtains drawn, by her bedroom telephone, standing only to go to the toilet. She leafed through the same issue of *McCall's* three times until a drop of blood smeared across the slick page. She had bit her cuticles to bleeding.

At Thanksgiving, her mother invited KJ to join her on Martha's Vineyard, but KJ refused. She did not dream of asking her mother to come to her. Her mother would never leave the island, not until the oceans rose and covered the land with seawater. Jack's sister, of all people, invited KJ to join the family in Cambridge, perhaps laboring under some delusion that she could connive her brother and his wife to reconcile. KJ said she'd attend, went as far as packing a bag for two nights, but never left the Scarsdale house. What if Buckles came home to find an empty house? KJ sat cross-legged on the floor before the television in Buckles' room to watch the Macy's Day Parade and chatted with Buckles as if she were there and was six or seven or eight years old. Their favorite balloon was Popeye. KJ cradled Buckles' old teddy bear in her lap and sang, "I'm Popeye the sailor man." She ooohed and aahed at floats, bands, and balloons to the imaginary companion who was her kid in pink Dr. Denton's. KJ cautioned Buckles that she would ruin her eyes so close to the television. They were excited to catch a first glimpse of Santa Claus.

After the parade, she turned knob to OFF. The picture imploded to a white dot that vanished.

Downstairs, KJ remained motionless in a Queen Anne armchair in a darkened room. Twice she hallucinated the phone ringing, but lifting a receiver she heard only a monotonous dial tone, a fact that did not prevent her from repeating "Hello? Hello?" several times before hanging up the dead line.

Ghosts, spirits, hallucinations, dreams, delusions, and nightmares stalked KJ from room to room in the empty house. Buckles here at 6, Buckles there at 10, Buckles there again at 14. She was at the top of the stairs dressed for her first day of school in the blue checkered skirt she'd been so terribly proud to have selected herself; there she was swimming, maybe at 4, shrieking delight whenever Jack tossed her into the air, refusing to climb out of the pool until she mastered a backstroke flip-turn. KJ saw her daughter at the kitchen island spreading cream cheese on an English muffin, every surface smooth and even.

Every turn proved a dead end. The local police, the Dobbs School, a private eye, the San Francisco police, the San Francisco priest, the newspaper ads all across the country, every door opened onto a blank wall.

Her divorce lawyer, a man named Blatt, chosen from the first page of attorneys in the Yonkers and Westchester Yellow Pages, cautioned her about financial losses if she flat out walked away from the house. "You'll have to defend a charge of abandonment." Blatt's concern was her money; KJ's concern was what little remained of her mind.

KJ knew she had to create a new life. Hope was killing her.

Buckles' birthday had been bad; Thanksgiving worse. Christmas might kill her.

She rode a commuter rail to meet with a Manhattan real estate rental agent, looked at three places to assure herself she was being sensible, then returned for a second look at the first apartment she'd viewed. The three partially furnished rooms were on the twelfth floor. *Partially furnished* was a real estate euphemism for hideous cast-off furniture scattered around a coffee-stained carpet that might once have been the color of gold but now was the color of strong mustard. All three apartment windows offered a direct view of cream-colored brick and darkened windows across an alley, but if she wrestled open the third window and twisted her neck east, she could see the Manhattan tower of the Queensboro Bridge.

It had been advertised to have *rivr vws*, but the important point was that she could move in immediately.

Forging Jack's name on the deposit check was easier than she thought it would be.

August 1967

LINDA THE WAITRESS BROUGHT BUCKLES a fresh lemon slice and another pot of water. Buckles folded the lemon in a white paper napkin and thought how she might brush her teeth with her finger and the rind, as her mouth and tongue felt like an old woman's flannel pajamas.

Then a skinny old lady who might have worn those pajamas occupied the counter seat beside hers. She was no truck driver. Her feet did not reach the floor, either. The old lady leaned in to peer closely at Buckles. She smelled of antiseptic.

"Three sugars is quite a lot of sugar," the old lady said. "Those pretty teeth will rot and fall out."

Buckles dropped a fourth sugar cube into her tiny teapot for spite. The old lady was missing two teeth on her left lower jaw, so maybe she knew what she was talking about. Then again, who was she to give warnings? Once she was in San Francisco, Buckles would be done with old ladies forever. She put that on her mental list of things she had to do along with meeting Lawrence Ferlinghetti the amazing poet and licking LSD off a sugar cube.

Buckles sipped her tea, too weak, too sweet, and too hot. Her used teabag had hardly stained the water. She wished the old lady would leave her alone.

"My grandson and I noticed you," the old lady said. "We're over there." She gestured with her pointy chin where a few thick black hairs sprang from a mole. "He's Felix. I am Dorothy. Friends call me Dot."

Buckles stole a look at Felix. A little older than she, the boy sat sideways in a booth, his spine as curled as a question mark, his head as low as his raised, bent knees. Curly black hair tumbled over his eyes, ears, and shirt collar. The beginnings of a beard colored his cheeks like stuffing torn from a cheap mattress. His green-and-brown camouflage T-shirt bagged two sizes too large; his olive drab Army vest was made of heavy canvas. It had a million pockets. Dope peddlers in New York loved Army-issue vests because they kept their inventory sorted in those pockets, downers here, crank there, reds, 'shrooms, maybe a glassine envelope of coke in a fourth location. His vest's campaign ribbons and insignia had been removed with a seam ripper that left imprints of darker material surrounded by stringy threads. Felix was the kind who needed to shave twice each day, a nuisance he probably was avoiding by growing the beard. The boy studied the empty red vinyl seat of the restaurant booth opposite him as though his eyes could force the seat to give up mysteries. He idly scratched his knee through his paratrooper pants. Then he flashed the V sign to Buckles. *Peace*, not *Victory*, and she quickly turned away.

Buckles felt kinship. Felix was as miserable as she. Buckles was trapped in a world of rapist truck drivers and big-hair waitresses; Felix was prisoner in a world of busybody old ladies who smelled of antiseptic.

Dot whispered so close to Buckles' ear, Buckles felt her breath. "I call him 'Sweetboy.' I am his grandmother, sort of." She said: "We noticed you are by yourself. That's not healthy, dear. You're too young to be by yourself."

Buckles hoped that ignoring the weird old lady would convince her to go away, but at the exact moment Buckles was preparing to glare at her, a state trooper parked himself on the captain's chair to Buckles' left. Her tiny section of the zigzag counter was suddenly crowded with newcomers anxious about her wellbeing.

"That's the one," Linda the waitress said.

The trooper placed his Smokey Bear hat on the counter. His shaved head was waxed and gleamed. Buckles was considering never again shaving her armpits, but how weird was it to shave your skull every morning? Did men smear shaving cream all over their faces and heads, or did they use depilatory creams and polish their heads with candle wax? The trooper gestured for Linda to bring coffee. Linda somehow knew to also bring a slice of apple pie. Maybe Linda and Smokey Bear were old friends. Maybe all state troopers get free apple pie and coffee wherever they are in Ohio. The white letters on the trooper's black nameplate read *Higgenbottom*.

Higgenbottom stirred in cream before he pushed his untouched pie and a fork toward Buckles. If he looked in her tote bag and fished out James' marijuana, she'd spend the rest of her life in an Ohio prison washing sheets until bleach fumes eroded her brain, and all for a few crappy stems and seeds. Her stomach betrayed her by growling loud enough for the trooper to hear. The crumb-top apple looked awful good.

Shirtsleeve to wrist, Higgenbottom's bare forearm was covered by a tangle of ruddy hair, thick as bear fur. His eyebrows were bushy. Freckles were on him from the top of his bald head down his neck and the length of his arms. If Buckles had Big Bill's radio, she'd have pressed the button to say, "Breaker-one-nine, ginger-bear alert." That sounded so much like ginger beer, she giggled, a sure sign she was losing what remained of her mind. She was dizzy with hunger. The apple pie called her name.

"Linda 'spects you can't pay." Ginger Bear's smile was filled by teeth big as tombstones. He had enough teeth to spare. Would Ginger Bear lend a tooth to Smelly Old Lady? He touched the apple pie again. "Compliments of the people of Ohio."

Higgenbottom was the name of her Social Studies teacher in her first year at Dobbs. Everyone called him *Higgy*. Higgy was a total asshole, an asshole's asshole, a teacher who stood rigidly at attention to lead his class in the Pledge of Allegiance every morning with his hand over his heart and his belly over his belt. Louder than the PA system, Higgy teared up when the Pledge got to the part about God. Speculation was that Higgy was born wearing a starched button-down white shirt and his clip-on red bowtie with white polka-dots. Who'd have guessed the world had room enough for two asshole-Higgenbottoms?

"If you do not care for apple, Linda will bring you blueberry? Isn't that right, Linda?" Linda's arms crossed over her narrow chest. "But what I need to know is your name? What is your name, sweetheart? Do you have an ID? If we know your name, we can help you go home? You want to go home, don't you?" This asshole-Higgenbottom spoke perfectly ordinary sentences as if they were questions.

If she had had time to answer Higgy, she'd have told him she was never going home, but the words never left her because things right then that had already grown weird achieved weirdness escape velocity and rocketed into weirdness orbit.

First the old lady laughed like a tickled chicken. "Officer, why would my Caroline need an ID? The child is but fifteen." She snapped a silver dollar down to the countertop. "I'll have a piece of that pie for myself, young lady," she said to Linda. "But no crumb-top for me. I like my crust plain. It best be flakey, though. Is your crust flakey? Can I get it with a slice of warmed cheddar cheese?"

"She's been sitting by herself for hours," Linda said.

"That long?" the old lady said. "My, oh my. Our Caroline is an early riser. She is. Caroline, did you tippy-toe out of the motel room and sashay all the way over here from the motor court? That's our Caroline. Now over there is our Felix, her cousin. He did not hear a thing, either. Caro, did you go out for breakfast and forget money? Shame on you. Shame on you. I've told you and told you that you can't just walk around and expect the good Lord and kind people will take care of you, not even in Ohio where Christians grow tall and sweet as Ohio corn. My two grandchildren are taking me to our family reunion in Des Moines. Isn't it precious how they look alike? Two peas in a pod, we all say. Peas in a pod." The boy in the booth was black-haired; Buckles was as blonde as a Beach Boys' lyric. Judging by coloring, they might have been separate species. "Caroline looks more like Aunt Cynthia than Aunt Cynthia did, God rest her." Her voice fell to a stage whisper. "That was Felix's mother. Died of leprosy in Borneo baptizing cannibals. Caroline never knew her, of course. We hail from Massachusetts and Cynthia lived in Ankeny before she went to do her ministry. That's Ankeny, Iowa, I am sure you know it, a stone's throw north of Des Moines." She cackled that laugh and her voice rose again to a volume that could be heard in Indiana. "Officer, you know how young girls are. Push everyone's limits. I'll be sure to give her a good talking-to."

"'Trooper,' ma'am?" the state trooper said. "Ohio State Highway Patrol?" His smile displayed even more teeth. He pointed to the badge pinned to his chest below his nametag. "That makes me a trooper? I am not an officer? Ma'am? The O-S-H-P?" He pronounced it *oh-ess-aitch-pee*. Any contest between the trooper and her old social studies teacher for World Champion Asshole would be close.

The old lady's wrinkled hand went to her scrawny throat. "I meant no offense, officer. But now see what you've done, Caro? You came here to deceive people, and now they are worried for you. This is the United States of America, one nation, under God, where people are kind, especially in Ohio. They do not deserve to be deceived. Ohioans will line up to help a girl on her own. Ohio is God's country, not like New York City. I pray for those weak sinners every day, I do. I pray that God will spare New York, I do, when His Kingdom returns. Christ is my Redeemer and He will bring his Kingdom soon! We will be embraced by holy light." She closed her eyes and swayed to rhythms only she could hear.

This was not weirdness escape velocity: this was intergalactic weirdness.

The old lady stood up to shout the praises of Iowa's blue sky, blue being the holiest color, and the yellow of Iowa's corn, the golden color of Jesus's crown. Truckers lifted their eyes from their breakfasts, scrambled eggs trembling on forks suspended before their half-parted lips until someone took off his John Deere hat and said, "Amen." That seemed to be the signal for everyone to return their attention to their home fries, but the old lady did not quiet down. "Linda here is a charitable woman, charitable. You have to be a charitable believer to summon Trooper Higgenbottom for help. I blame myself for all her trouble. You can't take your eyes off young girls, not for a second." She bent close to Higgenbottom's ear to say, "Girls nowadays … well unless they have the luck to come across good Christians like Sister Linda they cannot escape the snares of sin. Not in this day and age. So I thank the Lord for putting Linda among us. I do. St. Michael may be the Lord's Sword, but Linda is His Shield, I swear, hallelujah. I shall always remember her in my prayers." She pivoted to Buckles. "But Caro, fun is fun, but these good people need to get on with their lives. We need to move on."

Linda produced a second slice of apple pie, this time under a half-melted wedge of sharp yellow cheddar. Buckles stole a second glance at Felix. The boy was without success trying to sink through the linoleum floor.

The spindly old lady who said her name was Dot moved behind her to place her hands flat on Buckles' two shoulders, the way a real Grandma would, but no one could see those scrawny hands dig in like talons through a layer of heavy denim and the Sherpa lining of her vest. She struggled not to cry out. "Just you wait, young lady, until your mother hears about this." Then the old lady eased her grip on Buckles' shoulders, but her bent finger floated inches from Buckles' nose as if to warn Buckles she could have her shoulders painfully squeezed another time. "Just you wait." She cackled like a giddy chicken once more before she turned again to Higgenbottom. "May I pay for your apple pie, officer, while my granddaughter goes to the Ladies Room to wash that paint off her face? It is time for Caro to be fourteen again."

"'Trooper,' please? No, ma'am? I'll just enjoy the pie and pay for it, too?" He pulled the plate close to him now that Buckles had a slice of her own that the old woman would pay for.

The slice of melting cheddar cheese seemed disgusting, but Buckles saw no reason to let food go to waste. The cheese peeled away, but fearful someone might take the pie from her too soon, she cut a forkful so large it near toppled to her lap on its journey to her mouth. The apple pie was the best thing Buckles had eaten, ever. When you died and went to heaven, if you'd been good and said your prayers every day, God greeted you with apple pie from Perrysville.

Buckles pressed her luck. She barely drooled when she lifted her eyes to Linda and managed, "Choc 'ilk.'

The trooper said, "Caroline, are you sure you have no ID? I will need to see some ID?"

Eyes widening Buckles shook her head. Her only ID was a library card, and that was in her wallet, and her wallet was westbound aboard *Donna May*. Otherwise, all she had was a fake driver's license that said she was Florence Goodbody from Madison, Wisconsin. The crazy old lady named Dot said her name was Caroline. At that moment, she was Abigail Buckles Caroline Florence Goodbody Sinclair. Buckles swallowed enough pie to choke a medium-size house pet and brightly asked, "Grandma, is my ID back in the room?"

Dot laughed. "Just scrub that trash off your face, young lady, stop this foolishness about an ID. You can't keep running loose to pretend you are some filthy hippie. I would not stand for that. Your mother would not stand for that. Our waffles are getting cold. We need to get down to business, and right now business means a good breakfast and a clean face before we move on. Our friend Officer Higgenbottom knows that no fifteen-year-old girl needs any ID. Isn't that right, officer?"

"'Trooper,' ma'am? Trooper?"

Dot daubed a napkin into a glass of water and with two fingers scraped at Buckles' face. The mascara did not so much as smear. It needed cold cream, so the old lady used spit and elbow grease. Her pointy finger hurt. "I am so sorry for your trouble," Dot said to the trooper, reaching across Buckles to touch the Ginger Bear's forearm, an arm thick as Big Bill's, but without Bill's tattoo of a naked lady riding a red snake.

Linda, the Shield of the Lord, gnawed her pencil eraser; her eyes narrowed in doubt. Dot set her blue eyes on her and said, "You are positively the most Christian woman. I think you must be an angel. Tell us the truth now. Is God's hand on your shoulder? You are an angel, aren't you? That's right, now, isn't it?"

Linda's eyes glowed. At last, someone perceived her inner goodness. She retrieved a short stack of pancakes and a side of link sausage before floating off to minister to burly truck drivers.

Buckles was no longer lightheaded, but the aroma of real food was making Buckles even more ravenous. The last thing she'd eaten before the pie was half a cellophane wrapped chocolate chip cookie in Scranton. She sucked down her chocolate milk until it crackled through the straw. Linda delivered another glass of milk.

Dot lumped as if the force of a brilliant idea lifted her. "Officer, won't you join us? I suspect you are also an angel. An angel warrior, like Gabriel. I saw those wings on the side of your car. I can see them from here. Angel's wings through a rubber tire."

The emblem of the Ohio State Highway Patrol was on the side of Higgenbottom's car, a Crown Vic visible outside. Its motor hummed.

"I wish I could?" Higgenbottom said. He stood, hitched his pants, and made to leave. "'Trooper?'" he said to the old woman again. "I'm a trooper?"

"Felix!" Dot said, shrill as a fighter jet. Felix nervously untied and retied his combat boots. Several of the professional truckers lifted their dull eyes at this new assault on their morose morning silence. "Felix, you help cousin Caroline with her bag. You hear me, boy?"

Buckles slid from her stool with her fresh chocolate milk. They had put ice in it. Felix lifted her rainbow tote with two hands. He said nothing more. Maybe he was used to crazy. He stowed her tote beneath the booth's table where Buckles joined him.

Dot could not weight ninety pounds, but she had more pep than a squad of high school cheerleaders. She stalked Higgenbottom to the diner's revolving door, babbling all manner of trash about these children today, how being an officer must be just one thing after another, and how lucky his wife had to be because she did notice his wedding ring, and was he blessed to have children of his own?

"Five?"

Dot crowded herself into the same segment of the revolving door as the trooper. They were released into the parking lot's steamy August morning together. Dot prattled on about St. Louis and Six Flags and how a reservation would be missed if they delayed. They would swing south before they had to swing north again to the family reunion in the heart of Iowa, the beating heart of the Heartland. Did the trooper think that was a good plan? They had to deliver the boy in Ankeny because he had but one week's leave before he would be shipped out of San Diego to fight godless communists in Vietnam. Visiting Ankeny was just a family stop en route from Fort Dix to a troop ship, but Dot hoped to ride the roller coaster at Six Flags. "Do you think we can manage all of that?"

The trooper tried to extricate himself, but the crone in pale blue pedal pushers was relentless. He wiped his brow dry with his forearm before he cinched his chinstrap tight to center his Smokey Bear hat on his polished bald head.

Felix and Buckles watched through truck-stop glass so thick it took on a tinge of green that made the outside world vaguely purple. It was better than television, watching a silent movie of Dot's arms flapping wildly and the Ohio trooper trying to get away.

"Grandma believes that if she pauses for breath she'll fall over dead," Felix explained. He sipped his milk. Buckles laughed. "Don't laugh. She might not be wrong."

"What do you mean?"

"She is real sick. She thinks I do not know she does not have much time left. I don't know where she gets the energy. Maybe she thinks if she keeps talking, she will live forever. She kidnapped me off base. I am her only living relative, and we are not really blood, either. She married my grandfather. She was his fourth wife, or maybe his fifth. I can't keep track. To tell you the truth, I don't think she knows, either."

Dot bent from the waist to lean directly into the trooper's open car door, her bony hips behind her, her skinny elbows flapping like wings. Higgenbottom waved at her to step back so he might shut the door.

"Is she crazy?"

"I can't figure it out. The stories she tells can't be real, but then most turn out to be right on. Can I sip your chocolate milk? It looks good. I don't know why I don't drink chocolate milk more." Buckles nodded, and Felix lifted his straw from his white milk and dropped it into Buckles' chocolate.

Buckles took her eyes from The Grandma Dot and Trooper Higgenbottom Show to ask, "Are you 'Sweetboy' or 'Felix?'"

"Pussy," her sudden cousin answered. "Call me 'Pussy.' You may as well. Everyone else does. I kind of like it. Call me Pussy."

"'Pussy'? Really? What kind of name is Pussy?"

"It's a long story, though if you come with us, you are sure to hear it. Grandma hates the radio, so she demands stories to pass the time. They do not have to be true. With her stories, I can't tell what's true and what isn't. I don't think she knows the difference." He sucked a long swallow of her milk. "If you come with us, you need to know that the only thing Grandma likes more than telling her own stories is to hear someone else's. They do not have to be true, either."

"Does she ask every hitchhiker to come along?"

"You'll be the first."

"Then how do you know she will ask me?"

"Because when she saw you at the counter, she muttered how you looked like a runaway who needed help, but when that trooper showed up she said you needed rescuing. Most of the time, we head west. She thinks they are after us."

"Who?"

Pussy shrugged. "Everybody."

The Crown Vic rolled forward with Grandma doing a quicker and quicker sidestep, her head in the open window.

"Before you say yes or no," Pussy said, "you need to know the worst. I am twenty-two, dropped out of school, joined the Army, but then Grandma reclaimed me from Fort Dix. She thinks the Army is like a library; you borrow soldiers instead of books. They gave me a two-hour leave because she persuaded a colonel she was dying, and so we went for a burger off base. She never took me back."

"That doesn't sound so bad."

"It will be if we get busted and you are arrested. I am AWOL, not dodging the draft. It's a whole other thing. That's why Grandma is making me grow this beard. It itches and I hate it, but if the MPs have a photo of me, the photo is beardless. In a few more days I won't be AWOL, I'll officially be a deserter. That's a hanging offense, Caroline."

"Buckles. Your grandmother made that name up. I am nineteen," she said, lying. "What will happen?"

"What kind of name is 'Buckles'?"

"It's my long story. You'll hear all of it if I go with you." She smiled, pleased at how she could echo what he'd said to her. Pussy smiled in return. His smile seemed whiter because of his scruff of beard.

Pussy leaned forward. "Grandma's crazy but she is smart. Taking you with us might be camouflage. They are looking for two people, but if you come along we are an ordinary family of three."

Pussy wondered aloud if the trooper outside would have to put on his sirens and lights to escape from Dot. That made Buckles laugh again. The Crown Vic gradually rolled faster. Dot stood erect to draw a breath and the car took the opportunity to pull away. She chased it several yards down the tarmac before she stopped, turned, and, winded, slowly walked back to the diner.

"Are you going to Canada?"

"Don't ask me. There is no safe place. I am a felon, not a draft dodger. I volunteered before they could draft me when my family blew up. Grandma Dot got into her car and came to rescue me."

"Wait. Your family blew up?"

He shrugged. "It's another long story."

Buckles sensed there would be no immediate details. "How long have you been on the road?"

"Weeks. All that circling around takes time. We go like hell, but never get anywhere. We stop while she rests, too. That can be for days."

"Is her name really 'Dot'?"

"Short for Dorothy, like the Wizard of Oz, but she says it has more to do with her days as a champion backgammon player. That may not be a fib. She'll tell you that story. Count on it. It's her favorite story, so it is probably true, and she likes to tell it. The details change, but not all that much. Backgammon is the game on the back of a cardboard checkerboard, but it gets played for serious money. My grandfather, the one she married, my mother's father, he's gone, too. Dot and I have each other and not much else. Once she is gone, I will be alone. Unless I die before her, and then she will be alone." Pussy offered her a forkful of French toast dripping syrup. "Grandma orders enough food for three lumberjacks. She claims to be from Maine. I only just learned that. She picks at breakfast, and then goes off to throw up. She can't keep food down. She thinks I do not notice that she pukes, but I do. She's having a good day today, it looks like. Other days, not so good. Maybe you will bring her luck."

"My luck is bad."

"Then Grandma would say you are overdue to turn the die. That's backgammon talk for doubling the bet to force your opponent to quit or lose more, like a raise in poker. But in backgammon there is no bluffing. The board is open for anyone to see. The game is about calculation, nerve, and much less luck than people think." Pussy gazed out the window. "She is not lucky, though. She is real, real sick. You can smell it on her. I don't know what to do except stay close and go along for the ride." Subdued panic roiled at a low boil in his soft eyes.

The old lady labored in the sun as she crossed the last of the parking apron. "Shouldn't we go out to get her?"

"Only if you want her to kill us. She won't admit she is sick. If she accepts assistance, the cat is out of the bag."

They sat in air-conditioning and watched Grandma Dot stop twice with her hands on her knees to recover her wind under the August sun in air so thick it could be sliced by a breadknife. Pussy inventoried the breakfast table, his index finger moving as he spoke. "My French toast, Grandma's waffle, two slices of pie, your pie, milk, some very good chocolate milk, a side of crisp bacon, a side of link sausage, one egg over-easy, home fries. We have had enough coffee to float a battleship, but this carafe is full. There was a biscuit with gravy here, too, but I ate that. Dot took two spoons of oatmeal before she hacked into this bowl, so I'd leave that alone. When Grandma saw you alone at the counter, she ordered extra French toast even before she went to get you, so this untouched plate over here must be yours."

The French toast was made from thick bread with powdered sugar and a coating of crushed corn flakes laced with cinnamon. "Texas Toast," Pussy said when Buckles rolled her eyes. She took two slices of crisp bacon from his plate with her fingers, looked at Pussy for any objection, and then claimed a third.

Dot finally fell into the revolving door. Being immersed in the diner's cold air seemed to revive her. She burst into the restaurant bouncing on her toes like a boxer in blue pedal pushers and Tretorns. Someone shouted, "Hallelujah," but since no one knew if that was a joke, no one laughed. Two drivers solemnly added, "Amen."

When Dot returned to the booth, her smile vanished. A patina of perspiration set her sallow face aglow with no hint of health, and she coughed spasms into a cloth napkin before her fevered water-green eyes, hard as ball-bearings, rose to rake Buckles.

"You are one fast study, young lady. I admire that, but if you want to ride with us you have to take that crap off your face. I will not ride with a girl who looks as if she is ready to turn a trick. The last thing we need is to attract John Law's attention. Old John looks down on pretty young girls who make their living the old-fashioned way." Her tone dropped even further. "Why does every hippie girl insist on looking like a Berlin streetwalker? All they wear are pussy belts. Their snatch stays in the breeze." Grandma Dot's fork clicked against her plate several times as she cut crescents of waffle, though she ate only one bit that she pushed through a congealing puddle of melted butter. Her fork waved at the French toast before Buckles. "Remember, Sweetboy, a decent order of French toast comes with whipped cream. That's free wisdom for you. Pecans are nice, cinnamon goes without saying, and fresh strawberries are lovely, but these Ohio bumpkins ought to know that your French toast wants whipped cream. A decorative sprinkle of powdered sugar is no substitute for genuine whipped cream. Now here is a riddle for you both. What do you suppose they call French toast in Paris?"

"French toast? Do they call it French toast?" Pussy said, smirking.

"Don't mock me, Sweetboy. Don't mock me. Do you think people in Brussels call waffles Belgian waffles? Of course they don't. It makes no sense."

Pussy said, "Then what do they call French toast in Paris?"

"*Pain perdu.* It means 'lost bread.' It's how the frogs rescue bread gone stale. Eggs and milk for the basic batter, soak that stale bread, fry it up, and *voila*, your lost bread is born again. We need some upbeat gospel about stale bread rising from the grave. Something we can clap rhythm to." For a half second, Buckles thought the crazy old lady would stand and dance to begin her second truck-stop morning revival, but she sipped ice water while faint color crept into her face. "On the other hand, your Belgian waffles have been around for hundreds of years. Despite bumpkin belief, Belgian waffles were not invented at the World's Fair. Imitation, theft, and adoption are the basis of the America character, and Belgian waffles were imitated, stolen, and adopted. There's no such thing as Chow Mein or Chop Suey in China, either, but who gives a tinker's damn? Mark me, they'll put P.T. Barnum on the ten dollar bill one fine day. Fakery is the American faith, and out here in the toolies every hick has faith. Not for good works, mind you. Confess a belief in Jesus and you can be a mass murderer in the Bumpkin Paradise to Come. Now, your hotdogs are a more interesting story. German, of course, nothing but sausages from Frankfurt. Same country gave us sauerkraut. But came The War to End All Wars, hicks needed to wave the flag harder than usual, so nothing could be German. In America, when facts become inconvenient, we invent new facts. Patriotism can take you only so far, but no patriot would dare require anyone give up the ideal food for baseball. What else can fit in your hand, cost fifteen cents, and be thrown accurately twenty yards across four rows seats? Schlitz, Pabst, Budweiser, Piels, Stroh's, Rheingold, every last one brewed by Huns. No one stopped beer. So much for patriotism. On a sunny July Fourth at the ballpark people want their German beers and a frankfurter. Some genius with more brains than a Hottentot renamed frankfurters 'hotdogs'." Bits of breakfast impaled on the tines of her fork, she waved it like a conductor waves a baton. "I should make you write these things down, Sweetboy. In a better world, I'd be paid for what I know. I would." She sucked enough ice water up a straw to moisten her lips, rolled it around in her mouth, and swallowed. "Breakfast. How I do love breakfast. Breakfast reminds me of all the times I crossed the Atlantic aboard the Cunard and White Star Lines. You could get anything, but when I was with Omar we'd breakfast on scones or kippers. Omar insisted his scones be smeared with heated Irish butter and a half-teaspoon of currant jam. I was hustling backgammon in the Smoking Room. Omar hustled Bridge. Sharif, I mean. Omar Sharif. One of the most civilized men I ever knew. An actor, too, of course. I do miss the aroma of good Cuban cigars. I miss the taste, too. Cigars are how I worked my way into the Smoking Room. Women were not allowed, but they could not very well have a sweet young thing like me puffing on her Havana while wandering anywhere on the Promenade Deck. You must have seen *Lawrence of Arabia*." They stared blankly back at her. "The movie?" Neither of them had seen it. Grandma sadly shook her head. "You can't be that young. Nobody is that young. All right, *Dr. Zhivago*, then. That was my Omar, but back when he was playing Bridge on transatlantic voyages no one but me guessed he would become famous. He was just a handsome black-eyed boy with a knack for cards, like my knack for backgammon." Her eyes glazed with a past she alone could see, a past she likely was inventing, a past that nevertheless enchanted Buckles. Buckles and her entire generation may have sworn allegiance to Truth, but a good yarn hurt no one. Besides, a made-up story could contain more truth than any history. "We had our fling. Nothing that would inspire the poets. There was a storm and poor Omar was terrified, so I kept him distracted in my state-room. One thing led to another, naturally. People had red blood in their veins back then. Wonderful dark, dark eyes. A girl could fold herself into those eyes and forget every warning her mother ever gave her. Well, the *Aquitania* did not sink. Maybe it was the *Mauretania*. It's hard to keep them straight. Floating hotels, as good as The Connaught, but with the Atlantic Ocean out the front door instead of Grosvenor Square. Did I mention his eyes? When the storm ended, everyone who was not throwing up was eating scones with tea. Breakfast. Breakfast, how I love breakfast." She lifted a thin crust of whole wheat toast, but did not eat it. "Years later I learned all about breakfast at my diner, The Dot, in Reno. Breakfast all day. Mr. Andrew, my short order cook, was an art-ist. Michelangelo for statues, Chanel for clothing, Mr. Andrew for batter. I tasted his pancakes and hired him on the spot. It was the vanilla. People criticized and created gossip about the blue-eyed lady and her black cook, calling him every vile name you can think of and throwing my reputation into the mix. Truth was, he was a family man, and I have my principles about marriage. The Dot had customers around the clock because your true gambler never gets up to pee or eat. The action is all his biology requires." She went to put her crust of bread down, but did not. "It's a wonder of nature. If you ever meet a man who does not gamble, steer clear. Run. Run as fast as you can, dears. A man who won't gamble has no soul. Don't expect to keep him, but enjoy your time together. Your craps players quit at two-thirty in the morning, they want French toast. Your Blackjack players want French toast at noon. Your Keno girls walk on spike heels, so when their shift ends they rub their calves, tend to their blisters, and they want their French toast, no sugar. But try serving French toast without whipped cream to a slots player. Slot machines." She sniffed. "There's a game for imbeciles, not gamblers. Why do you suppose they call them One-Armed Bandits? You can train a monkey to play the slots, and the monkey has the same chances as you or me. Levers and gears like an elevator. Where's the thrill in beating an elevator? But you can be sure that, if monkeys played slots, at the night's end they'd be out for bananas and French toast. The trick to Mr. Andrew's batter was that dash of Mexican *bonilla* and unpasteurized buttermilk. I'd sell you both to gypsies this minute for a plate of Mr. Andrew's pancakes." Her eyes closed for a heartbeat. "Even a short stack. I gave The Dot to Mr. Andrew when I went back east. Just gave the place to him. Why not? His pancakes brought in the customers, so why not? It was only fair. He had a wife and two boys, and they stood by him as he stood by them. That's true love, you ask me."

Her untouched plate had congealed into a grease-stiffened mess. She drew breath as if she'd been sprinting as she asked, "Who'd like an orange juice?" She rearranged plates as if a stray orange juice might lay hidden under a paper placemat. "Don't mind me prattling on like this. Talk is what old people do. It's the best way to know each other short of doing time together in a jail cell." She touched her lips dry with a paper napkin. "What about you, Caro? How about a biscuit and sausage gravy?"

"Her name is Buckles."

"Buckles? What kind of name is that?"

"It's my nickname, like Pussy's is 'Pussy'."

"You told her your name is Pussy?" Pussy shrugged. "Where did I go wrong?" Dot placed her fork on the table and fastened those steely green eyes on him. "You need more deceit, boy," she muttered. "Buckles," she said, then repeated, "Buckles," as if her lips were trying the name on for size. She shrugged. "I like it. I do. Buckles it will be." She extended her hand. Dot's skin was dry, brown as Egyptian paper. "Christ, this coffee is sewage. A lizard would not piss in this cup. Are you a whore, Miss Buckles? Nothing personal, but I suppose we need to know."

"No, ma'am. I am not a whore," Buckles managed to say.

"No shame in it if you were, but it is nothing to brag on, either. Takes no special talent. I ran a semi-legal cathouse in Reno, too, back in the day, but I had to give that up when I met old man Leitner, Sweetboy's grandfather. He was a sap, but he was a rich sap; a boring old bachelor fart with a deep wallet makes the perfect last husband. Ambrose and his brothers owned a factory in Lawrence, Massachusetts, where they made tablecloths, but they went to canvas tents and uniforms when war broke out. That's World War One, dearie. They bribed their way into a government contract, and made a fortune. Ambrose would never talk about the Wobblies and the Bread and Roses riot because he and his brothers hated Bill Haywood. I was just a baby then, myself, of course. By the time I came along, Ambrose's brothers were gone, and Ambrose had the good grace to kick the bucket himself not very much later. A fishing accident. Ernest said it was the damndest thing he'd ever seen."

Pussy lifted his chin with renewed interest, then looked suspiciously at his grandmother. "Ernest?"

"Ernest Hemingway."

"The writer?"

"How many Ernest Hemingways do you know?" She rolled her eyes and refilled her coffee from the table carafe, made a sour face, then leaned to peer more closely at Buckles. "At least you don't wear eye-shadow in broad daylight. Only under-age whores want to look older. Any other whore will want to look younger. Men want them young. There are laws in America. Not that men give a damn about laws, but if they are caught with their hands in the honeypot, John Law comes down like the Wrath of God. Better to be in the grip of the Inquisition than be a baby rapist in jail."

Buckles thought of how Big Bill had gone from monster to coward. Was this the reason?

"Laws protect the weak, and young women in America are taught to be weak. A 'good girl' is an obedient girl. Buckles, remember this if nothing else, when a man shows up on his white horse with a promise to rescue you, he is already counting the ways he can play Hide the Sausage. So take his horse and skedaddle."

"She told you, she is not a whore, Grandma. And Buckles is twenty," Pussy said, adding to Buckles' fib. She was aging fast, up three years over her true birthday, five if you counted from the lie she'd told Big Bill. Dizziness passed through her at the thought of Big Bill's hands on her. She'd pleaded she was fifteen.

Her newly-filled belly was making her sleepy; either that, or her sleepless night slapping at Big Bill's hands was making its overdue claim.

Dot loudly burped. She washed the tiniest bit of waffle down her throat with the terrible coffee. "Tricking is no life for a young girl, though. Besides, with hippie girls giving it away, I am surprised the business is not done. Amateurs ruin everything. Amateurs ruined backgammon. Amateurs are ruining America." She touched the back of Buckles' wrist. "Don't you fret, dear. Most men are pecker-heads, including Sweetboy here, but he is young enough to change. There may be hope for him. He's twenty-six."

"Twenty-two."

"Twenty-six. Get used to being twenty-six. That's one year past being draftable. You were in a coma, remember? Be as fast a study as Buckles here. That seven-year nap in Switzerland is why you were never in the Army. Eisenhower isn't president, Kennedy was shot, and Lyndon Johnson swings dogs around by the ears. You missed a lot asleep in Berne."

"You were in a coma?" Buckles asked.

"Of course not," Pussy said.

"Don't contradict your grandmother. Of course you were. When he woke up, the doctors called it a miracle."

Grandma gently took Buckles' chin and turned her head left and right as if Buckles was a horse at auction. "I suppose you are coming with us, but if I see a speck of eye-shadow or eyeliner, I'll throw you right out. We need to look innocent. Right out the car door, you hear me? Won't even slow down. Fair warning. Where are you bound?"

"San Francisco."

"Well, you've got more balls than brains, my friend. You're lucky you are not dead in a ditch with your throat cut."

"Yes, ma'am." Buckles would never tell anyone about her night aboard *Donna May* and how having her throat cut had seemed preferable to being broken by Big Bill before he traded her to his friends in Kansas. She might change her mind and tell the story someday, but not this day. Her belly flipflopped; she unconsciously touched a bruise on her left arm.

"We're also headed west, for now," Pussy said. "I drive."

"I make no guarantees where we will end up," Dot said. "That's how the Edsel rolls. You climb aboard and in the morning you see where it brought you. Whatever happens, happens."

Pussy was right about Dot probably being crazy, but it was also plain she was sick and needed help. Dot's gray hair was wound in a bun and had what could have been a knitting needle sticking out like an old broken TV antenna. Her hair was lifeless gray. Dying. Knowing you were dying could make anyone crazy.

Grandma suddenly sent Pussy to the lavatory.

"But I don't have to go."

"Yes, you do. Sweetboy, see a man about a horse and do not contradict me."

Pussy left them.

"Quick, now. Girl-talk. Are you truly alone? We can't have some crazy boyfriend with a pistol following us."

"I am by myself, ma'am."

"No one is after you?"

"I don't think so," she said, lying. For sure, her parents were searching, but she'd covered so much ground in only two days they'd never find her. If police were looking, they'd be looking for a kid with her thumb out by the side of the road, not someone travelling with her cousin and their grandmother. If she was camouflage for Grandma and Pussy, they were camouflage for her as well.

"Call me 'Dot' or 'Grandma,' especially if other people are around. Lord, we put it over on that Higgenbottom-donkey, didn't we? I haven't had that much fun in a while. Five kids. He said it like he lost count. His wife must be bowlegged. Pussy would not have known where to start a scam like that, much less be put in the middle of it, but you picked up the ball and ran with it. Damn, how I like a quick study! Have you ever been on the grift? You are a natural."

Buckles wondered what *on the grift* meant, but she was proud to be a quick study and a natural, though she did not understand at what. "I'd like a ride, for a while, if that is all right."

"Don't be so damned polite. I'm not half as crazy as I act and I am not as old as I look. It's this sickness. It's killing me. It ties my guts in knots. Sweetboy hardly knows. But enough about me. I suppose you are knocked up."

Buckles knew what that meant. "No."

Dot sat back and crossed her arms with doubt, "Are you sure? It's not the end of the world, but if you are knocked up, we have a different set of problems."

"Yes, I am sure. I am not pregnant."

Grandma's whisper lowered to a hiss. "Nasty father at home? Creepy uncle?" The back of the old lady's dry hand stroked Buckles' smooth cheek. "Someone scared you badly, dearie. It's on you like white on rice, not to mention the yellow bruises on your upper arm. Those bruises will feel worse before they feel better, too. They'll want ice. They look nasty, and they look new, and in that torn up vest your tits are half out. I can see those arms and half your chest between the buttons. You may want to wear a shirt under that thing, if you own a shirt. Someone did you wrong, though. Why else would you come up for air in this pisshole-of-a-truck-stop with nothing but tea since before sunup and not a car in sight? If you didn't drop from the sky or crawl out of the corn, someone dumped you here. I don't need the details. They are always ugly and always the same. So here is some free advice from your Grandma Dot: wash the poison out of your life even when you think the poison is what makes you who you are. Be whole. Pain is no private treasure. It's just pain. Let it go. Are you injured somewhere I can't see? We are just us girls here. Tell the whole truth."

Buckles touched the exposed bruises on her upper arm. "I tripped," she said.

Dot fell back against the rear of the red leatherette booth and sighed. "If you say so, yes, dear, but I doubt it. We passed a dozen kids like you on the road, alone, or two or three at a time. You might be the first natural blonde, though. They hold up cardboard signs in crayon. 'Frisco.' Here's some news for those nitwits. Never call San Francisco 'Frisco.' The natives will hang you."

Pussy reappeared but never had a chance to sit. Grandma dropped some crumpled bills onto the table, said she'd meet them at the car, and left them while she hurried to "take a whiz."

Buckles asked, "Should I call you Felix, Pussy, or Sweetboy?"

"Yes," he said, laughing. "'A rose by any other name would smell as sweet.'"

"That's *Hamlet*."

Pussy laughed again. "Close, but no cigar."

"*Julius Caesar*? I know it isn't *Macbeth*. It isn't *Macbeth*, is it?"

They each grasped a handle of Buckles' tote bag and walked across the concrete apron to the biggest car Buckles had ever seen, a two-door white Edsel convertible. The car had chrome hubcaps and seemed to float on cushy marshmallow whitewalls. The cream-colored vinyl top was down. Two crimson and cream-colored leather bucket seats were in front, a rear seat wide as a park bench was in the rear. The Edsel's fins were like a flying shark's.

"When I first saw that car," Pussy said, "I did not believe it, either."

"It's no pregnant roller-skate, is it?"

"Pregnant roller-skate?"

"What truck drivers call a Volkswagen," Buckles explained with an air of superiority at using an expression she'd learned less than ten hours earlier when Big Bill, before he went crazy, had explained the chatter on *Donna May*'s CB radio. Grandma Dot said that Buckles was a fast study; maybe she was.

Pussy gazed at her with respect colored by skepticism. "Don't even ask about the gas mileage. This is a 1958 Edsel. Grandma swears she bought it new for less than a dollar per pound when they could not give them away. They only made a few. It handles like a boat with a broken rudder. It's a rare car. She kept it in storage for years, but she took it out of mothballs to come for me."

"It looks great."

"It's a heap of junk. Famous junk, but still junk. Whatever hasn't broken yet, will, and at the least convenient time. But that's Grandma Dot's style. Once she likes something, she won't give up on it. That includes me and maybe you. She sounds crazy until you check out her stories and find how much is true. I went to the Harvard Library. Omar Sharif really plays high stakes Bridge, so maybe he did it on luxury liners, but that would have had to have been before he was born. Grandma really did play backgammon, so it almost makes sense. The Hemingway story today was new to me, though. All I know about Grandpa was that he drowned, so it could be true."

"Stop dawdling." Dot had caught up to them. She went to the car's far side. "I'll ride this honey until it rolls over and its wheels go up in the air. Don't care if it is noticeable. There's a limit to what I am willing to give up."

Pussy dropped Buckles' tote on the back seat. Buckles climbed in after it. "Does the car have a name?" she asked.

Grandma pivoted on her hip to half face Buckles in the rear as Pussy shut her door behind her. While he circled around to the driver's side, Grandma quickly whispered, "Never tolerate a man who names his car or his penis. It means he thinks more of his cock than of himself, and you come in a distant third." Big Bill had forced her to meet Little Bill. Buckles' belly danced its Mambo again.

"Have you much clothing in that thing, dear?"

"Some."

"Sweetboy, you keep your eyes straight ahead while Buckles gets into something a little cooler than that vest."

Buckles slipped out of the vest, the fresh air cool on her exposed skin in the seconds it took for her to push her head into her loose

peasant blouse with the red embroidered neck line, her only garment that wasn't a T-shirt.

Before the Edsel carried them beyond the limits of Perrysburg,
Buckles fell across the big red leather backseat. Her head lay on
her tote bag as she rolled to her hip, her arms crossed, and drew
her knees to her chest. What with the rhythm of the moving car,
the hum of the whitewall tires, her stomach full, the sun strobing
the shadows of electric towers, and the sweet aroma of the joint
Grandma withdrew from the glovebox, before she knew it, hardly
thinking it was remarkable that the weird old lady was toking on
weed, Buckles Sinclair sank deep into a grey lake of exhaustion.

The Edsel consumed ruler-straight two-lane blacktop roads
through endless fields of corn and swaying dry grass. With the car's
convertible top down and humid August smelling richly of manure
flowing over the windshield, wisps of her own floating hair tangled
before Buckles' near-awake eyes. Her fallen star-spangled kerchief
lay knotted near her feet. Her denim vest was bunched under her
cheek, a pillow. Her face peeled off the Edsel's hot vinyl seat.

What would happen to her now?

When she sat up, she struggled against sudden dizziness. The
summer sun must have been having its way with her. All ten of her
fingers massaged her own scalp. Her trip was beginning anew. Her
throat was sandpaper.

Without facing her, Grandma informed Buckles that she
would require a cap. "It will keep your hair neat enough and the
sun from your eyes. That bandana thing is a trendy rag, dear, and
not much protection unless you are planning on doing stoop work
and need to stop sweat dripping into your eyes, so blow your nose
one last time with that American flag and throw it overboard. Sun
can ruin a woman. All those ads about tanned beach bunnies don't
show you their faces at fifty. A cap is the thing. But that blonde hair
worries me more. It screams, 'Look at me!' and our game is to slide
by unnoticed. I'd ask you to cut and dye it, but I'll admit that may
seem extreme for our free ride, so we'll cover it with a cap." She

said to Pussy: "Next stop, find a John Deere cap. In Indiana that should be about as difficult as scratching your ear. Green will suit you, Buckles. The first thing to do with a new hat is to soak it and rub in dirt so it looks like an old hat."

"What's wrong with a new hat?" Pussy asked.

"It looks new."

The Edsel was doing forty-five and was being passed by every other vehicle on the road. The old woman punched Pussy's thigh and told him to slow down anyway, then spun in her seat to face Buckles. "Take a hit of this. You'll feel better." She passed her joint to Buckles. "Avoid highways, Sweetboy. I can't very well inhale my medicine in full view of a state trooper. They are not all as dense as that hoople back in Ohio. Not that anyone expects an old hag with her two grandchildren to be smoking weed in an Edsel convertible on the back roads of Indiana, but why be reckless? We made Indiana while you were asleep, dear."

"Higgenbottom," Buckles said, "not Hoople."

"'Hoople' is an expression, Buckles. Major Hoople was in the funny papers when I was a girl. A 'hoople' is a fat idiot with a high opinion of himself. Our Higgenbottom was a hoople." Buckles laughed. "We could have sold that trooper ice in winter, and charged him a dollar extra for a charitable donation to Eskimos. I do believe that. I do. I near passed a collection plate to the diner congregation. That was the best tent meeting I've run in years. But even a Hoosier hoople might notice a whiff of herb on the wind above the aroma of Grade A Indiana horseshit, and I am not about to put the Edsel's top up when fresh air is so good a tonic. Maybe your beatniks would smoke herb in Indiana, but I don't suspect a single beatnik is still in Indiana."

"What's a beatnik?" Pussy asked.

"Tell him, Buckles."

"Before there were hippies, there were beatniks," Buckles said. "Poets and stuff, mostly."

"I *knew* you'd know," Grandma said, raising one skinny arm in triumph. "Can I pick 'em or can I pick 'em? Little girl, you remind me of me." She spun about in the Edsel's bucket seat as her hand reached into the glovebox to hover over a rattling vial of pills, but emerged holding only a fresh joint.

At a secluded bend in the road, Grandma called a halt. The motor ran while she squatted behind a row of mulberry bushes. Then Pussy took his turn to pee.

"The only advantage men have is to pee standing up," Grandma said. "God has one wicked sense of humor."

When it was Buckles' turn, she took the moment of privacy to tent her peasant blouse and peer down her neckline. Her left breast was scary shades of purple, green, and yellow. Her armpits smelled like a swamp.

Buckles never could have guessed at how full her bladder could get. Water ran from her for whole minutes. She was sure she'd emerge from behind the bush to see the last of the Edsel with the last of her pitiful belongings far down the road, leaving Buckles alone among sad cows, but when she stood, zipped, and rebuttoned the waist of her cutoffs, her companions were idly passing time under billows of fragrant smoke.

As the Edsel accelerated once again, Grandma said, "Sweetboy, tell our new friend how you got your name."

"You gave it to me."

"I mean 'Pussy.' You are a sweet boy, but Buckles needs to know why you are so damned proud of being 'Pussy.' Buckles needs to know your story."

"Do I have to?"

"Yes, you have to. The only radio shows we have are all Jesus all the time. I vomit enough without hearing a huckster selling God. A con is a con is a con, and religion is the oldest con there is. I'd rather spend eternity in Hell than buy a ticket into Heaven with a check made out to the Very Sacred First Church of Perpetual Bumpkin Broadcasting. A caveman once squatted around a fire, poked at some charred bones when the nitwit next to him asked what he was doing to make cinders flare so pretty, and so he told some cock-and-bull story about how the bones and fire sought a higher power and he was the intermediary. As a rule, the boys at the fire were cold, wet, hungry and had the ague, so hearing how their suffering would end in the sweet by and by was uplifting. That was when they gave the prophet a place closer to the fire and cut him a better cut of haunch from a wild boar. The prophet knew an easy gig when he had one. To keep the meat coming in, he wore feathers on his head. What fool would race through a forest stubbing his toes on tree roots when nitwits are fighting each other to keep you fat to tell them pretty lies?"

"Where were the cave women?" Pussy asked in his snottiest tone.

"Hauling water, doing real work. Don't be a wiseacre. Buckles has not had the privilege of hearing all I have to say, so you keep your lip buttoned." She toked her joint but did not pass it. "Stories are how we know each other, Sweetboy. I know your story, and you think you know mine, but Buckles here knows neither."

The point of Buckles' chin settled on her crossed forearms at rest on the spine of Grandma's front seat. Riding the Edsel with these two might be better entertainment than her stack of 45s and a record player. Indiana smelled like Ohio, and both places smelled of fresh shit. Her hair rippled behind her. She was able to ignore the waves of lightheadedness that passed through her. It had to be the dope and fatigue, right? Grandma bit into a pill that crackled as if she chewed on ice.

"My life could strip Gandhi of hope," Pussy said. "Everything went down the crapper at my sixth birthday party. Grandma remembers."

"The hell I do," Grandma said.

"But you were married to Grandpa Gaitreaux by then. He was there. He kept stealing my nose. It made me cry."

"Sweetboy, I was Gaitreaux's third wife, last in a line of skinny, flat-chested women too young for the old reprobate. When I came along, Ambrose was at an advanced age and did not have much use for a wife beyond casting an illusion of virility, more for himself than anyone else. We tied the knot, but I made him swear we would take regular separate vacations. That way, he enjoyed his reputation for having a way with young women, and I got to sleep with young men."

"I thought you had principles around marriage?"

"I do. As long as all parties play by the same rules, why not?"

"Who was that beautiful young woman Grandpa got?" Pussy asked, grinning.

"Me, you little snot." She punched his thigh hard enough for him to wince. "But I never attended your birthday parties. Came April, I was in the Berkshires pursuing a sex life with newly met strangers."

Buckles listened hard as Felix's story unfolded. Telling stories did more than pass the time, even if the stories were made of lies and exaggerations. The kinds of lies and the kinds of exaggerations told as much or more than truth.

Pussy moved on to how his mother, Renee Gaitreaux Leitner, was a mainstay of volunteerism in Metrowest, a clot of wealthy suburban communities valued for their proximity to Boston and their public schools the equal of the prep academies that dot New England.

Buckles kept mute about her former life at Dobbs.

Rich white people had abandoned Boston in search of the good life in Wayland, Weston, Natick, Westwood, and Norwood. "It was the fifties," Pussy said. "That was what people did."

Grandma snorted. "What kind of explanation is that? The bastards barred Jews, coloreds, and made certain damn few Irish got in, too, though they had to ease up on the Irish once the micks took control of Massachusetts. The symbol of the Mass Pike is still a leprechaun, for God's sake. That's the Irish sticking a shillelagh in the Brahmin's eye. You'd think that road connected Stockbridge to Killarney."

"Aren't Brahmins a kind of bull?"

"Yes, Buckles, they are. But in Boston the word refers to religious refugees from Britain who infected Indians with small pox and claimed God gave them the continent. They've conducted business the same way ever since."

"Are you done?" Pussy asked.

"The truth is the truth," Grandma said. "A good story needs plenty of background and context. A good digression helps everyone."

"But that digression has nothing to do with how I got my name," Pussy said.

"Telling tales is an art," Grandma said. "We have plenty of time and it is a lovely day. May as well tell it all." She rolled the yellow sleeves of her blouse to her forearms. Her skin was crisscrossed by blue and red veins. "All right, Sweetboy, get on with it."

He sighed. "Our lawn parties were famous. Our backyard lawn sloped to a running stream. No one refused an invitation. Dad hired professional bartenders; pretty college girls dressed as French maids carried platters of *hors d'oeuvres*."

"Cardboard platters," Grandma muttered to Buckles. "Even Johnny Leitner was not stupid enough to trust that crowd around silver. He'd count spoons when the guests left. But those college girls went home with plenty of bruises pinched onto their derrieres."

"You said you were never there, so how would you know?"

"That's men. I know men."

"Is that you giving more context?"

"No. It's a fact of life. Just shut up and talk." Grandma passed a fresh joint over her shoulder. Buckles closed her eyes to draw a long hit. The marijuana left her nicely mellow. Her heart, which had been flippity-flopping ever since she opened her eyes, slowed, though her vague sense of paranoia persisted. It was nothing to worry about. Weed could do that.

"By my sixth birthday, I was sure the annual invasion of our yard was because I was a celebrity. I was special," Pussy said. "Born on April Fool's Day. Doesn't that tell you everything? But the actual reason everyone congregated in our backyard was that my father celebrated the Boston Sox weekend home opener, usually in mid-April. We delayed my party so baseball and I arrived together."

Grandma interrupted again. "You are doing a better job, Sweetboy, I'll admit. Details are good, but Buckles will want to know that, when Renee's waters broke three days before her due date, her doctor urged her to hold on two hours to spare you the humiliation of being born on the Day for Fools. Now, Renee was much too proper to be foulmouthed, but even though she was in labor back on her elbows with her legs up in stirrups, she spit through her teeth, 'Get this fucking kid out of me.' You see, Sweetboy's older sister, Sheila, had taken thirty-six hours to come into this world. Renee was having no part of that again. I heard she tried to lunge across a table of sterile instruments to perform her own epidural, but on the doctor. Or maybe it was to apply the forceps to his privates. The date of your birth, Sweetboy, was a choice your mother made for you."

"And you know all this how?"

"Renee told me, of course. Isn't that obvious? Women talk. They don't have to be great friends to share information, and technically I was her stepmother."

"I thought the two of you hardly spoke?"

"There was some Zinfandel involved. I forget which cousin we were burying. Funerals can be hilarious."

She asked if Buckles knew what an epidural was, and when Buckles lied and said that she did, Grandma waved her age-spotted veiny wrist for Pussy to resume.

"The season's first Saturday home game for the Sox was Dad's excuse to immolate huge slabs of beef, pork ribs, and Fenway hotdogs. He had a brick grill built on our flagstone patio just for that. The year I turned six Dad was keen to show off his new color projector TV in the living room. It was his Christmas gift to his family. People traipsed in and out most of the day to marvel at the picture even if the TV was crap. There was no way to balance the colors. Our screen was stained with so much magenta, Buffalo Bob looked like a ghoul. For the party, Dad climbed a ladder to fiddle with the antenna, but the Fenway grass stayed blue. I grew up thinking that baseball infields were supposed to look blue."

"Why did he like the Red Sox so much?" Buckles asked.

Grandma explained. "Around Boston, the Red Sox are a religion, Buckles, because they always find a way to lose." Grandma snorted. "The leprechaun may be Catholic, but in every other way New Englanders are fatalistic as Cotton Mather."

"And what is cotton matter?" Sweetboy asked.

"Not what. Who."

"An old boyfriend of yours?"

"Tell him, Buckles."

"He was a preacher for the Pilgrims," Buckles said.

Grandma whooped and emitted her chicken laugh. "I knew it! I knew you'd know!"

Pussy added how back in the day an added attraction was the general belief that no Negro would ever wear a Red Sox uniform. "They were the last team to integrate," Pussy said. "Almost a decade after Jackie Robinson."

"Who is Jackie Robinson?" Buckles asked, but the flow of air through the open car sucked her question away over her shoulder. Had she spoken at all? Dobbs made her smart on book learning, but left her stupid as a rock when it came to knowing life.

The Edsel glided through big shadows cast by white clouds. Wind in the Edsel's rear seat rose to the volume of a jet and then sank to a whisper depending on the car's speed or how hard Buckles' heart pumped blood through Buckles' ears. The day grew warmer, so she considered removing her peasant blouse, but being bare-chested in a convertible was likely to frustrate Grandma's plan to pass unnoticed. Her thighs would by day's end flame red with sunburn. She unlaced the neck of her peasant blouse to its limit so it fell open. That left her slightly cooler and relieved irritating pressure on her bruised boob.

"The guests brought me Red Sox T-shirts, Red Sox caps, Red Sox lunch boxes and a few fielder's mitts. Dad tried to play catch with me once, but after five minutes gave that up. Sheila, my older sister, was the athlete in the family. Dad was bragging about Sheila a month before he blew everyone up."

"You're getting ahead of yourself," Grandma said. "Who is losing track of his story now? The art of telling a story, Sweetboy, is to use digressions to illuminate one point at a time. The point is why you are called 'Pussy.' That's why storytelling is an art." Grandma swiveled to face Buckles. "Johnny Leitner didn't murder anyone, but the damn fool did kill them all."

"Now you are telling my story."

"My car, my rules. Follow the signs to Decatur. Go slow."

"We passed the turn to Decatur while Buckles was asleep."

Grandma sighed. "That was Decatur, Indiana. I am talking about Decatur, Illinois. There are Decaturs everywhere you spit. He was an admiral in the Revolutionary War."

"Did you know him, too?"

"Very cute, Sweetboy. When you get out from behind the wheel, don't think I won't slap you silly just because we were once roommates."

"She farts in her sleep," Pussy said over his shoulder to Buckles.

"I may fart, but Sweetboy keeps nudie and muscle magazines of men under his mattress. You didn't think I knew that, did you?"

Buckles' head spun. They talked at a gallop. Keeping up was challenging. The marijuana was blossoming into a giggle fit, but since she was sure that if the giggles started she'd be unable to stop them, she pinched the loose exposed flesh of her thigh to study the speed with which color returned to her sunburned flesh, the surest measure of how much pain she'd suffer later. If skin stayed lobster red after a pinch, she was fried. Baby oil and iodine were her preferred tanning mix at the family pool; what tamed the sun in a speeding convertible?

Pussy missed a turn and backed up a hundred yards to follow a one lane tractor road between fields to Decatur. "My mother, Renee, prepared ambrosia every year, but every year that became crusty from the sun. No one ever touched it."

"Ambrosia?" Buckles asked. "Sounds like something that can get a person stoned."

"Not in that crowd, Buckles," Grandma said. "Sweet, sticky, fattening, made from marshmallows, oranges, pineapple, tapioca, and shaved coconut in whipping cream." Buckles was being assaulted by the munchies. A bag of Hydrox and a jar of Skippy would do for her. She'd have more acne pockmarks than the surface of the moon, but scooping a few Hydrox through peanut butter was worth any number of pockmarks. A Snickers Bar would be good, too. Maybe she'd run a Snickers through the peanut butter. "Ambrosia will leave you with an ass the size of Montana."

"Sheila worshipped our father," Pussy said, quick to avoid Dot's digression into nutrition and hips. "She was eleven the year I turned six. Grandpa Ambrose would pinch his own thumb between two other fingers and tell me, 'I got your nose.' I'd beg Grandpa not to leave me disfigured for life. '*Please please please* put my nose back!'"

"Ambrose did not need a drink in him to be a mean, stingy, sadistic prick who would torture a six year old boy," Grandma said. "He produced tears for a hobby. God rest his black heart, he met a bad end."

"You're interrupting, again."

"No story goes in a straight line. I told you, 'My car, my rules.'"

Pussy sighed. "Knock yourself out. I suppose this is the fish story."

"In fact it is the fish story." Grandma turned three-quarters to face Buckles. "Ambrose and I met when I went to Havana to gamble. It was what I did when I lived in Reno but the casino pit bosses knew me. In Nevada it is illegal to gamble and win too often. You are supposed to lose at games of chance. If you win and win often, you obviously are not engaged in a game of chance. Ambrose went to Cuba to trawl for blue fin marlin and young women, so we hit it off. He lured me in by flashing a lot of money. Marlin had more sense than I, but I was young and money looked good. We drank white rum at *El Floridita*. Mary invited us for a nightcap at *Finca Vigia*, Papa's villa on the hill. The place stank of cats. Mary was the last wife, cute as a button. We stayed for a week and were sober some of the time."

"Hemingway again?"

She ignored him, but went on. "Ambrose and I married right there in Havana. Papa was best man. Two years later, when I was off to revisit Innsbruck, Ambrose hankered for cigars and fishing. He stayed with Papa, of course. Castro was still up in the mountains nearby, but Papa had nothing to fear because Fidel adored anyone who wrote well. He adored writers as much as he adored baseball players. Ambrose drowned. Papa's letter to me filled in the details. Ambrose was drunk when he hooked a damn fine marlin, but had left his safety harness unfastened. The marlin was too much fish. The reel locked, and the cheap stupid bastard refused to let go of his tackle, an Ugly Stick and Avet reel I had given him. Grandpa Ambrose went over the side and skimmed the surface like a drag float. When the marlin sounded, Grandpa Ambrose followed. Unlike Ahab, he never rose to beckon for anyone to follow."

"Who was Ahab?" Pussy asked. "Another buddy of Hemingway's?"

"He's the captain of the ship in *Moby Dick*," Buckles shouted into the wind.

"I begin to like you even more, young lady," Grandma said. "In the same letter, Hem told me how he and Hotch poured Midori off the fantail of the *Pilar*, almost as much as they drank. 'The sun was hot. He had courage. We drank to his fine death,' Papa wrote. If I had half a brain, I'd have kept the letter, but I threw it out with the morning trash because I knew that Ambrose had never written a will, so I expected to inherit every dime. Renee's panties twisted into a knot over that; she did not like thinking her Daddy's fortune was going to the harlot who seduced her father but was dallying with a downhill racer in Austria when her father drowned rather than let go of his fishing gear. I had to get to Massachusetts because they'd be hiding assets fast as they could get their hands on them. There was jewelry that had been given to me and I wanted the pieces, heirloom stuff. Johnny Leitner, Satan's own lawyer, could squeeze a nickel until the Indian choked. I eventually got my share, but that cost me time in goddam Arborside. I should have known better to agree to that, but I did."

While Buckles tried to ask what Arborside was, Pussy said, "Well, Mom had a point, didn't she? You did seduce the old man, right?"

Grandma sucked on her teeth as if in pain, reached to her stash in the glovebox, thought better of it, and said, "Of course I did.

But take it from a grifter, there is no such thing as seduction. The word was invented by proper young ladies suffering buyer's remorse. What can you say about a woman who buys a dress, puts on her stockings, does her hair, spends hundreds on Chanel, rouges her face, stains her lips, and spends another fortune on black underwear in hopes someone will tear the works off her? Comes the harsh morning, she tells herself she was seduced rather than admit she enjoyed a roll in the hay with the sweaty sack of shit wheezing in her bed." Grandma's fingers curled a set of quotation marks in the air. "Trust me, dear hearts, no man or woman can be 'seduced' unless they want to be."

Pussy laughed. Grandma kicked at his thigh hard enough to make his leg go pins and needles. "Not funny, Sweetboy. Not funny." She pressed her hand to her side and sharply inhaled. "Well, get on with it. Get on with it. Lunch is overdue. Get on with your story. I'll tell Buckles all about Arborside when it is my turn at storytelling. But last I heard, we were in the Leitner backyard immolating beef." Grandma chewed the remains of her most recent joint and picked shreds of marijuana from her teeth. The Edsel rolled past millions of rows of corn. "I'm not sleepy," the old woman murmured. "Keep talking."

"Are you sure?"

Grandma punched his thigh again.

"At the party, Mom announced 'The Felix Parade.' I was clueless, but I was very proud. Ice cream cake and three Fenway Franks churned in my stomach, but a parade would keep me from being sick. Every guest snapped on a paper mask of Felix the Cat, the kind with an elastic band that pinches back your ears. The masks had big black punch-out eyes and the cat's big grin. Mom dropped a yellow record on a portable phonograph, and music started.

> *Felix the cat*
> *The wonderful, wonderful cat,*
> *Whenever he gets in a fix*
> *He reaches into his bag of tricks …*

"Even Sheila, my sister who hated being out of the spotlight, clapped. The baseball fans abandoned the TV picture of Fenway with blue grass long enough to snake around the backyard in a sort of conga line, slapping tambourines, bashing cymbals, ringing bells, and grabbing each other's behinds. I had a cowbell and a drumstick and walked in front." Pussy sighed. "It was the last moment I can remember being totally happy. My life began to crater from there. My life peaked when I was six." Grandma gently snored and farted twice. Pussy went forward anyway. Even in her sleep, her grandson obeyed her. "Once the Felix Parade ended, most guests left. Dad settled down to drain a bottle of Chivas Regal with his oldest friends. I was drowsing in my mother's arms when Uncle Stevie proposed a toast. 'To Felix the Cat!' he said and raised his glass to me.

"Sheila shouted from the family room, 'More like Felix the Pussy!'"

Buckles laughed. "The name stuck, right?"

"Pretty much, but I liked it, too. I loved Sheila. That day, she not only named me Pussy, but earned a Princess phone for enduring me, a private line with a pig-tail extension cord that reached into a closet with a door. It was her private phone booth. The one obstacle to perfection in her life was her baby brother. When no one was looking, she'd punch me in the solar plexus. Punching did not count as bad behavior, provided no one saw it."

"Nothing is bad behavior if no one sees it," Grandma muttered, proving she was at most half asleep.

Buckles had always wanted a baby brother, though not for punching. "Why on earth would a sister do that?"

"Don't know, exactly. Maybe she was fond of the shade of blue and pink my face turned when I could not catch my breath. She believed I was unconscionably stupid, needing ongoing reminders that she was five years and seven months older than I was, practically six years, so we could not ever, not in a million bazillion years, be peers. She once explained to me how the nuns had found me in a smelly dumpster and that if I did not do whatever she demanded the instant she demanded it, I might be returned to where I came from, a world of rats and spiders. My family was not Catholic, but everyone knew Catholic nuns were weird."

"I was born Catholic," Buckles said. "I was even baptized."

"Lucky you." Grandma breathed and lifted one arm to shield her eyes.

"According to Sheila, since Mom was allergic to cat dander we could not have a real pet like a puppy for Sheila to love, so they kept me." Buckles wanted to laugh, but did not. Brothers. Sisters. She knew nothing. "I was her retarded cretin spazmo idiot brother, soaking up the attention that was rightfully hers. Even a retarded cretin spazmo idiot should have been able to see the cosmic injustice of her being ignored for a few minutes. If I did not have the decency to crawl off and throw myself into traffic, the very least I could do was to leave her alone with her Princess phone."

Pussy spoke in a dreamy voice that suggested he was not exclusively in the present. In the Edsel, time, memory, and distance moved at different speeds.

"Now I was sure that being a retarded cretin spazmo idiot was nothing good, but I also hoped that being Felix the Pussy brought some better status. After all, it was Sheila's name for me, and the name made people laugh. But a few days after my birthday barbecue, I found my cat mask in tiny, unflushable bits of cardboard floating in the toilet. Mr. Nobody, my mother's explanation for everything that had no explanation, had done the job. Then, a few days after the party, Mom drove the family wagon to an emergency meeting at a Natick coffee shop because the keynote speaker for the Town Hall Speakers Program had canceled his talk about the dangers of communism in the public schools. My mother was Chair of the Speakers' Committee, so she sped away to confer with the same patriots who'd required kindergarten teachers to sign Loyalty Oaths. Sheila was supposed to be minding me while Mom was gone, but a thunderstorm was brewing. Electricity was in the air, an aroma I recognized from the time Sheila put flashlight bulbs in my ears, stuck copper pennies in my nose, and connected them with an unbent paper clip soaked in lemon juice that she put in my mouth."

"Why would she do that?" Buckles asked.

"For her junior high school's Science Fair. It was an experiment to see if low voltage could electrocute a retarded cretin spazmo idiot. When the flashlight bulb did not light up, she kicked me because I was not trying hard enough. I had ruined her chances to win the first prize, an important step on her way to Yale, the Nobel Prize, and world domination."

Grandma snorted in her seat. "She was not as smart as you seem to think."

"She was not stupid, either. Let me finish, Grandma. You asked for this."

"Go ahead. This story goes on forever. I've created a monster."

"I was at the front door wishing my mother's station wagon would magically appear in our driveway. Raindrops fat as jellyfish crawled down the glass. I knew they were jellyfish because Sheila once told me how if they got in the house, like the Blob, they'd digest me into raspberry jam. Lightning flashed. Thunder drew closer. The big projector TV in the family room flickered, the screen imploded to a tiny white dot, and then went out completely. I was terrified, so I broke the rules."

"What rules?" Buckles asked.

"Sheila's rules. I went to her door and shouted, 'I'm Felix the Pussy!' Then I opened the door and saw Sheila upside down on her shag carpet as if peering at me through the top of her skull. Her legs were bent at the knees and her feet crossed at the ankles on her messy bed. Her pink Princess phone was tucked under her chin so her two hands were free to go wherever she needed her hands to be. Her unbuttoned blouse was yanked up. I saw her soft, pale belly and her nipples. She said, 'Hold on, Norman. I'll be right back,' then popped to her feet and said to me, 'Do you want to know what pussy is?' She unzipped her slacks fully before she stretched her white panties down with her thumb. 'That's pussy, you fucking idiot. Get out of my room before I tell Mom what a pervert you are.' I wondered how she'd lost her penis. What had she done wrong? If Grandpa could take my nose, maybe someone took her penis."

"Freud is an imbecile," Grandma said, suddenly fully awake. Had she been asleep at all? "I once asked Sigmund if he had ever suffered vagina-envy, and he became so terrified at the idea that he bit through his cigar."

"Sigmund? You knew Freud, too?"

"It was Vienna. The best people mingled." Grandma ignored Pussy's snickering.

Pussy said, "But that's the story of how I became 'Pussy.' I do like the name. I do. And I did love my sister. I truly did."

The Edsel crawled west through the quiet lawn-lined streets of Decatur, Indiana along Route 224. It was a town of vast open spaces, lush shade trees, and a cluster of no-nonsense two-story brick buildings in the shadow of a central clock tower.

Grandma said. "Welcome to downtown Decatur, located a convenient five hundred yards from out-of-town Decatur. There was a Howard Johnson's around here somewhere, but I do not see it. Jack and I bummed a meal there. There's always a ptomaine palace near a courthouse. Lawyers will eat offal. Try down there." She pointed to the deeper shade of what might be the center of town.

"Jack?" Pussy asked.

"Kerouac."

"I should have guessed," Pussy muttered. "He must have been one of those beatniks."

"In fact, he was. Buckles, lace that shirt collar. You do not have to choke, but you're showing just a tad too much tit."

Nothing escaped her. Nothing.

The burgers were thick, charred, ran with juice, and were topped with fat cuts of beefsteak tomato, a lettuce leaf, and soft squares of cheddar. The French fries had been cut from genuine potatoes that very morning; the diner specialized in homemade ketchup served in a brown ceramic pot with a long, slender spoon. Grandma held forth on how ketchup was America's sole contribution to international cuisine, a sauce through which sulfur dioxide was bubbled in order to kill taste buds. "It was invented to disguise rancid meat," she explained. Then she ordered a slice of Boston Cream Pie with three forks. She did not taste a morsel.

After three quick trips to the lavatories, Buckles offered to pay for her lunch, but Grandma slapped her wrist. "You've been adopted." No one was ready to climb back into the Edsel, so they explored beyond the town square of shade trees surrounding the Decatur bell tower. While Pussy waited on a bench outside a general store smelling strongly of dust and mothballs, Grandma and Buckles found a 3-pack of white Dickey T-shirts small enough to fit her.

"I like black," Buckles said.

"When you join a motorcycle gang, you can wear black. When you travel with me, white. Do you need bottoms?"

"I think so."

"Get the half-bikini things, then. They are not Granny-panties, but you are not getting anything skimpier on my dime, not while you are walking around in shorts cut two inches from your crotch. White, too. No red, no blue. Not even pink. Decent girls dress decently, and we are on the road and have to appear to be decent."

Back at the Edsel, when Pussy cracked open the passenger door, Grandma said, "Buckles should drive. I'm the back seat. Sweetboy rides shotgun."

"I don't have a driver's license."

The old woman sighed. "Did I ask you to drive the Indianapolis 500? You know how to operate a motor vehicle, don't you? Turn the key, put it in gear, step on the gas, steer. The pedal on the left makes it stop. Driving is not nuclear physics."

Buckles nodded. She'd never paid attention to the gauges and dials on her mother's car, but the rest seemed easy enough: start, pedals, steer, stop. Pussy helped her adjust the seat. When she did as Grandma said, the engine howled while they went nowhere.

"That doohickey has to point at the D," Pussy said and showed her how to put the car in gear.

"Well, at least you were not lying," Grandma said. "A woman has to know her own limitations, and only an idiot keeps them secret from her friends. Go slow on the turns until you can handle the car without tipping us into a ditch or running on a sidewalk, and learn to brake without slamming your nose into the dashboard." Grandma wearily climbed into the rear seat to lay with her face to the rear cushions, her bony hip to the sky, the same position in which Buckles had slept through the morning. "Sweetboy, make sure she does not kill a cow. Look for rooms tonight. I'll be kinked up from napping in the car and I already need a bath. Take some place off the main highways but clean. No hot-sheet operations. You know what to look for. Now hand me some of my medicine. One pill ought to do it."

They jerked to a start and jerked to a stop several times, but by the time the Edsel reached the western edge of Decatur, Buckles thought she was doing pretty good. Turning was tricky, though, so she kept their speed no faster than a brisk walk. She only scraped the curbstone three times, once knocking over a wire mesh trash can that bounced into the street, but after that they were out of town, the road was more or less straight as far as anyone could see, and driving became even easier.

Grandma's sleepy voice came from the backseat. "Don't get over-confident, kid."

As long as Buckles focused on controlling the car, she did not have a single mysterious dizzy spell.

Life was a marvel. She'd left home three days ago, and now here she was driving a convertible. She'd crossed Pennsylvania with a grave robber and a dog named Sandy, spent a night slapping and kicking at the hands and arms of the scariest man she hoped ever to meet, learned from Grandma she could bamboozle an Ohio state trooper and get away with it, her stomach was filled with sweet cherry Coke and a pretty good burger, a crazy old lady in powder blue pedal pushers and a half-buttoned yellow blouse was snoozing in the back seat of the biggest car ever made, a boy who needed a shave sat beside her in camouflage paratrooper pants with his left leg over the transmission hump and her bare right leg in case he needed to brake for her, the glove box was filled with loosely rolled joints and vials of blue and pink pills. Her pack of fresh white T-shirts and new panties lay in the back on the car floor beside her rainbow tote. She had made it to Indiana and a town that last week she could not have found on a map.

A tiny bit of her wanted to call her mother to brag.

They were doing more than 25, a sane speed since the speed limit was 50, and she understood *limit* to mean the upper extreme of how fast she should go.

"What happened to Sheila?" Buckles asked without taking her eyes from the road.

"You may as well finish, Sweetboy." Grandma's weary voice was slurred. "Organ grinders tell better stories to their monkeys, but you are in it now, so finish. Notice how we are way past the story of how you obtained your name. Stories lead to more stories, so just be done with it."

Grandma Dot's voice drifted off in the middle of sentences.

"Sheila's reputation preceded me in school. Teachers in September would ask, 'Are you Sheila Leitner's brother?' And by November they'd send notes home expressing disappointment at my failures. Her name was engraved on three silver cups and one plaque in a trophy case next to a half dozen collapsing footballs in the trophy case in our high school's lobby. Her senior year basketball team won its state division title, but her ticket to college was volleyball. She was captain of a squad that swept the state championship. She earned a full scholarship to Colby College.

"But none of that stopped boys I knew saying Sheila's greatest claim to fame was blowjob lips. My sense of family honor got the living crap beat out of me whenever I rose to her defense. It was stupid. Facts were facts. Shelia had navigated high school by giving head to the right boys at the right time. Sheila went down only on team captains or honor students, ideally boys who were both. I think there was a Trigonometry teacher in there, too. She was wildly popular."

Her eyes still closed, Grandma mumbled, "Don't judge. No risk of pregnancy and not too much discomfort. Good head ends with Kleenex, a sip of water, and Listerine."

"I think she just liked to hear boys moan," Pussy said.

Buckles focused on the road, grateful no one asked her opinion on the matter. Up until last night aboard *Donna May*, her experience had been limited to a single boy at Dobbs when a hand-job did not go far enough. Oral sex did not repel her; it drew her. It seemed disgusting, though, especially Big Bill's descriptions of just how he'd wanted that to proceed. Sex confused her.

"Sheila bragged to me about being a technical virgin until her sophomore year at college when a hockey wingman with a 3.8 GPA scored two goals. Hours later, despite taped ribs, he scored Sheila. She made it a hat trick."

"How could you know that?" Buckles asked.

"She told me, of course. We had no secrets. She could not wait to come home to tell me she finally lost it. I loved my big sister and she loved her baby brother."

Buckles had a boatload of awkward questions about sex. It was one of the reasons she'd wished for an older sibling, either a brother or sister. To have asked for details from a classmate at Dobbs was social suicide. Not that she could have asked, but her mother's experience was plainly limited. Buckles was not eager to hear what her Mom knew because that had to be about Daddy, and the whole idea of sharing what her mother and father did in their big bed was so icky Buckles just could not think on it. *The Village Voice* was clinical, but it at least had informed Buckles of enough for her to lord it over her mother. With a wife who was one step away from a nun, no wonder Daddy's eyes wandered. Perhaps she would someday ask Grandma Dot about whether she'd had an orgasm with her dipshit lacrosse forward, Spencer, but all she recalled was a pinch of pain and a few seconds of discomfort. He could not have been much of a lover, but Buckles had no basis of comparison. Maybe someday she would have the courage to ask Pussy.

"Colby is in Maine. There was a photo of her I wish I still had, snowflakes twinkle on her eyelashes and her in white fur earmuffs and a rabbit fur jacket. Then Grandpa Ambrose drowned. That was when Grandma and me became housemates. And that's about it until the end."

"That was before Johnny-boy had me sign the commitment papers to Arborside," Grandma said bitterly. "It was the only way he could get his mitts on his wife's family's money. I agreed to pretend I was old and feeble and they had to lie about my age to get me in. Johnny assured me Arborside was a great deal for me, and he said I could take it back anytime I wished. He forgot to mention the part about having me declared *non compos mentis* at a hearing I did not attend, the son-of-a-bitch."

"What's Arborside?" Buckles twisted in her seat to look at Grandma. The car would have swerved into a tree if Pussy had not grabbed at the wheel. The Edsel was venturing as high as 35 now and had, with Pussy's assistance, steered around a tractor pulling an empty rick. Big Bill had pushed *Donna May* to triple digits. He must have been crazy in more ways than one.

"Arborside is a home for elderly people," Pussy said.

"That's like saying Joliet is a rest stop for murderers on their way to Hell." Grandma struggled to sit up. "But it is on me. I signed. The next thing I know, I am begging for extra toilet paper, eating lime Jell-O, and playing Parcheesi with old ladies who think the back of the checkerboard is a pretty design. It's backgammon. It's not a design. It's goddam backgammon, the game of kings and queens."

Buckles could not bring herself to ask what Parcheesi was or what that had to do with the other side of a checkerboard. It occurred to her that this moment was the moment when her education, her real education, began.

"But I outfoxed them."

"Do you want to tell us that story now?" Pussy asked. "Your car, your rules, right?"

"No. No. I hate when you are right. Maybe tomorrow I'll have the energy. Finish up, Sweetboy."

Buckles discovered the Edsel's directional signals, blinking left, then right, then left. They were fun, and proved useful when a flatbed of manure slowed to make a left turn in front of her. Instead of stomping down the Edsel's brakes so hard that Grandma rolled off her rear seat, Buckles could flash a signal and simply go around on the right. Buckles also noticed that if she flashed her headlights, something she'd seen Big Bill do, sometimes an oncoming car would flash back. Moving cars talked to each other. She blinked her lights at every oncoming car as the Edsel progressed at a steady speed on a very straight two-lane blacktop. They were passed by crazy drivers who roared across the double yellow line on her left, rolled down a window and yelled curses at her. Grandma hardly looked as she raised her skinny arm and her middle finger to each of them.

"Sheila matured into a big-boned Nazi fantasy of a Hitler Youth poster, a woman whose pelvis could carry the next generation of the Aryan master race. She looked like the St. Pauli Girl, the one with the pigtails on the beer. Sheila had muscles from pulling third oar of an eight-woman crew. They rowed on the Kennebec. She was a dirtier blonde than you, though," he said to Buckles, "but I never grew taller than five-six, three inches shorter than Sheila the Aryan Wet Dream."

Grandma snorted disdain. "For God's sake, we need to stop soon. I never heard anyone drag out a story so badly, and I lived at Arborside among the walking dead in flannel nighties and baby-blue plushies. My bones ache as bad as my ears ache, listening to you."

A paper roadmap in Pussy's hands crackled in the wind. "I know you think that going from Decatur, Indiana to Decatur, Illinois might be fun, but we took our time with lunch and Buckles drives a little slow. We're south of Champaign. Do you want to zig-zag again? I don't think we are being followed, but who knows?"

"Champagne in Champaign," Grandma Dot said. "The idea has a certain appeal."

They came to a motor court, The Tuscola Arms. The driveway proved much too narrow for Buckles even at 5 mph. She flattened a terracotta flower pot. Backing out, her first try at reverse, she overcompensated her steering and shattered a second pot.

"I don't know how to go backwards," she said.

Pussy started to explain, but Grandma told him to shut up. "If Buckles is as smart as I think she is, she will never need to go backwards." Her bony hand grasped a front seat and she pulled herself up. "Welcome to Tuscola," Grandma said. "Aren't you going to tell Buckles the finish?"

"There is no 'finish.' Dad blew the family up. It was an accident."

"Oh you tell a hell of a tale, you do. Every story could end like that. 'Then they died.'" Grandma began to hobble into the motel office, but paused long enough to retrieve a vial of pills from the glove compartment.

"Is she all right?"

"I told you. Bad days and good days. Today, not so good. She smokes a lot of grass and tries to stay off the pain killers. I think her hips are arthritic. Wherever we stay, Grandma always goes in first to be sure my photo is not posted on a wall." Pussy went behind the car and opened the trunk to ready their luggage while Grandma emerged with two keys for adjacent rooms.

She bent beside Pussy to fiddle around in the Edsel's trunk until she emerged with a tire iron in her fist raised over her head. Buckles thought for a second she was going to be murdered, but Dot smashed the Edsel's rearview mirror, then hit it twice more until what was left of it fell to the car's carpeting. "A woman makes better time if she never looks back. That's as much a driving fact as it is a philosophy. No charge, Buckles. Thank me when you are old. Keep your eyes on whatever is in front. Looking backward can become a bad habit."

Grandma walked awkward and stiff to the rear of the Tuscola Arms. The Edsel followed her, creeping slower than the old lady. The car would be invisible from the road. Buckles cut the engine; they pulled up the Edsel's top.

It was late afternoon. They were as yet the only guests at the Tuscola Arms. The two rooms faced a small swimming pool surrounded by a cyclone fence. Inside the fence, woven vinyl lounge chairs in yellow and green were scattered on the pool's cement deck.

The water's glassy surface reflected the sky's mounting clouds and the perfect blue beyond them.

Dot advised them to eat, though she herself was not hungry as they'd lunched only a few hours earlier. Pussy placed Grandma's small suitcase from the car trunk into her room, came out and shut her door behind him. Pussy hauled his duffel bag, Grandma's purchased addition for his disguise as a serviceman soon to depart for Vietnam, into the other room. Buckles stood with her rainbow tote at the door behind him.

"There's only one bed," Buckles said.

"Looks large enough."

"That's not what I meant."

"I know what you meant. Trust me, you have nothing to worry about."

"I can sleep in the car. Or at the pool on a lounge."

"The mosquitoes will eat you alive. You'll have dengue fever by morning. If I leave you in the car, Grandma will have my head on a pike. Look, Buckles, what we can do is cross the parking lot to that diner." He pointed across the road. "I am thinking an open-face hot turkey sandwich. Maybe stuffing and cranberry sauce if they have it. I could use a walk, too. We'll talk bed rules. If you still are still worried after that, I'll sleep in the tub. Or you can take the tub and lock the bathroom door, if that suits you." He smiled.

She did not feel reassured.

Though the diner was part of the motel complex, for some reason it seemed far, far away. Her strange dizziness returned. Too much sun? Beyond the pool's cyclone fence, restless weeds taller than she rustled. Anything could hide in there, even Big Bill and his truck.

The blast of cold air through the diner's open door was sharp. She should have pulled on one of the new T-shirts or risked being in their room alone with Pussy while she pulled on her jeans jacket. Pussy seemed nothing like Big Bill, but how could she really, really know? Her father, her lacrosse player, Big Bill—men were never what they seemed. She would lock the bathroom door if she bathed and maybe when she slept in there, too. Bathrooms always had locks. She needed to bathe. The idea of being behind a thin wooden door and naked made her shake.

Buckles slid into her side of a booth as she swept back her hair which fell loose again over her eyes and shoulders. She was glad to be rid of her American flag kerchief, but she really did need a John Deere cap, or at least a scrunchy. Her fingertips massaged her scalp. Her hair had not felt this grungy since the weekend her Girl Scout troop slept in the woods to eat a thousand 'smores and cultivate pimples.

"You're a real pretty girl," Pussy said as if he'd just discovered something nobody knew and thought Buckles would be pleased to hear it.

But she wasn't. *You're pretty* only meant *I imagine a dozen ways to put my penis inside you.* They had spent a day in the sun in an open car with an old lady, but most of the time Pussy had talked and talked and talked about why he was called Pussy. Could Grandma have brought her along so her grandson could have sex? Buckles had learned to drive with Pussy's leg draped over hers so he could press the brakes if she screwed up; they'd smoked more and better dope than she had ever had before, but none of that gave him the right to tell her she was pretty. Being with Pussy was better than being with pathetic James trying to get her to jerk him off while he squeezed her chest like twin loaves of bread dough, but what could Pussy want? Why had he said she was pretty?

Despite the diner's air conditioning, she perspired. Her tongue ran over her upper lip and came away salty. She planned the route she would run from the diner and Pussy and Grandma into those tall weeds on the pool's far side. She could hide there. She'd steal a steak knife so she could pop out of the weeds to kill anyone who came after her. Anyone. What if Big Bill showed up? He could have followed her, right? What if he was waiting for her in the weeds?

She tried to clear her head. This wasn't her. She *liked* Pussy. Why was she planning to cut his throat?

For several seconds, she allowed her largest problem in all the world to be the choice between a grilled cheese sandwich with or without tomato. She sipped more ice water, but her mouth was all flannel again. She could not swallow.

Pussy was prattling on. She must have missed something while she had concentrated on quelling the panic that rose in her like an unrestrainable water spout.

"I don't think Grandma will mind if I tell you the rest without her hearing it," Pussy said. Her elevated heartbeat was slowed by Pussy's voice. "She already knows it." Buckles forced herself to listen.

"I'd have quit college but if I did I'd be humping an M-15 through the jungle and burning leeches off my balls with cigarettes. Mom said to Dad, 'Pussy will find himself,' but Dad doubted it. I commuted to school and lived on a legless couch in Mom and Dad's basement. I brought people down there when I could find someone."

"Girls," Buckles said.

"Girls once or twice, but mostly boys. That's the part of 'the rest' Grandma knows and wants me to tell you. She doesn't miss much. She found my muscle magazines, right? The old lady is a lot of things, but none of them is stupid. Crazy, for sure, but crazy is not stupid."

"Oh my God. You're a homo?" Buckles' blue eyes went wide.

"Not the word I'd choose, but yeah, I am. Homo. Queer. Fag. Take your pick." Pussy sucked a chocolate malt up through a straw. "That's why you are perfectly safe sharing a bed with me. It is also why Grandma was desperate to get me out of the Army. So now you know my big secret."

"But you don't, you know, swish. You don't lisp. You don't wear girls' clothes."

"Those are stupid clichés, Buckles. The point is that I get excited by men. Only men. The right men. Boys hide *Playboy* under their beds; I hide muscle magazines. Sheila knew that, too. Like I said, we were close. At about the time Mom accepted the presidency of the New England chapter of an organization devoted to liberating child sex slaves from Guatemala and Cambodia, she and Dad were thinking of adopting another kid. They had the wherewithal, Dad thought I was a washout and liked the idea of a third chance, and Mom was hot to rescue some kid from a banana republic or an opium den. I'd have a brother, Sun-Yat Leitner or Esperanza de Jesus Leitner. But none of that happened because the house exploded."

"What?"

"The house exploded."

"How?"

"No one could tell my father anything. He skipped the part about getting a construction permit for the pool he was putting in, hired a few non-Union laborers, and the backhoe he was driving crushed an underground gas valve. Gas flowed for a day into the basement. I was trolling for men in Boston when Sheila came home as a surprise. The best the Fire Marshall could make of it, Mom and Dad were upstairs when Sheila opened the front door and hit a light switch that set off a spark. She was caught in the blast. Mom and Dad might have been suffocated before the fire so probably never felt a thing, but Sheila blew fifty feet across the front lawn before she burned to death."

Pussy ordered bread pudding.

"Puss, I am so sorry."

He shrugged. "Sheila used to call me 'Puss.' I liked it. You can call me that. I'd like that fine." He picked raisins from his bread pudding and segregated them on his plate. "Then I found out I was inheriting nothing because Dad was in hock to his eyeballs, so I decided to outfox the Army and join up before being drafted. Supposedly, if you volunteer, you get more options. Ha. Dad's voice was in my head telling me, 'Be a man.' Dad never knew for sure that I was queer, but he suspected. That's why he was eager to adopt a boy. Maybe he was right about the Army. I was trying to please him after he was dead."

"What happened?"

"Nothing changes. Anyone who tells you being queer is a choice or a disease is an asshole. I realized that if I bumped into a guy in the shower, even by accident, I'd get stomped to death. Then Grandma showed up at Fort Dix driving that ginormous car." He ate all the raisins he'd separated at the side of his plate and stared off into the distance over her shoulder. "Buckles, life turns on a dime." He focused his eyes again on her and snapped his fingers. "Boom! Just like that, you are alone in the world. My family was gone."

Recrossing the parking lot in the mounting heat and humidity, Buckles believed she'd been poisoned at the diner. Blood pooled in her feet. Her legs weighed a ton each, and while she wanted to go one way, her legs wanted to go another. She grasped Pussy's elbow, and fell into him. The sun was two hand's width over the horizon, but the world went dark.

"What if he comes back?" she asked.

"Who? What if who comes back?"

"Big Bill."

"Is he the man who raped you?"

"I wasn't raped."

"Grandma said you'd deny it. It's okay. Well, it's not okay that you were raped, but you are safe now."

"I wasn't raped. Don't think that."

"When you slept in the car, your blouse rode up. There are purple bruises on your chest and arms. Grandma guessed it was rape or at least a beating. You're okay now, Buckles. He can't get you."

She denied it a third time. "I was not raped."

"Then you must have put up a hell of a fight."

"He robbed me."

"It's only money."

"But what if he comes back?"

In their room, the fan on the faulty air conditioner squealed a regular rhythm.

"He can't know where you are."

"He might have followed me."

"He drove a big truck, right?"

"Yes, *Donna May*. *Donna May* is the name of his truck. It is white and has red flames painted on the engine. You can hear the horn for miles."

"It would be hard to sneak around in a big truck, right?"

That made sense, but it did not matter. "But Big Bill might still come back. He might. What if he comes back?"

They stood in half-light because Buckles would not let Pussy completely shut the door, but then he scooped her up in his arms as if they were honeymooners, kicked the door closed, and took two broad steps to the bed where he dropped her. He sat close to her, hip to hip.

But dropping Buckles onto a bed and sitting close were the wrong things to do. She twisted and struggled, punching his arms and face rolling from him. "Let me go! Let me go!" He tried to still her by embracing her, another wrong thing to do. Her teeth broke the skin on the back of his hand. He pressed the edge of a pillow-case to the oozing blood, then removed her rubber sandals from her churning feet. He was able to trap her beneath the blanket and the crisp top sheet, pulling them to her chin. Restraining her was another mistake, but there was nothing better. Teeth clenched, eyes wild, her head twisted from side to side, *no, no, no, no, no, no.*

How could she have been so stupid? Last night was not done with her. It might never be done with her. None of the night was clear in her mind, though the details swam up from nowhere, a sound, a smell, an image, hot bubbles of relentless terror boiling through her fear. Big Bill might have taken her any way of the ways he'd detailed to her, invaded and broken her, then thrown her away onto the highway.

She struggled under the motel's bedding. She needed to run. She needed to run right now. She was wild to run, but Pussy pressed the blanket tight under her chin. She twisted, unable to free herself. Run. Big Bill had described exactly what he would do to her cunt, her ass, and her mouth, but now she needed to run from Pussy because Pussy did not understand that nothing could stop Big Bill. Big

Bill was lurking outside their motel door. Eyes red and wild, he'd be on the other side of every door she would open. He would kill Pussy first, and then bend and break Buckles. She needed to run. Big Bill's bicep had been thicker than her waist and he'd made her squeeze his arm where a naked lady rode a red snake. His hand pressed at her neck when he pushed her head into his lap. He licked her face; his breath was foul; his T-shirt stank of sweat. Her jaw had locked so tight the muscles of her chin still ached. Her neck went stiff. She thrashed and kicked at the motel sheet. Why didn't Pussy understand that Big Bill waited behind the door? He would tie her in the dark back of his truck, lock the door, and come back to her whenever he wanted more. When he was done, he would sell her. That was why he waited on the other side of the motel door, to claim what he owned. He had handcuffs and ropes and would sell her after he did all he wanted. Big Bill owed money to men in Kansas and would pay them with Buckles. Big Bill's teeth crackled on white pills. It sounded like he chewed ice. What if Pussy was holding her down while he waited for Big Bill? Men laughed about all the ways they could use a girl, taking turns or all at once, twisting and bending her this way and that. When they were done, the girl was broken.

The stupidest girl in Westchester, Abigail Buckles Sinclair, all her life safe behind a wall of well-tended green hedges ran from safety. Now she was trapped under a motel sheet that smelled of bleach, the prisoner of a crazy faggot Army deserter named Pussy. The biggest lie of all was safety. There was no safety.

She heard herself say, "What if Big Bill comes here?"

"He can't."

"You don't know that. Stop saying that. You can't know that." She kicked at Pussy again, but her leg was bent funny and could not move freely beneath the tight blanket. When had Pussy stolen her sandals? How could she hope to run as far as the weeds without shoes? Her face was wet with what might have been blood but tasted like tears.

Pussy restrained her until she was exhausted. "Do you want to shower?" he asked her. "A shower might calm you. A hot shower."

To do that she would have to take off her clothes. Her voice rasped, "Did you lock the front door?"

"Yes, I locked the front door."

"Check. Check now. Check."

Her wide eyes peered at him over the blanket's edge. Pussy made a show of attaching the chain lock.

"Look outside for *Donna May*. Look through the window. Don't open the door. The truck has eighteen wheels, I think. Big Bill has a radio and can talk to everyone in the world. He said I was his Little Cherry Lollipop." Pussy looked through the slats of their window blinds. They smelled of dust.

Buckles curled on her hip. Her knees drew to her chin.

Pussy sat on the soft bed's edge. He recalled his sister Sheila first learning to read. He could not have been older than three. She would practice when they were alone, her warm voice wrapping around him, his head on her thigh. He'd sink into sleep smooth as warm milk.

When his hand went to Buckles' shoulder, she did not shrink from his touch. They explained to him that the fire had burned his parents and Sheila *beyond recognition*. His family was sealed in three caskets that lay on parallel gurneys beneath three white pall cloths. Good people waited to stand close to him, people largely unknown to him, people whose gentle hands made small circles on his shoulder or his back. He imagined what his family looked like in their caskets. It was impossible not to imagine them burned black and bald and their ears and noses burned away. He did not tell Buckles how alone he'd felt when he was in the empty stretch limo that trailed three flower-laden slow-moving hearses. On a morning exploding golden light, he'd dropped lilies onto three polished walnut coffins laid in crumbling brown earth.

Buckles, too, was alone.

She slowly quieted, her legs twitching like a dreaming dog chasing dream-rabbits. Stripes of day filtered through the Venetian blinds, igniting dust motes that sparkled like Buckles' hair, striping the floor with bars of sunlight that climbed the far wall as the sun sank closer to the earth.

Pussy's hand passed before her face. Her breath warmed his palm, but she did not stir. Her china blue eyes remained opaque, wall-eyed.

His new sister slept with her eyes open.

November 1967—April 1968

I F BUCKLES WERE DEAD, KJ would know it. Never mind how, she would. Daughters vanished, scattering like dandelion puffs on summer wind. That was true. Every silly, frightened, and deranged woman claimed a mysterious connection between themselves and their vanished daughters, but in KJ's case none of that applied. KJ *knew* Buckles lived, as unequivocal as the day the kid kicked at her from inside KJ's womb.

She stenciled personal rules onto plain typewriter paper and taped the paper flat at four corners to her white refrigerator. Martin Luther nailed his theses to a church door in Wittenberg with less determination.

> *No alcohol alone.*
> *Make the bed every morning.*
> *Wash your face.*
> *Eat.*
> *Bathe.*
> *Never-ever lose faith.*

At first the rules were difficult, but gradually they became routines. If she could not follow her own rules, how could she expect Buckles to respect her? Routines were easy; rules were hard.

She was happiest on the long nights she sank into magical thinking, awake, flat on her back on the gray wall-to-wall carpeting, her arms and legs spread-eagled, a mother crucified by the Summer of Love. She spoke to Buckles, certain her daughter instantly received her thoughts at any distance, equally certain the voice echoing in her head was Buckles' immediate response. In this way, they talked. A day would come when she would say to Buckles, *Remember how we spoke?* And Buckles would say, *I knew that was you.* KJ offered wisdom about boyfriends and how easy it was to be confused by the difference between being wanted and wanting; they talked about politics and how men in charge screwed up everything because testosterone deranged the mind, a nasty trick of evolution that was long past time to correct, but would never happen while men controlled so much; they talked about simple jobs and how important it was to have a job because a woman without a job would come to believe she needed a man to take care of her, and how that never lasted because what men did was leave.

KJs clothing grew too roomy. She found a car service willing to take her to Scarsdale and wait while she balled what she wanted into a few cardboard boxes and hijacked three pairs of sensible shoes. Everything she wanted from her former life fit in the back seat of a taxi. Jack never saw her coming or going.

One late afternoon she lay on the floor in the apartment's non-light and yielded to anger and a wave of sadness that came from nowhere but rose to overwhelm her. She'd been too civilized. Rage should have left her howling. Had Buckles been with her, she'd have slapped the kid silly. *You stupid stupid stupid girl.* She sat up to discover she shouted alone at no one in darkness.

Near midnight she wandered until she found a pizza joint near her. This was the entire point of New York City, it never closed. Nothing ever tasted so good. She sat on a stool at a counter and ate two hot slices with her fingers off a paper plate, her palate blistering. She was anonymous and accountable to no one. As a student, she'd signed in or out of a Wellesley residence hall; as a wife and mother she was responsible to Jack and to Buckles. The moment Buckles had vanished, KJ had been bringing the kid her food, leaving notes about where she could be found, when she'd be back, and how to find her in an emergency. Being given over to others, KJ's life was utterly stupid. Buckles might know a lot about her mother as a mother, but nothing about her as a woman. She sent Buckles a telepathic note of apology, acknowledging the kid had been right all along, promising when they met again, things would be different.

Ma Bell connected her kitchen wall phone. The 212 area code made her a full-fledged New Yorker. She dialed her own number just to hear the busy signal.

Furniture from Bloomingdale's came helter-skelter into her apartment. The bills went to Jack. Sweating delivery men waited for instructions, but when none came placed her new furniture where they stood. The apartment took on the ambience of a doctor's waiting room, a coffee table here, a lamp there, a flowered sofa that faced a wall from a distance of four feet. Her taste was hideous, impaired by what she discovered was a rattan fetish. Four pillows and a queen-size bed with its mattress wrapped in heavy plastic found their way to the bedroom. *Her* bedroom, she corrected. She needed to revise how she thought about her space. *Her* bedroom lacked linens. Lying nude on the heavy plastic wrapper felt like a kinky fetish.

She too easily neglected her own rules, discovering she needed to bathe when she became convinced a dead ferret was decaying in the walls and then tracking down the aroma to herself. She might have showered more, but believed that walking jaybird naked through her place was an important break with her past, a declaration of freedom. People should be nude as often as possible. Arms out, she spun from one room to the next. She enjoyed dizziness. It would not have surprised her if she peed in every corner. It was evening, her lights were glaring bright, and she had not yet considered window treatments. Anyone across the alley could watch the naked blonde doing pirouettes. Uncaring, she gave the place two more twirls, then inspected herself in the full-length mirror bolted to the bathroom's door.

The Grief Diet was carving her down to the bones. When had she developed cheekbones?

Breakfasts could especially cast her into a funk, a possibility that could spoil a day before it started. She drank vile instant decaf and stared into a translucent Corning Ware bowl white as disease where Cheerios floated in a puddle of watery skim milk. Instant decaf? Why was she drinking brown hot water? She dumped breakfast and the coffee down the drain, then threw the Cheerios box into her trash. She sat at the table a time, her knee bouncing until she yielded to dialing Charlotte.

"Come and see the new place," she said.

She had not told Charlotte she was leaving Jack, fearing Charlotte might talk her out of it. Charlotte endured an adulterous husband for the sake of her two sons and her club memberships, so surely would want KJ's life to validate her own. She lived for alcohol-soaked flings with young men, a choice that always appeared thrilling until KJ sobered up to look hard at it. Still, she was lonely.

Flurries were predicted, but it was not bad for a lunch in early December. Charlotte would take a commuter train.

KJ set sheets and bath towels over her windows with masking tape, then tore open a half-dozen brown boxes in search of a decent outfit, decided she had no such thing, and so pulled on old slacks that gapped at her waist and sagged in the seat. She found the discolored ivory sweater with a cowl collar from a consignment shop she'd never worn, but kept. With the sleeves pushed to her elbows, it fit like a flour sack.

Charlotte arrived with a bottle of dark vermouth, a pint of cheap rye, and a jar of Maraschino cherries. "My traditional house-warming gifts," she said. Her smart leather jacket slipped from her shoulders to the floor as she swept past KJ. She smacked her lips in the air in the vicinity of KJ's ear.

"Your cupboards are bare, Mother Hubbard," she said, opening and slamming shut each of them. She then dumped a full jar of apple sauce from KJ's refrigerator into the small galley kitchen sink, rinsed the jar clean, and used it to mix Manhattans.

"Desperate times, desperate measures." she said. "Do you think Mr. Mott knows his jars are perfect cocktail shakers?" She stirred with a butter knife, dropped four cherries into the jar, thought for a heartbeat, then added two more.

"It's early," KJ said.

"It's cocktail hour in Paris, darling," Charlotte said. She drank directly from the jar and then passed the jar to KJ while she did that thing she did with cherry stems, knotting the stem with her tongue. She sorrowfully shook her head. "Your refrigerator is empty. Eggs, bread, and milk. If there is an atomic war, you can trade French Toast for steak." She looked at KJ critically. "Where did you donate your ass? Will they take mine?"

KJ sipped the very good Manhattan. "Crying and throwing up work better than two weeks at a spa."

Charlotte draped herself the length the couch that faced a blank wall, lifted her feet from the floor, and balanced the unsteady apple sauce jar on her stomach. "God, I love this place." Her finger-tips stroked the upholstery and she sighed. "Only grown-ups can live with white. And your bare bed looks positively ferocious. Never put a pillow on it. Before you throw away the plastic cover, have some kinky fun. Baby oil. Lots and lots of baby oil. Get laid, Kelly Jo Sinclair. It's good for you. This is the 60s. Simple, anonymous, casual sex is all the rage. I read that in *Time*, so it must be true." She threw back the rest of her drink with a single swallow and immediately popped to her feet to begin a fresh batch, four parts rye to one part sweet vermouth.

Charlotte's chatter could be wearing. At least Charlotte did not ask for word of Buckles; there was nothing amusing or clever to say about Buckles' disappearance. Charlotte's chatter danced a deliberate circle around the edges of KJ's despair.

"Never divorce a lawyer," KJ said. "Jack is bleeding me white because legal delays are in his favor but time costs him nothing. He says one thing on Monday, then by Friday says something else. Meanwhile, my lawyer's bills run sky high. Jack has a lawyer, too, but Jack's lawyer is charging him next to nothing. Professional courtesy."

"Don't you know about the sharks that did not eat the drowning lawyer?"

"God, who doesn't?"

"Stick with dentists. Laughing gas puts life into perspective."

"Blatt, my lawyer, charges in six minute increments. If I call him and ask how the weather is, it costs me seventeen dollars and fifty cents to find out the sun is shining."

"Where did you find this shyster?"

"The Yellow Pages."

"Oh, well, how can you go wrong with that?"

"Blatt said moving out could be construed as my abandoning Jack. That makes it easy for him to claim the house."

"You walked away from the house?"

"I'd have to give a crap to stay. I don't."

"See? That's why you'll go back to Scarsdale, sooner or later. Men have all the cards." Charlotte was still slugging Manhattans from an apple sauce jar. She bent once more to peer again into the refrigerator. "Wine? My god, we have no wine. You'll need a case of reds and a case of whites. Everybody gets back together. Girls like us have too much to lose. You will. Besides, what can you do? You can't type, you have no experience, and that means you have to be a sales girl. But no sales girl can make the rent on this place. You'll need to go home, so you may as well have a good time while you are free, out and about." She opened a cupboard. "Have you heard about food? They sell it in stores. Bread, cheese, chocolate? I can't get over how much weight you've lost. You look as though you've been vacationing in Andersonville."

"Nothing to it. Turn your life to crap and pounds will melt away."

They stood side by side, pelvic bones flush against the lip of the kitchen pass-through to what might someday be a dining area if anyone made tables that small. In New York City, single women, if they ate at all, ate standing over a sink, went out, or called for delivery to eat whatever was delivered over the sink.

"We need to fatten you up. But maybe a little exercise first."

KJ was unable to guess what Charlotte had in mind. "I hate when it gets dark early. At least the snow in the city lets you believe we are in a movie."

Coat collars high, footprints in the snow trailing them, they hiked south on Fifth Avenue, Store windows dressed for the holiday blinked stars, animated nutcrackers, waving Santas, tinsel, and flying reindeer. At Rockefeller Center, the Christmas tree and its twinkling lights soared above the statue of reclining Prometheus overlooking the skating rink.

"Exercise."

"I've never been on skates," KJ said.

"How can you have never been on ice skates?"

"The Mississippi River in N'awlins doesn't freeze over. At Wellesley I was an in-door kind of girl."

"Were you, now?"

"I was studying."

Charlotte sighed. "I thought all blondes were given ice skates at birth, like Sonja Henie. Color in their cheeks, gliding and all. Do you want to do something else?" Charlotte gazed longingly at the ice.

"I'll watch. It's all right. It's good to be out."

Charlotte rented skates, installed KJ at a table where she ordered cocoa, and tiptoed onto the ice after saying to KJ: "You work on reviving that southern drawl; it's sexy. And for God's sake, buy a better pushup bra. You look like you are twelve and that makes me look fifty. We can't go anywhere for drinks if men think I am your mother." She soared away in a graceful glide, a leg raised in perfect horizontal alignment behind her. Snowflakes sparkled on shoulders and hats, glistening as they melted. To KJ's amazement, Charlotte did a little something with her feet and began to skate backwards. Who looked twelve now?

KJ's cold hands circled a steaming mug of cocoa. Charlotte would inevitably land them in a dark bar, and that led KJ to recall how alcohol, close on misfortune, had destroyed her mother. Every daughter scorns her mother until she reaches an age where they can forgive them. Would Buckles ever grant forgiveness?

Skaters came from her left, passed, and left to her right, endlessly, a spinning parade of the untroubled. Charlotte, for all her expertise, managed a collision with a young man in a tweed suit and a wool tie. He could not have been thirty. Handsome in an elegant way, his jaw and forehead belonged in profile on currency. He had a red beard and a long woolen scarf. Too young and too rich, he was perfect for Charlotte. They collapsed in a heap; Charlotte girlishly laughed, the young man laughed, and when they tried to stand they slipped and fell again, Charlotte on the ice beneath him.

She skated to the rail and said, breathless: "I caught you one. He's German, but speaks almost perfect English. He returns to Berlin in three days. Ask him to teach you to skate."

"I couldn't."

Charlotte shrugged. "Well, I am not throwing this one back."

"Don't screw him on the ice."

"What a marvelous idea," Charlotte said. Cold had colored Charlotte's cheeks holiday red. "Are you sure? He's got more going on than Atlas back there."

KJ laughed. "Atlas is out front, That's Prometheus. He was a titan."

"Smarty pants. He doesn't look all that titanic to me. The banker has a tight tush, too."

"And how do you know all that?"

"I fell on him."

"You fell on him twice. You groped him?"

Charlotte had a half smile on her face as she pushed off to re-join the circling skaters.

At that exact moment, in a terribly ruthless flash, KJ grasped that she would have to break it off with Charlotte. She would only undermine KJ's determination to forge a life of her own and start again.

KJ took a long swallow of her cooling cocoa, the tiny marsh-mallows sliding sweetly over her tongue. If they did not have lunch soon, Charlotte would miss her train. She waved to her friend. She would miss her. Behind and over her, Prometheus passed the torch of knowledge to humankind.

Days of pizza and spaghetti and mindless celebrity magazines ran together. KJ took stock of herself in the mirror on the back of a bedroom closet door. Self-deception was impossible. The skin at her throat was firm. Her Mommy-pouch had vanished. Her belly was taut; her waist had narrowed; her hips still flared; her breasts were less than perky, but they were nothing a forty-year-old woman needed to be ashamed of. KJ was not young, but she far from old.

One fashion for youth was to show a lot of skin and wear clothing that clung to a woman's body; the other was to be shapeless and braless under baggy clothes. She could do shapeless. She stepped into her underwear. Unless someone drew close enough to see the faint crow's feet at the corners of her eyes, KJ could become anyone she chose to be.

She withdrew a scissor from her bureau, hesitated only once, and then her hair fell about her feet like skeins of golden yarn.

Naturally, she botched it. She looked like a blonde orphan from Dog Patch.

In the morning, KJ made her appointment for a full day at Elizabeth Arden. KJ insisted the appointment was an emergency; she had to come in that very same day. They acquiesced, but required an enormous premium on an already obscene charge. She offered up Jack's office address; Mr. Sinclair would pay for the pedicure, manicure, and the heated stones the length of her spine during the full body massage. She passed on the mud bath in favor of a cucumber facial.

She spent most of that day listening to herself breathe and thinking of absolutely nothing while various strangers worked their hands and fingers with exact precision over her scalp, neck, body and feet. A Monsieur Henri shaped and feathered her botched hair. He did not understand a word of her New Orleans French, but spoke fractured phrases as if he dropped out of language class in a Newark high school; he was nevertheless a genius with scissors, a comb, and a dryer. They verified that the staggering bill would be accepted by Jack's firm before they allowed her to sign it. She added a hundred dollar tip and two hundred dollars' worth of skin creams, powders, paints, and brushes she knew she'd never use, and exited the red door at Elizabeth Arden with a pixie cut and a delicate green frosting. For the pleasure of feeling eyes on her and to feel her power as a woman, this last time she'd ever appear in public dressed like a woman of position and power, she sat on a stool at Hurley's, the bar at the base of Radio City. She sipped cranberry juice and vodka, wondering how many people wondered whether she was a celebrity down from the NBC studios. She pretended she had a spot with Carson on *The Tonight Show*. She'd joke with Johnny about stupid men and runaway daughters. Three soft-spoken men each in white-on-white dress shirts, cufflinks, and well-tailored Hong Kong suits offered to buy the pixie blonde drinks, but KJ smiled, uninterested. She invented a serviceable lie about a German banker she was schedule to meet, a story planted in her mind by Charlotte and her ice-skater, and left Hurley's fully aware they'd surmise she was an expensive call girl. Sex. The vodka burned through her.

Two days later, what was left of her emerald highlights and hair color Jack called "impudent Chardonnay" yielded to Miss Clairol. Monsieur would have wept. The slender green-eyed brownette who peered at her from her bathroom mirror sucked on her lips to flush them red, then rolled all the cosmetics she'd bought into three ruined towels. The entire mess found its way into a trashcan. She purchased an inexpensive ratty gray knit hat. Pulling it over her ears it felt like the cloche she'd worn as a teenager.

She'd liked herself back then.

A few days after New Year's 1968, on a cloudless afternoon beneath an ice blue sky, KJ walked downtown, her chin drawn back and firmly tucked into a black woolen muffler under her peacoat. Walking endlessly through Manhattan had become a habit. Her coat collar was high. Each time she rounded a corner, her eyes teared in the sudden blast of a clawing wind. Her nose ran. Late January could burn away every thought and all her grief.

She stepped into The Grand Bookstore on lower 4th Avenue to escape the cold—and into the friendly familiar musty aroma of books. If books had been Catholic martyrs, the Grand's basement and sub-basements would have been catacombs, a dark labyrinth without rhyme or any reason. She spent an hour in dim light on a park bench they'd set in an aisle near stack of books on the occult, a topic that held no interest. As she was about to step back into winter, on impulse, she asked the cashier at the door, a kid not much older than Buckles, if they were hiring. The girl hardly lifted her eyes from the volume of Walt Whitman.

"The pay sucks," she said. "Don't I know you from my poetry class?"

"I don't think so."

The cashier looked dubious. "But I know you from campus, right? You go to NYU."

KJ smiled and took the application on a clipboard and a pencil. She was not about to deny being an undergraduate. The application was a five-page literary quiz. "You have to do it here," the kid said. "And you have to do it now."

The Grand called two days later. "Did you really attend Wellesley?" an excited effeminate male voice asked her. "You did not miss a single question. You must be the last person to ever hear of Lady Ottoline Morrel. No one gets that question right. And you're forty! All we ever see are snotty kids who think they invented reefer and sex. You simply have to come in for an interview. Have to."

She met Nat, the manager, in his tiny basement office. The walls were smoked glass from the waist up, protected by Roman shades that unrolled from the ceiling. Nat could have been anywhere from twenty to fifty. He had a nervous habit of raking his dark hair off his forehead with his left hand before it immediately fell back over his eyes. He detected the residue of her New Orleans drawl and, as if revealing a secret, whispered that he himself was from the South, Texas specifically, now forsaken among damned Yankees, though had he stayed in Lubbock, if he had not hanged himself he would have been lynched by of a band of high school football players or drunken oil riggers. Like everyone in New York, he'd done one thing while planning success at another; unlike most, he'd succeeded. "I'm a dancer," he said, though these days, he was giving his knees a rest, which was why he managed a used bookstore. "It gets me out of the house. I danced in revivals of *Music Man* and *Mame*. They seemed to close before they opened. We died in Hartford. We bombed in Boston." He rustled the pages of her application. "And believe me, when you bomb in Boston, you've bombed enough to leave a crater."

KJ surprised herself when she said: "I plan on being a novelist."

"I knew it. I knew it! Most of my applicants are nice college kids, but they are kids. We get customers who expect a bookstore clerk to have read *Vanity Fair*. You'd have to be a writer. I knew it."

"Thackeray," she said. It was like a patella reflex: hit her knee with a rubber mallet, and her leg kicked; say *Vanity Fair* and a Wellesley graduate said *Thackeray*. "I am not a writer, yet."

"No, no, no, dear. In New York, you are a writer the moment you say you are." Nat giggled. "I nearly moved to New Orleans when I left Lubbock. Fleeing from Lubbock is a rite. Lubbock. Death in life, I swear. Lubbock leads to spiritual death, but for me it would have been a short trip into the grave with dirt on my face. Being queer in Lubbock is like being a missionary among the cannibals. Eventually, you get sprinkled with paprika and thrown into a pot. May I call you 'Kelly Jo?' That sounds down home. You'll fit right in at the Grand. I just know it. We are going to be great friends. Mr. Cassiopeia, my astrologer in Rome, is never wrong. His phone consultations cost me a week's salary, but I subscribe four readings each year. Cass said new exciting things would be happening, and here you are! You'll have to meet Eugene. He writes plays and is an absolute scream. But he gets non-speaking roles on TV soaps and he is there on the set. It's a scream. This month, for one or two hours each day someone darkens his eyebrows and powders his face before he sits in a jury box under klieg lights. It's hilarious. He swivels and barely moves his eyes. Eugene plays Juror #4. We have lunch parties at 1:30 when he is on, and you have to empty your wine if the camera catches him scratching his nose. He does that on purpose. We wait for it. Eugene has Gregory Peck's profile. Look for the man in the second row with the bushy eyebrows and cheekbones that shamed Mount Rushmore. That's Eugene. Just not his eyebrows. None of Eugene's plays have ever been produced, but they should be. Sometimes we all share spaghetti and salad and everyone reads a part from a manuscript. It's not always bad, but then he takes back the pages and rips them into small squares he calls 'mouse TP'."

"TP?"

"Toilet paper." She laughed more at the speed that Nat flew from one idea to the next than anything else. "Even if you don't take the job, you'll come to the next script party. Eugene's script parties sometimes need a female voice, and here you are a writer who has heard of Thackeray. Bring pages of your own book. You'll have to read to us. Or we'll read your stuff to you. All the writers do it. It's like dancing in front of a mirror. You have to forgive yourself to get better." Nat prattled on with a lilting lisp, trying to impress her with why she should want a bookstore job even though he could not pay a Wellesley graduate what she was worth. "The Grand is fabulous because the people are fabulous. It's my job to find fabulous people. That's you, dear." He blinked like a brown-eyed rabbit. "There's some heavy lifting now and then, book cartons from estates, of course, but we do that kind of labor together and make a party of it. No one is being paid enough to do hard work, least of all me." He was trying to sell her the job, the opposite of what she expected, which was to be begging for a chance, just a chance, to show what she was worth, which in her mind was very little.

"The store's shelves go on for miles. That's not an exaggeration. A collector dies, we buy books by weight, and then inspect every volume. We need people who know the difference between Mrs. Dalloway and Minnie Mouse. Rare books almost never happen, but we do discover secret love letters in envelopes that still reek of perfume hidden tucked into the pages. Those letters make me weep. Positively weep." He leaned closer and his voice dropped. "You are the first person in years to know not only Lady Ottoline Morrell but Vita Sackville-West, too." He sat back, his eyes sparkling. "Can you imagine how few people know them? My absolute two favorite lesbians, better than Gertrude and Alice."

"Stein and Toklas?"

"Oh God, I am falling in love with you! Are you gay?"

"I don't think so."

"Well, we can't all be perfect."

He was flattering her and his enthusiasm was overblown, but what of it? His voice rasped down to an intimate whisper. "We had a dozen college boys who applied for this job, but college boys never last, if you know what I mean." He rocked with laughter when KJ whispered in the smuttiest tone she could muster: "That's the trouble with college boys. They never last."

"Oh we *are* going to get along," he said and touched her wrist.

She'd fantasized Madison Avenue; she'd fantasized magazine work. But a job in hand was nothing to sneeze at. No clerk in a bookstore ever became rich, but she'd have some money trickling in, money untouched by Jack. Someone was willing to pay her for what she could do!

Her first day on the job, Nat ushered her to the coffee urn in far corner of the basement near the employee lockers. He crayoned her name above a wall peg and looped her coat onto it. "Wear denim pants, if you want. You look fabulous in a wool tartan maxi-skirt, but you are overdressed. And get flats. Those two-inch heels are fine, but you'll have days where you'll be on your feet the entire day." Nat paused. "The pashmina, though, I am not so sure." He chewed his lip. "No, definitely. It has to go."

It was like having a girlfriend of a different sort. What man knew what a pashmina was? "What's wrong with it?" It was pink and gray and she liked how it looked beneath her coat.

"It says, 'Greenwich, Connecticut.' A woman might wear it to hide her hips, but you don't have that problem. Your chin isn't wrinkled, is it? You want to say 'hip Greenwich Village.' A sweat-shirt will do. Dress down a little, KJ. This is a bookstore, a famous bookstore, but this isn't as upscale as Scribners on Fifth, thank God. We aren't even Brentano's. God knows we are not Shakespeare and Company, and we are friendlier than The Strand, our only com-petitor. You look positively fabulous, but you can't intimidate the customers. Get an NYU sweatshirt. Everyone will believe you are a student. You have the looks."

KJ was joking when she asked: "Should I rip a hole in the shoulder seam?" But Nat considered the question seriously. He said it was not necessary. "I like you, Kelly Jo Sinclair."

"Kelly Jo when I am south of the Mason-Dixon. KJ in the north."

"Good enough! KJ it will be! Let's have lunch today, just the two of us. I promise you all the gossip about the people we work with and all the sordid details about my sorry life if you tell me the dirt in yours. And we'll pick up a sweatshirt for you."

"Can I wait on giving up my gossip?"

The puckish grin submerged in his eyes. "So you have real se-crets. I have none of my own, so I am jealous."

They found her NYU sweatshirt just off Washington Square, the first sweatshirt she'd ever owned, even from when she'd been at Wellesley where sweatshirts had been for male cheerleaders with megaphones or brawny men who threw medicine balls at each other. It was the most comfortable thing she'd ever worn, doubly so without a bra. Two days later she bought two more, all three identical, violet letters on pale gray, baggy and two sizes too large. The sleeves had to be pushed to her elbows to prevent her looking like a gorilla with broken shoulders, but under her heavy wool Navy pea-coat, the coat collar raised, she passed as an undergraduate commuter on the downtown bus.

Nat set her work hours and duties, though he was more a part-ner than a boss. Her duties seemed to mostly be to accompany Nat on three-hour lunch jaunts rather than sitting on a stool behind a counter to answer inane questions from semi-literate customers.

What is that book by what's-his-name? You know, it has a greenish cover and isn't by Faulkner but the other one, not Fitzgerald, but the other other one.

KJ's real value lay in identifying valuable assets buried in crates that came from estates. In a dark recess of the basement, with a small silver claw hammer, she pried back wooden slats that cracked and left splinters in her fingers. The aroma of the veiled past rose in a dusty cloud about her. KJ lingered over marginal notations, often no more than an exclamation point beside a poem that had no special meaning to her, but must have to someone, somewhere, sometime. Once, an unsigned, undated, yellowed love letter slipped into her lap. The pressed rose crumbled to dust as she touched it. The linen paper been folded and refolded many times. The fountain pen ink had faded to brown. Someone long dead called a weekend "glorious, but never to be repeated." KJ's eyes filled; her nose detected the last delicious scent of rosewater. She lingered over the letter for a long while, a voyeur of dead passions, considered keeping it, but returned the fragile paper to the page in the book where it was meant to stay.

Near every day Nat and KJ braced their shoulders against the rusted stubborn fire door into the alley on the store's back. Her sneakered feet went winter numb in slush. They often marched through streets sloppy with gray rain, light snow that settled on their eyelashes and glistened on the heavy blue woolen shoulders of their stiff Navy pea-coats. Nat had straightaway obtained a coat identical to hers; they must have looked like twins. She never minded the feel of his arm encircling her waist, protectively close without being sexual. Their hips bumped.

At the 14th Street Automat, they dropped coins into slots to open small glass doors set in the walls to slide food onto their serving trays. KJ preferred mac-and-cheese or a crock of baked beans browned under a layer of molasses; Nat was capable of eating a single forkful of lemon merengue pie and calling that single bite his lunch. "You should eat the rest," he'd say. "You're skin and bones."

They talked about everything; they talked about nothing. "If anyone asks, just say we were on the upper west side auditing someone's library. Say they had a lot of Twain. Everyone had a lot of Twain." If they were robbing the store with those three hour lunches, no one seemed to care.

"Do you secretly own the store?" she asked, but his eyes twinkled and he did not answer her.

Brisk sunnier days, they strayed further south. Being south of West 8th Street with Nat was like being with the mayor of Greenwich Village. He was better than any tour guide could hope to be. Melville lived here; there was The White Horse Tavern where Dylan Thomas drunkenly roared stanzas while pissing into a urinal filled with ice. At McNulty's Tea Shoppe on Christopher Street, Nat regularly purchased Mu Tea, an herbal brew he insisted had curative powers. McNulty's smelled of licorice, tea, and heaven; KJ wondered if the wrinkled Chinese clerk who called Nat "Mr. Nathan" could vanish beyond a beaded curtain and reappear with love potions or untraceable poisons. "Actually, Mr. Wong could do that," Nat said. "I can get you a discount. He's one hundred and eight years old, you know."

Nat gifted her with a small package of Lapsang Souchong, a heavy, smoky tea Nat insisted could only be sweetened with unrefined honey. He also insisted on paying. "I know your salary, dear heart," he said. He bought her a bamboo tea strainer and made her swear to burn any bags of Tetley or Lipton she might own. "Life is too short for bad tea," he said. Tin or aluminum infusion balls were the Devil's implements, aluminum causing impotence, senility, and baldness. "You may as well brew your tea on the engine block of a Chevrolet."

At Christopher and Greenwich, they'd duck into Sutter's French Bakery. Biting a croissant was like having her tongue swim in rendered butter. The window was streaked by condensation. Nat never took more than a small bite of a Napoleon. He'd offer the rest to her, she'd nibble, and then he'd drop the remainder into a trash barrel before slapping his hands clean of powdered sugar.

Outside the bakery, Nat waved to the shrieking whores imprisoned in the upper stories in the Women's House of Detention, a tall red brick box that loomed several stories over Greenwich Street. The whores shook their bare breasts. "Tertiary syphilis," Nat explained. "It makes the girls crazy when it reaches the brain."

He regaled her about the life in the shadows beneath the West Side Highway, the strip of elevated highway between the city and the Hudson docks at the river-end of Christopher. The rotten piers creaked with the rise and fall of tides; rats the size of small dogs skittered over cobblestones. "That aroma you detect is not the ocean," Nat said. "It is New Jersey. And the boys wearing black leather, seatless chaps, motorcycle caps, and mascara are for sale. Rough trade. Pain and sex. They cruise for customers in the old truck trailers."

KJ did not understand the charm. "How is pain fun?"

"It's playacting about power. Every once in a while someone gets carried away. That's what makes trolling the trucks thrilling. The risk creates an adrenaline rush. Better than poppers. Dare the universe and win! But you want to be careful."

"Me? Why would I ever be there?"

"Don't knock it until you try it," he said, rolling his eyes at the phrase that would become a frequent byword between them.

Buckles must have had insight to these lives, though her mother would never believe she had first-hand experience. Her copies of *The Village Voice* left suggestively open to the personal ads had shocked the Scarsdale housewife, not so much that crazy things were going on in near public view, but that her child knew of them. KJ was from New Orleans, after all, but by being a voyeur to Nat's life, KJ was catching up.

Visiting Nat was not like a date, nor was it like visiting a woman friend. There was no sexual tension; there was no bitchy competition. He was a brilliant cook, and visits were about food, companionship, wine, and endless talk. As KJ did, Nat lived up-town, a short walk to the Ansonia Hotel, a decaying gingerbread of a building on 74th Street. But unlike KJ's view of blank walls,

Nat's penthouse on Central Park West commanded views of all of Manhattan.

Whenever her cab delivered her there, a uniformed doorman touched his white gloved hand to his hat brim and opened her taxi's door. Once he came to know her, without calling on the intercom, he turned a key in the private elevator that allowed the car to rise to the penthouse. The elevator was a wooden box the size of two coffins with panels of polished wooden inlay that smelled of lemon oil and butcher's wax. It creaked slowly higher passing every other floor until the doors parted to a tiny, private vestibule where three scones shed muddy yellow light. Nat had placed a three-foot bronze sculpture by the elevator, smirking Pan on goat legs playing his pipes. The figure was reiterated again and again throughout the penthouse along with painted griffins, twining serpents, and what she learned was a pruning kind of parrot called a Bird of Paradise. "It's not a phoenix," he said. "No ashes to rise from. Yet."

His formal dining room was dominated by a high-gloss finish walnut refectory table that could seat ten beneath a twelve-armed pewter chandelier. All his floors were darkly stained matching parquet, most covered by tapestries of scenes from Greek and Roman mythology. "I robbed the Cloisters," he giggled. The corners not occupied by urns with dusty ostrich feathers arcing over the clutter were occupied by dim torchieres. The burgundy-red walls were hung with the gilt-framed oils, pastorals of barefoot shepherds, their flocks, and ominous storm clouds. And everywhere, on every surface, there was the cloven-hoofed satyr, Pan, playing his pipes, eyes devilish, his inviting smile promising imminent destruction.

On her first visit, he handed KJ a corkscrew and asked her to choose a white wine from a refrigerated rack while he fussed over a salad of spicy bits of crispy duck, honey, vinegar, cherry tomatoes, mandarin oranges, and three kinds of lettuce. "Something quick," he said. No man KJ knew ever delegated the choice of wine to a woman. They sat on stools at the island in Nat's kitchen, a room large enough to hold a six burner gas range, two ovens, and a refrigerator the size of Connecticut. Copper cookware hung free above a double stainless steel sink. The tiles on the island's top were hand-painted periwinkle blue on porcelain white.

KJ thought the wine was better than good, dry and tart, but Nat pronounced it dreadful, smacked his lips, and assured her that the next bottle would be better. He lifted salad onto her plate and said: "I am ready. Let's have the story of your life, and don't skip the good parts."

"If you mean smut, there is very little. None, practically."

"I won't insist. But remember, you can't shock a New York City fag." He refilled her wine glass.

She described how her husband, Jack, and she, stopped dining together. "We refueled at the same time, then dashed off our separate ways."

"But you must have loved him, once, right?"

"I suppose I did." It was an effort to recollect the feeling, but Nat's wine made that a little easier. When Jack asked her to marry him, she thought herself lucky. "The problem was that Jack thought I was lucky, too." Nat laughed and stabbed a three-tine silver fork at his salad. "My mother was adrift on a sea of Gordon's Vodka, so Jack's mother managed our wedding. She chose the church, my dress, and the menu at the country club. His mother thought I was lucky, too. Lucky to have Jack and her."

"You are kidding!"

"She said as much at the bridal shower to my entire Wellesley crowd. I was so stupidly young, I thought that she was right. Jack's mother wrote a collection of lies for the *Times* Society page. I had to be someone worthy of her boy. She called my father a war hero."

Nat's eyes held her over the brim of his wine glass. "Was he?"

"Maybe, but that's a stretch for a low-level American diplomat who'd been blown to pieces in the Blitz a year before Pearl Harbor. He may have been a spy."

"Oh, now *that* is glorious. Why would you think that?"

KJ shrugged. "He went to Yale. Spies come from Yale."

As she grew used to it, Nat's wine had less bite. She nibbled on the grainy peasant bread Nat had baked a day earlier. She remembered but did not mention how when they said their vows, Jack's hands had been slippery with perspiration. "We served New York State champagne and cold Maine lobster tails on beds of cracked ice and romaine lettuce."

"Domestic champagne is swill. I suppose they sculpted the mayonnaise and sprinkled it with paprika."

"It was Miracle Whip."

"Heathens. You were sold to heathens."

"Jack was eventually summoned to the law firm in Manhattan. Very white-shoe. We left a stuffy Cambridge apartment and took the four-bedroom Tudor in Scarsdale. Jack's people had arranged it for us to buy."

"You did not pick it out?"

"No, but it was a lovely place."

"No children in all those rooms?"

"No," she said, lying.

KJ had been 23 when they'd drugged her unconscious so Buckles might struggle into the world. KJ awakened believing that the wizened baby they placed in her arms could not have come out of her. She wept for a week as her hormones ran amok, sure her lack of maternal feeling marked her as unnatural, a punishment visited on her by God for her sin of adultery with the one man in her life who'd come before Jack. After two weeks of indifference, they'd named the infant Abigail.

She told Nat about her first lover, Chester. "You asked for smut," she said, smiling, sipping the wine. "Chet was a Psychology professor. He seemed wise. I threw myself at him."

"Oh, thank God, I was beginning to wonder if you grew up without sin."

"I was nineteen; he was twice my age, thirty-eight, married, and had two children. Chet cried whenever we made love. He'd talk about how much he loved his wife, and I was so stupid I thought that was okay. I swear, I was in bed with a weeping man who loved his wife. I didn't think that was creepy for years. I don't think Chet ever realized how creepy that was. It was creepy, wasn't it?" Chester had been soft in the middle and his short beard scratched her neck. It was amazing the details that stayed.

"Were you looking for your father?" Nat asked. "The dead spy?"

KJ considered it. Her upper lip had no feeling. Nat had perceptions no one in her life had ever. He already knew more. "Two kids and a wife. I think that may have been an attraction, a guarantee that I'd never do anything truly stupid like show up on his front door to declare eternal love." Did Jack's women think of KJ as their safeguard? Did Jack talk about her when he was in their bed? Did he ever weep with regret? "I wonder how many students Chet slept with."

"Probably all of them," Nat said.

She laughed.

"No. It's probably true, if you think about it. Rangy professors need to break the monotony of their lives. A college campus is more arid than the desert, but every year a new crop of young people shows up. If you are surrounded by youth, it's easy to believe you are not aging. Then one day you look in a mirror, so the next smiling young face is the face of your savior. Eugene explained that to me when he talked about his professor. It sounds exactly right. The professor gets to feel young, the student gets to feel wise. Eugene's professor taught history."

"Eugene's professor?"

"At Brown. Or maybe Harvard. Some place like that. Eugene can be vague on the details. Everyone worth anything sleeps with a professor, or wants to. But the truly bold do it. I suppose there are some teachers who exploit their power, but no one can be exploited unless they are willing. There's a balance of power, there. A career for a grade. Ask Eugene when you meet him. He has theories inside theories, and they all sound correct even when they contradict each other."

Nat cleared their plates, poured two snifters of Sambuca, a syrupy licorice-flavored liqueur that slicked and burned like a comet down her throat. Three coffee beans went into each snifter, for "health, happiness and prosperity. *Salut.*"

They carried their drinks to a room where they sat cross-legged on a drafty oak parquet floor. The room was huge; had they sat on the furniture they'd have been too far from each other. Nat started a fire that popped and crackled in a stone fireplace. She'd never realized fatwood could be purchased at Gristedes.

They peered quietly at the growing flames until Nat said, "I came to New York for *the life.*"

He stressed the words in a way there could be no mistaking his meaning.

"Coming of age in Lubbock may as well have been a death sentence. Texas could persuade a boy like me that he was so defective that suicide was an act of civic duty." Nat worried a fingernail and his eyes went cloudy with distance. "My father sold tools. He believed Lubbock was the fulfillment of God's Paradise on earth designed to show sinners all they'd miss in the afterlife if they did not heed The Word. I was confused because I was having wet dreams about boys, told my father, whose advice to his son was to pray, do pushups, and take cold showers."

"Did it work?"

"I learned to masturbate in a cold shower," he said bitterly.

Nat flicked his Pall Mall into the fireplace and reached for another. Smoking and talk with no laughter was a new level of intimacy between them. Life did not have to be hilarity followed by new hilarity.

"There were bankers and oil men, cutthroats and cattle barons," he said. "The kind of men who could snuff out a boy as soon as they were done with him. And they would. Believe me. They'd make sure if I did not die in some arroyo, I'd die in jail."

KJ kept her doubts to herself while Nat worked through his stage credits. Sambuca slid his tongue beyond logic. He'd either have to be fifteen years older than he said or have started dancing when he was five. "Cyril Ritchard wanted me for *Peter Pan.* The original Lost Boys were dancers in the chorus. And he wanted me every other way, too." KJ never challenged him. Friends do not challenge friends; they help create them. "Of course, Mary Martin got the part. She was wonderful, too."

Nat said he'd arrived in New York and was taken in by an older man named Harold. Harold discovered Nat at an audition. "He was a Broadway angel just so he could get close to chorus boys. The old pervert kept me, but loved me in his way. When he died, he left me this penthouse. His money came from commodity trading, and don't ask me to explain because I don't understand it. Harold always was studying weather charts and taking positions in corn or pigs or wheat. He was also a perfect bastard. We saw other people, we were open, but we were eventually devoted to each other. It's nice to know who you'll be going home with after the party. I had to fight his sister and brother over his will. They accused me of swindling him, but the fact was that Harold loved me and promised to take care of me. Which he did." Nat peeled a shred of tobacco from his lower lip, swirled his Sambuca, and crushed his cigarette into a pink marble ashtray with yet another goat-legged bronze satyr playing pipes perched on the tray's lip.

He refilled their Sambucas and put a pack of open ice cream between them. No dishes, two spoons, that gush of cold sweetness, and then Nat took a deep breath.

"Being queer is tricky. Faggot laws are made for police who need an excuse to shake people down. As long as nobody straight gets harmed, they can beat every florist and decorator they can find. Being a fag is worse than being a streetwalker. At least streetwalkers make a profit. But being queer in New York is better than most anywhere else, even New Orleans or San Francisco. We've got Fire Island and the Village, of course, but the truth is that queer culture, the bookstores, the movie theaters, the dance clubs, and even the D&D Building make New York New York. Everyone knows it. That's why the cops hate us so much. I mean, we aren't living the high life in Queens, are we?

"Did you know the Ansonia has the Continental Baths in the basement? Nothing but men in towels moving through eucalyptus mist into tiny massage rooms. Everyone knows what is going on. How could anyone not know? Even Bette Midler wears a towel. The vending machine stocks KY Jelly and Snickers bars. The Baths advertise in the straight and queer papers. The ads don't say *No*

Women, but it is understood. New York would turn into Wichita without its queers." His tongue snaked pink around a spoon of Breyer's Vanilla. "What could be more miserable than being a vice cop? You cruise public toilets looking for a dick in the wrong person's fist. Lubbock was bad and I will never regret leaving, but Hell itself is the Delancey Street Men's Room." His smile wobbled and his eyes lighted with sudden concern. "Does 'dick' offend you?"

"I've heard the word before. Who is Bette Midler?"

Nat's grin steadied and he became radiant. "Just the most fabulous singer in New York. Forget your piano bars. This is New York. You never heard of her because you are straight, KJ. I need to corrupt you more. They will be singing her songs at bar mitzvahs eventually, but right now the Divine Miss M plays the Continental where cut and buff naked men grope each other and shine with mineral oil. Midler wears a sarong and sometimes a towel, too. She does campy dick and cock jokes between numbers. It's so New York. Where else can you go to get wet, naked, take some 'ludes, and hear the best singer in town?" He patted the back of KJ's wrist, a touch of camaraderie. "You'll have to come with us. We know people, or at least the people that will look the other way for five dollars when you show up. You'll have to wear a towel, of course, but with your figure—no offense—you will pass. Certain things have to be experienced: Paris, roller coasters, and The Divine Miss M."

"Me? A towel?"

"You look closer to twenty than forty and your hair is short as a boy's. Just keep the towel above your breasts. You'll be just another boy in the mist. Besides, everyone will be looking at Midler. Her knockers will convince you that you had a hormone deficiency when you were eleven. That's the baths, for you. This is New York, dear heart, where everyone is planning on becoming someone else. Not that anyone will ask, but if the towel slips, we can always say you just had the surgery and you are a little shy."

KJ awakened before sunrise, face down against a thin carpet, a faded tapestry actually, showing Dido and Aeneas. Her mouth felt like damp flannel. His back to her, a few feet away, Nat lay curled in a fetal position, snoring lightly. She pushed herself to stand and tucked her shirt into her jeans and let herself out. In the elevator, she wondered how many points Buckles would have awarded her for sleeping on the floor beside an aging homosexual dancer?

She must have passed a test. Soon after, another evening at Nat's, friends who claimed to be in his neighborhood arrived with bottles of cheap screw-cap red wine. It went with the bowls of spaghetti and meatballs, both of which were sources of adolescent-boy jokes and general hilarity heightened by the hashish in the sauce. *Your balls are bigger than mine, but I have the longer sausage.* KJ was the only woman in a crowd that waxed and waned between twenty and thirty.

She dressed like a moth seeking to be invisible against the gray bark of a dark tree. Her dyed brown hair was cut above her ears, her blonde roots hidden beneath the gray knit cap she pulled below her ears. With half-shoe basketball sneakers, shapeless jeans, and T-shirt, she looked like a college student with contempt for lipstick.

The inner circle sat cross-legged on an area rug that was a reproduction of the Unicorn in Captivity, the tapestry at the Cloisters, which made for leering puns about how the beast was safe at Nat's as there were no virgins. They jostled each other to sit on the horn, which would not have amused KJ were it not for the hash in the spaghetti sauce. They passed joints and drink at what KJ was meant to believe was a spontaneous party that promised to become an orgy. Pizzas appeared, gifts from the Pizza Fairy. Someone played show tunes on the piano, and the circle of friends hushed the chatter for each of the baritones taking his turn at *On the Street Where You Live, I Enjoy Being a Girl,* or any tune recorded by Johnny Mathis. Whenever a joint came to her, KJ at first passed it from one hand to the other and then to anyone nearby, but Nat was having none of that and whispered to her to inhale a toke and hold it until her breath exploded. She'd not smoked dope since a giddy afternoon when she'd been a teenager in New Orleans. Her ears happily thrummed.

Nat sold her hard. "KJ is simply brilliant. Brilliant. A great novelist in the making." He managed to make the tale of her bookstore interview epic. "My astrologer, the fabulous Mr. Cassiopeia in Rome, that same day predicted change and opportunity for me, and so I knew it was KJ as soon as she popped through the door. I practically chased her down the block. I swear, I expected to see a comet."

KJ's memory was that of a pimply female clerk, already quit, who had handed her an application and a short answer test. The party flowed around her. The meatball jokes seemed more clever. The unicorn jokes became hysterical. More pizza and more jug wine arrived with every cluster of fresh guests. If there was a Pizza Fairy able to deliver ever more pizza, the Wine Fairy was twice as productive.

That night she first met Eugene, who could never, ever be "Gene." After thirty minutes of talk, he pronounced her Most Gracious Fag-Hag of New York, a title Eugene assured her was more hotly contested on the Upper West Side than Miss Subways, Miss Rheingold, and Miss America. But as men paired off and began to vanish in groups of three and four, she began to feel uncomfortable. What if she were invited into a room? She was not ready for that. Nat noticed her discomfort and suggested she might want to leave. "No one will think any less of you."

In the private elevator, Nat said: "By *fag-hag* Eugene is flattering you for being nonjudgmental. The Lost Boys of Midtown really want a mother, and you, my dear, shall be our Wendy."

"That makes you Peter Pan."

"Well, if you insist." He grinned. "Just remember that Eugene has white-hot good looks and a mind that is scorching brilliant, but will someday ask you for money."

"What should I do?"

"That's up to you, dear heart."

"Is he a con man?"

"No. Nothing like that. He wants to see his plays produced, and is always in search of angels. Do you want to go back upstairs? The orgy will be starting soon, but if you take off your shirt some of these boys will be struck impotent. Naked girls are terrifying."

She was unsure if he joked.

So KJ became Wendy for the Lost Boys of Midtown, a place near the second star from the right, but located from river to river between West 4th and 78th Street. Kelly Jo Sinclair, an only child, found herself with a dozen talented siblings, all men whose lives percolated self-created drama. They whispered their hopes and intrigues, and sought advice from their nonjudgmental sister. The nuns in New Orleans had warned her that homosexuality was a depraved, shameful practice that displeased God so much He brought holy fire down on Sodom, yet these New York men were unashamed, creative, smart, inventive, talented and cultured. They had no designs on her. Why would God hate them?

If being a fag-hag meant being accepted by talented people, she'd stitch shadows to their feet and risk God's displeasure and the eternal flames of Hell.

Eugene was black Irish, unspeakably handsome, lifted weights, and ate little but vegetables. Charlotte would have opened her veins at such waste of masculine flesh, discounting his preference for sex with men as a mild shortcoming. Soon after Nat described KJ as a soon-to-be great writer, KJ and Eugene agreed to be perfectly frank about anything and everything. "Writers cannot be shy. Kissing and telling is ethically irresponsible, except for writers. We ask personal questions even of strangers, and most strangers reply. It's amazing. Eventually, writers betray everyone they know. It's expected."

Eugene said the old Royal he brought her had been taking up space in a closet, a block of black iron that now sat on her kitchen table, stolid as a library lion, beside a squared-off pile of white 18-pound paper and a sleeve of carbon paper. They drank cheap wine and spent a Sunday afternoon cleaning the keys with a solvent and a toothbrush, picking grime from the O, lowercase E, and Q with toothpicks. That was when Eugene asked KJ how it felt to have an orgasm.

"I am hardly an expert."

"No one is. I keep reading it is like a sudden sneeze, but that does not tell me what I need to know." He smeared a clot of inky grime from his thumb onto a paper towel. "I can't experience a female orgasm. Is it really like a sneeze?"

"Not in my experience. And believe me, that is very limited." Inky fingerprints smeared on their wineglasses, which were in fact grape jelly jars. Eugene was being earnest; she felt obliged to answer as best she could. "It's not about a man's technique, though. At least not for me, anyway. It's much more about how I feel for a man." She blushed, thinking of how she'd faked orgasms for Jack "Or how intense my fantasy is."

"Like masturbation?"

KJ hesitated, then nodded. "That's all you're getting about fantasies today."

"How many men have you been with, KJ?"

"Two," she said honestly.

"I did not mean at the same time. I mean total."

"Two."

"My God, you are a saint. Really? It's nobody's business but yours."

An idea nibbled at her mind. "Eugene," she said. "Are you working up the nerve to sleep with me?"

"God, no. I'd die of panic."

She kissed his cheek; he colored like a schoolboy with a crush on his teacher.

To keep the platen's rubber supple, Eugene lifted it from the carriage and gently rubbed the platen with olive oil. His hands glistened. "Let it set overnight, then wipe it down with a dishrag. If you are ever with a man who wants a better hand job, it's the same motion, from the wrist, not the elbow. It's not as if you are pumping water. But use baby oil and no paper towel. Paper scratches."

"I could have guessed that."

"Mink gloves work." He stated it as a fact, not a joke.

KJ made a mess of her fingers installing a new ribbon before she inserted her first blank sheet into the carriage to clack out *The quick brown fox jumped over the lazy dog.* She typed the sentence a second time. Every key responded with snappy action.

Weeks later, that first clean sheet still in the machine goaded her daily at breakfast. Breakfast came to mean a toasted English muffin, a touch of peanut butter with honey, tea from McNulty's, and a mocking white sheet of paper with every letter of the alphabet informing her about some damned dog and a fox. Her imagination offered no escape; she was imprisoned by reality. She knew nothing more dramatic than her daughter's disappearance and its fallout, and her perpetually ongoing divorce, and she was unready to write about either. KJ still sat up startlingly awake from dreams that left the clutch of her daughter's icy hands burning on her shoulders. Buckles was sinking into time's abyss. Nightmares kept her afloat.

One night in mid-February, a week after Nat's semi-annual spaghetti and salad party for the returning cast of the Ice Capades and their two week stand at Madison Square Garden, Eugene and KJ opened the French doors to step out onto Nat's flagstone terrace. The building behind them broke some of the clawing wind that rose from the black void that was Central Park. They faced uptown. A pewter quarter moon floated behind wind-strung clouds. Eugene braced his elbows on the rusting guardrail to face her. Below, twin rivers of headlights flowed, ruby red north and diamond white south crawling on Central Park West. The city was under a few inches of snow already gone soot-gray.

"Your skater was handsome." The night of the pasta party Eugene had left early with a skater, a boy no older than 20. They kissed at Nat's front door. It was not the first time she'd seen two men kiss, but it was the first time she'd seen Eugene with his tongue so far down another man's throat.

"Werner is dumb as a rock, though if leg muscles were brains he'd be Einstein. He'd have made the Olympics if it weren't for a sprained ankle at the very worst time. He is Austrian, and he speaks just enough English that we managed to make it through breakfast before I wanted to drop him out a window." Eugene looked straight at her. "Are you jealous? Would you join us when the show returns to New York? They'll be back in late spring. Werner would not be unhappy to see you in our bed."

Eugene's sincerity never failed to touch her. "No," she heard herself say.

Eugene shrugged. "It was just a thought. The one woman I've been with was a friend in high school. She wound up hating me because she expected to turn me. When that did not happen, she was insulted. I was born this way, KJ. We are what we are."

"So no one can change?"

"I didn't say that. But if you deny who you are, it can feel like you are very briefly in control. Then when the truth returns, it all blows up in your face. Guaranteed."

"That sounds like the sad voice of experience."

"It is, it is." But Eugene was grinning. Love gone wrong was friendly terrain.

Encouraged, KJ asked what seemed indelicate. "How do you know with a man how it will work? That you are, I don't know how to say this, 'compatible'?"

"Who will pitch and who will catch?"

The metaphor made her laugh; it was exactly what she was asking.

"We'll experiment. I'm open, in case you are wondering. Nothing ever feels right; everything feels right. A lot of the boys advertise. At the moment, cruising code is all about bandanas. They aren't fashion accessories. More like semaphore. Blue bandanas hanging from the right hand back pocket of a boy's jeans means he wants to pitch. On the left, it means catch. If the bandana is red, it means mild S and M, maybe some restraint. Stuff like that. And yellow ... believe me, you don't want to know about yellow."

"Oh God. Really? Yellow?"

As a defense to the cold, Eugene folded his arms tightly over his chest. "The bandana code won't last, though. Something new will come along. Keeping up is part of the Queer Game. And it is a game, like fashion. And the Queer Game is all about fashion."

The wind sliced through KJ's sweatshirt. She moved closer to Eugene. He seemed oddly stiff, so she lifted his arm around her shoulders, for the cold, she told herself. His arm tightened on her. "I've never seen Nat take a friend so quickly, much less a woman friend. You're brother and sister. He loves people thinking that about you, you know. Buster called you his sister and he did not correct him. You know Buster?"

"Buster? Buster?"

"His last name is Brown, Like the shoes. It drives him crazy to be called Buster. He says he does not live in a shoe with a dog."

"What's his real name?"

Eugene thought a bit. "I don't think anyone knows. He's all about appearances, denies being queer, but shows up. One of those fags filled with self-loathing and denial. That doesn't stop him from showing up when it suits him. He wears suits all the time. Button down collars and crimson ties. He's a banker with a wife and two kids, but none of us know anything about them and I am fairly sure they don't know about us and Buster. Everyone wants a family. We can't choose our parents, but queers build their own family, sometimes more than one. Speaking of Buster the Banker reminds me. Would you like to get in on a project of mine?"

"As long as I am not the project."

"Don't be crude, KJ. I need money. Buster can't steal it for us, though he has promised to manage it. I need someone with brains enough to manage everything except the money. It's about a show. Well, a club and the show we will mount in it."

"Does it have a chance?"

"As long as we don't do O'Neill or Strindberg, maybe."

"What is it?"

They went back inside. Out of the wind, her blood rushed to warm her extremities. Eugene wrote an address on a napkin. "Meet me for lunch on Tuesday." Eugene spun back into the thinning crowd and thickening smoke.

Later, while she cleared dishes and packed leftovers and picked cigarette butts off soiled plates, Eugene and his lover of the moment paused at the front door. He raised his eyebrows inquisitively. There was no mistaking the invitation; it seemed to be becoming his habit. She shook her head.

Eugene's persistent invitations were reviving tension in her, and though a good deal of her was ready, and though anything physical with Eugene guaranteed no deep emotional entanglements, KJ still favored the feel of extra space in her bed. Even a meaningless ménage à trois was several steps too far into kinky. It sounded too busy.

At Tuesday lunch over a salad of broiled salmon and balsamic vinegar, Eugene offered KJ the manager job.

"I know nothing about running a club," she said.

"No one does. But at least you have a head on your shoulders."

"Pay?"

"Be serious. I was going ask you for money, but won't. I ask all my other managers for money, but at least you'd be the real manager."

"When do I get to talk with Buster? I've never met him."

"Maybe never. He's so far in the closet his closet has a closet. He worries about being outed." Eugene promised her name would appear on the bronze plaque he would put up somewhere. "Benefactors on the wall encourage people to add their own. Like the museum and the opera."

"But this is a nightclub."

"For now. By the way, how is your book coming? I'd love to read some of it."

"It's moving along," she said, lying.

KJ accepted his offer. Her impossible contradictory feelings for Eugene were taking her through an emotional terrain for which she had no map.

Tense weeks after Martin Luther King was shot, the revolution at last came to New York. After days of student occupation of administrative offices where spat-on desks and hurled files fluttered from windows, on a chilly April night, New York's finest erupted from subterranean passageways beneath the campus of Columbia University. They were allegedly evicting the trespassers nervy enough to object to their school's plan to level a neighborhood to erect a gymnasium; they were in fact enjoying the rare opportunity to deliver a lesson to rich-pansy-assed unwashed hippies who lived the high life on Mom and Dad's money.

A phalanx of helmeted cops pocketed their badges to become anonymous and kicked ass. Their polished broughams, truncheons, nightsticks, and fists broke bones and split scalps. Students dragged by the hair from the Low Library were more fortunate than those dragged by the feet whose eggheads bounced on concrete steps. By morning, on Amsterdam Avenue, St. Luke's Hospital Emergency Room was overwhelmed with bleeding college students.

Composed of Columbia trustees who rooted for the Lions and certified Pulitzer Prizes, the editorial board of *The New York Times* claimed the school was building a better city. The *Times* blamed the fracas on *off-campus radicals,* an accusation that suggested every Columbia and Barnard student had been duped by well-funded persuasive subversives loosed in America by powers unknown. Only outside agitators could seriously oppose the construction of a tax-free Manhattan real estate empire run by Columbia, an empire rivaled only by the other tax-free empire run by the Archdiocese of New York. Student demands for justice and peace collided with that university's God-given right and mission to accrue wealth and power. The Grey Lady assured the public that the uprising would pass and made no note that every cop in every news photograph was not wearing an identifying badge. It was part of an international conspiracy that ran from Vietnamese peasants squatting in rice paddies to anarchists running amok in Berlin, London, and Paris. No such activity could possibly be the consequence of the spontaneous rise of a new age. New York's beefy Blue Line was all that stood between America and chaos. They did their duty by kicking the living shit out of the little bastards.

KJ could only wonder how Buckles felt, then concluded her daughter would risk any danger in the cause of justice. It was her nature. An irrational conviction settled in KJ's heart: her missing daughter was in Morningside Heights.

She told Nat she was leaving the store and might not be back for two or three days. She was not asking permission.

"Right now?"

"Right now."

Nat reached for his jacket. "I'll go with you. Where are we going?"

"No."

"You're staying in town, though, right? No jets or trains?"

"No jets or trains."

"Not your divorce?"

"Nothing like that." How could Nat understand that she believed the daughter she'd never told him about needed her?

She hailed an illegal cruising taxi. *Black Peal* was a response to licensed taxi drivers who became blind to black people who needed cabs willing to travel north of W 72nd Street. Their motto was *We Aren't Yellow.*

Delivered to W. 114th Street, KJ sat on a park bench on the north end of the traffic island that divided Broadway. She faced north. The main campus was to her right. At her back, crocuses and daffodils rose through the black soil. People cared for this patch of dirt. Tulips would emerge soon. Spring and new hope was emerging.

It was two mornings after the riot, but students still milled about the street, stunned and indignant. They'd been swatted flat by ham-handed cops who had more regard for mosquitoes on a summer night on the Jersey Shore.

KJ still believed that mothers and daughter shared an unaccountable connection. Didn't they bleed at the same time every month? They spoke telepathically all the time, whole conversations in KJ's head. Buckles knew all about Nat and his friends. She shared her mother's excitement about Eugene's prospects. Her daughter's spirit enwrapped her, a palpable aura of comfort.

She twice walked the full perimeter of campus, from 114th Street to 120th Street, littered by torn, crayoned oak tag signs and fluttering bits of colored paper, loose flyers that had been taped to fences, benches, buildings, and windows that snagged at her ankles, now trash like enormous flakes of multicolored pastel-colored snow. Sidewalks on 114th had dark spots and wider puddle stains of what had surely been blood. The black metal gates at all the entrances to the campus except Broadway and 120th street were chained and locked.

Buckles' spirit was everywhere. KJ sprinted to catch and spin to face short, long-haired blonde girls whose hair cascaded like strands of golden silk. She lost track of the times she shouted "Buckles!" only to be captured in the dull eyes of a stranger as a lunatic. Why else would this crazy woman ask: "Do you know my Buckles?"

KJ went through the only open gate to linger on the periphery of a crowd clustered around the statue Alma Mater. A stenciled sign was propped in her lap: *Raped*, an idea that made KJ tremble. She was helpless to protect her daughter. Speakers on the granite steps of the Butler Library shouting into bullhorns that the cops were sure to come again, Vaseline was the best defense against tear gas. Earrings and belts had to be discarded so the pigs could find no grip. An organization KJ had never heard of, the Students for a Democratic Society, was America's best hope against racism, exploitation, and the imperialism that devastated Puerto Rico, Nicaragua, Guatemala, and was making Mexico a gangster state. The university was part of it.

Triage in the Emergency Room at St Luke's had separated injuries early morning two days ago. Split scalps, broken arms, twisted wrists, and cracked ribs were deemed not life-threatening, but the Admitting Room floor remained sticky with blood, the air pungent with disinfectant. Buckles' voice called to her a dozen times, but when KJ turned she'd see no one. No one knew any kid named Sinclair, Buckles, or Abigail, but that meant little because the hospital stopped creating records when clerical workers were needed to apply bandages. Had her daughter been treated and released? She asked dozens of bandaged and bleeding kids. Their eyes dulled with pain.

Returned to her 114th Street bench, KJ wept without restraint, rocking, unnoticed, just another one of New York's addled lunatics seeking trouble, this one on a Broadway bench following a police riot.

Then on the ground between her unlaced black sneakers, she saw a glint of light off a cheap earring in the dirt. It had not been on the ground at that spot earlier that day. She was sure of that. She'd have seen it. It was the kind of bauble Buckles adored. She'd come home from her trips to the city with mountains of crap, cheap costume jewelry, beaded strings or bent spoons fashioned into rings, and this earring was the kind of thing that always caught the kid's eye. KJ spit on her fingers and rubbed a smudge of dirt from the earring to hold it close before her eyes. A turquoise stone was set in elaborately hammered, tarnished silver. Navajo? If Buckles had been to the southwest, she might be on her way home.

Yes. That made perfect sense.

The earring must have belonged to Buckles. It was a promise from God. Buckles had been right here at this bench in search of her mother even as her mother had searched for her. They'd heard the same voices, felt the same presence. Hadn't student leaders told the girls to discard their jewelry? Buckles would have done the smart thing. Her daughter was many things, too bold by half, but she was far from stupid. She'd dropped her earring as a promise to her mother among the daffodils.

KJ slipped the earring into her sweatshirt's belly pouch. She staggered south, dazed, unable to take more than a dozen steps before she paused to withdraw the earring again, fearful she'd somehow lost it.

Home was long blocks south and east, but at 112th Street and Amsterdam, KJ was drawn into the immensity and cool shadows of the Cathedral of Saint John the Divine. She'd never been there. KJ was nominally Catholic and the cathedral was nominally Episcopal, but the earring was God's unmistakable promise. Buckles was still on the earth.

Though KJ had never been a believer, she felt the need to pray. The nuns taught her that God would hear not only the pious, but also the troubled, the sick, the lonely, and the fearful. She was all of those things. God would hear her.

Blocks long, the cathedral was made of polished stone and sheer concrete. Befitting a house of God, the work was never done and was projected to last at least a hundred years. KJ was immersed in deep, cool shadows. No wall was without its carvings, angels and disciples turning on each other, alive in the stone of walls in alcoves, atop pillars, in ribbed vaults, spires. She walked through a tumult of red, blue, green, and yellow light, sunlight filtered through God's eye, a round stained-glass window set high above the altar's back wall. Her soul swelled to fill the air laden by the wax-smell of holy candles. She was embraced by Christ who extended His arms down from Heaven.

He would restore Buckles to her.

She lighted a vigil candle, crossed herself, genuflected and crossed herself twice more. The found earring, tight between her palms, was her sign of God's promise. She placed it among the steadily burning candles, knelt again, prayed, and rose, comforted.

Rivulets of sweat snaked through the patina of plaster dust covering the bare shoulders and deep copper arms of a black boy swinging a sledgehammer. It was late May, hot as hell, though the basement was cooler. The dust seemed not to bother him, but his figure stirred KJ.

The boy was half her age, perfect for Buckles assuming the boy liked girls, which was unlikely. A black David swinging a hammer, Michelangelo would have worshipped his burnished copper skin, his impossibly white teeth, his ear-to-ear beard, and his perfectly shaved head. The single strap that held up the bib of his overalls gapped over the muscles of his hairless chest. The veins of his forearms popped. The perfect V that was his torso vanished into his waist. He'd swing, and a piece of the wall crumbled into the growing pile of plaster at his feet. He wore thick leather ankle boots and a workman's tool belt. He eliminating walls in the basement of what was to become The Box, Eugene's new night club.

KJ rubbed irritating dust from her eyes. She imagined those muscles yielding under her hands, and shut the idea from her mind. She was becoming a rangy bitch, an inappropriate status for the Mother of the Lost Boys, not to mention a moment earlier entertaining the idea of the boy with her own daughter.

KJ spent her free time either at The Box or on the phone with Buster. Neither of them liked the other. Buster was too much like Jack's associates, charming, accomplished, and ready to stab anyone in the back. Like them, Buster distrusted women with even a smidgen of power. It puzzled her that Eugene and Nat did not see Buster the same way she did. Maybe they had slept with him; that might put him in a different category.

KJ was unhappy with herself reducing her every consideration of people to be who had slept with whom. It was like being a high school gossip in a world with real sex. Maybe if she lingered at one of the orgies she could sleep with all of them and get past being judgmental.

The Box was still a dark cellar, but once the non-supporting walls were gone it would be a club in-the-round with narrow wooden chairs and tables the size postage stamps. They hoped to be licensed for 125 people and would stuff in another 25. None of the dust-covered crew was drawing pay, but for reasons she understood, working for free was ordinary. She was no different from any of the workers in that way.

The painful pressure of the metal chair on her bottom was a reminder of how much weight she had shed. For a decade, she'd worried about middle-aged spread; now she was down to less than what she'd weighed as a college girl at Wellesley. She embraced the metal back of her chair, the point of her chin resting on her folded forearms, what was left of her breasts against the chairback.

"Could a girl just pass a happy day watching that man swing that hammer? My my my my." KJ had not noticed the elegant woman who'd tiptoed through the basement's gloom and plaster dust. "Why mount a show? I'd buy a ticket to watch John Henry over there at work. All they'd need is a popcorn machine and taffy apples. It's the tool belt." She paused. "Definitely the tool belt."

KJ extended her hand. "KJ. Short for Kelly Jo. I'm the club manager. Or will be when we open. Which at this rate will be three days after forever."

"Just the person I need. Who would I see to join the company?"

They kept their eyes on the young man hammering at the walls. Somewhere in the murky space a boom-box played classic show tunes, not the score best suited to swinging a hammer. Marijuana smoke drifted in plaster dust.

"You'll want Eugene. We're hoping for an opening by late May at the latest, but I don't see how we'll do it. The space has to be cleared before we install seats, lights, or get a popcorn machine. You may be a little early for casting." She sneezed. The dust in her nose was killing her.

"Call me Ginny. Can I at least buy you lunch and pick your brain?"

How had Ginny got in? The doors were chained and locked. Buster said he gave money to a building inspector though they lacked permits to begin. She expected the ceiling to crash down on them at any second. Only a few people were allowed in, which did not stop the hopefuls who had hear a rumor of a secret opening. Nat speculated that Greyhound ran special fares for hopeful queers from Sandusky to New York to The Box.

Even with his penthouse overlooking Central Park, Nat had more money than she'd have previously guessed. She wondered if being bookstore manager was camouflage to make his younger friends believe that he was the same as the florists, bit-actors, and other wannabes making their assault on fame. She suspected he owned the bookstore and answered to no one. The penthouse was just more of his luck, luck he shared promiscuously.

"I could watch John Henry over there swing his hammer all day long," KJ said. "But my lungs will try to cough their way out of my chest if we stay here." KJ tore her eyes from the rhythmic sledge-hammer long enough to look at Ginny. She had a bobbing Adam's apple. "God, is that you, Eugene?"

"'Ginny,' please. Call me Ginny when I'm in drag." Ginny sighed. "What gave Ginny away? It's who I am today. It changes whenever I wake up."

"You're too pretty."

"It's the pearls. I knew it. Too much?"

"You're drop-dead gorgeous. The makeup is perfect," KJ said, lying. Ginny wore a curly but short blonde wig that must have cost a week of KJ's salary, but Eugene was black Irish. His whiskers could not be hidden by facial powder unless she applied it with a trowel, and she was too elegant to look that cheap. "You look terrific. I mean for a woman. Well, for anyone. You look terrific. Not flamboyant, just terrific."

"Flaming faggotry is not Ginny. Shrieking and hugging is not what Ginny does. All that gushing leaves me exhausted. And, no, Eugene does not have a woman inside longing to get out, so there are no plans for any surgical alterations. There are uptown doctors who will do that, now. No one has to fly to Sweden." Ginny shut her eyes theatrically. The touch of color at her lids emphasized her modest lashes. "I enjoy drag now and then. For the freedom. What do you think? Should we run a drag revue? A good drag revue takes in baskets of money."

"We won't be doing one of your plays?"

"Maybe someday, but not if we want to sell tickets, dear heart. An unknown play by an unknown playwright? Why not open in a church basement in Rego Park? I can dramatically challenge the fundamental questions of existence another year. Eugene O'Neill's position is safe because nothing packs the house like heels, fake tits, and feathers."

The club's sole door, a violation of fire laws, lay at the end of a narrow alley between two brick buildings. At least the crash bar worked. KJ made a mental note to do something about the alleyway's rusting dumpster and metal trash cans. Hip-decrepit ambience could go just so far; scurrying rats were never charming. They'd sworn to the Permit Gods that The Box would have more doors, but Buster's budget did not yet allow serious plans for that to advance. The place would be a firetrap if he did not get a move on.

Ginny walked as if she'd been born on high heels. KJ felt suddenly drab in black Converse sneakers, her gray NYU sweatshirt, and her faded jeans beside a crossdressing man on her four-inch silk Ferragamos that matched her black clutch. The red miniskirt was hemmed three inches above her knee, not quite as short as the fashion, but short enough to show a lot of shapely thigh in fishnet pantyhose. Ginny looked at least as good as Buckles, but where Buckles was a teenage girl, Ginny was a young woman in her prime who, only incidentally, had balls at her crotch.

Luigi's was a cliché of a spaghetti place, red checkered table-cloths, faint gold wall sconces, and an ill-lit mural of the bay at Naples. Nat insisted it was the inspiration for the spaghetti dinner in *Lady and the Tramp*. Red candles puddled scarlet wax over Chianti bottles stitched into straw baskets. Fat rivulets of condensation zigzagged down the frosted storefront glass window. The bread was crusty, the butter frozen into patty-size bricks on small squares of foil. Despite Luigi's air redolent of oil and garlic, KJ detected a trace of Ginny's Chanel #5.

Too late for lunch and too early for dinner, the, place was near empty. They chose a table in the restaurant's center. Ginny sat demurely at a chair's edge as the waiter slid her chair beneath her. She settled three-quarters sideways in her seat, a fan of her fingers brushing by her cheek. Eugene and the rest of Nat's friends ordinarily sat in full masculine display, a left leg in Brooklyn and a right leg in Hoboken—"Highlighting the junk," Nat called it—but Ginny sat pigeon-toed, her legs together as if her strict grandmother had taught her to be ever-mindful of nasty boys eager to stare up her skirt. Ginny's legs crossed at the ankles. Her hand smoothed the line of her miniskirt.

"You make quite the lady," KJ said.

"I'll bet you say that to all the boys."

Ginny's voice leveled breathy as Jackie Kennedy, never faltering into a falsetto. KJ had come of age as the head-turning wild-haired blond ingénue from New Orleans, but here she was with a man dressed as a woman who could turn more men's heads than KJ ever had hoped to.

Ginny's fingers ran back through her blonde wig, a studied, cultivated habit. The wig's shoulder-length ringlet touched her shoulders. KJ did not reveal that Ginny's wig was very near KJ's own hair color before she'd cropped and dyed her hair to never again be taken for Mrs. Jack Sinclair, the lawyer's good wife and mother who drove a station wagon that needed a muffler and whose vanished daughter went to a prep school in Westchester.

"In the womb, we all start the same. That's why men have nipples. Sex is about parts, but gender is about everything else. Gender is about learned mannerisms. It can't be that so many gay men lisp unless that kind of speech is learned and adopted. It's how so many of us know each other. Sex can be altered with a scalpel, but gender can be changed with a decent pair of nylons."

"And a lisp."

"You understand." Ginny smiled. She asked for a red.

KJ picked clean he innards of a crusty warm slice of bread. "I am sharing bread, pasta, and wine with a man dressed as a woman who is telling me biology may be defied." The waiter uncorked a bottle of Bardolino, showed KJ the label, and though she had no idea what she was looking at she nodded. He splashed a finger's worth into KJ's wineglass, she sipped, approved, and only then the waiter filled Ginny's wineglass.

"See?" Ginny whispered. "He took his best guess from our gender cues. He assumed you were butch and I was femme. You taste and approve, you get any cork if it crumbles, but only then is my glass filled. It's a gender-based ritual. People want rituals because they tell them what to do." She smacked her lips. The wine was short of spectacular, but good enough. "What a lovey pair of dykes we make."

"So we are pretend lesbians?"

"You know the old joke, KJ? What do gay men do on a second date?"

"I have no idea."

"They fuck for the second time."

KJ smiled.

"What do lesbians do on a second date?"

"I have no idea," she said again.

"They plan a garden."

KJ laughed but asked: "Why is that funny?"

"Because there is truth in it. Biology requires women to plan. DNA is immortal because it replicates itself. I don't care if it was a bolt of lightning from God's own finger or an accident of static electricity, but long ago lightning struck a strand of a protein that experienced the thrill of a lifetime. A billion lifetimes. It slithered through mud looking for more hot DNA, not to replicate itself but to get it on with a stranger. Zap! We have been pub-crawling on Friday nights ever since. Sexual attraction is nothing but DNA screaming, 'This one! That one! That one! All of them!' It's the Mud Puddle Sweepstakes. New combinations means new life."

"And female DNA doesn't scream?"

"It does, but it has to be far more picky. Women's DNA seeks the best it can get—brains, looks, longevity, and wealth. If you are going to invest nine months and a single egg to make a person, and carry that person on your hip for a few years, you have to be picky. Men, however, can spray once and move on to spray and spray again. It's not terribly fair, I admit, but biology isn't about justice."

"Wealth?"

"Wealth is evidence of better DNA. A diamond pinky ring for some girls is all they need to know."

"That sounds primitive."

"It is."

Nat paid the running tab at Luigi's. The only people who knew that were Eugene, KJ and Buster. Buster complained that there was no need to feed every stray fag who wandered into The Box, but Nat agreed with KJ that people who were working without pay deserved a meal at the very least.

The tines of KJ's fork twirled pasta against her spoon. Unable to halt her curiosity, relying on their writer's pact that no question could offend, she asked: "Why would you want to be a woman? Trust me and my mother; it's all about discomfort. Menstrual cramps are called 'The Curse' for a reason, though I suppose that's not a problem for you. Herring bones in your underwear to hold a boob in place was developed by The Spanish Inquisition. Plucking your eyebrows, high heels, and corsets are torture compared to a soft flannel shirt or this sweatshirt I have on."

To mention childbirth would have been an invitation for Ginny to ask what her experience was, and KJ was unsure she could lie to her about it. She was not yet ready to share the fact of Buckles with any of The Lost Boys, not even Peter Pan himself.

"I have no desire to be a woman. Did you know Jewish men at morning pray to thank God they are not a woman? I am definitely not a woman trapped in a man's body. Gender dysphoria depresses adolescents into suicide if the kid isn't lucky enough to find acceptance. Church, family, and country all tell the kid he is an irredeemable pervert. That may be Nat's history, but thank god it was never mine."

"Gender dysphoria?"

"I forget. The vocabulary is not in the forefront of everyone's mind. Dysphoria occurs when a person's body and mind don't agree on who or what the person is."

"That sound awful."

"That's why so many teenagers kill themselves."

"But you are a drag queen."

"No, I am a female impersonator. Drag queens strut. I don't strut. We'll stage a revue at The Box that starts with tits and feathers under hot red and yellow spots. A dozen queens will enter in headpieces big as Carmen Miranda's. You know, the Banana Queen. It's campy fun. The next number will ease into a hotter red spot for our plagiarized Bob Fosse choreography of 'Hey Big Spender,' then we'll segue into a white spot solo on a single member of the cast singing 'Someone to Watch Over Me.' No headdress for her, maybe a simple black dress with sequins on the deep neckline and some falsies that will make everyone in the club wonder. She'll be our most important female impersonator. Just before intermission, we'll do the Can-Can. We can't afford six musicians, but we will need them, so I hope we have a decent sound system. I can't talk to Buster. All he says to me is to talk to you. As long as we finish the revue with 'Mame,' everyone goes home happy. The straights will come to gawk and drink, but they have to leave impressed enough to send their friends. Maybe when they get home they'll have sex in a new way."

"You have it all figured out."

"Yes. This is my dream and I am not making it up as I go along. For your exclusive information, I wear women's clothes to see if Ginny can pass. I don't pirouette in front of the mirror and I don't sing *I Enjoy Being a Girl*. Crossdressing is something I do for me, not for an audience."

"Size 12?"

"Ten if I don't have to let out the bust."

"What's 'camp' mean? 'Campy fun.'"

"God, KJ, when you fell off the turnip truck at 72nd Street last week someone should have given you a guidebook. Read Susan Sontag. That woman is scary smart. She says camp is a style at the center of male homosexual life. Sontag says that the life is an overstated lark about exaggerated masculinity. No one lifts weights to get strong, they lift weights to look hard. In New York, New Orleans, and San Francisco everyone understands gay men are being camp. But if a knuckle-dragger reaches under a skirt and finds an unexpected pair of testicles, all bets are off. He will beat someone bloody. Camp puts people on notice about what lies north of a thigh." KJ laughed. "Queers exert what power they have through camp. The best drag queen wins, because anything worth doing is worth doing to excess."

"Sounds like a motto."

"It is. Straights pretend to be disgusted but they are fascinated. The idea of being penetrated leaves the average knuckle-dragger dizzy with fear. Queer sex must be powerful, powerful shit. Suck a single cock and you're queer forever." Ginny thought a moment. "Except blowjobs in jails. They do not count."

"Because jail sex is about power, not affection."

"Damn, KJ, you are smart. I'm not so sure, though, that the situation is any different in every suburban bedroom. There's an element of power in heterosexuals getting it on."

"But power is not about you?"

"Never. The more quietly I pass, the happier I am." Ginny's bread sopped up sauce in a very unladylike way. Her chair tipped backward, and then she stood. "You might want to fill your glass while I pee."

"Where?"

"The Ladies Room, of course. Do you want to come with me? Women usually go together. When they can."

"I'll pass on that experience. No offense. Feel free to pee in privacy."

Ginny glided away. Even her viola-shaped bottom moved in the right way. KJ wondered what shops sold falsies for buttocks. Ginny and Eugene were mesmerizingly smart. It stirred her, even if they were wrong. They had mind down solid, and body as much as anyone could, but neither Eugene nor Ginny ventured into spirit. KJ would consider all that was said at some time or other, but she might just as easily choose not to think about it all. Eugene and Ginny might occupy a single body, and all the rhetoric strained to make that duality unified, but unity was a very masculine condition. The cold fact was that women could go on undisturbed by ambiguity, accepting contradictions or ignoring them.

There was no explaining that. It lay beyond thought and speech. There were so few female philosophers because there were so few questions worth thinking to death.

At Ginny's return, the waiter hurried to withdraw her chair again. Ginny acknowledged his courtesy with the faintest of smiles as she settled back. The waiter glowed with obsequious pleasure. KJ's head spun as much from the wine as the talk. She buttered a heel of bread. "Why don't we make the club's toilets unisex?"

"Not even New York is ready for that. Maybe someday, but not in 1968."

"How about putting an extra john or two in the Ladies' WC? I hate standing on a long line while men are zipping along."

Ginny's lips pursed. "That's brilliant. Talk to the plumber and tell Buster we'll sell more beer if women can move faster through a lavatory. The best toilets in New York are at Radio City. Art Deco.

Gray, black, and white. The Rockettes are good, but the Rockefeller Center pissoir is better." Ginny's hand hovered over the wicker bread basket, but never descended. Eugene would not have hesitated; Ginny was more careful about her figure. "Every morning I wonder who I should be when I walk out the front door. I don't always have a choice."

"You're less a drag queen and more the Caterpillar in Alice in Wonderland. The one smoking a hookah."

"If you remember that, you also remember that the Caterpillar sits on a magic mushroom. The Alice books are written by a man who also had two identities. One was an Oxford math professor named Charles Dodgson; the other was Lewis Carroll, a pedophile who made up stories to delight his neighbor's little girl. Her name was Alice, of course. Alice Liddel. He took several semi-nude photographs of the kid before her parents became uncomfortable."

"Why did they allow that?"

"They were Victorians. The worst was unthinkable because they had no vocabulary for scandal. All they had was the scandal. That mushroom made a person larger or smaller depending on which side they ate, and naturally it was round, a mathematician's paradox. No sides. Alice asks which side is which, a question that has no answer. She needs to get larger. But before it can answer, the Caterpillar sucks on its hookah and metamorphoses into a butterfly. Hashish will do that."

"Hashish?"

"What do you think was in the hookah? Oregano? Poor Alice has to experiment. She nibbles at two alternatives with no obvious distinctions. Will she grow or shrink?"

"That's my life."

"That dear heart is everybody's life." Ginny's wrist settled to the checkered tablecloth. Her crimson nails matched her miniskirt; her cuticles had the perfection that came with a patient orange stick. "Eventually, to find your way, you have to rip yourself a deeper bite."

KJ liked who she'd become, but she was sure she could not remain an invisible gray moth forever. What might she be next? Hawk, hamster, or hyena?

She felt herself falling into Ginny's limpid dark eyes.

All right, she'd nibble.

Ginny's lips were a subdued coral. A crescent of that color was a crescent imprinted on her wine goblet. Ginny asked for a second bottle, this time a Valpolicella. "I discover more when I am Ginny."

"Like what?"

"Look at this wine. The color is beautiful. Straight men would call it red, maybe dark red. On a good day, they might distinguish light red from pink. They own the world, so they don't need to see more. They see only what they want and so that is what is. Gay men might see cherry or crimson. But women, especially female impersonators, can see burgundy, cherry, scarlet, cerise, ruby, carmine, rose and flame. It's a richer world than anyone knows, if they are just bold enough to look. And what can we make of green, the color of your wonderful eyes? Jade, sea, juniper, olive, and sage." Ginny's voice became softer.

"Ginny, are you flirting with me?"

"Maybe. I am drunk enough. Two bottles and two people? We may set records for Luigi's."

To change the topic, KJ asked: "What about suffering? I was raised Catholic. How about instead of DNA replication, we are born to suffer?"

"Did you bring Tolstoy to lunch? Are we drinking vodka? Suffering is a Russian thing. There is simply no virtue to it. Suffering is suffering. If you insist on suffering, see Benny."

"Who is Benny?" KJ's face had not gone this far AWOL since she'd drunk with Charlotte. Her mind wandered of its own volition into an imagined bedroom with Eugene, or Ginny, or both of them, an impossibility made imaginable by intoxication, a threesome with two bodies, so much less complicated than the reality that would require three people.

"Benny is the guy at the end of Christopher Street who will beat you black and blue for fifty dollars. He has plenty of customers. He wears doeskin gloves and promises to leave no permanent marks. Unless you want them."

"Christ suffered for us." In her mind, the good sisters who first educated her cheered their fallen star pupil.

"The most fucked up people I know are queers who want to be good Catholics. The only sin is gratuitous cruelty. Hippies have it right. Go after the cosmic fuck and forget anything else."

A plate of olives and sharp cheese appeared. Neither of them could recall ordering it. KJ's head was floating in the direction of the moon in the wall mural of the bay at Sorrento, or Naples, or wherever it was that a gondolier in a striped shirt could stand in a boat and sing to the moon. Her head bobbed like a birthday balloon against the tin ceiling. She did not want to leave quite yet, but more wine would have put her on a gurney.

"How about an aperitif?" she said.

"Amaretto or Benedictine? First one to throw up pays."

"Nat's buying," KJ said. "They'll find us dead in the gutter."

"The boys at the morgue are in for a surprise."

Amaretto flowed down her throat like syrupy almonds set afire.

KJ was perspiring. Ginny, on her second Amaretto, seemed to be talking to no one anywhere. KJ was imagining sliding her tongue across that hairless chest. Did Ginny shave her chest? she wondered. To distract herself, she asked: "How did you realize you were gay?"

"Wet dreams, dear heart. I was sure I was defective and thank God I did not hang myself. Being gay is not culture. It is biology."

"But the mannerisms …"

"Yes, there is queer culture, but not every homosexual lisps, minces his walk, or wears girls' clothes. Look at Buster. It's about where and when you are when you learn how to be who you already are. Ancient Athens, Christopher Street, or Provincetown."

"What about femininity? Your favorite fag-hag is having some doubts about herself. I think I am losing track of where I belong."

"Really? It's a whole other thing, not a simple opposite at all. Femininity is a performance. That's why a drag revue will make a gazillion dollars. Are you in crisis?"

KJ was sure she could stand, but was uncertain about getting to the door. "No crisis. Just wondering about myself while I was appreciating John Henry with his hammer. He looked awfully good, but may be half my age."

"That's no crisis. It's good news. When you stop looking, you're dead." Ginny gestured for the check and signed it. "I have to get back to The Box."

"John Henry?"

"No. Buster business. Well, John Henry, too."

Luigi's spun. KJ steadied herself by placing her hands on her chair's back.

"You'll need a cab," Ginny said. She took KJ by the elbow, walked her out Luigi's door, and stood beside her with hand in the air until a taxi stopped. Light snow peppered the air and landed like jewels on Ginny's shoulders and eyelashes.

"Why not come to my place for a late dinner?" KJ said. "Pick something up."

Ginny bent to kiss the air near KJ's ear and whispered. "Don't deny yourself, dear heart. Get some dick." Ginny's grin was the same as Eugene's, white and perfect.

Get some dick? What did Ginny think her dinner invitation was about?

KJ made it home with a cab driver begging her to stop him if she needed to puke. She leaned against the cool metal wall of her elevator, staggered down the hallway, and fell sweating across her unmade bed.

But sleep evaded her. Restless, she thought she'd have to find a way to sleep with Eugene, which she knew would be impossible, but she wanted to. She needed to spend a night wrapped in another person. It was about flesh. Not mind. Not spirit. Body. If she were gentle and took her time, he might give in. They would be two people in the bed, at least three souls. That might prove glorious.

She awakened in the small hours of morning with a world-class headache, then surprised herself and masturbated for the first time in more than a decade. That made the headache worse. When she went to shower, she pulled her sweatshirt over her head to discover her armpits were rank. There are hangovers and there are hangovers, but then there are wine hangovers. KJ shut the hot water and lifted her face into the ice-cold spray so her cupped hands could funnel the equivalent of a gallon of water down her throat. The throbbing in her head eased. When she staggered back to her bed she half-expected to find Eugene.

The only thing tangled in her sheets was regret.

That same week, Eugene was recalled to his soap opera. The trial was back in session. Eugene and eleven other actor-jurors hurriedly signed a guarantee for five days' scale work with options for five days more if the writers figured out a way to send a woman to prison though she'd been found innocent of murder, a murder the TV audience knew she did not commit insofar as the victim remained alive but captive in a villa on a luxurious rockbound island off the coast of Barcelona with a lover whose face never faced the camera.

The Lost Boys of Midtown gathered at Nat's to watch the show and throw popcorn while giggling through the preposterous action. Eugene never spoke, but if the cameras passed over his face the game required that you choose between swallowing a Quaalude or inhaling a popper, amyl nitrate. The pills were mixed with M&Ms in a Florentine glass candy dish. No one could explain the show's plot, least of all Eugene, who reported a lot of griping on set that the trial was escalating costs because every one of the jurors was earning scale, though the show's ratings soared. They sold a lot of soap.

Nat took command of auditions for the No-Name Revue at The Box. He gave KJ a raise so she could work fewer hours at the bookstore but draw the same salary, reinforcing her suspicion he was the bookstore's never-seen owner. If there was an owner, they were robbing the poor bastard blind, of course, but Nat taught KJ to understand that theater-people considered strict honesty a liability. "Sophocles swindled patricians," he said. "It's in Aristotle. In the *Poetics*."

"There's only tragedy in *Poetics*."

"Well, if he had written more, he's have included a long section on swindling patricians."

Nat's small ad asking for talented crossdressers drew a line outside the place that went down the alley and around the block past Luigi's door. KJ spent days standing in fresh slush, her feet turning to blocks of ice, reassuring men in heels that they'd have their chance. There were a dozen Marlene Dietrichs and what must have been twenty Carol Channings among several Judy Garlands until Nat appeared in a chinchilla coat, went down the line, thanked each of them, and told most of the hopefuls to go home. Her reassurances that they would have their chance proved untrue.

The TV trial ended with a hung jury, a term the Lost Boys of Midtown found hilarious. But it also meant Eugene might be called back for a third time. KJ, Nat, and Eugene made plans to open, which meant they went into rehearsals though The Box lacked seats and anything more than basic lighting.

Nat took to wearing Italian loafers and a soft black fedora, and walked with a wooden stave he used to bang out time. When the undated proofs of the first printed programs arrived, KJ was startled to see her name with the credit *Associate Producer* one line below Eugene's name. Nat had edited the proofs. He'd proclaimed himself Dancing Master.

Buzz about the forthcoming revue rose. Every seat for opening night was promised at least twice. There would not be a paying customer in the house.

August 1967—Tuscola, IL

TWO PALE CRESCENTS OF PUSSY's butt peeped above the elastic waistband of his camouflage boxer shorts. Buckles spied on him while pretending to sleep. Cursing softly, he fiddled with the rabbit ears of their room's television. Both Tuscola stations seemed only to broadcast fuzzy electronic snow.

Buckles swung her legs out of bed but stopped to slap at herself beneath the blanket. Her clothes were properly fastened. Pussy claimed to be a fag, but you can't be too careful. Men lied. They lied all the time.

Pussy was about to offer her first shower when, before he could claim gallantry, Buckles snatched her tote and dashed fully dressed across the room to become naked, safe behind a locked bathroom door. Nudity was a luxury.

The shower spray was so hot she could barely endure it. Grit flowed from the folds of her body where no grit should have been able to settle. After a time, she threw a towel onto the tile floor, stepped from the tub, then swiped a clear space through the condensed mist on the mirror. The purple-yellow bruise on her breast had faded to more yellow than purple, but her arms would not be clear of Big Bill's handprints for a while. Her mind, well, maybe never. No shower could be hot enough.

Wrapped in a second large towel, she peeled cellophane from the pink plastic razor the motel supplied. She had no shaving cream, but the bar soap worked just fine until she nicked a spot on her knee, a spot she often cut at home no matter how much Extra Creamy Barbasol she used. Her knee must have been built wrong.

That stupid song by Scott McKenzie failed to mention drug-crazed truckers tearing the flowers from your hair with plans to sell you to rapist criminals in Kansas. The song said nothing about strangers grabbing your tits. *The Village Voice* omitted mention of the road monsters hauling smack, speed, and crystal over America's highways. Buckles composed indignant letters in her head. People needed to know. *The Voice* and *Rolling Stone* should print her letters on their front page. Buckles was owed an apology.

Naked and by herself in the bathroom mist, she started to cry at the hopelessness of it, but then stopped herself. Self-pity not only sucked, it did no good. She would never cry again. Instead, if she ever saw Big Bill or anyone like him, she'd be ready. She'd need a knife, at least five inches of sharp steel, maybe seven. For now, all she could do was seize control of her shakes before her shakes seized control of her.

The trickle of blood scabbed at her knee. Buckles unrolled her last clean black T-shirt, a pair of the panties Grandma had paid for, and stepped into her cutoffs. Her boobs were too tender for a bra. She had to bend from the waist to use the motel's blow dryer bolted to the wall. That made her scalp feel so good she balled her Star-Bangled Banana Bandana and threw it into her rainbow tote. Once again, Buckles looked like the envy of every girl at Dobbs, a surfer girl in an ad for Breck Shampoo. The real reason she hated her hair was that it brought her unearned praise and unwanted attention.

When she stepped from the bathroom, Pussy was dancing from one foot to the other. He barely had time to shut the door behind him. He peed noisily. "You're as bad as my sister was," he called through the door. "What is it with girls? Who needs three towels for one shower?"

She brushed her hair until Pussy emerged with the broad white towel she'd left on the floor wrapped around his waist. He asked her to turn away, which she did, sort of. With her fingers over her eyes she peeked into the mirror to see Pussy's pale behind vanish into briefs and baggy camouflage pants. Whatever Army basic training was about, it left Pussy with ropey arms, a washboard belly, and a muscled ass. His black hair, shaved clean by the Army, was growing long enough to hang over his eyes. His beard was coming in thick as a poet's. He yanked tight his clanking black garrison belt and told her she could turn around, never guessing she'd seen the whole show.

When they checked with Grandma, her green eyes peered out to them from beneath the edge of her blanket. Her room was cold. The air conditioner rattled.

"I'm calling a rest," she said, her chin above the bedsheet. "We are taking the day off. This rat hole is better than most, the Edsel can't be spotted from the highway, and that diner doesn't look half bad. It's not the Ritz, but if the bugs do not eat you alive, you two can swim in that pool tonight." The many times Buckles slipped nude into the pool behind her parents' house, she had been alone under a slim moon. It would be different to skinny-dip with Pussy. Maybe this was what it was like to have a brother. "You two can have some fun while I catch my breath."

She struggled to roll to her hip without moaning and gestured with a limp wave that was a dismissal. "Bring my medicine from the car, get yourself some breakfast, and get back to me. Don't forget the pills." She sucked on her teeth as if stricken by sudden sharp pain. Pussy opened her purse.

"Without the bandana," Pussy said in the parking lot, "you look like a movie star."

Buckles had heard it before. You were supposed to blush and smile and deny a compliment, but if Pussy was going to be her brother, she wanted something different. No more bullshit. "All my hair ever did was make life harder. My mother has the same problem. It's the only thing we ever agreed about. If you tell dumb blonde jokes, I will have to hurt you."

"Then no faggot jokes about lisps."

They stopped to shake hands. "I had a Chemistry teacher tell me not to worry if I did not understand how to balance chemical equations because blondes never needed to know. So I aced every test he gave us just to piss him off. I got an A. Everyone was after me for cheerleading. I love swimming team because when you are in the water you are completely alone. Can't even hear crowd noises. I love my morning workout in a pool, but I hate cheerleading. Hate it. Hate cheerleaders, hate cheerleading, hate football, hate pom-poms, and think twirling a baton is psychotic."

"Tell me how you really feel about it."

"It's not funny, Puss." She grabbed the diner's door handle. "My prep school pep squad makes me want to vomit through my eyes. Boys tell me really stupid jokes and I have to smile when what I want to do is punch their faces. The worst are the pimply assholes who think they are cute when they ask me to prove I am a real blonde."

The Illinois August morning air was already hot and damp, the diner felt nearly as chilled as Grandma Dot's room. She wished she'd worn more than a Dickey T-shirt, cut-offs, and her sandals. Socks would have helped. Gooseflesh rippled over her thighs. No one seemed to notice the hippie girl and boy who took a booth by the plate glass window.

Pussy buttered two slices of raisin toast. She had Sugar Pops, but when Buckles reached across the table to take his second slice of toast from his plate, he said nothing, as if they had spent a lifetime gobbling from each other's plates.

"Pussy, why don't you just tell the Army you are queer?" Buckles said, whispering. "Wouldn't that get you discharged?"

"I could not do that."

"Why not?"

"It's complicated," he said, shrugging. "In my head, it's all about my father."

"But he's dead."

"Not in my head he's not. Besides, the Army won't believe me. I took an oath. They'll put me in a stockade and have my head cracked open with a shlock." He answered the question forming on her lips before she uttered it. "That's a padlock in a sweat sock. They beat queers with them."

"You're being stupid."

"Probably."

"Your grandmother looks pasty," Buckles said over their second coffee.

"Good days and bad days, but this is the first time she has ever said she wanted to take the day off. She'll bury both of us, though." Buckles was not so sure. "She is right about one thing, though. This looks like a good place to hide out."

"I am sorry about last night."

"What for?"

"I think I was a little hysterical."

"You were a lot hysterical, but I was glad to be there for you." He shrugged. "Forget it."

Buckles was forgetting nothing any time soon. "You make me feel safe. Did I really sleep next to you all night?"

He nodded.

"And you held me. Now I can say I spent a night in a boy's arms."

"Just leave out the part about me being a homo. There's not a lot of status in that for you. So you're a virgin?"

"Mostly. Technically." Pussy looked at her skeptically. "All right. No."

Pussy laughed and then became solemn. "Let's be Hansel and Gretel. We'll drop breadcrumbs everywhere we go, and fight witches. I'll have your back and you'll have mine."

"You lie; I'll swear," Buckles said.

"If I ever get a tattoo, that will be what it says. Our motto. For life."

They shook hands. They were suddenly solemn, bound into a permanent unit.

"Where is Grandma taking you?"

"I haven't the slightest. We go back and forth and north and south, loop the loop across the country because she thinks we have to lose people who may be following us. Nobody is following us, I am sure. We go in circles to lose ghosts. We were all the way to Nebraska when she had me double back to the East. We might have gone as far as West Virginia except that we saw you in Ohio. I think having you aboard has given her a new strategy. We're not just running from MPs. Grandma thinks someone is following her, too. She may be a little paranoid. Maybe a lot paranoid. Don't ask her who 'they' are. She'll just say 'the boys.' I can't figure out what that might mean unless it means 'the mob.' But that's totally crazy. Why would gangsters chase a sick old lady who ran from a geriatric home? Don't ask about her sunglasses, either. They are cheap crap, but she keeps them on her at all times. Says they are valuable. Cheap sunglasses."

"I like her, though."

"She does not know how to be mean. She invented a past for herself when she was in that place. I think her stories gave her status. At least people listened to her. Now she believes her own stories. Grandma is her own invention."

Pussy purchased three jelly donuts and stopped at the Edsel for Grandma's medicine, a vial of pills that rattled like an infant's toy, and three bomber joints that could get them hard time anywhere in America.

Perspiring in her cold room, her sheets damp with that sweat, the lights growing darker every moment, Grandma recollected the slippery feel of the clay beneath the outcropping of rock at the Tahoe lake house. She felt the mud on her hands, more real than the cheap sheets under her fingers or the television across room, its screen dull with static and electronic snow. The metal cashbox that had waited twenty years would have to rust undisturbed a few years more. Its grave was shallow and damp, which hers was likely to be as well. She was sure the loaded revolver in the box was no morphine dream. It was a .38. These things existed as sure as her diamonds that could become the cash money that bailed out the Edsel, bought her medicine, and paid for rooms at the Tuscola Arms.

She clutched at the glasses looped at her neck. If she could see better than a brick she'd count the remaining stones again, but the

fact was that her eyes, like most of what was left of her, were no longer sharp enough to distinguish between a gem and a rhinestone.
Her guts burbled like lava, her bowels readying to erupt without
warning again. She'd need to sprint to a toilet to escape her own
mess. Dot had gotten this far by pretending that the prairie fire rag-
ing in her innards was the sign that her body strained to fix itself,
but she could no longer kid herself. The rat in her belly was surely
Death, gnawing its way free.

Dot needed to live a little longer. Just a little. Sweetboy needed
her protection, but she could only protect him by telling him everything she knew. He was a good boy, a sweet boy, an unassuming
boy, and while he was not an idiot, his innocence left him vulnerable. Who else would volunteer for the Army knowing full well
that being queer was less than a career advantage in the military?
Sweetboy had the heart and mind of an eager puppy in a world that
ate dogs.

But this Buckles had summoned up guile at a moment's notice.
The kid might be just be the ticket. The blond hippie's presence in
the Edsel might turn the odds in Sweetboy's favor; maybe they'd be
able to drive in a straight line at high speeds, looking like regular
citizens going from one place to another and wanting to get there.
Ditching the Edsel would be the smart move, too. It was about as
inconspicuous as a cockroach swimming in a bowl of milk, but the
car was dear to her and the girl might add the camouflage they
needed. Sweetboy's beard grew too slowly, but the blonde kid might
make all the difference in a tight spot. Look how she'd distracted
that fool trooper in Ohio. With the blonde hippie in the car, they'd
be just another family on the Great American Highway on a route
from Here to There.

Her room was chilled enough to store porterhouse at Buckhorn's.
That was in Denver, or was Buckhorn's in Chicago? Details evap-
orated faster than piss on a hot rock. The gaps between what she
knew, had forgotten, and what she thought she knew were widening into chasms, and some of it could never have been true at all.
The erosion of her mind terrified her more than death. Marijuana

and morphine opened fissures in memories that she pasted together with dreams, inventions as necessary as salt to soup. She suffered galloping CRS. Can't Remember Shit, the disease with no telethon and only one dismal outcome.

When Sweetboy's asshat-father blew his family to Kingdom Come, Dot violated one of her cardinal rules. She'd taken pity on Leitner's only son, Felix.

She'd been a fool.

Like everything else, it was a long story, made more complicated by her inclination to the joys of deceit. Ambrose had brought home his fourth bride, Dot, but to maintain peace in the family the old man tacked ten years onto her age on their American marriage certificate, the original having been lost in the files of a drunken Justice of the Peace in Tobago. With the flourish of a pen, instead of being twenty-two years older than his bride, Ambrose was made to seem a mere twelve. That judicious lie rose up to bite Dot on the ass after Ambrose followed a marlin to the bottom of the Caribbean. After a suitable period of mourning during which she'd shared a small room with Sweetboy, John Leitner hired an ambulance-chaser to parley the falsehood about her age with another falsehood. Dot's grief at the demise of her aged husband had worsened non-existent senility. Lies designed to keep the peace in a family now all dead had leveraged her into Arborside, God's Waiting Room in the Berkshires.

To be sure, Dot had signed the papers willingly, figuring three hots and a cot in the countryside might be just the ticket until things settled, but in the pack of papers the shyster slipped in front of her had been a Power of Attorney triggered by Leitner's death. The idea was to have her declared *non compus mentis* to protect Ambrose's fortune, but Leitner could not know that he and his family would all go up in smoke simultaneously. The iron gate at Arborside clanged irrevocably shut welded by a web of legal documents she herself had signed.

Arborside owned her. In exchange, she owned cloth slippers that flopped off her feet, a thin pink flannel housecoat missing two clear plastic flower buttons, and a wooden crate filled with the accumulated crap of a lifetime they put in a storage shed behind the main building. No one but Dot knew that in the stored crap were diamonds she had set into cheap, plastic sunglasses.

In winter, Dot shuffled to the windows close enough to cloud the glass with her breath, wrote *Help* backwards with her index finger, then stood back to watch the glass go clear. In spring and summer, those slippers slapping at her heels, she followed well-trodden grass paths to abrupt ends at stone walls or to the black rusted gate where she waved at passing cars until a polite, soft-spoken orderly the size of Mont Blanc hoisted Dot, kicking, over his shoulders. She'd flashed a passing Mercedes once, but baring her chest earned her only a week's promotion from yellow to blue Valium that left her mind awash in petroleum jelly.

So a world-class backgammon champion was consigned to endless rounds of Parcheesi, proof that God had a mean streak and a meaner sense of humor. Dot was world-class, or had been. She was sure of that. That was why *Dorothy* was known as *Dot*. Parcheesi was backgammon for simpletons. At Arborside, she had played with "the girls," a knot of sweet, senile, frequently incontinent women who gazed at each other each new day with no flicker of recognition.

When the Leitners exited this world, Dot breathed a sincere prayer for their two children and believed she'd walk out of Arborside. The Director, however, a pissant in a cheap plaid suit had other ideas. He informed her that the Power of Attorney had devolved to him. She need not worry about her wellbeing for she would be a ward of the Commonwealth for as long as he said she was not ready for independence. Arborside would collect a monthly stipend for her maintenance. They moved her to a shared room with an unfortunate woman who spoke no words but stared out their window and whooped whenever she saw a bird.

Then, as if rising from the ashes, Sweetboy's letter arrived. Her prayers for his immortal soul had been premature.

When the Leitner house exploded at three in the morning, Sweetboy had been out, a stroke of luck Dot fervently hoped meant he'd been getting laid. He wrote how he had decided to find a new home, new purpose, and new family in the US Army.

The boy was plainly deranged by grief. A stint in the Army could leave a man blind, without his legs, maybe without his face, but a loop of stout rope over a sturdy rafter above an unsteady chair had swift finality, if he did not screw it up, which Sweetboy almost certainly would do. Dot knew Sweetboy was queer as a blue three-dollar bill. Why else would a healthy teenage boy hide muscle magazines of beefcake glistening with mineral oil under his mattress? The Vietcong and his barrack mates posed equal risks to his life.

Men bewildered Dot; in any war the young needed only to put their bayonets through the ribs of the flaccid old farts who sent them off to die for national honor or credibility or some other horseshit, and then get back to the more rewarding life of fornicating for fun. Even the most dedicated soldier in Hitler's Wehrmacht should have found lying between the trembling thighs of some Aryan *fräulein* superior to freezing his ass off at Stalingrad.

Instead, old men unfurled flags and wrapped them around intangible ideas before sending youth off to a very tangible grass-covered hole in the very tangible dirt until their mothers received a very tangible bit of parchment as a very tangible keepsake of a son who'd perished.

Unblushingly, the old men called it duty and sacrifice. What it was, in fact, was wholesale murder. John Phillip Sousa was a goddam war criminal.

She had to go to Sweetboy's rescue. Departing Arborside required cunning, scheming deceit, calculated ruthlessness, and money. She had plenty of wealth in the form of shiny rocks, and that meant Takooshian, her old fence in Boston, assuming he still lived. With cash, she'd liberate the Edsel. With the Edsel, she'd hightail it to the pine wilds of New Jersey where Sweetboy was taking basic training.

Grandma was unsure how she'd spring the boy, but any plan had to begin with a break from Arborside and a bus ticket to Boston. The rest, she had been sure, would come to her.

If she could have lifted the other Arborside residents by the ankles, she'd have shaken them until coins fell from their pockets, but the nickel and dime wagers at Parcheesi mounted up once they raised the stakes from cough drops to nickels. When Bebe suggested canasta, Dot could have kissed her, but said, "You'll have to teach me to play." Those old ladies might forget their children's names, but canasta was acid-etched on their souls. Dot's marks forked over genuine folding money reeking of Frangipani or Bain de Soleil, the money from a fragrant sock in the back of a bureau drawer. If any orderly and or nurse cared that in the TV room Dot was winning more than Maverick, they made no mention of it.

Dot also hoarded her allowance from the weekly candy and cough drop run. More nickles and dimes, but like Boy Scouts in open air on a diet of beef, her quarters quickly matured into dollars, and her dollars, God bless them, aggregated to Benjamins.

Knowing she was close, one night she snuck out to the storage barn behind the trees to retrieve her Audrey Hepburn sunglasses. She swiped at cobwebs, stepped over mouse shit, and made her way through the smell of mildew, dust, and time. She liberated a rusted shovel from a rotted rope dangling over the barn's back door. It brushed against the single lightbulb that dangled bare from a rafter. The swiftly shifting shadows gave her a spot of vertigo. Her luck was with her; her crate was on top of two others. She pried loose the top. Her stored dresses smelled as if she had been buried in them, so she realized she'd need new, but she fished out the sunglasses, relieved that they existed at all, having trembled at one terrible moment that in her bouts with Valium and medicated delirium she'd invented the sunglasses. She returned to the residence with her clenched fists in her flannel bathrobe's pockets after spitting on her palms to clear them of rust from the shovel.

On the next run to the mall, Dorothy slipped away to drop three precious quarters into a phone to call Arturo's Body Shop in Lawrence, the dirty little decaying factory town north of Boston. Even at her age, it was nothing for a world-class backgammon champion to remember every telephone number she'd ever need.

Arturo organized platoons of under-aged Dominican boys to boost cars from nearby Andover, specializing in Mercedes, Audi, and Cadillac. The gang could strip a car faster than Biblical locusts denuded hillsides in the Promised Land. Arturo supplied allegedly legitimate body shops that in turn charged their customers standard prices, about three times what Arturo charged. Everyone was happy except the insurance companies.

The Edsel, the last thing she'd purchased with poor drowned Ambrose's money, was a road yacht. Her heart had a soft spot for it. Like Dot, the Edsel had lain low, drained of fluids, peacefully rusting while awaiting resurrection. It was true that the Edsel was dangerously conspicuous, but Dot was not about to ride to Sweetboy's rescue in a station wagon. Partly about style, her decision had as much to do with the grating pains in her hips, back, and neck. The Edsel had plush seats.

Her heart leapt when Arturo Jr. said her car was under a dust-covered tarp, but her heart fell to learn that Arturo himself, his blessed father, was with Jesus. "One second the old man was blowing cigar smoke in my eyes and calling me stupid, the next he falls onto his face. He went all blue, jew-know?" He pronounced it *jew-know*. Arturo Jr. asked: "When jew need it?"

"Immediately," she said. A flubbed answer because her anxiety to ride to Sweetboy's rescue leeched into her tone. "I also need some medicine."

"What kind of medicine?"

The car back to Arborside would be leaving the mall in minutes, so she had no time to discuss alternatives. "Morphine," she said. "The kind in pills."

And heard Arturo Jr.'s low whistle.

"You don't fuck around, do you, lady? How many pills? That can cost. Heroin is easier."

"I don't like needles."

"You can smoke it."

Dot shook her head. There was no regulating the strength of a powder prepared by criminals and cut with quinine or baking soda or who knew what.

"Can you get morphine or not?"

"This is Lawrence. I can get you whatever you need. Bring money. I'll get you fixed up. I don' like talking on the phone."

Like a jackal that smelled fallen prey, Arturo Jr. picked up the stink of hot money. For all he knew, she might have been running girls, guns, or smack. All the same to the little dirt-bag whose father had cut a deal Dot hoped he'd honor. But Arturo Sr. was worm food, and Arturo Jr. did not believe that honor and obligations passed from one generation to the next.

Dot agreed to triple what she'd agreed to pay his father for holding her car. Her medicine could not be priced. She was being buggered, but what else could she do? Complain to the Better Business Bureau? Vietnam was no playground. Sweetboy could be shipped out before she could make it to Fort Dix.

Arturo Jr. would dismantle the Edsel down to the bolts in search of bricks of cash or cocaine or heroin, and when he found nothing he'd do it second time.

Three days later on an Arborside fieldtrip to the movies, she vanished in the dark theater, made a phone call to summon a car service to the Stockbridge bus station. She slept eight hours on the bus, peeing without touching the bus's toilet seat, a posture that left her with wet sneakers and shaky legs. A coffin had more space than the pisser on the Trailways. In the predawn gloom of Boston's South Station, bus fumes stung her eyes. She collapsed into a cab and uttered the name of the only hotel she could remember.

The Omni Parker bellman seemed skeptical that her luggage would follow in a day or two, but at least no one could accuse a gray-haired bundle of knobby elbows and knees wearing a droopy flannel housecoat of being a call girl. She had enough folding cash tucked into her sneakers to pay for two nights in advance. Cash elevated her status from *homeless and crazy* to *eccentric and rich*, the Omni's specialty. The bellman showed her the suite that had been Babe Ruth's favorite, a detail about which she cared not a flying fig and doubted it was true, anyway. He flipped lights on and off as if electricity might be a mystery to the old lady. He had not lifted a bag, but she tipped him a dollar—in quarters.

Early morning room service brought a half bottle of chilled chardonnay and six oysters, a service available to the rich and eccentric. Then she puked before laying back in near-sleep in a warm tub. She wondered whether Babe Ruth's bare ass appreciated the unforgiving porcelain any more than her own boney bottom.

At daybreak, she pinned up her hair, looped her sunglasses on their beaded cord around her neck, and faced the day. She was burning through the little cash she had. She walked slowly to Downtown Crossing, becoming breathless only once. She purchased a beaded straw bag from a pushcart, then in Filene's Basement found three pairs of pedal pushers, red, pale blue, and mint green. The salesgirl called them Capri Pants but goddam pedal pushers were goddam pedal pushers. She stepped into the green pair before tightly rolling the others into the bag, then hooked herself into a new white brassiere she barely needed but without which she would feel naked, and then tugged her head through the collar of one of two new cotton pullovers, a boat-neck collar with a thread of lime green embroidery at the neckline. Finally, she stepped sockless into a pair of very white canvas Tretorns. On the street, she dropped her Arborside flannel nightie into a trash barrel, and only then made a second breakfast of a doughy pretzel chosen more for the salt than for hunger. She washed the pretzel down with a can of Fresca, waited, and was pleased that nothing came up.

Across the street from Filene's Basement was the Jeweler's Building, so decrepit the only thing holding it up was the two taller buildings on each side. Behind an unspectacular glass door was a framed floor directory. Takooshian's was still on the fourth floor, one of three jewelry merchants well away from street crowds, smash-and-grab hoodlums, and the eyes of police.

The elevator groaned like her bowels.

If the largish woman behind the counter found stones embedded in cheap plastic unusual, nothing in her expression showed it. She poked one loose, snapped on a bright white overhead light, and peered at it through a jeweler's glass on a square of black velvet, turning it several times with a tiny wooden pick. Even Dot's failing eyes saw how light danced in the gem as if alive. The woman grunted.

Dorothy, perched on a wooden stool, asked: "And how is Sevan?"

"You know my father?"

"You must be little Kohar."

The woman's dark eyes widened with wonder. "No one has called me that for a very long time. I am now 'Gemma,' but, please, Kohar if you will."

"Your father. How is he?" Dot asked, expecting the worst. Everyone she'd ever loved was dead or dying. People fell away; life went on. She'd join them soon enough.

"My father is with my mother, bless them both."

"Passed then?"

"No. They are in Boca Raton. How did you know him?"

Dot brightened. "May they thrive a hundred years more. We did some business in the old days. It was of little significance. My name is Dot. Your father and I shared a mutual understanding. He needed stones, I required money, we did business."

"Will you have tea?"

Dot risked skipping the social nicety and apologized. She had to depart soon, a matter of being on a certain commuter train to Lawrence from North Station. Did Kohar conduct business as her father had done with trusted customers? No paper, cash, and an honored inviolable handshake?

Kohar insisted on telephoning her father. Friends from the old days did not appear at her door every day. Dorothy must stay even if Kohar herself had to close the shop and drive her to Lawrence.

In a back room, Kohar whispered in Armenian into a telephone. Kohar returned to explain. "My father could not come to the phone. He grows old. His hips, his knees … I talk to my mother, she talks to my father, he talks to my mother, and she talks to me." She shook her head in wonder at her father's perseverance over bad luck. "Eighty-six, may he live forever, but he sends you his warmest love and respect. He asks if you still win your finest stones playing chess."

"Sevan's memory must be failing. Such a pity. My game was backgammon."

Kohar pressed her palm to her ample chest. "Forgive me, grandmother. His memory is perfect. The fault is mine. Not five minutes ago, he said backgammon! Of course! How could I be so stupid?" Kohar smiled broadly. Dot had passed a test; she was indeed the woman from the old days who could be trusted. "Come. Let me see the stone once more, since you are pressed for time. Are you certain I cannot offer you tea?"

"Perhaps a cup. But the train, alas, will not wait."

Kohar brewed strong tea in a small stone pot from leaves in an infuser and a kettle on a hot plate. Then the two women dickered, but not bitterly. While Dot had been cooling her heels behind the gate at Arborside, her diamonds had tripled in value.

Kohar shrugged her shoulders and said that if her father were with them, he would murder his own daughter for being overly generous, but to honor old friends is a daughter's duty and privilege. "You cannot make new old friends," Kohar said. She dropped two sugar cubes into her Limoges teacup on its matching saucer that sat on an engraved silver service that might have been etched by Paul Revere. She could offer two thousand for the one stone. As for the other eight stones, she'd have to look at each, though if they were as flawless as this one and weighed as much, they'd all be worth roughly the same, perhaps more if someone were to want matched stones for an elegant heirloom piece. "More than that and my two boys will lack bread."

Dorothy did not want her children to go hungry. She thought of the irony if the stones were to journey from an heirloom piece in a white gold setting to loose stones embedded in plastic sunglasses only to be rejoined in a new heirloom piece. "Three thousand," she said. "Each."

"All of them?"

"Two. But to honor your father, take the best two."

They settled on twenty-seven hundred each, cash in fifties and hundreds taken from a backroom safe. Kohar dropped the money into two large manila envelopes marked Interoffice Memo, the envelopes fastened by a loop of red string. The envelopes nestled below the folded clothes on the bottom of Dot's straw bag.

In the near-empty mid-day commuter railroad car, Dorothy lifted her feet onto the straw bag. She had not moved this much this quickly in years, and though her legs ached and her hips throbbed, she felt pretty good. At the Lawrence railroad station, she dropped coins into a payphone to summon Arturo Jr. As agreed, he'd deliver the Edsel and her medicine. She sat in the sun on a distant bench to redistribute her money, what she'd owe Arturo Jr. in a single envelope along with some extra, the rest buried deep in the beaded bag beneath her pedal pushers. It would not do to have the little thieving shit see her entire bankroll. Pedal pushers. She wondered if she could manage to ride a bicycle.

The Edsel's engine was a throaty hum; the paint glowed; the chrome gleamed. The little weasel had done a decent job. "Your medicine is in the glove compartment in a vial. All I could get on short notice was fifty morphine pills. But they are the real shit. Be careful with that morphine shit, too. You got pills and capsules. You need it quick, you open the capsule. You can chew the pills, too."

"Why?"

"It will work faster. I got to tell you, lady. The people I know say you should want heroin."

"I'm old fashioned. My money is up to date, though."

"Ain't you gonna look?"

"Are you going to screw me over?"

"Why would I do that?"

"Then I don't have to look."

He counted her money, licking his fingertips every third bill, then climbed into the passenger seat of a pickup that had followed the Edsel to the station.

Her trembling hand found the vial. She rattled it like a baby's toy, then extracted one. She knew they would be hard to replace so she would have to allow herself very few and only at the worst times. The pills were off-white or blue. She took a smaller pill and her teeth broke it in half along a slit cut into its surface, then chewed it. Morphine suffused her like a lover.

Eager to ride to Sweetboy's rescue, she nevertheless sat at the railroad terminal for her first pain-free hours in months. She'd have to drive the resurrected Edsel back to the Omni Parker. It had been a while since she was behind a wheel, and she could not risk being stopped any police. It would take time for that first high to pass. She was suddenly in no hurry.

Once the buzz faded, Dot drove precisely, squinting to see over the steering wheel, actually using her sunglasses as sunglasses. Driving was like riding a bicycle or swimming, impossible to forget, and that every other car in Massachusetts passed her with a driver raising a finger to the old lady on a highway doing forty in a while convertible was simply evidence she was being justifiably cautious. The Edsel's brakes pulled slightly left, but not terribly so. She kept the top down, the same as when Arturo Jr. had delivered the car, but she also had the air conditioning vents blasting directly at her face. The radio worked, even if there was nothing worth listening to. If there was a big band station, she could not find it. She hummed *Chattanooga Choo-Choo*, *In the Mood*, and *String of Pearls* while she mourned Glenn Miller's passing and tried to recall a medley of Dorsey Brothers' hits.

If the hotel doorman remembered the old lady that a day earlier appeared in a housecoat and not much else, he showed no sign of it. He slid behind the wheel after he placed her straw bag on the sidewalk, never realizing that the bag that looked like it belonged on Revere Beach held a year of his salary, enough drugs to put the entire hotel staff on Cloud 9, and that the sunglasses casually hanging on a cord from the old woman's neck were worth enough to send three kids to college. The car squealed around a corner into an underground garage.

Maybe the Edsel was a mistake, too unforgettable, but be damned if she would travel ever again on a bus that reeked of shit, cheap perfume, and unwashed bodies.

Room service delivered a crisp bacon, lettuce, and tomato sandwich. She managed to keep down half of it by scraping away the mayonnaise and sipping from a small bottle of Perrier with every tiny bite.

She was ready to ride to Sweetboy's rescue. If not her, who?

Dot refused to back up the Edsel until she spoke to the man in charge. The sergeant at the Texas Road Fort Dix gate had a face like the back of a bus rear-ended by a Mack truck, but also managed to look as if he would cry. He had standing orders for pacifist Catholic priests, pointy-headed professors, anyone wearing sandals, your hippies or other subversive types, but he had no orders for little old ladies in lime green pedal pushers. Someone was sure to tell him to use initiative. The old lady was FUBAR, strictly FUBAR.

Dot propped her bony hips against the Edsel's front fender and dropped the Edsel keys down the front of her blouse. The keys damn near slid to the ground, she was so thin, but the gesture gave her the upper hand.

The sergeant summoned a lieutenant.

The lieutenant summoned a captain.

The captain summoned a major.

The major summoned a lieutenant colonel.

The sandy-haired lieutenant colonel was an aging college boy with a face deeply lined by all he had seen. Two months earlier, he'd lain semi-conscious while his wounds were bound in an air-conditioned tent in Cam Rahn Bay, a base noted for its pink sand beach, gentle surf, and its officers' mess specializing in steak and lobster. He'd arrived in country a green captain with the First Air Cavalry, became a major when he signed for a second tour, and fought with distinction in the Ia Drang Valley where the ARVN motherfuckers fired something—he never knew what—that ripped four inches of his thigh right off his leg but somehow left his balls, bones, and femoral artery intact, the artery strangely visible and pulsing with his tenuous life. The wound gave him his ticket home, a clean bed at Walter Reed for weeks, a limp he'd have all the rest of his life, a Purple Heart, and a pair of silver oak leaves.

Nothing he'd studied had prepared the lieutenant colonel for a war lacking front lines, a war for which territorial capture was meaningless, a war where enemy supply lines snaked south down the Ho Chi Minh Trail through countries allegedly neutral that therefore could not be bombed, occupied, or disrupted by any ordinary military tactic. The Army knew how to win wars; but the rules did not apply in Nam. The only trusted rule was to kill them all and let God sort them out later. He'd become overly familiar with the chatter of BARs and the shredded gobbets of men who'd stepped on claymores or were caught beneath a Bouncing Betty. He'd ordered his own men to pacify thatch-roof villages by burning huts to the ground with flickering G.I.-issue Zippo lighters. And as a captain he had ordered men to open fire at a child of ten.

The kid had come running at them up a dirt road. Its hands were in the air when a bullet found the kid's Semtex vest, evaporating the kid in a flash of violent pink light. They could only speculate if the kid had been a boy or a girl. Having been right about opening fire on the little gook booby trap did not, however, put his mind at ease. He had six children of his own, and all this time later he was still getting little sleep wondering what the kid's last moments were like, full knowing the men behind him would blow him up when he drew close to the Americans, and full knowing the Americans would shoot him dead if he drew too close. It was the dilemma of every soldier: death at his rear, death before him, death if he stood his ground. The Fort Dix head sawbones held that eventually time healed all wounds, though the lieutenant colonel seriously doubted that particular bit of military wisdom. He had found a home in the Army, but he no longer wished to lead men. Becoming a full bird colonel was for some war lover, not for him.

The old lady was a welcome distraction, but her car, that outlandish very American bone white convertible, was more than that, a sign as sure as God's Rainbow was for Noah that the lieutenant colonel was back in the real world, the blessed home of the brave and free. An ember of his forgotten life glowed anew. The absurd car brought back long lazy days in western Tennessee beneath a jalopy polished with multiple coats of Blue Turtle Wax, of cars with open engines, days of white wall tires, wire hubcaps, polished chrome pipes, and double-barrel carburetors that sucked in nitro fuel faster than a boy drank milk, memories he'd thought extinguished beneath the stink of jungle rot that lingered in his nostrils and mixed with the smoke of a firefight. The Edsel revived memories of sultry nights scooping the loop in his own modified Ford while scheming to lure willing cheerleaders into the rumble seat. Boys headed for VMI dreamed of gallantry and sacrifice, not blowing up children laced into explosives and prodded to run directly at the enemy, hands raised and shouting the only English it would ever know: *No shoot no shoot no shoot.*

The lieutenant colonel's fingers stroked the Edsel's satiny finish with the same tender reverence with which he stroked his wife's bare back, so when he politely asked the old lady if he could sit in the driver's bucket seat simply to enjoy the feel of the red leather, and she said: "Knock yourself out, colonel," he did not correct her on his rank. He cautioned her, as much as he admired the Edsel and appreciated her generosity, he hoped Miss Dot, as she asked to be called, appreciated he would not hesitate to do his duty. Either move the vehicle or a tank would crush it flat.

Dot sat in the passenger seat beside him and played her rarest card, always a last resort; she told him the truth. She whispered that she was dying, a fact her grandson did not know and trusted the colonel would not tell him. She only hoped to set eyes on him for a few moments before her final breath. He could look it up, but she was sure that Private Felix Leitner's records indicated he was an orphan. As she was his grandmother by marriage, no blood relative, a hardship leave was out of the question. Did the duty of an officer and a gentleman require denying a woman her dying wish? A few hours, no more.

The lieutenant colonel emphasized that Private Leitner was not at summer camp, but his heart had softened too much at this chance to sip virtue, so he telephoned a company clerk from the sentry post and held the wire until the file was found that could verify that Private Leitner, a recent enlistee, had listed no living relatives and had no known next of kin. Private Leitner was at that very moment hauling ass and a 40-pound pack in high humidity through a pine forest and over the red clay mosquito-infested terrain of a 15-mile obstacle course.

The lieutenant colonel gave an order and returned to Dot to explain they would need to wait a short while, but her grandson would be delivered to the gate. While they waited, he wondered if it might be best to take the Edsel from the center of the access road. Knowing she had bagged him, Dot asked that he drive the car onto the road's shoulder for her, and it was not lost on her that the lieutenant colonel's hands gripped the red steering wheel tenderly as a lover. The Edsel's throaty purr made the lieutenant colonel grin. He lowered the top for her and they waited for Sweetboy while he explained again his rules for what amounted to an instant leave for the recruit. Twenty minutes of privacy in her car as long as Dot, Private Leitner, and the Edsel stayed within sight.

Parked with the top down, the musty smell of pine in summer rose around them. The lieutenant colonel's hands circled the wheel while they chatted about his two daughters, four sons, and his wife, Lurline, whose peach pie was worthy of worship. He had attended VMI in Lexington, Virginia.

"God's own country," Dot said.

"You know it?"

"I know it well," she said, lying. "Peanuts, hogs, and the beautiful Blue Ridge." Summarizing all she knew about Virginia in a single phrase.

Dot swore no one would ever learn of his kindness, at least not from her. He was right to fear a long line of filthy peaceniks appearing at the gate tomorrow all demanding to visit soldiers. "The price of no good deed goes unpunished," she said, realizing she'd mangled the cliché but unsure exactly how. The half dose of morphine she'd swallowed a hour before when she first caught sight of the gate was not done addling her mind.

Sweetboy himself finally trotted up, his fatigues dark with perspiration, his face streaked by grime. They exited the car to greet him; Sweetboy snapped a salute at the lieutenant colonel, still bewildered at having been snatched from his unit, expecting some form of discipline, and amazed to see his grandmother. His pack dropped to the ground and raised a small cloud of dust. The lieutenant colonel grinned at the fulfillment of his own good deed, his first deposit on his debt at the Bank of Karma.

Without cracking open the car door, Dot tumbled Sweetboy ass over tea kettle into the passenger seat. He fell under the glovebox with his boots in the air. Grandma hurried to the driver's side, put the car in gear, hissed, "Stay down," and then shouted gaily over her shoulder, "Back by dinner!" The lieutenant colonel's mouth gaped open, but by then Dot had the Edsel's rear tires spitting gravel and raising white smoke. "Keep your head down in case the cocksuckers shoot," she said, floored the accelerator, and, roaring, the car fishtailed onto the dirt road.

Five miles away, beyond the immediate reach of Fort Dix, Sweetboy explained once more to Dot that he had never been drafted. He'd enlisted. He'd be AWOL and then declared a deserter. Did Grandma understand that? They needed to obey the rules and turn around. Canada was a refuge for draft dodgers, not deserters. She was making him an outlaw. "I took an oath, Grandma."

If she had not believed the entire US Army was in hot pursuit, Dot would have stopped to slap Sweetboy silly. There's no disguising the Edsel, so Dot relied on her conviction that no Army man would willingly admit he'd been bamboozled by an old lady in tennis sneakers. Oh, they'd surely come after Sweetboy, but not until that lieutenant colonel found a way to cover his ass. That meant they had a few hours to build a lead.

Compulsively checking her rearview, Dot near rear-ended a slow-moving flatbed hauling rusted appliances west of Philly. Her vision was going to shit. Though she did not relax, she settled down to the speed limit. The morphine was wearing out, and so she coaxed Sweetboy into lighting a joint she instructed him to take from the glovebox.

She'd seen no pursuit, a fact that did not mean there was none. Like the return of the pain in her gut, she knew they came after you. Always.

Dot squinted at Buckles and Pussy from beneath the motel's cotton bedspread. The bright day behind them blinded her. She took no pleasure from the sunny warmth; sultry summer weather in the Midwest was evidence of God's Divine perverse humor. In the devout Midwest, such days could end with barns dismantled by the wind, houses flattened, aluminum roofs peeled off mobile homes, trees uprooted at the roots, and hail that in seconds crushed a year's unharvested crops left in fields naked to the Lord's mercy, which did not exist. Dot was sure she would see God soon enough. All she prayed for was that He grant her an audience long enough for her to call Him to account.

Her blackout curtains still drawn, as the door closed behind them the room became an ink-dark freezer. They placed a rattling vial of morphine pills and a brown bag with three sugar donuts on her bedspread. Grandma set the three donuts atop her sheet on the bit of wax paper while Sweetboy selected her first joint of the morning. She coughed weakly, then offered Sweetboy and Buckles hits. They each declined. The smoke filled her and while it did not eliminate her pain, it kept her pain far off, throbbing on some distant horizon.

Sweetboy persisted in being one of life's innocents. Bitterness was unknown to him. The boy had courage enough, brains enough, and was clever enough, but with his soul that of a kitten still blind at birth, he lacked necessary guile.

But Buckles? Life would come at Buckles fierce as it had come at Dot, fierce as it came to all women who chose not to be ornaments. If needs be, the kid would eat her own wounded. If Sweetboy were not a twink, Dot would have hauled them before a JP to seal the deal, but then neither would have been happy for very long. Buckles and Sweetboy had shared a room; Dot wondered what had happened between them. Twinks married, didn't they? It did not sway them from being twinks, but why expect miracles?

Grandma sucked powdered sugar from her fingertips while Buckles pulled a chair close and tugged a corner of Grandma's blanket over her own feet. Grandma said she approved of the strawberry jam filling. She said, "Grease, dough, and sugar are more inspiring than brandy," then licked her fingers clean a second time. When she was not burning up, she was freezing. They offered her hot coffee, but she was sure the acid in her belly would not take it for long.

Only three things relieved Dot of her pain: marijuana, morphine, and stories. Morphine encased her pain in someone else's feather pillows; marijuana dulled but did not free her from pain. But stories told well, especially her own, could take her mind to long ago and far away, places where pain existed, but where pain had no province.

The blonde kid was the find of lifetime, about as likely as rolling double sixes three times in succession, as unlikely as her blue eyes that with the smallest shift in light might go from turquoise, to purple, to the color of polished steel. Buckles reminded Dot of herself, ballsy enough to run off, no easy decision for an American girl who had not a single callus on her hands, and who was neither pregnant nor fleeing some family monster. Someone had paid plenty for that smile. She was no honest twenty-one. Dot guessed eighteen, even seventeen. But Buckles had developed none of the tics of a girl who'd lived through the worst of what life had to offer. No wave of uncertainty polluted her voice; she pushed level to the end of every sentence and her voice did not quiver with rising self-doubt unless the kid had a genuine question. Her gaze remained dead level and never dropped to her fingers; her knees did not bounce with nervous energy. Buckles did not stare at her feet, blink through a lie, mumble, or hunch her shoulders awaiting the next blow. Whatever had put her broke and alone and bruised in a truck-stop was bad luck that would fade in time, but it also stood as Dot's good fortune.

After two days, Dorothy knew Buckles was her last best hope to keep Sweetboy safe once Dot was gone. A story was there, one she wanted to know for reasons beyond gossip. Buckles' story would more than pass the time, but when she suggested Buckles go ahead, the kid's eyes became saucers and Sweetboy quickly said: "No. She is not ready."

Dot pulled herself up. Buckles' wide eyes remained unreadable in the darkness. Dot realized that Sweetboy knew something she did not. His tone, a tone she had never before heard, disallowed any disagreement. Had she underestimated the boy? Had Buckles cultivated Sweetboy's spine in a single night?

She wanted more than ever to know what had transpired in the room beside hers, but she said "All right. Unless you want to watch television game shows, why don't I tell my story?" She knew there was too much to tell, some of it had sunk into the morass of time and memory, and some of it had never happened, but her choices were to either dose herself with her dwindling supply of morphine or keep her jaw flapping. Her story could keep Death at arm's length for a while more.

She drew and held smoke from a new reefer. This time, Buckles took a hit, though Sweetboy did not. The lighted joint balanced delicately on the lip of an ashtray, smoke curling into the air. The dim motel room took on the atmosphere of an after-hours night-club in Memphis. The sparking pinwheel that was what was left of her mind slowed and accelerated, and though Grandma was near flat on her back, vertigo lifted her as in flight.

GRANDMA'S TALE

"Money is swell, but most suckers don't know how to get it or what to do with it." Dot's mind always outran her mouth. There was too much to say and never time enough to say it. "Just spend every nickel. Someday, you'll be flat on your back and broke, but no matter how broke you are, your memories stay yours forever." She toked her joint. The tip glowed cherry red. "A man named Nick taught me to make money, and man named Bertram taught me to spend it. Ambrose, my only husband, was too stupid and too mean and too old to learn those tricks. His heart was a rock. But I married him for his wallet, not love. It was a wrong turn on a road that took me nowhere."

Her past was a cataract tumbling through and filling her, most of it false, though she believed every bit. Time, morphine, and sickness had turned Dot's mind into its own mark. She believed everything her mind told her was true, no matter how preposterous.

She gestured to Sweetboy for her sunglasses on the nightstand. The two kids leaned in closer. "Audrey Hepburn wore a pair like these in *Breakfast at Tiffany's*. I had these made to imitate her, but Hepburn was too refined for rhinestones. She was no Texas cheerleader about sparkle and glass. Neither am I. Look here, children. Look hard. My rhinestones are not all rhinestones. See there. Some have light."

Grandma pointed to the pockmarks on the left that marked where the stones she'd sold in Boston had been. She handed the glasses and the beaded neck cord to Buckles. "Those are diamonds, dearie, about fifteen carats worth, total. The right side holds worthless glass, but the left is worth at least twenty grand. When you get in trouble, which you will if you have any heart, soften the plastic with a cigarette lighter, pop a stone free, and sell it. Unless you are fencing the Hope Diamond, no one gives a rat's ass where a diamond came from. No one cares about a stone's history because any diamond large enough can be recut. If anyone asks, you tell them your Grandma gave the stones to you and that she brought them from Europe sewn in her coat while she ran from Hitler. You're fair enough to pass for Polish or Swedish, and because the rich will pay for drama, they will imagine all the details they need about borders, barbed wire, German shepherds, and how your diamonds freed your relatives from death. It's the best kind of scam. You don't need to say a thing. The marks will do all your work for you."

"Is that how these got here?" Buckles asked, wide-eyed.

"Don't be ridiculous. I'll tell you the truth another day. But if you are on the grift, and we all are, all the time, every last one of us, then you need to know that marks pay for drama because they have none in their own lives. They lack the heart to live, really live. If you do not invent stories for them, they will invent their own, so you may as well be good at inventing drama that does you the most good. Like that idiot Higgencoop."

"Higgenbottom."

"Yes. That genius. We twisted that Ohio hoople like a licorice whip. And without a moment to rehearse. That's when I knew you were the one."

Buckles was pleased she was the one, but could not guess the one of *what*.

Dot's mind rambled like Red Grange. The children needed to know about the stones, not how she obtained them or how clever she could be, or why she knew of Red Grange and loved Audrey Hepburn, or how an Ohio trooper named Chickenlooper was an idiot. Buckles and Sweetboy needed to know what they needed to know, and Dot had no time for extra trimmings. She thought about beginning again, but said: "Water."

Sweetboy braced Dot's pillows. Grandma rearranged herself to look them in the eye, sitting up, not flat as a stiff on a gurney.

"When we get to Tahoe, you won't find more in the box." She'd jumped ahead, and knew she had to explain. "It's time you knew we are headed for Tahoe. It's a lake in the mountains near Reno. That's in Nevada, but half the lake is in California. On the southern end you'll find Emerald Bay. There's a metal box buried there on the footpath. Follow the pencil map I drew on the brown paper in the Edsel's glove box. Stay as close to the water line as you can get. If you slip on goose shit, you are doing it right. Our shack probably collapsed or burned, but there's a slate rock flat as a billiard table. Wood rots, but slate lasts forever. Like diamonds. You'll find the box under the slate."

Her quavering voice floated within the room's shadowy recesses, addressing not only Buckles and Sweetboy but the shades of men and women pressing in behind them.

"But what is *in* the box?" Buckles asked.

"Never you mind." Grandma rolled to one achy hip as something taut and hot in her guts snapped like the cable on a bad bridge. It burned like a son-of-a-bitch. She drew hissing breath between her teeth. "Life gave me crappy dice and all of a sudden I was playing goddam Parcheesi for cough drops. Maybe one of the five best backgammon players in the world, locked up with old ladies who played Parcheesi for cough drops." She seized control of her breathing ceiling and licked her lips before correcting herself. "Three best."

"I know Parcheesi," Buckles said. "Is that like Backgammon?"

"Yes," Sweetboy said. "They are close."

"Sure. Like Go Fish is close to Poker." Grandma glowered as Sweetboy started to explain backgammon. "Will you shut up, or will you piss away my time?"

They promised to listen, though Sweetboy rolled his eyes, patronizing Dot to score cheap grins from Buckles. Had her grandson the fairy been in the kid's pants? She should have left the little ingrate with the killer bugs flying through the pines at Fort Dix.

"The War to End All Wars ended when I was eighteen. The boys in Orono signed up. That's in Maine. The damn fools came back missing only an arm or leg, if they were lucky. Less lucky, they lost their eyes or their face. Least lucky did not come back at all. You hear me, Sweetboy. Whenever your country says it needs you, they blow a bugle and wave a flag. All it really means is that old men want young men to die for them. You get one ride on this merry-go-round, and if you don't come away with the brass ring, at least try to stay on your pony.

"My father, Dr. Charles Lewis, indulged me. His wife, my mother, left the world in the flu epidemic. Doc took Mother's death hard. I always called him 'Doc.' It was not a warm relationship. He was a good doctor and like all good doctors he considered Death to be his personal enemy. Losing my mother was a personal defeat. He was a decent enough man with sideburns who smelled of Lilac Vegetal and twirled his mustache with lemon-scented wax. He was a man of science trapped in a town of storekeepers, lumberjacks, potato farmers, and lobstermen. Put three Orono townsmen together and you might count twenty-five fingers, but no more than that. Men's fingers in Maine have a way of disappearing. Doc was no sawbones who owned a sharp scissor; he had a genuine medical education from Johns Hopkins. He must have felt very alone."

"Like playing Parcheesi when he should have been playing backgammon?"

"Child, you astound me." Grandma patted the back of Buckles' hand and shredded the last donut. "Our housekeeper did more than keep house—her name was Ella—but no one in Orono was stupid enough to criticize the man who delivered their babies, cured their children's fevers, and stitched their wounds. If Doc Lewis slept with his housekeeper and never saw the inside of a church, what of it?

"Doc was too old and tired to go elsewhere, but I was suffocating. Europe was out. The continent was still in ruins, but he agreed I could spend two weeks in New York. He had conditions, though."

"What kind of conditions?" Buckles asked.

"The usual. Not in so many words, but I agreed to keep my legs together."

"Why didn't you just run away?"

Grandma stared at Buckles over the lip of her water glass. She was learning more about Buckles than Buckles was learning about her. Her rough hand settled on her coarse sheet. "It just was not done, dear. It just was not done. I suppose Doc expected I'd come back and get around to popping out children soon enough. He arranged a hotel that included chaperone service to young women alone in the city. Doc had a black Ford, and he drove me to the railroad. A porter carried my portmanteau. On the platform, Doc pecked me on the cheek. That was the very last time I saw or touched him. Years later, I tried to visit, but he was gone. If you ever get to Orono, visit his grave and tell him I did just fine."

"What happened?" Buckles asked, wondering what *portmanteau* meant.

"The Boston & Maine carried me to Boston; the Downeaster to New York. The city was the dream in a marvelous dream, but it was overpowered by the stink of shit and gasoline. Cobblestone streets! I never saw so many cars and so many horses in one place. I stowed my bag in my hotel room and went straight to Delmonico's, a place my father recommended because innocent girls could be safe for a meal. Nick was a busboy. I did not return that night or any other to the hotel. For all I know, my luggage is still there." She cackled. "My father's opinion of Delmonico's may have been somewhat off."

"But what did you do for clothes?"

"Clothes? Didn't need any for a week!" Her chicken-laugh caught in her throat, choking her. She was unsure if she still spoke. It was possible the morphine put her to sleep in midsentence, but she peered at the wavering block of shadow that was Buckles and noted the kid was still at her bedside. She and Sweetboy needed to know what to do next, but here she was babbling about her father and his housekeeper and horseshit in the streets of New York. At least the memory of Nick kindled new life in her.

"Nick taught me backgammon." They'd been naked on his Murphy bed when Nick taught her to rattle a dice cup or why to turn a doubling cube. It was a mercy to his neighbors, the only time the bed was not bouncing off the floor or the walls. If you want to learn about anything—fine wine, cutthroat games, or the intricacies of any art—learn your lessons naked. You will never forget them.

But she'd be damned before she'd tell the kids how Nick's black eyes had penetrated her as deeply as Nick himself on his bed in his third floor walk-up in Murray Hill. He'd been twenty-four, with obsidian curls cascading from a widow's peak over his forehead. His bottomless eyes were as black as his hair. That olive skin stretched smooth and tight over his chest and abdomen. If she closed her eyes right now, though she was in a chilled motel room with a rattling air conditioner in Tuscola, Illinois, and though it was fifty years later, and though the air was thick with the eddying smoke of weed, she could still smell Nick, that mysterious mix of licorice and cinnamon and sex and lemon pomade that still owned her.

They had dined off a warped plywood board they placed over a four-legged bathtub, which, being in the middle of the kitchen, also served as their sink. Now and then they saved enough to go to a souvlaki place where he introduced her to white *sangria* made with cracked ice and peaches and lemons. They sucked the meat from mussels in garlicky Greek paella. When Nick touched her under the table with his hand or her foot, those gold candle flames dancing in his eyes, their faces inches apart, her knees turned to jelly. It was all she could do not to hurl him to the restaurant floor and have her way with him.

More importantly, she was soon beating Nick at backgammon. Where he saw blots and dice and luck, the blots sang their music to her. The checkers never lied. No mystic, Dot had no better explanation for her talent. She accepted it and made a point of telling no one.

A day came when Nick entered her name in a tournament at the Commodore Hotel. She finished second. She still remembered the blunder that cost her first place and a $25 prize. She'd rolled double fours and could have maintained a winning block, but she chose to run her blots for the excitement of a running game. She never repeated that stupid mistake. She'd wept with frustration. The tournament organizers were relieved they did not have to present their trophy to a slip of a girl. Allowing her to play was scandal enough. But that tournament made Dot and Nick bold enough to try the salons.

First Dot lost a lot, then lost less, then won a bit, then won quite a bit more. In the salons, they learned about side bets where far more was at stake than prize money. As her reputation grew and she was recognized, they learned how Dot could lose a tournament but win more if Nick bet against her at odds. Deliberately losing went against every grain of her personality, but there was an art to that as well. She had to seem to play to win; they had to arrive separately and pretend they did not know each other. It was a dangerous game, to be sure, but one night she and Nick brought home one hundred dollars as a single night's profit at a time when Nick's rent was $18.50 per month.

They rendezvoused at Keen's, a steakhouse where tables reflected electric lights in deeply burnished dark wood and a peculiar collection of clay pipes used by great men were in a case by the door. The restaurant staff was amused by so young a couple so obviously the wrong sort, but they had no trouble honoring the wrong sort's money. The burgundy was rich, the steak was rare, but they never made it to the cheesecake. Home, they fell on each other like wolves and did not leave the squealing Murphy Bed for three days. Mrs. Felipé from downstairs saw Dorothy emerge from the building, crossed herself, and rolled her eyes. It was good to be that young. Her skin had been pale as a doily, his as dark as an olive. They must have made a beautiful picture.

She squinted at Buckle's shadow with envy; all those good years lay in front of her.

"I was becoming too well known. Our opportunities were drying up. We decided to sail for Europe. I was not yet twenty. It was just after the war. If you ask me which war, Sweetboy, I'll kick you out the door now and talk only to Buckles."

"I did not say a word."

"Don't deny it. I heard you thinking." She rolled to her other hip and suppressed a groan. "In the days before White Star merged with Cunard, transatlantic voyages featured Bridge, Cribbage, and Whist at sea. Fares became suddenly cheap when they tried to lure back transatlantic tourist traffic. They paid celebrities to voyage and attract passengers. It took every dime we had saved to book First Class to Liverpool and buy the clothes I'd need to look the part. Nick needed only a dinner jacket and two starched shirts, but I needed gowns, day dresses, evening wear. The works. It was a good plan. It takes money to make money. If I lost, we'd have to swim home. But with six or seven days at sea, it was a certainty we'd find at least four pigeons."

Grandma hacked into a wad of tissue until her throat was clear. She looked, but saw no blood. Wheezing like a pipe organ, she risked a deeper breath. A dull sheen of perspiration dampened her florid cheeks as she settled limply back against her pillows. Buckles and Pussy exchanged an anxious look.

"The boat wasn't three hours out from New York when we found a new problem. Women were not allowed in the Cigar Room, and the Cigar Room was where the game was played."

"What did you do?"

"Be brazen, dear, be brazen. I summoned a deck chair, set it by the door, and puffed away on a delicate Cohiba. Passengers were scandalized by the irreverent flapper. The crew had a problem. Allow the girl into the Cigar Room or leave her to smoke in public? But I persisted, and they solved their dilemma by giving in. I was ushered to where no woman had gone before. Vaulted ceilings, stained glass skylights, gold fixtures, green and white marble inlay on octagonal playing tables. I think we were on the Mauretania." The ships blended in her mind. Franconia, Mauritania, Queen Mary, all sisters of the doomed Titanic and Lusitania. In First, no stench of diesel reached the highest decks. The air was fresh from wind passing beyond sliding glass deck doors. Their staterooms had been far enough above the waterline to open a porthole for fresh salt air. "Even when we crossed in summer, on deck I covered up with two woolen blankets, tied on my hat, and sat on a canvas recliner with a steaming cup of broth. The North Atlantic is damned cold."

What was left of her mind was trapped in the middle of the Atlantic in the Twenties. It was forty years ago. What could she leave in? What could she leave out?

"Where was Nick?" Buckles asked.

"For our scam to work, we could never be seen together. I was supposedly a recent orphan traveling to join an uncle who did not exist."

"Did you like cigars?"

"Cigars are vile. Smoke enough of them, and you wake up with a bad case of glue-mouth, though if you dip an end into Cherry Heering, you'll find them tolerable. I had to rinse my hair clean of smoke every night, and slept sitting in a cabin chair waiting for it to dry. The cigars were never more than a prop, part of the show Nick and I concocted to lure the marks into believing that the sweet young thing had blundered into a man's game by accident and then somehow took their money by dumb luck. That lie would keep them coming back. I once took two grand from a single player because I fluttered my eyes with doubt whenever I doubled, and he'd redouble just to see me flutter my eyes again, the pinhead. After a few trips, once the crews knew us, Nick bought their silence by giving the Head Steward twenty percent of our take. It was cake, it was so easy. What man would confess to his wife that the orphan flapper with the cigar on the Promenade Deck took him for a bundle?"

Sweetboy started to speak, but Grandma gave him a look that could wilt lettuce.

"Were you that lucky or did you cheat?" Buckles said.

Grandma crowed. "You're catching on, kid. I knew you were a quick study." She cackled again, then said to the darkness, "Backgammon won't allow you to cheat. Like chess, it's all there to see on the board. You can't load the dice because no roll, like a seven in Craps, is better than all the others. It's why the game requires dice cups. Different tactics for every new situation. Like life." There. She'd finally said something worth saying, but could not stop herself from adding more. "If backgammon were pure luck, you would not have the same champions year after year. The game's genius is in the gambling and psychology. In backgammon that means the doubling cube. Over days at sea, luck will even out, but the psychology never does. You can teach a monkey to play cards, but you can't teach a monkey to bluff. But put the smallest stake on the table and you're no longer playing the board; you're playing your opponent. A three game backgammon match can be played for fifty dollars a game, another fifty for winning two of three, and a hundred bonus for sweeping them all. But the doubling cube can multiply those stakes to serious money before a mark knows what hit him. If you are a grifter who can't empty a deep wallet on an ocean cruise, stay in port. Go to church. Play Bingo."

Her belly growled. She persuaded herself that was from hunger, but it had to be something else. She had no appetite. Dot would endure the tortures of Hell to make Buckles understand. The kid could not know enough. "Look, smart women have to press their advantages. Like your hair. It's an asset because men want to believe blondes are dumb and gullible. They'll underestimate you every time. So press that. Act dumb and gullible. Suck the tip of your thumb if you need to. Press that advantage until your opponent is on the run, turn, trip him up, grab him by the nose, and kick him twice in the ass." Buckles thought of her mother, her father, and the bitch from Connecticut, April. "The good Lord made men and women equal, not the same. What we do with what we have is up to no one but ourselves."

She was satisfied; it was a second thing worth saying.

"How did you learn all that?"

"By losing a lot of Nick's money." Grandma's laugh became a blood-spotted wad of phlegm she spat into a tissue. She waved Sweetboy away for water while she waited for the return of her breath. "We lived on beluga and Taittinger. I played the helpless green-eyed ingénue with bobbed chestnut hair under a broad white hat and a modest veil. A purser said I had the heart of a lion and the soul of a shark."

Was she speaking or thinking? It was as if she were struggling to swim through a turbulent blue tide that threw her back from land to suck her into a deeper, bluer undertow. The kids could not know what Taittinger's was. Why did she bring that up? Better champagne brought only a better class of hangover. Enough of the stuff and you'd demand mittens on the cat.

Her mouth and mind veered out of control. They did not need to know about Baum, but before she could stop, she had embarked on that tale.

"Ten hours from Liverpool, Nick arranged a last game against the same man who'd been a prime patsy the entire trip, Herr Baum, a Swiss banker. I think I was twenty, same as Buckles here, or at least same as she claims."

"I am twenty," the eighteen-year old said.

If Buckles was twenty, then Dot was 106, but she had not asked nor would she. She'd kept mum on any dispute on Buckles' age in case they were arrested. It would never do to have the cops learn how she and Sweetboy knowingly transported a minor across state lines. Maybe Buckles was a minor, maybe she wasn't. Best not to know. Besides, when Dot played backgammon against the Swiss banker, she must have been 26 or 27. What story ever improved by strict adherence to the truth?

"At one point in a match with Baum, I doubled the stake, but Baum was a smart player. He knew enough to cut his losses and declined. Later, Nick let him know that I believed Baum could have won, which was not even slightly true. His game was dead in the water. Nick was goading Baum by making him think he'd quit too soon. Look, anything is possible; a plow horse has four legs and a tail, but nobody bets on it to beat Whirlaway. Baum scoffed at the Greek boy who belonged in steerage but traveled with a young woman clearly not his wife and certainly not his sister. They arranged to resume the lost game, but with colors reversed. I'd take the losing position and win."

Buckles wondered what a Whirlaway was, but even in the dim room Grandma's eyes glowed with life. Buckles did not dare interrupt.

"At Baum's request, there were no onlookers. That seemed pointless to me. I could not understand what Nicky was about. No onlookers, no side bets at odds. How could Nicky hope to make money from my playing Baum's lost position? It was hopeless. A fool's proposition.

"Baum was a Nazi sympathizer. Hitler and his bullyboys were just starting to come out from under their rocks, but nobody took the wallpaper hanger seriously. But Baum was Swiss, a banker returning to Zurich. They take everything seriously. Baum was partial to cream-colored shirts, and he sported an opal stickpin the size of your eye through his gold cravat, all very daring for a banker. The sea tossed the ship like a cork, but at two in the morning anyone not holding their head over the rail was in the forward ballroom at the end-of-voyage gala. A stout man, Baum settled into a leather armchair bolted to the deck of the Cigar Room and kissed the back of my wrist. Wind whistled; spray and mist covered the Cigar Room's thick external glass. Baum had seen me plenty of times puffing on my Cohibas, but being a gentleman he asked my permission before he rolled a Macanudo against his trouser leg, snipped off the nib, and passed one end of his cigar above the table's small alcohol lamp. We arranged the checkers to where his game had gone irretrievably sour, the position at which I had doubled and he'd wisely conceded rather than accept a higher loss. We spun the backgammon board and I resumed his lost game.

"Baum spilled a 5/4, and nodded with satisfaction. His first roll only increased the advantage. Ordinarily, I'd have resigned to cut my losses and move on to the next game in the match, but that was not part of Nick's proposition. My only chance was to roll doubles, a matter of sheer luck, not tactics. My first dice came up 3/2, a weak roll. Bad became worse. Baum loaded his dice cup, but first looked to Nick. 'May I double?' he asked. 'It is unclear to me the precise nature of our wager.' He'd attended Oxford. His voice held only a trace of his native German, likely why his family chose him to sail to New York to assure people of the safety and anonymity of Swiss banks when stock markets were tanking the world over. Swiss banks pay no interest, of course; they charge depositors for anonymity and safety, not at all a bad deal when the world is turning to shit.

"Nicky leaned close to my ear and breathed 'Win this.' But his voice frightened me. That night with Baum, there would be no second game. Conceding was out of the question. This was no match; it was an isolated do-or-die game. In backgammon, that's a crazy person's proposition.

"The ship surged through rough seas. Distant waltz music faintly came to us on the wind. I'd never been seasick, but that night I was queasy. The feeling was completely new to me.

"Baum's soft fingers turned the doubling cube, an invitation for me to quit, like resigning in chess, preserving dignity. But I accepted the double. What else could I do? At least the rules were that he could not double again, at least not unless I doubled, and I was not about to do that in a game that was lost. He touched off the fine ash of his cigar into a glass ashtray. The newly exposed tobacco blazed cherry red. When he lifted the alcohol lamp beneath his snifter to warm his brandy and inhale the heated aroma, his round face was haloed in golden light. 'You know Cuvée 1888, *fräulein*? It is near as exquisite as you.' I smiled, but my attention focused on the board. I now owned the doubling cube, but I dared not use it. Baum was too rich and too good a player to be bluffed and shut out. My position was miserable. I'd need to roll miracles.

"Then I smacked down a 4/3, a great turn of the dice that opened up a new option." Her trembling voice rose. She was more alive in her past than she was in the cold motel room, Baum more close than Sweetboy and Buckles. "I could maintain an anchor in Baum's home board and play a conservative back game while I hoped for his luck to reverse, or I could shift to a blitz, my only real chance at a win even if it left my scattered blots vulnerable. It was very risky."

Buckles did not understand a word, but was thrilled. "What did you do?" she asked, her imagination saturated by golden light, cigars, the pitch and roll of the sea, far off ghostly music, and the dark-eyed Greek who'd been Grandma's lover.

"I played to win, of course. Play to win. Play to win, Buckles. Press every chance. We're women and do not play to cut our losses, but to win. I blitzed. Did you know that Cuvée smells the same as crushed flowers in Carcassonne?" Now who gave a damn about flowers in Carcassonne? At this rate, it would take a week before she got to the lockbox buried on the shore of Lake Tahoe. What else was the point of all her yammering?

"His next roll was no catastrophe, but he was unable to take advantage of my vulnerable position. Another small miracle. None of my blots went back to the bar. His face went pink as a pet pig's." She laughed so hard she gagged. Pussy lifted her shoulder higher on her pillow. "For the next three rolls, I attacked his blots and ran mine. Baum did the same. No defense by anyone, just a Hell-bent dice race. When Baum rolled a 2/1, he was for the third time unable to take advantage of my vulnerability. He muttered in German.

"When Lady Luck is on your side, she's like sable on your shoulders. My 4/4 was a powerful double, overdue, if you ask me. Doubles mean you toss the dice a second time, a free turn. Our games drew even. If he rolled his fair share of better numbers, I'd lose my chance, but neither of us believed that could happen. Luck was with me. I owned Fate and Chance. Remember this, Buckles. If you know nothing else, remember that luck has momentum. When luck runs with you, press it. Press it hard. It will leave you soon, but while you have it, press it.

"I doubled, blind to any notion of what wager Nick had made. Herr Baum's eyes shifted from me to Nicky and back to me. Then he conceded. 'It would have been my great pleasure, *fräulein*,' he said, delicately touched his lips to my wrist, and added in French, '*Formidable.*' His pocket-watch read 4:30 in the morning. He handed Nicky the opal stickpin, and then they went together to the purser to cash a check."

"That's quite a story," Sweetboy said.

"It's not yet done. No story is done if it has no point." Grandma believed it had a point. She hoped it had a point. Dear God, what if her story had no point?

"I parted a glass slider to the open deck. Mist, rain, spray, no matter. I needed fresh air. The wind had lessened, but the ship still surged forward through rough seas. We must have been doing twenty-five knots. The rain hissed on the black water. *Goodnight Ladies,* the music insubstantial and faint, floated on the air from the forward ballroom. Clouds parted enough to scud across a new moon so silver it seemed hammered from sterling. The ocean was on fire the color of mercury. I tightened my shawl at my shoulders and touched the lapis pin at my chest. I remember that pin. I miss that pin. Now I'd have Baum's opal, as well. My mind cleared. I had never felt more alive.

"When Nick returned, he tried to put his arms around me, but I was having none of that. I asked if he had lost his mind.

"'We won,' he said. 'What difference?'"

"What exactly did we win?"

"'Six thousand. And the opal. It's worth at least half that.'

"I said, 'My God. Pounds or dollars?' and Nicky said, 'Pounds.'

"I kissed him. I cupped his face in my two hands and kissed him. Then I said, 'You should have told me. How could you not tell me?'

"'Would you have played any differently?'

"'I would not have played at all,' I said. If he had won, we'd have owed Baum at least the six, unless Nicky obtained odds. But Swiss bankers don't give odds. They take them. I was giddy. We did not have six thousand pounds or dollars to lose. I peered at Nicky's silhouette, dark and opaque in front of my eyes, his elbows behind bracing him on the top rail. I asked how we could have paid if I'd lost.

"As if he were proud, Nicky said, 'Baum wagered for you.'

"The moon behind him, his face was in deepest shadow. For a moment, I did not understand. Then I slapped him. The impact ran the length of my arm. Nick did not wince, he was a strong man, so I slapped him twice more. 'Are you my pimp now?'

"'It was nothing like that,' he said.

"But it was exactly like that. It was that. It was that and nothing more.

"We made Liverpool by midday, only a few hours late. My luggage followed me to London and the Savoy. Two days later, an envelope was delivered to the concierge. My money. My full share, but no note. Nothing but cash. I never saw Nick again."

"But you miss him, right?"

"Not a bit, dear," Dot said, lying. "Not a bit." Grandma sipped ice water. "All this chatter makes me hungry." That was another lie. She'd never know hunger again. All she had left were stories, each clamoring to be told, in her mind a dozen baby robins begging to be fed.

She tried to swing her legs free of the blankets, but her hips seized solid. Pain crackled below her knees and calves as if her bones were Venetian glass. If she stood, she'd topple, so she settled back as if merely adjusting herself. Anything was better than the kids seeing her fall helpless. Sweetboy needed to believe he was of some use, so she said: "Get me some mushroom soup if they have it. Vegetable if they do not. There's always vegetable soup."

Dark shadows moved about her. As soon as the flash of light that was the open door extinguished, she clawed the vial of morphine

to her side and managed to open it. She could no longer see well
enough to know what dosage she was taking by color, and trying to
know that by feel was hopeless. She swallowed two with what was
left of her glass of water, waited a bit, then chewed on a third pill
as she fell back against her thin pillows and the rickety headboard.
She drifted buoyant into a blue fogbank of morphine dreams. Had
they left her in darkness or light? Her failing eyesight felt clear and
bright, though she could see nothing. The line between fact and
fancy blurred and then was gone. She had become her mind's own
mark, eager to believe anything and everything.

She wanted to tell Sweetboy and Buckles all they'd need to
know, but she was botching the job. She'd have to begin again
when they returned if they were to value her map, that scrap of
paper they might otherwise simply throw away. She was sure she
had told them about the map. It was the main thing. The map. Dot
felt most welcome in her past afloat on the gentle swells of morphine, but the map was their future. Did they know, really know,
how crucial her map was? When they returned, to make certain
she'd need to start her story again. This time she'd begin with a
moment that was certain and plod forward from there. Her mind
slid among decades and oceans while the kids walked a hundred
yards in search of soup. She needed to stop grasping the foolish lies
she told herself about Omar Shariff or Ernest Hemingway. What
was real? What was not?

She'd crossed the footbridge over the Truckee at North Virginia
and 4th Street to gaze up to the hills surrounding around Reno.
That much was certain. That was where she promised herself she
would make a life there. But the flash of memory of the mountains
reminded her of Innsbruck, and Innsbruck reminded her of Bertie
and times long before she ever saw Reno.

No one could invent Bertie. Bertie had been real. No one but
Bertie had the requisite gall to invent Bertie. Bertie affected as-
cots and ink blue flannel slacks and white scarves and pale blue
blazers with patch pockets and brass buttons. He paid lavishly for

manicures, and he quoted Noel Coward to be clever. When he was not wearing tasseled harem slippers, he wore custom-made Italian shoes soft as a baby's ass. And Bertie drank Moët, always oët, from a Baccarat crystal flute that he packed first whenever they moved on. "Nothing else is fit to touch these lips."

Brown as a nut, his gleaming thick blond hair was brushed straight back by twin military brushes. In his 50s, Bertie confessed to being 35 and looked it, while Dorothy had been 32 and admitted to 25. Perhaps she'd been 36. The years jumbled in the flume of her Morphine-flooded mind, but Bertie rose above the flood.

They'd occupied adjacent canvas deck chairs when he asked if she liked Mondrian, the kind of question the passengers asked in First Class to be sure their neighbor was the right sort. Or had he asked about Modigliani? They'd drunk bouillon, and when he detected what remained of her downeast accent, he said: "I abhor the Colonies, nearly as much as Herr Hitler and his gangsters." He'd been observing her win at backgammon for three nights running. "You're extraordinary, you know," he said, "but spare me false modesty or some nonsense about being lucky. I've heard that story you put out. Bound for the continent to visit a dying uncle, is it? You just happen to smoke cigars and turn a doubling cube like Satan's own croupier. Do I have it right?"

He offered to be her partner.

"Why would I need a partner?"

"Barcelona, Lisbon, Cannes, Monaco. Innsbruck, and my personal favorite, Bellagio on Lake Como." He pointed to a manicured finger for each place. "Bellagio grows less pleasant now that Il Duce favors it. The man is a peasant." He went on as if she'd already agreed to join him. "We'll need to start with your wardrobe," he said. His bouillon steamed. "A woman needs to own every room she enters, but she must do so without uttering a word. It's the fundamental premise of fashion."

They crossed the Channel and by railroad rode on to Paris. Montmartre was cold and wet; they'd shared a bed in the office of an abandoned loft that had been a dress factory where she confirmed that a woman in bed with Bertie was safer than a woman in bed alone.

The loft in Montmartre reeked of yeast and bread from the *boulangerie* three stories below. That first morning, Bertie summoned the cohort of friends he called the Cobbler's Elves. They came with sewing machines, tape measures, tailor's chalk, pins, pinking shears and bolts of satin and velvet. They stood her on a workbench in the center of the drafty factory floor and stripped her down to a white garter belt, white stockings, and three-inch heels, a nude a bride-to-be surrounded by twittering dressmakers debating how to drape a breathing mannequin. Filthy, bare, floor-to-ceiling windows admitted gray sunlight. Bertie deemed her hair an auburn asset with her jade green eyes, so there'd be no discussion of a cut, though it needed to be tamed. They adored that she was not curvy. Binding her breasts for years, she could not have been flatter if she'd been cut from plywood. Bertie passed judgment from a swiveling office chair, his back to the light, a silhouette beneath a curling snake of gray smoke rising from his Gauloises. When she begged for rest or at least to step out of her heels, he'd waved a hand and said: "Sleep is for the meek." They fortified her with cognac that she drank from the bottle. Naked and drunk, she'd slept on her feet.

The Depression that left drafty Montmartre factory lofts vacant also lowered hemlines to mid-calf and lower. Everyone was broke. Modesty was in fashion. Five years earlier, a flapper's chemise might endure no more than two nights of the Charleston, but now fabrics had to last while still seeming to conform to a woman's shape. The Elves stretched velvet tight across her hips, so tight that walking was difficult, but instead of letting the gown out, Bertie insisted that the design be gathered an additional inch. "Don't worry. You'll never break the line of a dress with underwear. You'll never wear underwear."

The Elves fashioned two strapless gowns of velvet, a pale rose for her complexion, green to match her eyes, and a silk pants-suit in sinful midnight blue to be worn with a satin cream slip that was part chemise on her shoulders through the grace of slack spa-ghetti straps. The three outfits required body powder in places she'd never applied powder. They sewed a stolen Chanel label into the suit. The sewing machines hummed to produce matching pairs of elbow-length gloves. The Elves managed the production in hours.

After the final fittings, they peeled her back to naked. She was allowed to collapse in sleep under a ragged blanket on the wooden floor. When she awoke, the Elves somehow produced three pairs of four-inch heels, each pair dyed to match an outfit, each pair a bit less blocky than the fashion. They had measured her feet while she slept; the shoes fit perfectly. Bertie insisted she wear the shoes until she could walk in them without tottering. The tissue he stuffed into the shoes staunched the bleeding.

Three days later, she and Bertie swept into the Grand Hotel du Cap, a hotel that by tradition reflexively never had a room available to any non-royalty at any price regardless of a person's financial status. "I have a friend," Bertie explained. "We are not paying a shilling, but go easy on room service." He then ordered beluga and a magnum of Moët to be delivered to the room. He forbid her to sit in the sun at the beach. She had to look like an angel wasting away with consumption. From their high window, she stared at the pebbled shore of the Mediterranean Riviera.

Dorothy wanted to wear the midnight blue suit a la mode Chanel, but Bertie thought it too mannish for their target, a mark known as much for his interest in women as for his backgammon. They went with the rose gown. "You have perfect skin, you know," Bertie said. Not only were her shoulders bare, but every step she took exposed her legs to her thighs, her calves made more pronounced by her heels. She was cautioned not to lose the pearls: they were real but on loan, a situation she understood meant they had been filched from an estate and had to be returned before their absence was discovered. Gown, gloves, pearls, shoes—she was otherwise naked. "Put some adhesive tape across your nipples. The casino can be chilly," Bertie contemplated her in a final critical examination. Then he thought a moment and corrected himself. "Never mind. Let your tits be."

They rode in a borrowed black Bentley. Bertie's friends were everywhere. Hitler eventually gassed most of them, but that night, she arrived by the grace of the Elves at the Grand Monaco Casino to place her gloved hand on an ivory and gold spiral balustrade. She descended alone to the casino floor beneath the enormous crystal chandelier. Light played highlights in her lush hair. She drank Chambord from a Limoges cup while scattering meaningless chips on a roulette table. Bertie knew his business. Every eye, men's and women's, came to rest on her, including eventually the mark, a man who'd escaped the Bolsheviks. They retired to his villa on a hilltop overlooking the sea and his vineyard. Under Bertie's eyes and the eyes of two uniformed stewards, they rolled dice under lanterns strung above a pebbled patio. His backgammon case was made of soft Spanish leather. The disks were ivory or ebony, each etched in gold with the Romanov crest. He was a perfect gentleman who played well, but not well enough.

She won 17,500 francs.

She'd once asked Nick if they could have paid if she'd lost. They were in the borrowed Bentley on the shore road as the sun rose behind them when she asked Bertie the same question. Gulls wheeled and called. "Not a centime." He held up his Moët. "Shall I pour some in your shoe?"

But Bertie and her gowns and her life in Europe before National Socialism swallowed all that was irrelevant to Buckles and Sweetboy, though they could stand to know Bertie's two secrets to life. "Never accept the first room the concierge shows you. And insist on the best of everything," he'd advised her. "It's simple. No choices, no errors." In a hotel fire, Bertie would have seized cash, clothes, and, once a safe distance from the flames, might have informed a firefighter that a sleeping Dorothy remained inside.

It ended at Innsbruck. Over breakfast on their chalet patio near Le Grand Hotel Europa, he removed the top from a tin of Hofbauer chocolates. Sunlight glared off the slopes. The sky was an unearthly violet. "Why is Mozart on the wrapper?"

"They are made in Vienna, dear. These days the choices are the Corporal or Mozart, so they go with Mozart. Herr Hitler remains disagreeable."

Bertie took a thickly buttered slice of spice cake with a spot of raspberry jam. Dot drank a third cup of dark tea poured from a silver samovar. Beneath the table, she toed off a shoe before she lifted her ankle into Bertie's lap.

"How do you feel about losing?" he asked, digging his fingers deep into the soft flesh of her foot.

"Hate it." The foot massage drained tension from her. "God, Bertie, if you ever decide to sleep with a woman, I hope it will be me."

"Don't be disgusting." Bertie drained his champagne. "Can you lose and make it look as if you tried to win? I can bet against you. Secretly, of course."

He had no inkling of how well she knew that game. They needed the money. They always needed money. Sterlet caviar did not come cheap. She said she could manage it.

"That's my good girl," he said, dropped her foot like a hot stone, kissed his fingertips, and touched the kiss to her cheek. "Not too much sun if you go for a hike," he said and left her.

A day later, followed by a smattering of applause, head low, she left the hotel's tournament game room as if she'd succumbed after a noble fight. She'd broken a block that she should have maintained and her opponent saw his chances and took them. It looked like bad dice but it was deliberate bad judgment. Back in her suite, she gorged on too many Godiva chocolates and drank Cointreau. She summoned her lover at the moment, a downhill racer whose name she could not recall, though his iron thighs were unforgettable. After a while, she kissed his lips and sent him away. Making love after giving away her chance at a 10,000 RM purse for which she had been the favorite did not sit well with her no matter how much Cointreau she drank or how much Bertie might have won wagering against her.

Naturally, she never saw Bertie again.

However, she did see a forlorn boy waiting with his oxblood brown leather luggage and camelhair coat in the hotel lobby. He wore a brown fedora and repeatedly glanced at his wristwatch. Bertie had managed to run out on two people at once, quite the feat.

He left Dorothy without two centimes.

The American Embassy reluctantly helped. Americans who could were fleeing Europe. The Wehrmacht soon would goose-step into the Rhineland and then the Sudetenland. Dorothy never knew, but she hoped Bertie's arrogance did not prevent him from finding safety back in Great Britain; but he was arrogant enough to believe his network of friends could prevail and he'd never need to wear the pink triangle. She could never be certain, but her heart knew Bertie and his friends were immolated in Der Führer's firestorm.

Safe across the Atlantic, Dot made her way to Nevada, took one look at Las Vegas and headed to Reno. Reno was hardly Monte Carlo, and Fremont Street was not the Grand Casino, but anywhere they tossed dice, Dot had believed she could make a go of it.

The flaming augur twisted in her side. She was unable to find and light a joint, so she swallowed another morphine pill dry. Why were they taking so long? She seemed unhinged from time. They could be spared her stories of Bertie, but could Buckles and Sweetboy understand her stories of Reno? Dot's Spot, her breakfast business replaced her scam about being the lucky ingénue with a gifted dice cup. The years carved marks on her, backgammon was no longer much of a game, and so she had to work for a living, though she was smart enough never to work for someone other than herself. But in that gambler's town where silver dollars clanked deep in every pocket, no bank offered credit to a former backgammon hustler, a woman no less. She instead took money from the kind of men you had to be crazy to take money from. The vig was a tapeworm, starving her to death no matter how much coin Dot's Spot took in.

When the war was done, the nearby Army base emptied, and the restaurant's business cratered. Her debt to the men with bent noses, however, did not vanish. They took the place.

Dot fled east to find new options. She gambled in Havana and met Ambrose where they drank gin and bitters with Hem and Hotch and Mary. At least, they said they were Hem, Hotch, and Mary. Maybe there was no one there at all. Her mind might deceive her, but her heart was always true, and her heart's truth told her she'd been with Hemingway, his cats, his drinking companions, his boat, his woman. In Cuba. Or maybe it was Bimini. Ambrose talked sword and marlin while Hem held forth on the many ways the Spanish were more cruel than Italians, but unlike Italians lacked all imagination. Germans were the worst though, a nation of philosophers and scientists that was also a nation of soulless bookkeepers that maintained Death's ledgers, creating exacting records of every man, woman, and child before shutting every soul into a furnace.

In her bed at the Tuscola Arms, Dot alternately felt weightless and then heavy, lighter, then heavy again, a bobbing balloon attached by rubber bands to a running child's wrist. She believed she could escape yet, float away to leave behind the burning in her belly, to be blissfully free if only she could order her mind. But her memories broke apart as fast as they coalesced, a flipbook with all the leaves but no two in the proper order. She blinked. In the motel room's utter darkness a port city's lights rose before her, its lights twinkling above an ocean's glassine surface in morning's half-light. The calls of following gulls surrounded her. New-born sun was fierce at her eyes. She drew a final easy breath, inhaling clean air thick with the memory of the waxen scent of votive candles beneath a mosaic that soared to the ceiling of a nave in a Lisbon church.

She'd never been to Lisbon.

Pain surged. She could not expel her breath.

Dammit, she was not ready. She was not done. How could she be done? She was not ready.

Death arrived neither as lover nor relief. No welcoming embrace lifted her from her bed. She did not move toward any far-off light. No voice from her past rose to welcome her. She was greeted by no one who had gone before. That which was Dorothy simply was no more.

Pussy and Buckles reopened the icy room to find Grandma Dot's corpse half fallen from her bed, her nightgown bunched at her waist, one impossibly bent leg tangled in her thin blanket. Her face was flat against the worn carpet, her skin gray, her green eyes wide open and dull as a carousel pony's.

They sank to the gritty carpet floor. Whenever they regained any composure, they'd restore eye contact and would again fall apart. Buckles struggled unsuccessfully to hold herself together, but she had to, as much for Pussy's sake as her own. Grandma deserved nothing less. Pussy had held her through a night of horror that would return to her again and again, she knew, a night that might never leave her. He'd held her. He deserved her at her best, now.

They had sworn to have each other's backs, and now it was her turn to step up. Buckles stopped Puss from running from the room to seek help. The old lady was past aid. If Pussy lost his head, he might lose all Grandma worked for. "We can't allow Grandma to have died for nothing," she whispered. The feedback loop of grief between them slowly lessened.

Buckles took stock, though she did not need to think. Pussy was a wanted man. They'd go forward in Grandma's car, smoking Grandma's dope, spending Grandma's money, running with Grandma's diamonds and head for Tahoe to find out whether Grandma's map was another one of her stories, or if there was a lockbox holding some sort of treasure. She presented her plan, fully aware it was no more than Grandma's plan, but without Grandma.

"Does that sound right to you?" she asked.

Wordlessly, Pussy seemed to agree. His eyes were swollen, red, a portrait of grief. Buckles' face was a runny mess as well. She struggled with an inescapable conclusion, drew a deep breath, and said: "We need to leave her and vanish." Pussy slowly nodded without stirring from his grandmother's side.

Buckles rolled Grandma's housecoat chastely below the body's knees. The corpse was already growing cold, but the corpse was no longer Grandma, she told herself. She held a full breath, stood, and grabbed the corpse by the ankles. "I can't do this alone," she said.

Pussy hesitated, then stood to lift the body by its shoulders. Grandma hung between them like wet clothesline. They swung her onto the bed and propped two pillows at her back. Her unseeing eyes were transfixed by something far off, something startling and distant, something invisible to the living. Buckles turned away, and with a gesture she'd seen in a thousand movies palmed Grandma's eyes shut. She shuddered, but the dread in the motel room lessened. Closing a corpse's eyes was for the sake of the living, not for the dead.

It was hard to say how much time passed. The monotonous rattle and knock of the air conditioner's bent fan was the only sound until the insistent wail of sirens invaded the room.

What now?

Buckles opened the room door the smallest crack, but a giant outside pressed back. She put her shoulder into it and as the door sprung free and banged out to hit the motel's white-washed wall, she lost her footing. She turned to see the last of the screen door bend like a paper clip and then fly off. The world had gone pearl gray beneath a low churning sky, eerie, green, and evil. Two boys struggled to throw lounge chairs into the motel's swimming pool's uneasy water. Buckles tried to take a few strides. Three times, the room door banged open and shut behind her, each time a sound that sounded final. She made a megaphone of her hands to shout to the pool boys, but the wind threw her words back at her. The taller boy, his mouth shaped in a perfect O, gestured wildly for her to look up and behind her over the motel roof.

Hail the size of buckshot peppered her upturned face and bare arms. Her sandals were no protection. Her toes felt the sting of glistening ice pellets. The air was rank with the aroma of freshly turned dirt. Stinging her like whips, her hair snapped around her face and eyes. An old tree beside the pool bent impossibly until a branch snapped like a twig and exposed raw wood; a flying branch flew through the air, a javelin that missed her by a few feet before it pierced the plate glass window of the office at the Tuscola Arms.

"Tornado!" she shouted to no one. "Tornado! Tornado!"

Wild winds whirled from every direction, snatching away her breath. She was pushed every which way except back to the room and Pussy. Pussy looked through the open door at her uncomprehendingly; then she made it into the room where Grandma lay dead. The door slammed behind her, then banged opened again, then flapped shut twice more, a crippled bird's one good wing. The latch was bent useless. There was no time to talk. God's darkest finger was curling from Heaven to find them.

Buckles tugged Pussy to his feet, and they sprinted to their own room, a distance of a few feet that against the swirling wind felt like a mile, but when the wind moved behind them it threatened to make them take flight. The motel's fragile windows rattled. They stuffed whatever they could grab off the floor into her tote and Pussy's Army duffle, and then returned to Grandma's room. Her door was completely gone, flown from its twisted brass hinges. Buckles scooped the Edsel's keys from the nightstand and looped the beaded cord that held Grandma's sunglasses around her own neck.

Pussy sank in grief to the floor beside the bed, but there was no time for that. Buckles kicked his hip, hard. Pussy still did not stand. She left him only long enough to haul his duffle and her tote through the whirling wind to the Edsel. The car trembled like a wet dog, eager to be off, but tethered to the ground. Buckles prayed for Grandma's luck, started the Edsel's engine, and backed over all manner of crackling branches, leaves, and windblown crap as she circled the swimming pool in reverse. The boys had fled. Torn free and snapping like a whip, the pool's cyclone fence remained tethered at one end. It writhed like a snake, worked itself loose, and soared away, a scythe.

Her new brother stood on the narrow cement curb, the tail of his camouflage shirt flapping. Grandma's corpse lay on the ground rolled in loose bedding between his legs.

"Help me!" he shouted.

Buckles pointed to the sky. "Leave her! Get in! Get in! Get in!"

Something hard had smacked the windshield and was blown away, but a vertical crack as long as her arm zigzagged through the glass. She was sure that driving fast to escape a tornado was not the safest plan, but she had no other. The convertible top was fastened, but pumped like bellows. It might fly off at any second. Buckles had been behind the wheel for her first time only a day ago, but Pussy was in no condition to take charge. He had yanked open the Edsel's passenger door and was struggling to load Grandma into the rear seat, but only the lower half of her body was in the car. He bent her like a bobby-pin, but the Edsel's door would not close against the wind. Grandma's head and torso bounced twice on the black macadam. Buckles' head swelled like an overinflated balloon. She forced herself to yawn to ease the pressure in her ears.

Grandma's spirit urged her to play for the win. *Push your luck.* Could her ghost be trapped on earth by a whirlwind? Buckles' opponent was a tornado; however slim, the Edsel was her only chance to get away. She would roll dice against God.

There was no time to persuade Pussy to abandon the body. What could they do with her? If they stayed put, the tornado would kill them. Even if they survived the storm, they'd be caught: a deserter, a runaway, and the corpse of an old lady in a car overloaded with marijuana and morphine pills. Why couldn't Pussy see their danger?

Yesterday Buckles had driven uncertainly. Not this day. There was no time for uncertainty.

"Leave her!" she shouted and near stood on the accelerator. With Pussy and Grandma in the open door, the wind could tear the car's vinyl roof to shreds. Her ears popped again.

In her panic, her left foot remained firmly down on the brake pedal and her right stood on the accelerator. The tires smoked and squealed, but the car only spun in a tight circle, the rear wheels wanting to go, the front wheels gripping the ground. The convertible roof threatened to fly off completely, but then centrifugal force flung Grandma free of the car and the wind slammed Pussy's door shut with Pussy inside, his head below the glovebox, his ass in the air above the seat. Buckles' hair pressed against the convertible's soft top, the wheels squealed, and once Pussy put his hand around her ankle to pull her foot off the brake pedal, the Edsel sprang forward like an unrestrained pit bull.

An opaque wall of horizontal rain drove straight at her. The passenger-side windshield wiper locked; the driver-side wiper cleared nothing. Blind, the car bounced over something Buckles hoped was not Grandma as they careened around the motel parking lot, one wheel falling over the lip of the swimming pool, the car engine roaring, the car going nowhere until by some miracle the trapped wheel lurched free and they skid across what was left of the Tuscola Arms, narrowly missing a collision with the motel building itself. The Edsel developed a mind of its own, the steering loose as a Playland bumper car, twisting in her hands left and right and back again with no effect as the tires spun on water. They sideswiped someone's pickup truck, caromed into an Impala, and fishtailed onto the two lane blacktop road before the front office. On the nearby diner's roof, the lattice of iron that held the sign that read EAT groaned, crumpled, sagged, and collapsed. Sparks showered the ground. The neon sign collapsed, a tarpaper tail like batwings soaring from the roof behind it. The tubing exploded; shards of fine glass rained down no different from the hail. Somewhere in Tuscola a church bell tolled wildly; then the church bell itself rolled lazily down the highway.

Pussy knelt on the passenger seat. He looked back. "Holy crap! Do you see that? Look at it! Look at it! I can see it! Holy crap!" Muffled by her popping ears, his voice sounded as if he was below deep water. "Drive! Drive!"

Freezing rain struck the convertible roof, a rising crescendo as if they lived in a drum. The Edsel weighed at least two tons, but the following wind lifted and dropped and lifted again the car's rear wheels from the ground. Buckles dared not turn to look because Grandma destroyed the rearview mirror when she advised Buckles to never look back, but Grandma had never told a story about being chased by a funnel cloud. Buckles seized Pussy's hand and put it on the wheel for the moment she twisted to see behind them. The biggest damn thing Buckles ever saw or hoped to see, a storm that was nobody's friend, blocked the sky from one horizon to the other. A single thick finger curled to the ground to pursue them.

It was personal.

She hunched her shoulders and her knuckles turned white as Buckles grimly held on, certain the car would flip into a cornfield and come to rest upside down, spilling her and Pussy through the vinyl top as easily as Grandma's dice cup spilled dice. Lightning strobed. Wind tore at her breath. Static electricity crackled in her hair.

Dumb luck and Grandma's spirit carried the Edsel west and south through the storm's heart. The storm itself passed north and east. Buckles pushed the car to 80 on the ruler-straight road, more than double her fastest speed only a day ago. Fire trucks and ambulances and police cars flew by them going in the opposite direction. No other vehicles were on the road.

An unnerving calm invaded her, as if she were somewhere else while she was in fact there, and she thought how this was one hell of a way to practice steering.

But then as if they'd passed through a purple curtain of water, a storm on one side and sun on the other, they were free of the rain. Thunder and lightning crackled behind them, going away. Buckles slowed the Edsel. A few miles more and they felt safe. The Edsel came to a halt on a rise overlooking yellow and green fields of what had to be corn, green and yellow fields the storm had bypassed on this lovely Midwestern summer day.

Buckles' forehead touched the red steering wheel. Her fingers cramped. She stopped panting when she rolled down a window to inhale air laden by the aromas of water and shit and good things that grew. Her pulse slowed. Distant sirens sounded what had to be an All Clear. The late-day sun hung above the horizon, a burnished gold coin.

"I got the glasses," Buckles managed to say.

"Where did you learn to drive like that?"

"Like what? I just went."

"You turned a perfect donut. When you get a car to spin like a top, it's called doing a donut because of the tire tracks. You did not learn that from me. If you ever rob a bank, drive the getaway car."

She was unsure if he were joking. "I don't have a gang." She punched his thigh as she'd seen Grandma do. "But I might, someday." Pussy almost grinned. That, she realized, was a good thing, so she punched him again.

"Grandma would have been proud of you. But now we have to go back for her."

She punched his thigh a third time, more lightly. Could she have a talent for driving, like Grandma found her talent for backgammon? Being a talented driver might go with being a natural grifter. Her first time behind the wheel had only been yesterday. She decided to never tell Pussy she had felt Grandma's hands on hers holding the Edsel's wheel. The crazy old lady might have been dead, but she had not quite abandoned them.

They'd surely never find her body, but for Pussy's sake they had to look.

The Edsel struggled back toward Tuscola. Emergency vehicles zipped past them in both directions. As they drove, Pussy took stock. In the glovebox was the manila envelope that held hundred dollar bills on top of a second identical envelope that held a several ounces of loose marijuana, a few fat bombers, and a torn package of Zig-Zag Rolling Paper. Whatever pills she had kept in that brown vial had gone with her into her room at the Tuscola Arms. There was the crumpled printed roadmap Pussy consulted. Beneath everything else was the hand-drawn pencil map with no place names on a scrap of brown paper torn from a grocery bag, creased so many times and refolded the paper had gone soft as cloth. Grandma's scribbles were meaningless to anyone who did not know it to be the shore of the California side of Lake Tahoe. It could as easily have been Lake George or Lake Erie. No X marked a spot, but a heavy arrow in red ink pointed to a point halfway up a bay.

The Edsel's tires eventually crushed debris where they were sure the Tuscola Arms had stood. The only surviving sign of the motel

was a hole in the ground that had been the swimming pool, now filled by sodden debris, twigs, and the branch of a leafless tree. One wall remained standing. Concrete had blown away; embedded iron bars stood naked, bent spears at attention.

They stepped out of the car. Buckles slipped the rhinestone-side temple piece of the sunglasses between her lips. Her seventh grade teacher had worn the same sort of eyeglass cord, and she had chewed on her glasses all the time. The teacher had seemed smart, though Buckles would bet she could not steer a perfect donut with or without the help of an old lady's ghost, and she doubted that her teacher's rhinestones were anything like the diamonds she and Pussy had inherited.

"What should we do?" Pussy stood beside her. "How will we find her?"

A fleet of police cars flashing lights and screaming sirens barreled over the nearby road.

"The only thing I know for sure is that we can't stay here," Buckles said. "They'll ask who we are and what we are doing here, and then we will either have to run or you'll be back in the Army." Pussy agreed. He was emerging from his shock and grief. It might return to him, later, but Buckles was ready for that. He'd been there for her. She could do no less. "What was Grandma's plan?" she asked.

"I guess she wanted to go to Tahoe, eventually, but we never went in a straight line and we never took major roads. We'd get just so far, and she'd make me turn this way or that, even going backwards to where we had already been. We'd made it to Omaha when she started to worry about the MPs, so we were headed back to Massachusetts, I think. We knew people in Massachusetts, so maybe that was why, but when we found you in Ohio, while you were asleep in the back seat she explained we would go west again because we no longer looked like the people the law was chasing."

"Omaha is in Nebraska. That's a big circle. I don't want to go in circles."

"Should we get rid of the Edsel? You can spot it from a mile away."

Buckles said "No," but did not tell Pussy she believed Grandma's spirit inhabited the car. How else to explain her driving skills or that they had driven through the heart of a tornado that devastated the countryside and taken her body?

The Edsel took them on a crawl north through the ruins of Tuscola. Air steamy as soup flowed through the car. They glared in skies already clearing to a blue so deep it seemed purple. Buckles accepted the magic and luck that was all about her. She'd press it. She had set out for San Francisco but had arrived in southern Illinois, with no driver's license but behind the wheel of a red and white Edsel convertible, marijuana in the glove box, and a spider web cracked windshield in front of her eyes. She'd escaped death with the guidance of a ghost that aided her to steer a perfect donut on the wet macadam of a parking lot glittering hail. There'd have been no other way to rescue Pussy, and that was what Grandma's ghost wanted from her. The convertible roof should have ripped away, but it held, another miracle she did not doubt had been accomplished by the spirit of the dead woman. Beside her was a lightly bearded homosexual boy-man Army deserter five years older than she in whose arms she'd spent a night but rose in the morning safer than when she'd closed her eyes. They shared a few thousand in cash, a lot more in diamonds, and they had a pencil treasure map scrawled on a creased bit of a bag from the A&P.

It was a fairytale.

No Beatles lyrics covered the situation; not even Bob Dylan had written a song with the wisdom she'd need. After three days on the road, Buckles understood the hippie-shit that songs laid down was utter bullcrap because the Big Bills of the world would bend you until you broke before they discarded your bleeding body onto the roadside. Grandma had it right. If you needed to accomplish anything like vanishing from the eyes of police and MPs, you took your best chances and then pressed your luck.

Puss lifted his eyes from the big roadmap. "How about Champaign? It's a university town. Just a little north. Maybe if we go there we can figure out what's next."

"We'll drink champagne in Champaign. Grandma would have liked that."

Mired in gloom, Pussy twisted the radio's chrome dial. The tornado left six dead, including an unidentified old woman wrapped in motel linens.

Buckles also fought a funk. She said on impulse: "That's not Grandma. Our Grandma rode that tornado to Oz. She'll be persuading the Wicked Witch of the West that even though she has no Ruby Slippers, she knows where to get a pair. Maybe they are in a lockbox at Lake Tahoe." Pussy's wan smile encouraged her. "She'll want an upfront down payment before she accepts Glinda's job to come back with the Wicked Witch's broom. No refund for failure to deliver, too, so Grandma won't really go to retrieve some witch-broom. She's not dumb. She'll hire the Munchkins to knock-off a cheap imitation. A broom is a broom, right?"

"How will she pay?"

"A percentage of the final take. The Lollipop Guild is always up for a discount."

"No magic?"

"Grandma makes her own magic."

"That's my Grandma, all right. So you figure she is traveling the Yellow Brick Road?"

"No chance. Suckers and marks take the Yellow Brick Road. Why risk apple trees that want to fight or poppies that put you to sleep when the Blue Brick Road is the shortcut. Glinda did not want Dorothy to know about that. Remember, no one in Oz messes with anyone named Dorothy. A Dorothy can bomb Oz with a farmhouse."

"Wait. Why didn't Glinda want Dorothy to take the shortcut?"

Buckles steered around a freshly dead horse. Could the storm have dropped it out of the sky this far from Tuscola? "Light us a memorial joint and I will tell you." Pussy rummaged through the glovebox for Grandma's stash. "See, Glinda the Good Witch is not a good guy. She just wants the Munchkins to think she is. They are all working for her. It's a scam."

"How is that?" Pussy said, gasping. Trapped smoke smoldered in his lungs.

"No Goody-Two-Shoes who travels around in a pink bubble is going to send our Grandma on a wild goose chase to a phony wizard who then sends her on a suicide mission."

"Suicide mission?"

"How long were you in the Army before Grandma sprung you?"

"Two weeks. Sixteen days, actually."

"When you were a soldier, Puss, if some general told you to bring back Ho Chi Minh's beard, would you go?"

"Not a chance." Pussy leaned his head back and exhaled.

"Glinda might fool your average Munchkins, but Grandma Dot has that covered." She risked a glance at Pussy and reached out for their joint. "Look, all Dorothy wants is to get home, right?"

"Right."

"And how does she do that?"

"She clicks her heels together three times and says, 'There's no place like home.'" Buckles goosed the gas. The Edsel rattled like a defective coffee grinder. "That noise is the muffler," Pussy said. "We must have run over something that knocked it loose. It's dragging."

"I didn't hit the dead horse. Maybe when we sideswiped that pickup?"

"Possible. I forgot that."

The exhaust pipe clattered against the undercarriage and scraped the road, spraying sparks beneath the Edsel until the pipe clung for a final moment before spinning and clattering onto the road behind them. Buckles twisted her neck to see, but the muffler became invisible around a gentle curve. The car thundered like Odin's motorcycle. At least the engine had not fallen out. Yet.

"We need to take the top down," Pussy said. "Otherwise, exhaust fumes will kill us."

"That's a pleasant thought."

"Does the crack in the windshield bother you?"

"Not too much."

They learned the frame that held the ragtop was bent, so they had to crush the top into the well behind the rear seat. It settled in with an ominous pop. Whether the top would ever rise again without a pry bar was an open question. They'd look damn silly if it rained.

These were the Edsel's final days, Buckles thought, and swatted a mosquito that thought to suck life from her neck. Preparing to shake itself into a pile of junk, the car sounded like a farting Drum and Bugle Corps. There was an excellent probability that if the engine was turned off, it would never again start. The lost muffler would rust forever by the side of the road; the windshield had several spider web-shaped cracks; the passenger door had been battered out of shape when the car caromed through the parking lot of the Tuscola Arms. The rearview mirror was, of course, long gone, a casualty to Grandma's philosophy of never looking back. Grandma's driving lesson was akin to throwing a non-swimmer into the deep end of the pool, though instead of drowning Buckles had been set loose with a three thousand pound weapon that moved at 70 mph. Still, Buckles was the girl who had turned a donut when she did not so much as know what turning a donut was. She wondered if she could do it again?

Repairing the car would be crazy, though Pussy might not be ready to release the Edsel. It was too much like releasing Grandma. The Edsel was a liability, enough wrong with it that a policeman might stop them on the road as a matter of safety. Never mind the stash of marijuana and the cash they could not explain, Buckles herself was a runaway driving on a fake Wisconsin driver's license that said she was twenty and named her as Florence Goodbody. For all Buckles knew, Grandma had stolen the Edsel on the same day she came into the diamonds. They'd never know the whole story, but Buckles guessed the diamonds were not a gift from a grateful loser at backgammon. That is, if she truly ever played backgammon.

One thing was undeniable: Grandma's weed was potent shit. The landscape spun like a Merry-Go-Round skipping gears. Her upper lip was on holiday far from her face. Her mind and voice were only tenuously connected, her jaw flapping. Her brain believed that if her jaw stopped flapping she would immediately die.

"Go with me on this," she said. "It is complicated. If all Dorothy had to do was click her heels three times, then Glinda the Good Witch was really Glinda the Pink Bubble Bitch."

Without exhaling Pussy said: "Dorothy had some things to learn. Glinda was doing her a favor."

"That's crap. That's what teachers say. No one suffers for their own good. Light us another joint, Puss."

The Edsel crept north through farmland where stolid Jersey cows and skittish brown horses trotted beside them to the limits of their world, a barbed wire fence. What tornado? Where?

In the outskirts of Champaign, the fields yielded to tree-lined streets, low red-brick buildings, and narrow lawns. They passed a few chain motels, the kinds of places with Pussy's photo thumbtacked to an office bulletin board. Other than a coffin mill by the railroad track that gave Buckles the creeps, Champaign seemed to have no industry except for a very large university. Buckles knew NYU students filled the streets and sidewalks of Greenwich Village, but the University of Illinois was more like Central Park with classroom buildings and hippies in expensive Earth Shoes.

The sunlit town seemed unaware that a killer tornado had raked the land an hour south. Buckles sucked in a deep toke, held it, gasped, then drew one more before she helicoptered the roach away. Pussy had his own joint. It would not do to smoke in an open car. Local police might have ideas about that. Her head whirled.

"I like dogs as much as the next girl, but not enough to get killed for that little rat-ass mutt."

"Rat-assed mutt?"

"Toto. Toto. Pay attention, Puss. This is deep. Dorothy wakes up in Kansas with her whole Oz crew looking down at her all creepy while they stare at her boobs, making believe they are concerned, when what they really did was to lock her out of the root cellar to offer her to a tornado, like some virgin thrown into a volcano. Her parents, wherever they are, gave her to people who claim to be her grandparents, but they never mention her mom and dad. She's a slave who does chores. Her only and best friend is a dog. The moral of the story is supposed to be, 'There is no place like home because everything life has to offer is in your very own backyard.' Pure propaganda, Puss. That's just code to make sure good slave girls don't run from their farmer owners. If Dorothy doesn't escape Kansas, she will be forced into doing the horizontal bop in a pigpen with illiterate farmhands her entire life."

Pussy was at last laughing. Buckles felt herself surfing the crest of a wave of her own making. "Over the rainbow my pale ass. Do you remember what Dorothy says to the Wicked Witch when the witch turns the hourglass? The Witch says, 'First the dog and then you!' and Dorothy says, 'Toto too?'"

"I remember that."

"If you say that backwards, you say, 'Oot, Ot Ot.'"

"Why would I say it backwards?"

"Don't know. Why not?"

They sank into helpless giggles. Grandma might be dead, but in her battered Edsel her survivors were very much alive.

April 1968 and 1974,
New York City

KJ's PHONE REELED HER UP from deep sleep. She had yet to install a bedroom extension, some part of her wanting her life to remain temporary, a state of mind that did her no good, leaving her uncommitted to the moment in which she lived. The white Princess phone in the kitchen had had a cord that stretched to the floor. The cord had kinks in it that could never be set right.

She needed to bathe. She took a whiff under her arm and immediately regretted it. Two steps from the kitchen she was brought up short as the sex dream she'd been having revived for a last tug back to her bed. Her partner had been Eugene, but then it had been Ginny, and then Eugene again. She picked up the phone filled with hope.

But it was Jack, her soon-to-be ex, calling.

"They shot King, the uppity bastard. He was asking for it, Peace Prize or not." In their best days, they'd never discussed politics. KJ's role at his firm's cocktail parties had been to nod agreement while Jack intoned pronouncements in a tone that promised his profile would soon be carved onto Mount Rushmore as soon as they sandblasted Teddy Roosevelt to dust. After all, any president not on currency probably did not warrant being on a mountainside, either. "Stay home from work. You have a job, right? Stay home today."

Jack was still yammering when KJ slammed the phone back into its wall cradle, lifted it, and dialed.

If she had not called Nat, he'd have called her. Nat agreed with Jack. He had been instructed not to open, but Nat did not giggle or joke about a paid day off. The bookstore's metal riot shields had been routinely padlocked to the ground and covered the store's windows and front door. If she wanted to take shelter at his place, she could, but he did not see how she might safely cross Central Park on foot. "You can get a cab, but expect to show the driver a hundred-dollar bill. Stay put. If the phones don't go down, I'll call later."

That brought the reality home. Nat was too frightened to go out. The world was unsafe and uncertain.

Her small black-and-white television perched on her kitchen counter brought at first sketchy reports, then more detailed. King was on a Memphis motel balcony when a single rifle shot found him. Stokely Carmichael, the young leader of Students for a Nonviolent Society, was calling for violence. Black America set oily fires in Newark, Detroit, Los Angeles. One expert speculated that Black troops in Vietnam would throw down their arms, shoot their white officers, commandeer transport ships, and set course to California to join the uprising. Shattered store windows left city streets glittering with shards of glass. Lines of men and women like a bucket brigade at an inferno passed canned goods from a supermarket to waiting trucks. Mayors pledged that looters would be shot to maintain order, a euphemism that guaranteed white America that the preservation of their liquor stores in Black neighborhoods was more important than human life. KJ looked for but found no report on New Orleans. Watts in Los Angeles was in flames again. So were Louisville, Washington, and Baltimore.

Nat called her twice. With little to say, it was enough to hear each other breathe.

New York by the next morning was eerie. John Lindsay, the mayor, had walked the streets of Harlem and though Newark across the Hudson burned, New York escaped the worst violence. The rifle in Memphis had changed nothing except to bring to light what white America had always known but pretended it did not.

KJ's life had for months alternated between hours at the Grand and hours at The Box until Nat pretty much told her to spend all her time managing Eugene's project. They saw each other solely at show rehearsals. She missed their long walks and the dusty peace of the bookstore, but the arrangement made her certain that Nat owned the place. For reasons she could not guess—taxes? a lover? a silent partner?—he'd never say as much, but would simply tell her that his boss, the invisible nameless owner, had approved his request for her release time with pay. The more time she spent in The Box, the more absurd the arrangement seemed.

The Box went slowly from being a dingy cellar to what felt and looked like an ill-lit open club that lacked seats, doors and sufficient ventilation. KJ begged Buster for money to install bathroom fixtures, a fifteen-foot bar rail, better glassware, and a smoky back mirror. Buster insisted everything was delayed or on back order or was sitting on a truck dispatch dock because union guys wanted bribes, hated homos, or simply were unable to find The Box because its sole entrance hidden down an alley and was on no street map of New York City. Buster claimed he greased the palms of a dozen officials to expedite a liquor license, though not a bottle or bit of glassware had yet to be delivered. "At least things are good with the fire marshal," he said.

"Don't we need a certificate or something?" she asked.

"It's coming."

A health inspector was promised they would take measures to prevent the spread of disease, and Buster siphoned money to four precinct cops. "They'll look the other way for anything and everything," he said.

It all left KJ frantically uneasy. She slept fewer than six hours each night, tossing endlessly, replaying spools of what-if scenarios through her mind. What if this happened? Or that? Or this other thing? Or some possibility she could not imagine? She'd march herself through them all, sit up in bed, turn her pillow to the cooler side, force herself to close her eyes, and the merry-go-round of what-if would start again. She did not so much sleep as pass out. When she told Nat she was sleepless, he said: "Ah, the theater!"

She learned a lot watching Nat work. The satyr of self-indulgence occupied the center of a circle where no personal excess was extreme, but being in The Box he transformed from a hedonist's hedonist to an unrelenting perfectionist. Drag queens wept. Whenever the Dancing Master pointed his silver-pommeled walking cane at someone for being less than their best, they accepted that Nat was right. He drew performances from them they themselves did not believe they could achieve.

KJ had placed the ads and had the flyers printed. Stacks of them were in a dark corner, and then as if by magic started to appear on walls and lampposts from river to river, from Wall Street north to 125th Street. She never saw who took the flyers. Buster appeared one late afternoon and moved carefully through the dust and gloom to sit on a crate beside her. Nat was supervising four men who were balanced on unsteady ladders while suspending lights from the ceiling. The lights ran through cycles from hot red to yellow to green to spotlight white. The choreography would change depending on how the lighting fell.

"Advance ticket sales are promising," Buster said, "but do you think it wise to hire a second bartender?"

"Only if we seriously intend to pour drinks," KJ said.

Buster sighed. "As long as he knows he doesn't get paid until we actually open."

She had promised the job to someone in a starched white shirt and bow tie. He was clean-shaven and had short blonder hair. He had impressed her because so many applicants wore their hair over their collars. KJ liked men to look crisp. She turned to Buster to say holding pay back was no way to insure that the boy would remain available, but Buster had slipped away.

When Buster spoke to her by phone, he could be a condescending prick, though she had to concede he had a head for business and seemed to get things done. She was too tired to be tactful. Nat heard KJ's complaints without comment, then reminded her that Buster lived with one foot in a world where men wore neckties and polished shoes. "My idea of bookkeeping is a cigar box. Leave it to me and we'll be overwhelmed with debt to men with broken noses. Learn to get along, KJ. We need him almost as much as we need you."

The day came when the Dancing Master dismissed the cast from rehearsal early. Instead of fourteen hours, they were sent home after eight. "Go home," he said. "I want you to rest. Take care of your costumes. Take a day off. We open the day after tomorrow, so soak your legs in ice, then take a hot bath and work your thighs. Raise your legs above your head." The cast twittered. Nat smiled, the joke inadvertent. "Well, that, too, if you insist. Just stay sharp. Rest. Sleep. Shave where you need to shave. Depilatory strips are better than razor burns. If we are not ready now, we will never be. If we can't get chairs, we'll make history by becoming the first opening night to be standing room only." The show was ready, even if the theater was not quite. Nat clapped his hands in dismissal, the cast burst into applause and then scattered like children at recess.

Nat put an arm around KJ's shoulder and leaned close to whisper: "Let's find Eugene and Buster. What would you say to the Russian Tea Room?"

"Hello Russian Tea Room," KJ said brightly. The weeks leading to this moment now had been like being at the bottom of a swimming pool. This would be like exploding to the surface after holding her breath a very long time.

"Our Fate is with the Show Gods," Nat said. While she waited outside, he made two phone calls from Luigi's, and then they tumbled together into a taxi.

The Tea Room's waiter was deferential, the walls green, gold, and scarlet, the colors of the Romanovs. Nat and Eugene waved away menus. Buster, the stolid banker in a pinstriped wide-lapel charcoal-gray Brooks Brothers suit and high-polish Broughams, squinted at a menu down his narrow nose like a disapproving Baptist deacon who lost his pince-nez.

They had arrived for high tea, which meant two kinds of caviar, blini, and a bottle of Veuve Cliquot in a silver bucket swimming with ice. Buster never chose anything other than the high tea, but did caution Nat about spending too freely. Nat stuck his tongue out, ordered an additional bottle of vodka, and said: "This is no time for Nedick's." They sipped fragrant Darjeeling tipped into crockery from a silver samovar while the wine and vodka chilled. "We have worked too hard to hold back. Eat, drink and be merry, for we open in two days."

Eugene scooped the black caviar onto a blini, a kind of crepe. "Nicholas and Alexandra were the last of the Romanovs. They were executed in a basement in Ekaterinburg. Their children, too."

"Enlightening," Buster said. "We needed to know that. Appetizing." Though no morsel found its way through his narrow lips, he lifted a napkin to his mouth.

Nat turned to KJ. "I knew Anastasia. She was an old lady, by then. She said she survived because the bullet meant for her heart was stopped by the gems her mother had sewn into her dress. They thought they were being exiled, but they were being shot. She lay on the floor with her dead family. No one noticed she was breathing."

"That's a myth," Buster said.

Nat rolled his eyes. "You're a real joy to have around. Why not loosen your tie?"

The wine went down faster than Pepsi. Then the foursome slammed back shots of Mamont peppered vodka. "No sipping," Nat said. The stuff was molten flames. KJ's eyes teared.

While they scooped larger portions of caviar onto blini, Nat asked what everyone thought of the order of the acts, but KJ begged off offering any opinion. The programs were printed. Any change could only mean a correction under the lights, and even she knew that would seem terribly amateurish. She said as much.

"This why the Most Gracious Fag-Hag of New York is our manager," Eugene said. "She knows something about everything and, when she does not, she relies on good sense."

"As long as we avoid a cost overrun at the printer," Buster said. "Please."

"Mr. Cassiopeia said our opening will be auspicious. Mercury goes out of retrograde tomorrow, so we are on a cusp. He never fails. I called him twice this week. My God, those calls to Rome cost, but his voice was clear as a bell, as clear as if he was sitting here." They ordered a plate of soft cheeses and assorted olives, refilled their cups from the samovar, and Nat wished they had ordered cold borscht but bemoaned the perils of sour cream. "It goes straight to your ass." They were drunk enough to laugh at that. Nat prepared food; Nat paid for food, but except by KJ, Nat never was seen eating food.

"Can't we stop obsessing over the show?" Eugene asked. "We've done all that can be done. It's time to talk about how terrific we are." They cheered and slammed back shot glasses of vodka as if they were Soviet commissars. KJ became tipsy. She focused on squeezing bread pills from a pumpernickel roll baked with salt and onions, dipped in caraway seeds.

Buster stood unsteadily. "My real job needs me. They get testy after a while. I'm allegedly at lunch."

"Work kills everyone eventually," Nat said kindly and reached for Buster's wrist, but Buster shook him off and made his way to the Tea Room's front door and 57th Street.

"Is he as much of an asshole as I think?" Eugene asked.

"Yes, but he can do percentages in his head. Handy when you leave a tip. He may be nervous about a colleague coming in and finding him with us. He's that deep in the closet, poor boy. He has a wife. He has kids. His bank is two blocks from here."

"It's self-hatred," Eugene said. "Some queers are like that. They believe they are victim of sick compulsive behavior, and they are too weak to control themselves."

KJ said she thought she understood.

"Can we get back to drinking, now?" Nat asked.

"But does Buster's wife know?"

"Mrs. Brown?"

"I hope Mrs. Brown knows," Eugene said. "Life in a shoe is hard enough without a secret like that from your spouse. His real name is Trevor."

Nat shrugged and tried again to steer the conversation into channels where he knew more. "Should The Box keep a supply of poppers?"

"Let's do a week before inviting a drug charge."

"They are perfectly legal. Part of every First-Aid kit. What if someone in the cast has a heart attack?"

Eugene smiled. "You're expecting several thousand heart attacks? I suppose we ought to be prepared."

KJ asked what poppers were.

"You have to get out more." Nat explained that poppers were a drug capsule that broke open and when it did, the capsule popped. "Like the weasel." They were also called Amys, short for amyl nitrate, a golden inhalant that dilated blood vessels for cardiac victims who needed to jump-start their hearts. The drug offered a very short rush, just seconds. "But that rush pumps a great erection." Nat described clubs where the dance floor was in a glittering golden cloud. "It's fairy dust. The same color as this Cliquot label. It also relaxes the muscles of the anus …"

"I don't need to know that part," KJ said. The boys looked at each other knowingly, but the talk had taken on momentum of its own. While Nat went on about muscle relaxants, her mind strayed.

Sex had vanished from her life. What had been shut off in her? She was physically whole, but not masturbating, though she'd awakened more than a few times with her hand and a pillow between her own legs. On some level, she needed sex. She liked the *idea* of sex. She hungered for closeness and the touch of another. Was it possible for her to bed Eugene? Could they persuade each other it was writerly research? KJ slowly closed and slowly opened her eyes.

"And they can make any troglodyte appear attractive. Knuckle-draggers believe a three-piece suit and a Maserati constitute irresistible allure. Take some Amys, and being irresistible is a lot less expensive than a Hong Kong suit."

"That's Buster's thing," Nat said and curled his pink tongue around a silver spoon to lick it clean of sour cream. "I mean, who in New York City needs a car? You take a taxi or if you are driving to Fire Island, you rent a car for a week."

Eugene seemed to ignore him. "Young people are stirred by signs of success. A man can look like a toad, but that won't matter. A woman, on the other hand, has to work at being alluring."

"I could tell you stories," KJ said, opening her eyes and leaving her passing fantasy. Her face was flush. They'd think that was the alcohol. It wasn't.

"Go right ahead. We love gossip," Nat said.

But Eugene again ignored him. "Wealth and power are about allure, the only asset that works for women as well as men. A guy will shower if you're lucky, but a woman will dye hair, shave legs, armpits, cunts, wear curlers, wigs, falls, apply depilatories, tweeze and pluck, color her lips and shadow her eyes, powder cheeks, rouge nipples, apply perfumes, paint mascara, stuff her bra, squeeze into a girdle, squeeze into CFM heels, body powder, pay for manis and pedis, and invest in surgical deceptions to present an illusion of youth. Men can age gracefully, but a woman holding on too long becomes as grotesque as Gloria Swanson in *Sunset Boulevard*."

"Like the cast of a drag revue?"

"A drag show is a parade of exaggeration. Who women think they are and could be. That's why we sell tickets to women. The show's final revelation, when the entire cast bares chests, reassures women that the strutting beauty they have applauded all night is no threat, only men in disguise. Drag queens can strut and pout and dance, but never, ever, bear a child. That part of allure remains in reserve."

"CFMs?"

"A high heel shoe. Boobs out, ass back, calves tight. The posture says Come Fuck Me, dear-heart. Allure is about advertised fertility. Long after it makes sense, mature women persist in deceiving themselves that they are as desirable as teenage girls."

"Nora Desmond clings to youth," KJ said, "but her instincts makes her disgusting. 'I am big. It's the pictures that got small.'"

"Such a great line," Nat said, trying again without success to steer the talk back to show business and away from philosophy, but the two writers, each with a snootful of vodka and heads bobbing on a sea of sparkling wine, were unstoppable.

"Do you know what a *merkin* is?"

"I have no idea."

"It's a toupee, but for a vagina. Goes back to the Renaissance. Queen Elizabeth's syphilis left her hairless. Everywhere. She inherited the disease from her father, Henry VIII. They knew all about syph back then. Elizabeth was the Virgin Queen. And now you know why the state was named Virginia."

"Was she really a virgin?"

Did Eugene know how sexy his intelligence was? Ginny, too, but KJ was a little too drunk to carefully make that distinction. She could take him in her mouth. Why not? How would that be any different from his gay lovers? A mouth was a mouth was a mouth. Jack had always pestered KJ for that; KJ had little interest. But that was Jack. This was Eugene. Eugene could tell her just what to do, and she would do it, love it, do it until he groaned, and then keep doing it. Her eyes closed longer than a blink. She shivered.

"No. But virginity was a matter of statecraft. It left no doubt as to the line of royal succession. Blame Eleanor of Aquitaine."

Nat rolled his eyes. "She's in one of the tapestries in my place," he said.

"Eleanor slept around," Eugene said. "Kings and princes left upside-down footprints on her headboard. She's the queen who invented chivalry."

"I thought that was Buster," Nat said.

"Different kind of queen." Eugene muttered. "Eleanor was the real thing."

"Buster would not see it that way," Nat said, laughing.

Eugene poured three more vodkas, holding the bottle aloft and pretending to squeeze the glass for the final drops. "An intact hymen was a guarantee. Royalty were promised at six and married at thirteen. They had to be chaste. The first night, witnesses came to the bed chamber to make sure no one slaughtered a chicken over the sheet to perpetrate a fraud. Common women were chattel, though, property of their husbands. Chivalry was not for peasants."

"Sound more and more like Buster."

The green, scarlet, and gold Russian Tea Room was unmoored from the planet and spun around KJ. Her eyes closed, but all that did was leave her spiraling in an abyss. Could her head spin one way and the room another? The throb of the universe pulsed through her, pushing her own blood like a tide within. Or was that the pulse of the universe throbbing? Eyes still closed, she made the mistake of imagining her chest flat and warm on Eugene's. It was a mistake because her nipples hardened. Her sweatshirt kept her secret. She knew Eugene's chest was hairless from having seen Ginny when she chose a plunging neckline. Straddling Eugene, she'd slowly trace the tip of her tongue over his clavicle and tease her way south to discover just how gay he was. Heat flooded her face. Heat flooded her everywhere. Eugene had abdominal muscles that tapered in a V to his narrow waist and lower. He was a walking anatomy chart. She'd tease every inch. Every damn inch. She'd take her damn time and take him in her mouth … a mouth was a mouth was a mouth. Why not? Vodka and champagne could have made Eleanor of Aquitaine one rangy bitch, but the effect of vodka and champagne on KJ Sinclair the peasant was to turn her into someone she barely suspected any longer existed. KJ sat in a puddle of her own making.

Nat abruptly pushed back his chair and stood. When Eugene stood, KJ sobered enough to realize she could not manage the moment into some private time with Eugene. She rose, wobbly.

The men put her in a taxi. They gave the driver strict instructions.

Home, KJ hurled herself across her narrow bed. Taking off her clothes would have been a complicated ordeal. Her armpits were swamps; her sweatshirt smelled as if something rank with fur had spent the night curled in it. The something with fur was she.

She fell into lovely wicked dreams.

By late afternoon KJ was antsy, at loose ends, and restless in ways that went beyond biology. Nat's good advice was to leave The Box for a day, but she took a long walk to the theater. The exercise and air would do her good. Her hangover liquidated in the growing spring day heat. There were buds on trees that dotted blocks in the city; birds that were not pigeons had returned.

But KJ's focus was their plan to pay for some sort of air-conditioning. They'd have to use early receipts for a bootstrap operation if they wanted audiences come serious summer when New York was sure to be trapped under a high pressure weather dome filled by auto and bus exhaust. Audiences might stay away in droves, and the cast might sweat their tits off, but Buster reasoned that if they flopped, spending money they could not replace made no sense. "We're leveraging our expectation of success," he said.

It sounded smart. *Leverage* was a word Jack used all the time, and while she hated to acknowledge it, Jack-the-prick remained her standard for business smarts.

She turned the corner into the alley beside Luigi's and first saw the padlock. Big, red, and heavy, the lock fastened a chain thick as her forearm. She pulled at it, which was stupid but had to be done. The rattling chain threaded through the door handle and across several feet to a steel hook newly hammered into the exterior wall. Chips of shattered brick lay at her feet. The yellow note glued across the door's seal said the premises were shut down until further notice.

That it made no sense. She tugged at the chain again. There had to be some mistake. She was the General Manager. It would be her job to get to the bottom of this newest mess. More than a hundred people had purchased tickets to the opening tomorrow. They had been told SRO, Nat's cagey way of generating that much more excitement, a plan that dovetailed nicely with the fact that they were yet to install a single seat. What were they supposed to do? Send the cast home and refund the money?

Buster had attended to every detail. Nat primed the pump with a gush of cash; Buster filled thick manila envelopes that went into the pockets of city agency bagmen. Buster had filled the bags of union bagmen. Nat joked that even the bagmen had bagmen. Men who did not know the uses of neckwear beyond a means to strangle people had demanded three no-show jobs on a payroll that had not yet existed. Buster had acquiesced; the no-show jobs were bleeding them white. People were lining their pockets with Nat's money. But he could not have infinite resources. If The Box did not soon bring money in, there was no telling if it could go on.

The padlock had to be a simple, typical, New York City screw-up. Or a shakedown, timed for the worst possible moment. Once they moved to ten shows per week, a tits and feathers revue would prove lucrative. Graft was a Golden Goose. Why drown the goose in the Hudson? Even the men with no necks were smart enough to understand that.

After a quick call from Luigi's, she went to Nat's. When she arrived at his penthouse, Eugene was already there. Despite Nat's initial giggled dismissal of the situation as a standard crisis for show business, both men grew worried when they could not locate Buster. Using his best actor's baritone, Eugene learned from the bank's switchboard operator that Mr. Trevor Brown had left the organization three weeks ago. Nat paled.

"I don't care if he is in the closet; we need to rattle his cage," Eugene said. "Do we have his home number? We have to have his home number. Do we have his home number?" Nat had a worn address book; Buster's home phone was circled in red, Nat's code for Do Not Call.

They called. A woman answered. Nat identified himself as a bank official and asked Mrs. Brown for her husband's whereabouts.

"I have no idea," the woman said. "But if you find the son-of-bitch, tell him his sons miss their father." She then abruptly hung up.

It took most of a day, but they learned the union guys never heard of him; the construction guys never heard of him; there were no seats because no one had contracted to rent them, sell them, or contracted to install them. There was no scheduled liquor delivery. Buster was not in a coma at any hospital. The police knew his name because his wife had registered him as a missing person, but once they ascertained that Buster abandoned his job a few days before he abandoned his wife, the police removed his name from any list of missing persons. With no evidence of foul play, it was not police business if a man walked out on his wife and kids.

Nat was unsure, but he calculated Buster had taken $250,000 of his money. Gloom filled the penthouse along with the certainty of being powerless.

The banker had vanished.

It was dark by the time they gave up searching for Buster. Nat would alert the cast.

KJ and Eugene left together. As the elevator door opened on the ground floor, Eugene said to her: "My ship came in and sank at the dock."

Uncle Sam for 2 Cents, Plain

COME THE SEVENTIES, THE WEATHERMEN declared war on the American Way. Fuck Thoreau. Fuck Gandhi. Fuck King. Fuck any other simpering pissant preaching nonviolence.

The first thought—and it is always the first thought—was to blame a Jew-Commie plot. The Feebs had long known that Yid-anarchists were in bed with Yid-bankers since the ill-fated day Trotsky persuaded the Rothschilds to fund the Worldwide Conspiracy to Control Everything Everywhere (WCCEE). Radicals with names like Hoffman, Abzug, Reuben, Friedan, and Kuntsler targeted draft boards, savings banks, and college administrative offices where egghead professors—probably Yids themselves—taught little bomb-throwing fuckers all they needed to know. In Chicago, Heather Booth, Amy Kesselman, Vivian Rothstein, and Naomi Weisstein encouraged women to burn their bras. This was not Hadassah. The Gang of Four became the core of the National Organization for Women, subversives who rejected the lessons of Biology and marched from the kitchen into the streets. Other hippie stoners emerged from under the protective rocks their parents had purchased for them to toss flaming pie plates smeared with dog shit, accidentally inventing Frisbees. The Days of Rage were loosed upon the land. The Weather Underground was a conspiracy of privileged white kids who assumed the right to blow up whatever impeded justice or threatened them. The Weathermen declared unity with The Black Panthers, dedicated uppity subversive Negroes who claimed Second Amendment Rights to bear arms and defend themselves from police murder. The Feebs eventually rounded those fuckers up. The Panthers they did not shoot they imprisoned.

The Underground swore to end racism, capitalism, and bring to a close American imperialism in Puerto Rico, Haiti, Honduras, Santo Domingo, Guatemala, Paraguay, Nicaragua, Panama, or anywhere else in the Western Hemisphere where US Marines fought brown people encroaching on the profits of United Fruit and Big Sugar. America ordinarily subverted governments in Chile, Uruguay, Bolivia and other nations few Americans could locate on a map. In the name of profit, the CIA intervened with its light hand, training gangsters in garish uniforms to discharge automatic weapons with their eyes open and to tie the wrists of blindfolded students with plastic stays before dropping them a thousand feet from American-made helicopters into Central American rain forests.

Though no one had ever figured out what in Holy Fuck the United States had been about in Southeast Asia, American policy in the Western Hemisphere was plain: no commie bastard could be allowed to interfere with any American's right to a decent cup of coffee and an unblemished banana for breakfast.

The subversives in America proposed the novel idea that the peons of South and Central America cultivate food they themselves could eat. Who would question that Carmen Miranda joyfully wiggled her ample Latin ass to a samba for the sake of Norte Americanos? *Chica chica boom chic-a-boom boom boom!* Besides any honest reading of the Good Book reveals that the poor will always be with us. God's plan is to keep brown people semi-starved with their noses in the dirt. Jesus may love the sinner and the poor, but Jesus never caught a whiff of a peon at the end of a hot day at stoop labor in a field fertilized with goat shit.

Unruly peasants defied Divine Will by diversifying what they grew. The CIA retaliated by poisoning the marijuana they grew by spraying paraquat over all of Godforsaken Mexico. Paraquat was the same shit they used to defoliate Vietnam to kill all plant life, exposing the Viet Cong to air attack, more proof of how war fostered innovation and progress. Who was smoking marijuana anyway? If junkies and poets coughed themselves dead, good riddance!

The peons, God bless them, embraced capitalism. They cultivated an alternative cash crop.

Coca.

Cocaine became bigger than oil in Texas. Cocaine factories popped up thick as groupies at a Rolling Stones concert. Cartels manipulated supply, demand, open markets, risk, reward, and profit margins for the white powder that went up rich noses in Los Angeles, Manhattan, Detroit, and Dallas. Would you rather have shares in General Motors or the Medellin cartel?

Sanity was in short supply.

In 1968, flag-draped black vinyl body bags stacked like cordwood on landing docks and in airplane hangars, so many American dead in the Tet offensive that no less a figure than Walter Cronkite, a TV news guy when TV news guys reported events instead of reading government handouts, the most trusted man in America, pronounced the war in Vietnam unwinnable. Lyndon Johnson ruefully observed that if he'd lost Cronkite, he'd lost the American people. Robert Kennedy was slain by an 8-shot revolver that somehow on tape was heard to discharge fourteen rounds, though no second gunman was ever identified or pursued, and plainly a hotel corridor packed with happy supporters could not create echoes. But Americans, weary of conspiracies within conspiracies, chose to believe that the world was one great grassy knoll breeding invisible assassins.

August of that same year brought homicidal police into Chicago's streets for the Democratic National Convention. Ten thousand snot-nosed kids met 12,000 cops in Grant Park, a ratio that left the cops short of ass to kick, a situation the cops remedied by kicking selected asses twice. Chicago's finest douched the streets with the blood of hippies, folk singers, yippies, and the other undesirables that had shaved beards and cut their hair short believing that if they appeared middle class their parents might vote for the poetry-writing Minnesota senator, Eugene McCarthy.

Elect a poet? In America?

Inside the convention hall, Senator Abraham Ribicoff, denounced Chicago's cops as Stormtroopers. The nation read Mayor Daley's lips on national TV. Spraying dry spittle, he cursed Ribicoff as a fucking kyke bastard.

Tricky Dick Nixon had run in 1960, but Republicans unearthed Dick to run again on his new promise that he had a secret plan to end the war. The plan was so secret not even Nixon knew what it was. The Peace talks underway in Paris were subverted by Dick to be sure no premature peace could lose the White House. Look, what was more important? World Peace or installing Dick in the Oval Office?

Nixon was obeying the wishes of The Silent Majority, the millions of Americans silent everywhere but in Nixon's head. Ordinarily, citizens who detected silent voices were prescribed Thorazine or Lithium, but in America if that person runs for President the person is celebrated as a descendant of Jeanne d'Arc, the frog who heard silent voices that led her to victory. Nixon's voices whispered for tens of thousands of American soldiers to die in the jungles, for millions of Asian civilians to be napalmed into fine ash while, and for law and order at home, a phrase that meant scrubbing America's streets of Black people and other unruly troublemakers. It was in the Constitutional clause that blessed the world with the Monroe Doctrine, the one about the Empire bringing Power to bear on black, brown, and yellow peasants who flung dried goat shit at rocket-shooting fighter jets.

· And so the Empire prosecuted its undeclared war. Credibility was at stake.

War was waged and millions died to prove the Empire would wage war.

The Sixties, perversely ended in 1974, when Dick, the only American president to willfully loosen his grasp on power for any reason other than death, said: "I am not a crook." But like his Vice President, Attorney General, and 40 other members of his band of pirates who claimed executive privilege, he was.

When Dicky mounted the gangway to his getaway helicopter on the White House lawn, he extended his arms in victory. A forced grin wobbled on his unshaven jowls. His eyes and scalp ached with hangover. It's a good thing he appointed a Vice-President so successor, Gerald Ford, who became the sole politician to hold the American presidency without receiving a single vote for that office. Ford quickly pardoned Tricky Dick, and said: "The American nightmare is over." No one understood that to mean anything more than that the nation could now return to the habits and policies that put the country into shit in the first place.

Communists overran Saigon. As the last American helicopter lifted from the roof of the American embassy, desperate collaborators, allies stupid enough to have believed in Uncle Sam's invulnerability and his reassurances that they would never be abandoned, dangled from helicopter struts as US Marines crushed their fingers with rifle butts. They fell screaming into the unforgiving arms of the mob below.

Disco balls and laser lights spun above dance floors where people once again touched each other while dancing. Nehru suits sprouted broad lapels; women wore scarves and business suits; hemlines fell near as fast as hippie icons dropped like fruit-flies in the Arctic.

Janis Joplin died of an overdose.

Jimi Hendrix died of an overdose.

Jim Morrison died of an overdose.

Otis Redding died in a plane crash.

Mama Cass died of heart failure while choking on a tuna sandwich.

By official FBI count, from 1970 to 1972, at least five bombs daily rocked America. *Five each day!* This was no lone-wolf terrorist. This was a transcontinental conspiracy.

The Federal Communications Commission further stoked the revolution when it inadvertently created Youth Radio by licensing FM bandwidth. The industry's panties went damp at the thought of new revenue sources, but here came the FCC with rules that might double costs.

The radio powerhouses went schizoid. AM tunes stamped out in the Brill Building or in Nashville were abandoned in favor of highly engineered multi-track sounds that buzzed the stir-fried minds of drug-addled youth—in stereo.

Goodbye *Venus in Blue Jeans*; hello *I Am the Walrus*.

Thankfully, J. Edgar Hoover, the *capo di tutti Feebs*, saw through it all. Well before he croaked, Hoover wrote:

> The morals of America are besieged today by an unprincipled force which will spare no home or community in its quest for illicit profits. I am speaking of the unquestionably base individuals who spread obscene literature across our land through the means of films, decks of playing cards, pbotographs (sic), "comic" books, salacious magazines, paperbacked books and other pornographic products. These forms of obscenity indeed threaten the morality of our Nation and its richest treasure—our young people.
> —*January 1, 1960*

In 1972, unequivocal proof that, when sufficient people beseech God that an individual have a heart attack, the man's coronary arteries turn to rock. He hit the deck beside his desk like a sack of wet shit cast off the Washington Monument. J. Edgar had been installed as FBI Director for Life, a job status hitherto reserved for the Pope and the Prince of Darkness.

General access to reliable birth control had effects more far-reaching than the invention of the rumble seat, an invention that made cars a fine and private place. Sundered by The Pill, fucking and pregnancy were no longer connected.

Goodbye Doris Day; hello Linda Lovelace.

Right in front of their disbelieving eyes bare-thigh mini-skirted daughters with suspiciously dilated pupils shook their

money-makers at bar mitzvahs, sweet-sixteen parties, and on wedding dance floors. As ever, the marketeers stepped in to turn a buck,
but they were as clueless as the last dinosaurs staring with admiration at a blinding flash of bright light in the sky that was nothing
less than the planet-killer asteroid that ended all known life larger
than a cockroach.

The marketeers worked hardest to co-opt black music into
white pabulum, but no one with hormones and blood and heart
could prefer Pat Boone to Little Richard. Boone's gang stole the
music and sucked the juice out of it. Good golly, if Miss Molly sure
liked the bone, who believed the poor girl wrapped her lips around
a porterhouse?

AWAP BOP A LUP BOP A WOP BAM BOOM!

New York City—1974

DIVORCING JACK FELT AS IF she were discarding a corpse by leaving it on the subway. A week before their court date, KJ accepted Jack's invitation to meet with him and no lawyers at the French steakhouse on 74th Street. Her moth-wardrobe of sweatshirts and jeans would not do. She was tempted to ask Ginny for advice, but Ginny would want to know the occasion, so she went alone to Bergdorf's. She'd dropped two dress sizes since she'd last bought anything, going from a 10 to a 6. She went with something that could be a business suit though it was killer-emerald, not business-navy. She found sensible shoes.

Standing outside the restaurant, she wondered why she was there.

The waiter seemed to know Mr. Sinclair, though KJ had never been inside the place. That fact was toxic. The place had to be one of his haunts, a place where he brought his women. He recommended that they share the chateaubriand for two. Medium rare, it would be nicely charred. "It's always good here," Jack said. KJ pretended not to notice that Jack's endorsement could only mean he'd been there time and again.

Before the steak arrived, Jack took both her hands in his, looked deeply into her eyes, and said: "We don't have to do this."

She folded Jack's smooth hands in hers, swallowed some water, and said: "She dumped you, didn't she?"

Her chair noisily scraped the floor. She was in the street before the bread basket was set on the tablecloth. She hoped Jack enjoyed his steaks. They'd been married nearly twenty years but the prick either forgot she preferred her meat medium-well or simply did not care enough to ask.

Blatt, her Yellow Pages attorney, stood beside her when a bored judge asked if both parties in Sinclair vs. Sinclair were sure their differences were irreconcilable. She was in the killer-green suit again. Blatt smelled as if he'd been doing backstroke in Aqua Velva. She braced her palms on the table, sure her legs could not bear her weight, terrified Jack would maneuver for yet another chance and another delay, but he did not so much as show up. His attorney lodged no objection. The gavel descended, and in courthouse hallway Blatt finally proved his value by holding a wastepaper basket while she puked.

Despite her job that paid a pittance at the bookstore, Jack promised he would pony up seven years of a modest alimony. She believed the shitheel. Jack's lies ordinarily were by omission, for example neglecting to mention his wandering dick loose in the land of new nookie, a habit that had him accidentally collide with Buckles in a way that three Sinclair lives took sharp turns. Only God knew the kid's whereabouts and what she was doing, but KJ's internal radar assured her that the girl was alive and making a life off her back.

Their best days done, KJ and Nat persisted in dining together at least once each week, but that became a hollow ritual, impossible without recalling The Box, its failure, and Buster's betrayal. Never-Never Land had never-never been; the lost boys who wanted to love other lost boys fluttered up the cone of silver light spilled to earth from the second star to the right.

Two days after the divorce, she was still emotionally rocky and so told Nat she had been married and was now divorced. He lowered the Venetian blinds of his glass-box office at the bookstore to say he was not surprised and wished she'd told him sooner. He did not ask about children. She tried being lighthearted, but in mid-sentence her voice caught and she wept. "I'm all right," she managed to say.

Two hours after sending her home, Nat showed up at her front door with two pints of Haagan-Dazs Rum Raisin. He had not wanted to tell her he was headed back to Lubbock, but this seemed to be a day to reveal secrets. "Just a short visit. My brother is ill." It was the first she'd heard of a brother. His attempt to sound jolly was a dismal failure. They stood on the sidewalk in front of where she lived while Nat waited for a taxi. "You'll need to manage the store for a while. Please water my plants."

Nat never returned from Texas. The penthouse was auctioned off, but she'd never learn what became of its furnishings. She kept a pothos because the plant could survive anything and the eucalyptus was in a pot far too large. Nat's share of the bookstore was purchased by a small group of businessmen. Part of the deal Nat negotiated was that KJ would get a raise and stay on and teach them the business.

She cried bitterly when Eugene fled to the West Coast for a fresh start. He departed fired with ambition, confidence, and purpose. KJ spoke to him by phone several times, able to distinguish Ginny from Eugene by simple voice tone, but there was less and less gossip to exchange because they lacked a base of common friends. They exchanged stories about strangers after they reached the limit to nostalgic talk about Nat, Ice Capades, and the fabulous boys who went in and out of Eugene's life but never stayed. The Box's failure had robbed him of hope. He was unable to get a decent agent in Hollywood. He was too young; he was too old; he was too pretty; he was not pretty enough. His Equity card did nothing for him. He went through three sets of publicity photos, the last set paid for by KJ. He stopped writing plays.

The gaps between their talks stretched longer and longer, the silent moments in the conversations they did have were painful, a hum on a long distance connection. The last time they spoke, Ginny joked about sending Christmas cards with photos of sad dogs, a rented family, and a mimeographed full-page newsletter of made-up happy events. Then she received a letter from a California friend whose return address meant nothing to her. He'd found her name in Eugene's papers. Eugene was dead, a suicide no one was willing to call a suicide. His ashes were scattered over the Pacific. He'd left no note. KJ failed at finding Nat to share her grief.

In the end, she was glad she never slept with Eugene. She wondered if all his talk about how none of us can escape our pre-determined natures and our genes was what finally looped the rope around his neck.

When that thought became too much to bear, she chose to remember that the most elegant and profound woman she'd ever known was born a man.

For slow years after the divorce, KJ might be window shopping, sitting on a bus, or in the lavatory at the bookstore when defeat immersed her in a pool of black self-pity. She was a worthless utter failure, a fraud moving among people who could not detect how utterly worthless she was. Her husband was gone, her daughter was gone, she had failed as a businessperson because she had failed to appreciate how much a thief Buster could be. The signs had all been there; she chose not to see. Her male friends were gone, too, dead or dying. Her only adult female friend had been Charlotte, and Charlotte was a lush who vanished with her husband the dentist and their two sons.

She drank herself into a stupor wondering if she should adopt a Korean baby or buy tropical fish, two plans she was drunk enough to think were equivalent. She awakened still at her table, a half bottle of wine spilled on her blouse and tacky on the floor. That night frightened her. Lonely women who drank spiraled into dark, unfathomable places. She was drowning.

A post-divorce fucking-frenzy might have been just the ticket, but KJ could no longer bring herself to believe she wanted anyone in that way. Awakening in a sweated bed beside some man whose name she did not recall filled her with loathing. She wanted something more than a bump in the hay. Something in her dimmed, flickered, and was going out.

The other employees at the bookstore were deferential to the old lady who was their boss, leading her strange life among the dusty stacks. She hired young women when the bookstore needed help and she tried to befriend the girls, but that seemed only to drive them further away. The one time she'd been invited for a drink with three of them, it had been an invitation they never dreamed she would accept. The foursome sat on high stools at a tall circular table and vainly searched for a conversation. There was no common topic. She tried talking about the tea shop on Christopher Street where Nat had taken her, but while they nodded and faked interest she realized that along with her enthusiasm for Mu tea and obscure novels she may as well have owned a canary. The girls eyeballed men half of KJ's age, then whispered among themselves. She left them at 7:45, claiming another appointment at 8, ashamed at having to see herself through those young girls' eyes, the old lady who opened and closed the cash register and who dyed her hair espresso brown, the color of a mouse.

So when a man came into the bookshop on a March day with a gun-metal sky that dripped rain, closed his black umbrella and strenuously shook it free of water, KJ was startled at her own reaction. Something in his manner and stance reminded her of her youth, her days as a New Orleans bobbysoxer running wild because her widowed mother could not be distracted from her plans to ensnare a second husband.

The stranger leaned his wet umbrella against the wall. The umbrella had an old fashioned bamboo cane handle shaped like the letter J. The afternoon remained murky with intermittent rain. The coat collar of his black double-breasted trench-coat was raised, the long belt undone dangling at either side. The coat was either unfashionable or a timeless classic; it was hard to say which, but something told KJ the man himself would never care. It was his coat, he liked it, it did a coat's job. His hazel eyes spotted by flecks of honey-brown were set deep beneath ebony eyebrows. They seemed to see everything. His nose was slender without being sharp.

She was gawking like a teenager as he placed his black snap-brim fedora onto a maple pegboard beside the front door. No one had used any of the four pegs in the hat-rack for years; did anyone know what a hat-rack was for. Hats? Who wore hats? His thick black hair was only slightly receding. It had no trace of gray.

He was unhurried, as if he were used to people who under-stood old-fashioned niceties took time. His gestures spoke. Those were his coat, hat, umbrella, and polished shoes, all cared for at a tempered pace. She'd have taken him for a professor, except that no professor she'd ever seen wore pale pink dress shirts with French cuffs extending two full inches over his wrists from beneath a sub-dued charcoal gray pin-stripe suit with precisely pressed slacks. His cufflinks were opals. A banker? A Wall Street type out for a stroll, unintimidated by rain, a little more uptown than most?

KJ experienced the weirdest sensation of knowing him from somewhere else.

He removed his gray kid gloves. Of course, his nails were man-icured. Why would she find that surprising? With a voice thick as syrup rumbling from deep in his chest, he apologized for disturbing her, but his time was limited. He was in search of rare chess books, a hobby in which he sometimes indulged himself, and since he was in New York on a brief business trip that had ended successfully and more quickly than he had planned, and with the rain delay at La Guardia, he'd seized his opportunity to explore The Grand.

"It's just as I always imagined," he said.

"We have customers from all over the world," KJ said, and im-mediately felt inane. He apologized for disturbing her a second time, and KJ was charmed that a customer thought to apologize for disturbing sales help, in her case a woman too old to be wearing jeans, swimming in her gray hooded sweatshirt.

"Anything by Philidor would be agreeable," the stranger said and straightened his tie that needed no straightening. He smiled through delicately thin lips. "Almost any edition, though anything before eighteen-hundred would be museum quality. I'd be obliged to donate it if I bought it." The light in his eyes went from green to brown and back again when he smiled. "Philidor. François-André Danican Philidor. The book is a classic, *Analyse du jeu des Échecs*."

His French was effortless. She heard strains of what might be Canadian Quebecois until she recognized the gravel of bayou country. He was no Parisian.

"There is no telling what may be hidden in the basement stacks."

"Philidor was quite a musician, actually a composer, as well. But he was also the finest chess player of his age. Music and chess are complementary. Chess players talk of great games as compositions."

"We had a run on chess books when Bobby Fischer won in Norway a few years ago. Since then, the demand has fallen off. You might be in luck."

"Iceland," he said. "Mr. Fischer defeated Mr. Spassky in Reykjavík. That's Iceland. I was there for games five and six." His teeth were very white; his eyes very deep. "Fischer won as black. It was quite exciting." KJ looked at him quizzically. "Well, it was exciting if you like chess." His smile was radiant; he almost blushed like a boy.

When she giggled in return, she thought of throwing herself under a passing bus.

As KJ led him to the basement stairs, she stopped and asked: "Have your tried the chess parlors on Sullivan Street?"

"Those kind people sent me here." The stranger took her hand. His grip was gentle. He bowed imperceptibly. "Pierre. Pierre Doucet. My friends call me 'Buddy'."

His touch robbed her of breath.

About the Author

Now settled in Haverhill, Massachusetts, **Perry Glasser** has roamed America, living in New York City, Fort Lee, Tucson, Des Moines, and Wichita. He was named a Fellow in Creative Nonfiction for the Commonwealth by the Massachusetts Arts Council and is the author of three collections of short fiction, *Metamemoirs* a collection of self-reflective essays, and the prize-winning novel *Riverton Noir* (Gival Press).

Books by Perry Glasser

Suspicious Origins
Singing on the Titanic
Dangerous Places
Metamemoirs
Riverton Noir
The Ghost of Amelia Parkhurst